SUPERSTITIOUS

SUPERSTITIOUS

R. L. STINE

WARNER BOOKS

A Time Warner Company

A Brandon Tartikoff Book

Warner Books, Inc., 1271 Avenue of the Americas, New York, NY 10020

 A Time Warner Company

Printed in the United States of America
First Printing: September 1995
10   9   8   7   6   5   4   3   2   1

Library of Congress Cataloging-in-Publication Data

Stine, R. L.
      Superstitious / R. L. Stine.
         p.   cm.
      ISBN 0-446-51953-7
      I. Title.
   PS3569.T4837S86   1995
   813'.54—dc20   95-11147
                                                                  CIP

For Brandon and Robert and Joan,
    with thanks
For Jane and Matty,
    with love

SUPERSTITIOUS

Prologue

Charlotte Wilson stares up at the ceiling. Pale yellow light from the street filters through the venetian blinds, spreading a shadow pattern of lines over her head.

Bars, Charlotte thinks. Prison bars.

The guy beside her stirs. She hears him muffle a burp.

His after-dinner burp, Charlotte thinks bitterly. I was dinner.

The blinds rattle as a gust of air sweeps over the bed. Fresh and cool. Charlotte sighs. The apartment smells so sour. Fried onions. Stale smoke.

"Do you smoke?" she asks, staring up at the shadowy bars, the cool air tingling her damp skin.

"No. That was just steam coming out my ears." He makes a joke. Then he adds, "You were great."

You weren't, she thinks.

You were heavy. I thought you were going to crush me. And what were those ridiculous walrus cries at the end?

His hand slides slowly down her bare stomach. Glancing down, she can see the white band on his finger where he has removed his wedding ring.

Married? Why not? she thinks. Am I surprised? No.

And what did he say his name was? Did he really tell me his name was John?

His hand slides lower. "What's so funny?" he asks.

"Just thinking about something."

She raises one knee. Scratches her thigh. I'm all sticky, she realizes. I need a long, hot bath. Lots of steam. A fog of steam. A fog to hide behind.

Her eyes survey the small bedroom. His suit jacket and trousers are tossed against the wall. His white shirt heaped over an open dresser drawer.

Her clothes are neatly folded on the chair beside the door. Skirt on the bottom. Sweater draped carefully over the chair back. Tights neatly rolled up beside the skirt.

So calculated. So passionless.

Why am I here? she thinks.

"I started a new job this week," she says.

Why should he care? Why am I telling him this?

His hand massages her. "Oh yeah?"

Can't he even pretend to be interested?

The blinds rattle. The shadow bars shift overhead.

"You work at the college?" His hand slides off and he pulls himself up, elbow on the pillow. His eyes meet hers. Dark, probing eyes. Damp hair falls over his forehead.

Is he twice my age? she wonders.

When he smiles, his eyes crinkle up. He isn't bad-looking, she decides. I'm not totally crazy.

"I got a job with a professor. I'm his secretary. Not a bad job. He's famous or something. I mean, the others make a big deal over him."

Professor Liam O'Connor. She repeats the name silently. She likes the sound of it. Liam. So foreign. So interesting.

She'll never call him Liam, she knows. She'll call him Dr. O'Connor. He has dark brown eyes. An intense face. Intelligent.

Does John remind her of Liam? Is that why she's here in his bedroom?

Not really.

He snickers. "So you bring him coffee and type his letters? That's an exciting job?"

She brushes his hand off her breast. Shivers. Her skin cold now. The venetian blinds rattling and swaying.

"He's a very interesting man. He's Irish."

How dumb does that sound? Very. She really doesn't want to talk to John anymore. They had a lot to talk about over beers at The Pitcher. Or was it Mike's Brewery?

Why do I hang out at these campus bars after work? Why do I let myself get picked up by these guys?

Good questions, Charlotte. Now sit down, open your notebook, and write an essay in three hundred words or less on "Self-Esteem."

No. No essays. And no more scolding myself. I'm getting my shit together. New job. New apartment across campus. New roommate.

I need to get home.

The box spring creaks as she pulls herself up. Lowers her feet to the floor. Shadows slide over the faded Oriental carpet. His black briefcase tucked beside the dresser.

"What do you do?" she asks. She remembers she asked in the bar, but he didn't reply.

"You mean work?"

"Yeah."

"Oh, this and that. A little of this. A lot of that."

The square briefcase gives him away. "You're a salesman?"

"Sometimes I sell. Sometimes I buy. Whatever." Very mysterious. Don't give anything away, John.

He reaches for her. His hand feels rough, hot against the cool skin of her waist. "Come back. It's early."

She stands up. "Got to go. It's been great. Really." She pushes her damp blond hair back over her shoulders with both hands.

She bends, picks his tie up from the carpet, runs it through her hands, examining the dark stripes. "Very conservative, John."

He laughs. Dry laughter, more like a cough. "The suit. The tie. It's just a costume. We all wear costumes—right?"

I seem to be naked, Charlotte thinks, dropping the tie.

She steps through the shadows, crosses the room to her clothes. She's tempted to pull open the closet door and see what kind of clothes his wife wears.

She picks up her underpants from the chair. Why did she choose the satiny black ones this morning? Did she know she would end the day in someone's bed? In someone's bed without a costume?

She can feel his eyes on her as she raises one leg, pulls the panties over her thigh. Go ahead and look, John. I guess that's why I came here.

"Uh . . . Charlotte?"

She smooths the top of the panties, reaches for the black tights, folded so neatly beside her short skirt.

"Charlotte?"

She turns. He's propped all the pillows behind him. Rests his head back against his hands, elbows out. Smiles.

Nice smile, she thinks. But a salesman's smile.

Well . . . he sold *me*.

"Uh . . . Charlotte? Before you leave? . . . uh . . ."

She lowers the tights. "Yeah?"

"Before you leave . . . How about a blow job, maybe?"

And I thought he loved me for my mind!

"I don't think so, John. I've got chapped lips."

They both laugh. Ha ha. It's so funny.

She's dressed and out of there a minute later. Feeling sticky. Legs kind of trembly. Face hot.

Starving suddenly. Should I stop somewhere and get a sandwich? No. I've got to get home, get into the bathtub.

She remembers cold Chinese food in the refrigerator. Leftovers she can shove into the microwave. A feast! Will Kelli be home? Is this the night she tutors that high school kid across town?

The wind shakes the trees. Whispers all around. Leaves flutter down and scrabble across the sidewalk, doing their autumn dance.

Lights blink in windows behind her. The old brick apartment building stretches the entire block. The long awning at the entrance flaps in the breeze. She glances up at John's window. Was he on the third floor or the fourth? No lights on up there.

She crosses Dale, heading to High Street. The street of dumb college-kid jokes. "Want to get high on High Street?" Lots of jokes about the corner of Merry and High.

She turns onto High. The wind turns with her. She shifts her canvas bag to her left hand and starts to jog, leaning against the wind.

She slows when she hears the steady *scrape scrape* coming up fast behind her. Turns to see two boys on Rollerblades, arms swinging, expressions serious, matching red and gray Moore State sweatshirts pulled down over loose-fitting jeans. Dark baseball caps turned backward.

Scrape scrape.

They glide past her. Don't even see her. Hurrying back to the dorm, she figures.

She suddenly feels old at twenty-six. I should try Rollerblades. Why haven't I tried them? Maybe they would change my life.

She stops at the corner and allows a dark station wagon to rumble past. A large dog, some kind of shepherd, sticks its head out the back window and barks at her. Three sharp, angry barks. Then, satisfied that he has given her a piece of his mind, the creature pulls back into the car.

The next street is Yale Avenue. The Moore State campus stretches beyond it. What a joke, Charlotte thinks—building a dinky college along a street called Yale. How could the college ever live up to the street?

She brushes a fat brown leaf from her hair and shifts the bag back to her right hand. Her eyes sweep over the familiar campus buildings. Silvery moonlight spills over the low, white granite Administration Building, making its pale green, domelike roof glow.

The old campus trees whisper and bend. Rising darkly be-

5

hind the main parking lot, the ivy-covered Language Arts Building looms, its brick steeple black against the purple night sky.

When Charlotte first saw the building as a seventeen-year-old enrolling as a freshman, she had mistaken it for a church. In the early days of the college, it had served as a chapel, she learned soon after. She had several classes inside its cramped, cracking walls during her four years on campus.

And now she finds herself working inside the old building. On the top floor, the office floor, just beneath the empty steeple.

Thinking about work makes Charlotte turn her eyes down Yale. On the next block, behind a pair of gnarled, old willow trees, stands the sprawling rooming house where her new boss has moved.

Liam.

Again, she pictures his brown eyes. So open and warm. The subtle cleft in his chin. The white curve of his teeth when he smiles. The slight Irish lilt to his "Good morning, Charlotte."

Oh, wow. Why am I thinking about him like this? Am I losing it totally?

Standing in the middle of the street, she squints into the darkness. Is he home?

She can't see past the trees.

Does he live alone? Is he married? Is he straight?

She realizes she hasn't learned a thing about him. A Man of Mystery. Well, give me time. I was hired only two weeks ago.

Approaching headlights snap her from her thoughts. She jogs across the street. The car rolls by, country music pouring from an open window.

Charlotte follows the curving cobblestone walkway that leads past the Administration Building, through the round, tree-lined open lawn known as The Circle. The college flag—a red script M on a background of gray—tugs against its flagpole rope as if trying to break free. The flapping pennant provides the only sound except for the scrape of her shoes on the cobblestones.

She thinks again of Chinese leftovers and a hot bath.

Low lampposts line the path as it curves between the trees. One of the lamps has burned out.

It's so dark, she thinks, as a figure steps in front of her.

A blur of purple. With a head. And arms.

"Huh?" A startled cry from her open mouth.

The canvas bag falls from her hand as the dark blur roughly grabs her by the hair and drags her off the path.

"Hey—*let go!*"

What is that *tearing* sound?

The searing pain shoots down her shoulders, down her back. Her legs give way. She collapses to her knees.

She knows her scalp has been torn away. Her scalp and all her hair. Ripped off her head. One effortless swipe.

No!

She sees the fingers moving toward her eyes.

Held by the swirls of pain, she cannot move. Her scream slips out as a feeble "Unh unh unh."

The fingers stab deep.

Her eyeballs make a soft *plop plop* as they are pried out.

"Unh unh unh."

She sees only red.

She can *feel* the red.

Her hands fly up to her head. She can feel bone up there. Bone wet with blood.

The top of her head feels soft, pulpy, like wet paper towels. Where is her hair?

The hot blood flows down her face.

"Unh unh unh."

Is that me?

She hears another low grunt as she is lifted off the ground. Lifted and then bent.

Bent back. Bent back.

"Unh unh."

The last sound Charlotte hears is the *crack* of her spine.

PART ONE

1

Sara Morgan cracked a crab leg between her fingers and pulled out a section of the white meat. "I like this place," she said, her eyes surveying the crowded restaurant.

Very homey, she thought. Very basic. Red-brick walls. Square wooden tables. White paper placemats. Menu chalked on a slate above the kitchen window. Waitresses in white aprons with big red lobsters stenciled across the front.

SPINNAKER'S. A hand-stenciled sign over the bar proclaimed the restaurant's name.

Sara dipped the crabmeat into the white china tub of butter sauce, then raised it carefully to her mouth.

Mary Beth Logan poked her fork into the broiled swordfish steak on her plate. "Back in Ohio when I was a kid, we didn't have seafood," she said. "No one knew about seafood in Ohio. Know what we had? Frozen fish sticks. That was seafood. Very exotic."

Sara laughed. She wiped buttery lips with her napkin, replaced the napkin on her lap.

"I didn't see a shrimp until I was twenty," Mary Beth continued. "I didn't know which end you were supposed to eat!"

Sara tried the coleslaw. Very sweet. "You didn't know how to work a shrimp? Mary Beth, I'm from Indiana. Even *we* knew how to work a shrimp!"

Mary Beth's green eyes flashed. "I grew up in the sticks."

"Huh?" Sara set down her fork. "Shaker Heights? Since when is Shaker Heights the sticks?"

Mary Beth tossed back her head and laughed. Sara had seen her do that a million times.

I've seen all of her expressions a million times, Sara thought. Except for the platinum streaks in her hair and the new, short hairstyle, Mary Beth hasn't changed a bit. We could be college freshmen, sitting in Daley's, talking about boys, boys, boys over cups and cups of very light coffee.

"I can't believe I'm here," Sara murmured. "I can't believe you and I—"

Mary Beth pointed. "You dripped butter on your sweater."

Sara lowered her eyes to the spot. She dipped her napkin into the water glass and dabbed at it.

Mary Beth swallowed a chunk of swordfish. "What color is that sweater? It looks great on you."

"Cranberry." Sara adjusted the cowl neck. She liked long, loose-fitting sweater-dresses she could hide inside. This one came down nearly to her knees. She wore it over black leggings.

"Where'd you get it?"

"I ordered it. From the J. Crew catalogue."

Mary Beth narrowed her eyes accusingly. She gestured with her fork. "You lived in New York City and you ordered from a catalogue?"

Sara shrugged. "It was easier. You know how much I like shopping." She hated to shop for any kind of clothing. It seemed such a vain activity. Adorning yourself. Admiring yourself in long mirrors. Asking strange store clerks how you looked in this one and that one.

Calling attention to yourself.

Sara wasn't shy. And she knew she was attractive. She just didn't see the point in calling attention to herself.

She quickly turned the conversation around. "I like your dress, Mary Beth. Talk about dressing for success. It's cashmere, right?"

Mary Beth tugged at one long gray sleeve. "On my salary? We're talking cotton, my dear." She sighed. "It's weird wearing dresses every day. But my boss doesn't allow jeans in the office."

"Your boss? I thought your title was Media Director."

Mary Beth shook her fork again at Sara. "Don't you know anything about colleges? Everyone has a boss. If there's a college media director, there has to be a director of media directors. Or a dean of media director directors."

They both laughed. Like old times, Sara thought happily. She could feel herself start to relax.

"I hope you don't plan to do any clothes shopping here in Freewood, Sara." Mary Beth spread sour cream over her baked potato. "The only thing you'll find are baggy Levi's and sweatshirts with big red Ms on the front."

"I could use a few of those," Sara replied. "Make me look younger." She sighed. "I feel so old!"

Mary Beth nodded in agreement. "Twenty-four is old around a college campus. But you still look eighteen. You should have been a model, Sara. With those cheekbones and those perfect lips. Of course, twenty-four is pretty old for a model these days. Face it. We're both past it."

They both gazed quickly around the restaurant. Mostly students from the college. Two middle-aged couples pressed into a booth near the bar. Professor types. Everyone else still has their baby fat, Sara thought.

"Sometimes I'm the oldest one in here," Mary Beth groaned. Her expression brightened. "Let's not talk about that. You're here! It's so exciting. How's the apartment?"

Sara cracked another crab leg. "Cozy."

"Does that mean too small? You hate it?"

Sara laughed. "No. It means cozy." She brushed her straight black hair behind her shoulder with one hand. She had soft bangs across her forehead, parted in the center, nearly down to her dark eyebrows.

"If you really hate it, we can try to find you another one.

Do you want to move in with me? I just thought you would want a place of your own. I mean, in New York you probably—"

"I'm fine. Really," Sara insisted. "I'm sorry I said it was cozy. I meant it was fine. Terrific. Just right."

Mary Beth shook her head, her streaked blond hair catching the light. "You hate it. I'm sorry." She stabbed at the potato with her fork. "At least it's a good location. Two blocks from campus. That's why I picked it. But I should've realized. I mean, you probably want a bigger place. To entertain friends and—"

"Friends?" Sara rolled her eyes. "Mary Beth—you're the only person I know here! You're it. You're my only friend."

Sara saw heads turn at the next table. She realized she had been talking loudly, felt her face grow hot. She lowered her eyes to her plate and waited for the strangers to stop staring and return to their own conversation.

"Well, you're still glad you came—aren't you?" Mary Beth's green eyes studied Sara.

"Of course," Sara replied quickly. "You know you saved my life."

"Well, you haven't told me much about . . . anything." Mary Beth nibbled her bottom lip. She pushed her plate away. Reached for her bag. Searched through it.

Sara glanced to the door as three people entered. An attractive, dark-haired man. Academic type, wearing a beige sweater under a tweedy sports jacket, patches at the elbows. A pleasant-looking woman in a tan raincoat clung to his arm. They were accompanied by an enormous hulk of a man, red-faced with a wave of white hair billowing up on his head as if he had been caught in a windstorm.

When she turned back, Mary Beth was raising a lighted match to a cigarette between her lips. Sara's mouth dropped open in disapproval. "You still smoke?"

Mary Beth shook the match out. "No. I quit." She inhaled deeply, let the smoke out slowly.

"Huh? Mary Beth?"

"I quit."

"But you're smoking."

"I know. But I quit. Trust me." She inhaled again, balanced the cigarette on the edge of her plate. "These restaurants—they never put out ashtrays anymore."

Sara rolled her hazel eyes. "You have to be the last smoker in America."

"No way," her friend protested. "Look around. College kids—they all smoke. They have Joe Camel fan clubs in the dorm. Really. They think they're immortal."

Sara's expression brightened. "Hey, I'm a college student again. Maybe I'm immortal."

Mary Beth shook her head, let out a long stream of smoke through her nostrils. "Graduate students are doomed."

"Mary Beth, you're still weird."

"And you're still the opposite of weird. You're . . . anti-weird." She stubbed out the cigarette, half-smoked, on the side of the plate. "See. I just quit."

The waitress cleared their plates. They ordered coffee. Loud laughter burst out at a table across the room. Four young guys at the table raised beer bottles high, then clicked them in a noisy toast.

"Just like New York, huh?" Mary Beth cracked. She pulled herself up straight, adjusting her long gray sleeves. "Hey, I want to hear some stories, Sara. I want to hear about the glamorous world of publishing. I want to hear about the nightlife. And all the interesting, fast-track people you met. I want to hear about Chip. And—"

"What about *you?*" Sara interrupted, squeezing the napkin on her lap with both hands. "What happened to Donny? The last time I talked to you, you and Donny—"

"I know, I know." Mary Beth raised both hands as if in surrender. "I was crazy about Donny. Donny was everything. Donny was God. He was crazy about me too. We used to have arguments about who was crazier about who."

"So?"

Mary Beth let out a bitter sigh. "I had to break up with him.

15

I had to break his heart." She tapped the fingers of her right hand on the tabletop. Sara saw that the fingernails were chewed short.

"Why? Come on. Spill."

Mary Beth hesitated. Finally, she leaned over the table, bringing her face close to Sara's. She spoke in a loud whisper. "He was hung like a hamster."

"Huh? Excuse me?"

"He had a little teeny one." Mary Beth raised her two pointer fingers, held them very close together.

Sara couldn't hold back her laugh. She covered her mouth with one hand.

"It wasn't funny," Mary Beth scolded. "Some nights we had to take a flashlight and hunt for it."

Sara shook her head, laughing harder.

Mary Beth reached across the table and grabbed her arm. "You know those experts on TV who say that size doesn't count? They're crazy. It counts. They should've asked *me.*"

"But—but—" Sara sputtered. Mary Beth could always make her laugh till tears rolled down her cheeks. Usually about the most serious subjects. "But you were in love with him!" she finally choked out.

Mary Beth let go of Sara's arm. She shrugged. "Love is *hard!*"

The waitress brought the coffee. Sara stirred milk into her cup. Mary Beth took hers black.

Sara wrapped her hands around the white china mug. She inhaled the coffee steam. "So you're not seeing anyone now?"

Mary Beth pressed her lips into an exaggerated pout. Another familiar expression. "Boo hoo."

Sara sipped her coffee. Still too hot. She reached for the aluminum milk pitcher.

"Your turn," Mary Beth announced. "Tell me everything. Come on. It's only fair. I rescued you."

"Not much to tell," Sara replied, staring down at the coffee mug. "I mean, too much to tell."

"Tell me about New York," Mary Beth insisted. "Tell me about your fabulous apartment in the fabulous luxury high-rise. Tell me about Concord Publishing, about all the famous authors you met."

Sara sighed. "It's all history." She flipped her hair behind her shoulder, straightened her bangs.

Mary Beth tapped the table impatiently. "Well at least tell me about Chip. When I phoned you in the spring, you were so serious about the guy. So what happened? Why'd you break it off?"

"Well . . ." Sara tilted her head to one side, her habit when she was thinking hard about something.

"Come on, Sara. Why'd you dump Chip?"

Sara sighed, took a deep breath, and started to reply. But she was interrupted by a shower of salt that sprayed onto her hair and over the shoulder of her cranberry sweater.

Salt?

She spun around quickly in her chair—and stared into the dark brown eyes of the man at the next table. He had turned too, turned to face her, the salt shaker gripped in one hand.

Sara brushed the white crystals off her sweater. "Did you just throw salt over your shoulder?"

The man's handsome face reddened. "I'm terribly sorry. Just one of my little superstitions."

2

"I tossed it over my shoulder. For luck. I didn't know you were sitting there. I should have looked first."

He had a slight foreign accent. Not British, Sara thought. Irish. Yes. Definitely Irish.

She stared into his brown eyes. Captivating eyes that crinkled at the corners. They stared back at her from beneath thick brown eyebrows.

"It's okay. I was just startled. I—" Why was she stammering?

Before she could finish her sentence, he was on his feet. Taller than she had imagined. Sweeping his wavy brown hair back with one hand. Scooting his chair back. Reaching for her.

Huh?

His hand was in her hair. Gentle. Warm. He began to brush the salt out. "I'm so sorry. Please forgive me." The woolly sleeve of his sports jacket rubbed her forehead.

"It's okay. Really." Her heart pounding. The touch of his hand making the back of her neck tingle. His eyes locked on hers. He lowered his face, concentrating on her hair. She could feel the heat off his skin.

She turned from his gaze and glimpsed two other people at his table. She had seen them enter the restaurant. A pleasant-faced woman, maybe thirty or thirty-five, with short, white-blond hair, dark at the roots, a nice smile. Across from her, the enormous hulk of a man, red-faced, a pile of white hair flying up from his head. He was finishing a beer, his big hand tilting the mug to his mouth, his dark eyes peering at Sara over the rim.

"There." Eyes still on her hair, he stepped back. "I think I got it all. What a shame to mess up such beautiful hair." He smiled for the first time. A warm smile, Sara thought.

He raised his palm. "Oh. Look. One of your hairs." He moved it toward Sara. "Take it. Quick. Wet your thumb and finger."

Sara hesitated. What was he talking about?

"Liam—" she heard the woman call softly. "Liam—sit down."

Liam didn't seem to hear her. "Wet your thumb and forefinger. Here." He handed Sara the single black hair.

She found herself obeying him. Licked her finger and thumb.

"Now pull the hair tight. If it curls up, you'll be rich. If it stays straight, you'll be poor."

Sara laughed. "I think I know the answer to this one."

She guessed right. The hair remained straight.

He leaned over her. "Too bad." He seemed genuinely sympathetic, as if he seriously accepted the verdict.

"Liam, give the girl a break!" the big hulk rasped. He had a hoarse, throaty voice.

"Okay, okay." Liam shrugged good-naturedly at Sara. He started to turn back to his table, then stopped. His expression changed. He was staring over Sara to Mary Beth. "I know you!" he exclaimed.

Mary Beth smiled. "Hello, Professor O'Connor."

He smiled back. "You're the girl with the video camera." He turned to the two at his table. "She did a video of me last week. Walking across the campus. 'Can you walk and talk at the same time?' That's what she asked me. No one had ever asked that question before."

The hulk and the blond woman laughed.

19

"It's not as easy as it sounds," Liam continued, turning back to Mary Beth. "I stumbled twice."

"You were very good," Mary Beth corrected him.

"A video about *you?*" the hulk rasped. "What was it? 'Strange Characters to Avoid on Campus'?"

Everyone laughed. The blond woman slapped the hulk's arm familiarly.

"It was a welcoming video," Mary Beth explained, her eyes on Sara. "We showed it to all the new students at Orientation. We don't often get such a famous visiting professor here at Moore State."

"Infamous, you mean," the hulk joked. He raised his mug, tilted it over his mouth, held it in midair as he realized it was empty. "Waitress! Miss!"

Still feeling the warmth of his hand in her hair, Sara stared at Professor O'Connor with renewed interest. She had seen a front-page article in the campus newspaper about the well-known folklore professor, author of several books, popular TV talk show guest, teaching a graduate seminar at the college this year. But she had only skimmed the first couple of paragraphs. Folklore wasn't exactly her cup of tea.

He is certainly good-looking, she thought. She liked the way he kept raking back his thick, dark hair, liked the way it fell back over his forehead. She wondered what it would feel like to brush her hand through his hair the way he had brushed hers.

She suddenly realized that Mary Beth had pronounced her name, had introduced her to Professor O'Connor. He took her hand, shook it twice. A gentle grip. His hand felt warm. Why was hers suddenly so cold?

"Nice to meet you, Dr. O'Connor." Was that my voice? she asked herself. Why do I sound so stiff, so nervous?

"Please. Liam," he corrected, still holding her hand. "Call me Liam." The brown eyes crinkled at the corners.

How old is he? she wondered. Thirty-five maybe? Hard to tell. She liked the slight Irish lilt. So pleasant. So charming. She pictured little leprechauns dancing under toadstools in emerald green grass.

He let go of her hand and motioned to his table. "Sara, this is my sister, Margaret." She nodded to Mary Beth and Sara. "And my new friend and colleague, Milton Cohn." Milton toasted them, raising the empty beer mug. A lopsided smile graced his red face. His white hair rose up like a blob of whipped cream on top of cherry Jell-O.

Colleague? Sara thought. He looks more like a professional wrestler. His hand, she saw, was nearly too big for the beer mug.

"I believe our food is arriving," Liam said, seeing the waitress approach, a large silver tray holding three dinners on her shoulder. As he returned to his seat, Liam turned back to Sara. "How were the crab legs?"

He noticed what I was eating? Sara thought. She felt her face grow hot.

"They were good," she replied, instantly feeling as if the answer was somehow inadequate. Not eloquent or interesting enough. "Very sweet."

Liam smiled. The waitress had to maneuver herself around him to set down the plates. "There is a tiny island off Samoa," he told Sara over the waitress's shoulder, "where the people always bury the crab leg shells deep in the sand after they have eaten the meat. Do you know why they do that? To keep the dead crabs from walking at night and coming after them for revenge."

"How interesting!" Sara replied awkwardly.

"It's bullshit!" Milton said loudly, pouring a shower of pepper over his rib eye steak. "Don't believe a word he says. Liam makes up half of it."

"Milton—Liam is a scholar." Margaret defended her brother, mock outrage in her voice.

"He's a bullshitter." Milton lowered his attention to his dinner, attacked his steak with violent slashes of the steak knife.

"Well, the crab legs are very good here," Sara insisted. "A real treat for me. I usually can't afford them." She realized she was trying to stretch the conversation, to keep Liam from turning away.

"Hey—are you looking for work?" Milton raised his eyes from his plate, gestured to Sara with the knife, his jaw flexing as he chewed.

"Excuse me?" Sara wasn't sure she'd heard correctly.

He swallowed, his Adam's apple bobbing in his wide neck. A football player's neck, Sara thought. Frankenstein's neck. "Are you looking for part-time work?"

"Well . . . yes," Sara replied uncertainly. *Do I look as if I'm broke? Is that why he asked?*

"She's totally broke," Mary Beth broke in.

Thanks a lot, Mary Beth. Why not pass my bank book around the table and we'll all have a look? She decided her friend was just trying to help.

Milton leaned forward to see around Liam. "My assistant is expecting a baby, and she's making the most of it," he rasped. He held a fat hand over his mouth to suppress a burp. Somehow he had gotten steak sauce on the side of his hand. "She's only coming in twice a week. I could use someone the other three days."

"Uh . . . I'd be interested," Sara replied hesitantly.

He's staring at my tits. Why is he staring at my tits?

"If the hours fit around my class schedule," she added. "I'm starting graduate work. In psychology."

Liam turned around. "That's interesting. Have you met Geraldine Foyer yet?"

Sara thought, shook her head. "No. Classes just started last week. I haven't met many people in the department."

"I'll have to introduce you," he replied.

Sara saw Margaret flash her brother an inquisitive glance. She turned back to Milton. "What kind of skills would I need for the job?"

"Can you walk and talk at the same time?" Milton asked, grinning his lopsided grin at Mary Beth. "That's about what it takes. It's just filing and answering the phone. Shit work for shit pay."

"Milton—we're eating!" Margaret declared primly.

Sara laughed. "That's exactly what I'm looking for." And then she blurted out, "What do you do?"

The question appeared to surprise him. He stopped chewing. "I'm the Dean of Students."

That's about the *last* thing I'd guess! Sara thought. Football coach maybe. Or head of security. But not the Dean of Students.

She was about to apologize for not knowing, when Milton climbed to his feet. He jabbed at his face with the napkin, tossed the napkin onto his chair, and started toward Sara. "I should properly introduce myself."

He took a step.

Two shots rang out.

With a choked gasp, he clutched his chest. His eyes rolled up in his head, and he started to slump to the floor.

3

Liam spun around quickly and caught the enormous man before he fell. "Milton—you really have a sophomoric sense of humor!" Liam declared.

Milton opened his eyes, regained his balance. He laughed. "That's why I'm still in college." He turned, grinning, to Sara. "I think I fooled you."

Sara swallowed hard. "I think you did."

Milton pointed to the bar. Two more loud cracks rose up over the voices and clatter of the restaurant.

"Shooters," Mary Beth explained. "Spinnaker's is known for its shooters."

Sara watched the bartender slap two more skinny glasses hard against a marble slab on the bar. Two more gunshot cracks rang out. Two young men in faded denim jeans and sweatshirts tilted the slender glasses to their mouths and downed the drinks in a single swallow.

Sara turned away to find Milton hovering over her, squeezing her shoulder. "Sorry if I scared you. I have a sick sense of humor."

"It's not sick; it's terminal," Liam cracked, his back to Sara.

Sara moved her shoulder uncomfortably under Milton's heavy hand. Is he apologizing or deliberately pawing me?

His hand slid off, as if he had read her thoughts. "If you

really are interested in the assistant job, come see me at the Administration Building tomorrow afternoon," he said. "Your name again?"

"Sara. Sara Morgan."

He nodded solemnly, memorizing it. Then he made his way back to his seat.

Sara's shoulder ached. Milton, she realized, didn't know his own strength.

Margaret leaned over their table and began speaking to Liam. Sara turned back to Mary Beth, who was digging into her maroon leather wallet to pay the check. "Let's split it," Sara insisted, reaching for her bag.

Mary Beth raised a hand. "No way. This is my treat tonight." She counted out three twenties. "You can take me out after you get your first paycheck." She leaned close and whispered, "Lucky break, huh?"

Sara thought of Liam, not Milton. "I guess," she whispered back.

"He looks like a gangster hit man," Mary Beth whispered. "But I've heard only good things about him. He just started at the end of last year. The old dean was caught totally naked in the back of a van with not one but—count 'em—two undergraduates." She snickered. "He believed in getting close to his students."

"Milton couldn't *fit* into a van!" Sara whispered, glancing back to make sure he couldn't hear. He was occupied in massacring what remained of his steak.

"Is he married?" she whispered to Mary Beth.

"Milton? I don't think so." Mary Beth narrowed her eyes at Sara. "Why do you care?"

Sara rolled her eyes. "Not Milton. Liam."

Mary Beth laughed. "No. Not married."

"Is he gay?"

"How should I know? I interviewed him for half an hour. He lives with his sister. That's all I know. The college gave them that big old rooming house. You know. The white one on the other side of Yale."

Sara bit her bottom lip. "I think I know it. Didn't Jessica Goldblatt and that red-haired girl, the really tall one, didn't they live there when we were in school?"

Mary Beth frowned. "I don't remember." The waitress took the check and the money. "He's kind of charming," Mary Beth commented, climbing to her feet.

"Kind of!" Sara exclaimed. "Know who he reminds me of? Daniel Day-Lewis. I rented *Age of Innocence* a few weeks ago. I've seen it twenty times. I actually bought *Last of the Mohicans*."

"You're sick," Mary Beth muttered, hoisting her bag onto her shoulder. "No. You're just such a romantic, Sara. That's even sicker."

"Don't you think he looks like him?" Sara insisted in a whisper.

Mary Beth shook her head, adjusted her skirt. "Daniel Day-Lewis? In your dreams!"

Sara reached for her bag. Started to stand up. Sneezed.

Liam spun around instantly. "God bless you!"

"Thank you." Sara felt her face grow hot.

"What day is it?" Liam demanded, his brown eyes sparkling as they locked on hers.

"Why?" Sara reached into her bag for a tissue.

"There's an old rhyme from Lancashire." His eyes went up to the ceiling as he struggled to remember it. "*Sneeze on Monday, sneeze for danger. Sneeze on Tuesday, kiss a stranger.* Today is Tuesday—isn't it?" he teased, drawing his face close.

He's flirting with me, Sara realized. This is definite flirting. "What about the rest of the days, Dr. O'Connor?"

"Liam."

"Don't encourage him," Milton called gruffly. "If he starts reciting rhymes from the Old Country, we'll be here all night."

"Hmmm . . . let's see." Liam ignored his colleague. He kept his eyes on Sara. "*Sneeze on Wednesday, sneeze for a letter. Sneeze on Thursday, something better.*" He took a breath and held it, trying to remember the rest. *"Sneeze on Friday, sneeze for woe. Sneeze on a Saturday, a journey to go. Sneeze on Sunday, your safety seek. For the devil will have you the rest of the week."*

Sara felt a chill as he completed the final words.

"Liam," she teased, "do all of your rhymes end with such frightening warnings?"

His smile faded quickly. "Yes. I'm afraid so."

4

"How are your pork chops, Detective Montgomery?"

He felt Angel slide up behind him, felt her arms go around his chest in a gentle hug. She smelled of oranges and onions.

"My pork chops are fine. How are yours?" He pressed the side of his face against her sleeve.

"Haven't tasted them yet." She moved away from him, crossed the table to the baby. Martin rocked in the high chair, humming contentedly as he dug his tiny fingers into the bowl of plain macaroni noodles in front of him, stuffing them into his mouth. His success rate, Garrett saw, was about fifty percent. Not bad for a one-year-old.

Detective Garrett Montgomery was always looking for new ways to be proud of his son. Angel had confessed that morning as they lingered over coffee that she had never expected Garrett to be such a doting father. "You even brag about how much he drools!"

Garrett had to admit he was surprised too. Having Martin was all Angel's idea. Garrett wanted to wait until they could afford a baby, until his job situation was settled, until they had some idea of what their future might hold.

But now he couldn't wait to get up in the morning to see what surprises Martin had in store. And he hurried home from the Freewood police station, eager to see how much the boy, his boy, had grown during the day. Having a kid around the house was *interesting*, Garrett thought. More interesting than staring across the room at Walter, picking his crooked teeth with a paper clip.

Angel fussed with Martin, picking stray noodles off the high chair table, placing them in his mouth. His little brown fingers squeezed a noodle into mush. He tossed it onto the floor.

Good throwing arm, Garrett thought. He's going to be athletic, like me. Garrett had been a track star in high school, until he messed up his knee. He had tried basketball too, but he had no shooting eye at all. And he had the *worst* time trying to dribble and run at the same time. Just because you're tall and black doesn't make you Michael Jordan.

Garrett still worked out every morning. He had put on a little weight, he realized—he weighed 180 now—but he was still pretty fast on his feet. Not that there was much call for a cop to be fast in this town.

At least he knew he'd never look like Walter, only twenty-five and already nurturing a potbelly that kept him a foot from his desk.

He pictured the box of Krispy Kreme doughnuts on Walter's desk. Walter with powdered sugar all down the front of his dark blue uniform. Garrett had to laugh. Walter was such a cliché.

He stared across the table at Angel. She had stains across the front of her loose-fitting blue sweater. Baby stains. "Aren't you going to sit down and eat?"

She dropped down to pick up the noodles scattered over the floor. "I want to get him another bowl first. This son of yours is a good eater."

Garrett nodded. "Of course he is." He forked up a clump of mashed potatoes. Cut off another section of pork chop. "The other white meat," he muttered.

"What's that?" Angel called from the stove. "What are you saying about white meat?"

"You know the TV commercial," Garrett explained. "For

pork. They're trying to tell you pork is good for you because it's white meat."

Angel dumped noodles from the pot into Martin's bowl. She shook her head. "I don't like to hear you talk about white meat."

Garrett snickered. "You have a dirty mind."

Angel grinned at him. "And you love it. Is that your gun, or are you just glad to see me?"

One of their shared jokes.

That's a marriage, Garrett thought happily. Shared jokes.

Martin banged the table impatiently with both fists. "Daaaa! Daaaa!"

Garrett imitated him. Banged the table. "Daaa! Daaa!"

Martin laughed.

"Two babies," Angel muttered. She placed the bowl in front of Martin, who grabbed at it with both hands. Then she slid into her chair across from Garrett. So graceful and light, he thought, watching her. She looks like a little girl in that huge sweater. She hasn't changed since we met at sixteen.

She picked up a pork chop, put on her pouty face. "You have to go in? Why don't you give all the criminals a break tonight?"

Criminals? What a laugh. The phone in the little, one-story station house behind the Post Office barely rang.

He swallowed. "Got to keep Walter company."

"But you're not on the late shift this month. Can't Walter manage by himself?"

"That dumb hillbilly? He can't manage a sandwich!"

"Where's Harvey?"

"Took his wife to a play. In Harper Falls. Her cousin is the director or something."

Angel frowned. "Harvey takes his wife to a play?"

"He'll sleep through it."

"Where do you take *me*? When's the last time you took me to a play or a movie or something?" Teasing, not bitter.

"Martin is more fun than any play."

She grinned at the baby. "True." She picked up her napkin

and dabbed at Martin's face. He shoved her hand away, raised both arms, and slid down to the floor, landing on his backside.

"Hey—I didn't know he could get out of that chair!" Garrett proclaimed proudly.

"He's a clever guy."

Martin struggled to push himself up to his feet. One hand got tangled in the bib that hung from his neck. Garrett read the label on the back of his red overalls. OshKosh B'Gosh.

"Are you wet?" Angel called down to Martin. "Do you need to be changed?"

Martin stood up, took a few unsteady steps toward the kitchen door. Angel jumped up. Garrett waved her back down. "Eat your dinner, hon. I'm watching him."

"Don't let him get near the stove. It's still hot." She scooped up a spoonful of potatoes, swallowed quickly. Having a one-year-old got them accustomed to eating on the run.

Garrett's eyes surveyed the small, cluttered kitchen, searching for other hazards. The faucet dripped in the sink. The Formica countertop was cracked. Only two burners worked on the stove.

Too small, he thought. This isn't a bad place. It's just too small. Every surface is covered. Every shelf is jammed. There isn't a spare inch to set down a pot or a cup.

Angel's father was a doctor. Angel had been middle class her whole life. Surveying the kitchen made the back of Garrett's neck grow hot. He couldn't step into their townhouse without feeling he had somehow let Angel down.

He and Angel both worked, but somehow they still couldn't manage a place to live as nice as the house she'd grown up in. If only he had more time to do some fix-up work, maybe give the whole house a coat of paint.

"I've been thinking a lot about what my brother said," he told her.

She had been mopping up gravy with a slice of bread. But she didn't raise the bread to her mouth. "Well, stop thinking about it. I really don't want to move to Atlanta. I like it up here."

"If I took that job at my brother's place, we could afford a house. With a yard. You know. A place for Martin to play."

She lowered the bread to the plate. "Detective Montgomery, I *know* what a yard is."

He laughed. He liked it when she called him Detective Montgomery. He wasn't sure why.

"I'm serious, Angel. We could have a better life. We could have a nice place. And maybe put away some money. For Martin to go to college."

Her catlike green eyes locked on his. She dabbed at the gravy, but still didn't eat the bread. "Are you forgetting something?"

"Huh? Forgetting what?"

"That you *like* being a cop. That you would *hate* being a furniture salesman. You think your brother is a jerk, remember?"

"I wouldn't be a salesman for long. I'd become store manager. Or I'd find something else. But I can't make any money here. And I'm not a real cop. I mean, this isn't a real town. It's just a bunch of houses and stores around a college campus. And that's what I am, Angel. I'm a campus cop. I'm like a crossing guard or something. I should ride a bike, not a squad car. A lousy little six-man police department to keep the college kids from jaywalking and getting high after the football games."

Angel twisted up her face at him. "Where have I heard this speech before?"

"You'll hear it again and again," Garrett threatened. "Until you agree that we should get *out* of here."

She scratched her forehead. Her high forehead. He loved her for her forehead. And her feline green eyes. "But I like my job, Garrett. And I'm in line for a promotion, remember? And I like my friends here. Okay, okay. So we're not living in a palace. But we're getting by."

"Your father never thought I was good enough for you. I'm sure he still thinks it!"

Where on earth did that come from?

He wasn't thinking that. Why did he blurt out those words? Had they been lurking all the while in some dark hiding place in his brain, waiting to leap out and startle them both?

Her mouth dropped open. The green eyes narrowed at him. "Go to work, Garrett. We're doing okay. Leave my dad out of it. I never think about all that, and you shouldn't, either."

Garrett reached for his uniform jacket. "Sorry. I . . ."

Angel's expression softened. She picked up Martin and held him up to Garrett. "Say good-bye to Daddy."

Martin automatically waved a pudgy brown hand.

Garrett waved back. He turned to Angel. "I'll call you later." Jacket over his shoulder, he started to the door.

But she swept in front of him, blocking his way. Swinging Martin to the side, she stood up on tiptoes to kiss Garrett's cheek. "Know what you need? A nice crime wave. It would cheer you right up."

Garrett laughed. "I'll keep my fingers crossed."

"Reba—wait up!"

"No. Keep running. Don't stop!"

The two girls jogged across Yale Avenue, their dark hair flying behind them like pennants, blue backpacks bouncing heavily on their backs.

"But I've got a stitch. I can't run anymore."

Reba Graham spun around, breathing hard, rested her hands on her knees. "We're going to be locked out. The dorm is probably closed already."

Suzanne Schwartz held her side, grimacing. "Why did we listen to those boys?"

Reba snickered. "It wasn't the boys. It was the grass. I still feel a little spaced."

"Jared was nice."

"He came on a little strong for me. He kept rubbing the sleeve of my sweater. Like he never felt wool before. I think he was stoned before we even arrived." She pulled Suzanne's jacket sleeve. "Come on. We don't want to sleep outside tonight."

Suzanne flashed her a devilish smile, her dark eyes catching the light of a streetlamp. "We could go back to their apartment."

Reba shook her head. "You are evil. Come on. Run."

Suzanne shifted the backpack on her shoulder, pushed her hair back off her sweaty forehead, and began jogging after her friend. She felt giggly. She had an urge to belt out the title song from *Oklahoma!* She had been in the senior production of it at her high school the previous spring, and she still remembered every word.

They turned into the campus. Made their way across The Circle. Thin wisps of black cloud rolled past the moon. Reba pulled several yards ahead.

"Hey, wait up—!" Reba was the athlete. Even when she was stoned. Suzanne was the couch potato. "Wait up, Reba! I can't run that fast!"

To Suzanne's surprise, Reba stopped short. Raised her right leg. "Hey—" A sharp cry.

Suzanne squinted into the dim light. "Reba—what's wrong?" Did she get a cramp? Pull a leg muscle?

"Yuck. I stepped in something."

Suzanne saw the girl first. Sprawled on the ground. At first, she thought it was a mannequin. The parts were all twisted, not in the right places.

But then she saw the dark blood, the bone where the skin had been pulled away, the guts pouring out from the torn stomach.

And she knew.

"What *is* this?" Reba pulled something off her shoe. "Some kind of sausage? I—*Oh my God!*"

Reba saw the twisted, torn corpse at her feet.

Not a sausage. Part of the girl's intestine.

I'm holding her intestine.

With a groan, she tossed it down. It made a soft *splat* against the walk.

Reba's stomach lurched and she choked out a high-pitched wail.

If she just screamed loud enough, Reba figured, maybe she could scream the whole hideous scene away.

5

Liam leaned on the window frame and pushed the wide front window shut with both hands. He peered out to the street, olive and gray shadows playing over the ground as snakes of cloud twisted over the hazy half-moon.

Turning back to the room, he watched Margaret pull off her raincoat and fold it between her arms.

"Cup of tea? Or do you feel like something a little stronger? Whiskey and soda, perhaps? Or a Bailey's?"

Margaret made a face. "Liam, you know I hate that stuff. It tastes like chocolate milk."

He tsk-tsked, then scolded her. "Never insult good Irish whiskey."

She sighed. "Is that one of your superstitions?"

"It's the Golden Rule!"

She didn't join in his laughter. She set the raincoat neatly over a tall, stiff-backed armchair. Glanced around the room. Still not sure where everything was. Would this drafty old place ever feel like home? At least her apartment upstairs was cozy and warm.

Liam shook his head at her. "Long dinner, huh? I know you hate sitting still that long." He clicked on a tall floor lamp. This red shade will have to go, he decided. Light spilled onto the floor but didn't light the room.

She yawned. Shook out her hair with both hands. "What do you think of Milton?" She didn't wait for a reply. It wasn't really a question. "He seemed jovial enough. But he makes me uncomfortable."

Liam crossed the room. He put his hand on her shoulder, rubbed the sleeve of her sweater, as if trying to warm her. "Because he's so big?"

"Big and gruff. He reminded me of a big goat."

Liam tossed back his head and laughed merrily. Margaret always came up with the most surprising pictures. "Like a goat?"

"Billy Goat Gruff. You must know that story."

Liam rubbed his chin. "It's Scandinavian." He crossed to the worn gray leather couch, dropped down gracefully onto the edge.

His brown eyes sparkled up at her, twinkling with amusement. "Goats can be good luck, you know. There's a goat's rhyme from the nineteenth century." He closed his eyes as he recited. *"Some may think it all a fable, when I say that in the stable I'm a doctor. And my scent—does many maladies prevent."*

Margaret shook her head. "And the malady lingers on," she murmured.

Liam winced. "The pun is the lowest form of humor."

"If you're going to sit there spouting barnyard poems, you can put up with one lousy little pun." She walked to the window. "It's cold in here. Look. The windowpanes are rattling. We'll probably both have pneumonia all winter. How do you remember all those old poems?"

Liam leaned over to the round coffee table in front of the couch. He lifted a glass decanter and poured himself a small glass of scotch. A faint smile played over his face in the dim light from the red-shaded floor lamp. "It's my business. The family business."

Margaret frowned. She brushed back the heavy crushed velvet drape and stared out to the street. Two girls came jogging by on the sidewalk across the street, backpacks bouncing on their backs.

They're really late, Margaret thought, watching them hurry toward the campus. Way past the curfew. They're going to be in big trouble if they live in a dorm.

"Did they have curfews in the dorms in Chicago?" she asked Liam. "I can't remember."

"No," he replied, sipping the scotch. "But these little Pennsylvania towns . . . they never change. Time stands still." Another sip.

"We were talking about Milton," she said, still peering out into the hazy night.

"Milton the Goat." He crossed the room, carrying his drink carefully in front of him.

"Those big hands. Is that what they mean by ham-fisted? His hands looked like big hams."

Liam snickered. "You can't get ham from a goat. Why were you looking at Milton's hands?"

Margaret turned back into the room. "It was hard *not* to! I thought he was going to *crush* that glass beer mug!"

Liam set his glass down next to the rabbit cage. She watched him poke a carrot through the bars.

"Milton is okay. I think he's an interesting man."

"Interesting? I saw you yawn during his endless description of his knife collection. I'm sorry. He just scared me. I'm not sure why. Maybe it's someone that big and strong, with those big hands, having a knife collection."

Liam snickered. "Well, with those hands, he can't have a *thimble* collection—can he?"

They both laughed.

Liam poked the carrot into the rabbit's face. "Here, Phoebe. Eat it. Come on. Eat it." He glanced back at Margaret. "This rabbit belongs in an Irish stew. Look at her. She'd rather eat her own pellets than a fresh, juicy carrot."

Margaret shivered. Stepped away from the window, pulling the drape back into place. "Liam, why do you keep that disgusting rabbit anyway?"

Liam paused before replying. "Four rabbit's feet. I need all the good luck I can get."

A minute later, a loud knock on the door made them both jump. Liam pushed the carrot into the cage and started across the room to the door. "It's so late. Who could that be?"

Margaret smiled. "Maybe it's Milton. Come to borrow a cup of Purina Goat Chow."

Liam stopped to check out his reflection in the mirror over the mantel. "Margaret, you're cruel. You really are."

Another knock. Three soft taps.

"Coming!" Liam pulled open the door. It took him a moment to recognize the woman on the front stoop. He saw her red-orange hair, disheveled, teased and tortured, falling over one eye. Then he saw her bright-lipsticked lips. "Andrea!"

"Hi, Professor. Hope I'm not disturbing you." She brushed her hair out of her eyes and smiled. A sexy smile, he thought.

He smiled back at her. "Not at all. Come in." He stepped back to make room for her to enter.

A rush of cold air accompanied Andrea DeHaven into the living room. Liam closed the door behind her. He turned to find her eyes lingering on him, a little too intensely, he thought.

She wore a long tunic sweater, iris purple, the shade clashing with her red hair and red lipstick. Purple tights under the sweater. Dangling black glass earrings. A rope of matching glass beads over her uplifted breasts, heavy-looking beads, clattering over the bright sweater as she stepped into the room.

Liam inhaled a sweet, tangy fragrance. Margaret can probably recognize the perfume, he thought. So strong. Did she *bathe* in it?

"Margaret, you remember Andrea DeHaven, our esteemed landlady?" he said with a smile and exaggerated formality.

"Yes, of course," Margaret said from the center of the room, forcing her own smile.

Andrea turned, noticing Margaret for the first time. She

39

gave her a perfunctory "Nice to see you again," then turned her watery blue eyes back to Liam.

How old is she? Liam wondered. Forty maybe? He tried not to stare at the pointy twin V's poking through the purple sweater. She'd be sexy if she didn't try so hard.

No. Check that. She *is* sexy.

She was a solid woman. Big thighs. He remembered that she had worn tight green slacks when she showed him the house in August. He remembered the slacks. Remembered her touching him as they moved through the rooms. Touching his hand, squeezing his arm. Friendly. Her hair brushing his cheek.

How many times had she mentioned she was a widow? At least a dozen. With so much sadness, right there, visible in those blue eyes that hung on his, as if trying to impart some secret message.

"I was on the next block, visiting an old friend," Andrea told him. "I was passing the house. I saw the light on. I thought I'd pop in for just a second and see how you were doing."

"That was so nice of you," Margaret offered. A voice in the distance.

Andrea stared at Liam.

"We're not used to having a landlady who is so friendly," Liam told her, suggestively.

"It's a little college town. Everyone is friendly here," she replied, lowering her eyes. She licked her lipsticked lips. "I've had my fingers crossed that you were enjoying the house." She raised both hands. Red, polished nails. Fingers crossed.

Liam reached out and tenderly took her right hand in his, fingers still crossed. "Well, it's certainly a pleasure to see you again, Andrea. Do you know why we cross our fingers?" He held on to her hand, the skin moist and warm, soft as a ripe peach.

"You see, the cross is a sign of perfect unity." He slid his hand over her crossed fingers. "The two fingers cross. In the center of the two lines is the perfect place to hold a wish."

"I never knew that," she gushed. He thought he felt her

shiver. She's too easy, he thought, letting go of her hand, lowering his eyes.

"What beautiful, long fingers," he added. "A sign of good breeding and long life."

She actually giggled.

"Liam—" Margaret from somewhere out in the dark reaches of the solar system. "Andrea didn't stop by to have her palm read."

Liam kept his eyes on the landlady's. "I wasn't telling her fortune. I was relating some ancient beliefs. You know, the Chinese put a lot of importance in the length of their fingernails. If you cut your nails too short, you were cutting off your life."

"It's all really interesting," Andrea said, glancing at her red nails. "Mine are fake." She laughed. Seemed to snap out of her Liam-induced trance. "I should be going." She swept her hair back again as her eyes surveyed the living room. "So everything is okay?"

"We're quite comfortable," Liam replied. "It's all still strange to us, but we're starting to feel at home."

"I'm having a little trouble with the faucet in my bathroom upstairs," Margaret told her, sitting on the sofa back, supporting herself with both hands. "It's dripping very badly. I can't get it to stop."

"We'll have to get a plumber." Andrea didn't sound terribly interested in Margaret's problem. She raised her eyes to Liam. And was that an actual wink? Or did she blink? "Your part of the house is okay, Liam? May I call you Liam?"

"Yes. All is shipshape. Andrea."

"And how are you enjoying your bedroom?"

He held back a laugh. Look up the word *obvious* in the dictionary, and you'll find a picture of Andrea DeHaven.

"The workmen did an excellent job. The new window solved the draft problem."

She nodded, letting her hair fall over one eye.

Very sexy, Liam thought, his eyes wandering to the V of her sweater once again.

"I'm so glad you're enjoying the house. I guess I'd better say good night." She glanced at Margaret, then turned to the door.

Liam followed her into the short entryway. I know what she's going to say, he told himself.

And then she said it. Word for word. "If there's ever *anything* I can do for you, please don't hesitate to call." Followed by one last meaningful glance.

He took her hand once again. Inhaled the tangy perfume. I'm only human.

She was obvious. But it worked. He felt aroused. Stirred.

"Chicago was so cold. It's nice to be in a warm, friendly place." I can be obvious too. "Good night, Andrea." He let his hand slide slowly off hers.

He watched her make her way down the steps, along the sidewalk. An undulating blur of red and purple under the hazy white glare of the streetlights. He couldn't help but think about the big thighs inside the purple tights.

Her perfume lingered in the entryway. Margaret snickered. "I thought she was going to tear off that hideous sweater and jump you right here. I pictured her on top of you, holding you down, humping away, smearing her lipstick all over your face."

Liam grinned. "You do have a graphic imagination."

Margaret cleared her throat. "It didn't take much imagination."

"Margaret, if you weren't here, I might've gotten lucky."

She narrowed her eyes at him. "Excuse me? *Lucky?*" Shaking her head, she crossed to the mantel. "We forgot to ask her if this fireplace works."

Liam sighed, rubbing his chin. "I'm sure she'll be back soon."

Margaret studied him, frowning. "Are you really attracted to that cow?"

"Cows have some pleasing qualities. There's a Welsh tale about a farmer's wife who was turned into a cow—"

"Oh, Liam. Stop! I asked you a serious question. Save the

charming folktales for someone who hasn't heard them all already."

"I was joking, Margaret."

"I wasn't. Are you attracted to her? To *Andrea?* Do you think you might—"

He shook his hand as if waving away her words. He dropped onto the arm of the couch. The leather made a soft whoosh as he sank into it. "No. I'm afraid poor Andrea will not have her way with me." He raised his eyes to Margaret's, hesitated. Then added, "I think I'm in love." Said lightly.

"You're kidding?"

He shook his head, his expression now thoughtful. "No. Not kidding. Not kidding at all."

Her mouth formed a small O of surprise. She removed her hand from the mantel to scratch the shoulder of her sweater, then returned it. Leaning. Studying him. "The dark-haired girl in the restaurant? The pretty one?"

Liam nodded. Didn't smile.

Margaret squinted at him. "What was her name? Sara? She's a little young."

"I don't agree."

"You don't think she's too young?"

A thin smile. "No. I think she'll do very nicely."

Margaret sighed. Her expression brightened. "Well, Liam— good luck." She made a fist, raised it, and knocked on the mantel, knocked on wood—very carefully—three times.

PART TWO

6

Garrett's black mood followed him into the night. What do I want to be when I grow up?

The question repeated in his mind until it became an annoying, unsettling chant. What do I want to be? What? What?

Not this.

He didn't remember driving to the station. He didn't remember where he parked the black-and-white. Probably in its usual spot in the Post Office lot. But he didn't remember.

And now Walter was saying something, but Garrett didn't hear him. Their gunmetal gray desks faced each other, pressed together in the center of the small, low squad room. Garrett leaned forward, squinted at Walter, tried to concentrate on what he was saying.

Walter Granger, his albino partner.

He was so white. So light. So bright. White skin, almost flour white. Almost ghostly, translucent. Topped by the straight, white-blond hair, so fine and light, like white thread. Crooked white teeth. White buck teeth. Even his eyes were pale. Gray eyes. Almost silver. Walter has no color, Garrett thought. He is anticolor. He is only light. And now he stared at Walter as if staring at a light, clinging to the light, clinging to Walter's brightness to keep himself from being pulled back into the darkness of his mood.

47

"How's it going, Walter?"

"Quiet." Walter finished his coffee, crumpled the cardboard cup in his hand, and tossed it in the wastepaper basket beside his desk. "Kinda boring, actually."

Kinda.

Garrett fumbled through the files on the desktop. All old news. "Anything happen this afternoon?"

Walter groaned and raised his feet to the desk. He had a hole on the sole of his left shoe. "Ethan had a seven-forty-two."

Garrett frowned impatiently. "Don't tell me numbers, man. You know I can't ever remember the damn numbers. What was it?"

Walter raised both hands in surrender. "Okay, okay. Sorry. You don't have to take my head off. A dog got run over."

"A dog? Where?"

"On Highlands. Across from the Stop 'N' Shop. A dalmation. Flattened his middle. He had a head and a butt, but his middle was squashed flat."

Garrett made a face. "Who ran him over?"

Walter shrugged. "If we knew that, it'd be a seven-forty-one. But this was a seven-forty-two—dog hit-and-run."

"Shit," Garrett muttered. He eyed Walter suspiciously. "You're making those numbers up, right? We don't really have a number for a dog hit-and-run—do we?"

Walter twisted his face. He actually looked hurt. "Course we do. We got numbers for everything. Ask Ethan. It's *his* case. Ethan thinks it was a truck. Probably a big semi. He don't think a car could squash a dog that flat. He said the guts were pressed right into the street. You couldn't scrape 'em up if you tried."

Garrett shuffled aimlessly through the files, just keeping his hands busy. "Ethan always exaggerates. Was that the only call today?"

"Yup. Unless you count Mrs. Flaherty."

Garrett sighed. "I don't count Mrs. Flaherty."

Mrs. Flaherty called at least twice a week to report that her husband was beating her up. Garrett and his fellow officers took the first few calls seriously. But it turned out that Mrs. Flaherty didn't have a husband.

"We need to start a fund," Garrett said, reaching for the morning newspaper, scanning the back pages.

"What kind of fund?"

"You know. Get people to contribute. Raise enough money to bring some criminals to town. So you and I don't have to sit here staring at each other all the time."

The irony went over Walter's head. He took Garrett seriously. "I kind of like it quiet, Garrett."

Garrett nodded thoughtfully. "Yeah. Me too." He found what he was searching for in the newspaper. The Jumble puzzle. He pulled open the desk drawer and retrieved a pencil. "Think Harvey's having a good time?"

"Where is he? At a concert or something?"

"His wife took him to a play."

Walter shook his head. "Harvey likes concerts better than plays. He says when he goes to a play, the people on stage talk real loud and keep him awake."

Garrett laughed. He eyed his companion. Had Walter just made a joke, or was he just repeating something Harvey had said?

Repeating, Garrett decided. He'd known Walter for two years and had never heard him make a joke or even come close.

Two years? Is that how long he and Angel had lived in this hick town? Two years next month in November, Garrett realized, lowering his eyes to the newspaper puzzle. Well. He had no regrets about leaving Detroit. No regrets about leaving Angel's parents two hundred miles behind.

Had he moved far enough away?

"Who's on patrol tonight—Duke or Jimmy?"

Walter scratched the back of his head. "Both, I think. They're both down on the duty roster. But they didn't call in."

Garrett pictured Duke and Jimmy parked in front of the Krispy Kreme. Heavy metal blaring on the squad car radio. The two of them sipping their black coffee, eyes out the windows, checking out the coeds.

He forced himself to focus on the puzzle. The first word was hard. FRRNOEIT. Sometimes he could unscramble them in a glance. But this one wasn't obvious.

Why did he like these word puzzles so much? He did the Jumble every day. It was part of his routine. Gave him a sense of accomplishment. He scribbled on the white margin of the newspaper page: TORNFIER. FIRETORN. No. Not right.

The Jumble, he realized, was the perfect cop's puzzle. You take something that's all messed up and you fix it, put it back together, make it neat. Order out of chaos.

He had just figured out the word and was writing it in the little circles when the phone rang.

Walter picked it up. "Station house."

Garrett lowered the pencil. Watched Walter's mouth drop open, his silver eyes go wide.

Walter jerked upright in the desk chair. "No shit. No shit. No shit."

"Hey—what's wrong?"

"No shit, Duke. Oh, man."

"It's Duke? What's going on?"

Walter didn't seem to hear him. Garrett jumped to his feet and leaned over the desk. "We got a problem?"

"No shit. No shit. Okay. Okay. Don't touch anything. We're coming."

The receiver dropped from Walter's hand and clonked against the desktop. Walter made no attempt to retrieve it. He stared across the desks at Garrett, making swallowing sounds.

Garrett leaned toward him impatiently. "Well?"

"We got a m-murder."

Garrett felt the back of his neck prickle.

Walter reached up to his collar. His fat fingers fumbled at his top button. "No shit. A murder. We've got to go."

"Where?" Garrett demanded. Was that the first question to

ask? He had dealt with one armed robbery in two years on the force. But a murder—that called for all different questions.

Walter gave up on the collar button. He spun around awkwardly and jerked his black uniform jacket off the wall hook. "The campus. The Circle. Behind some bushes, Duke said. Two girls discovered it."

His heart pounding, Garrett opened his bottom drawer, removed the service pistol in its heavy brown-leather holster. He strapped it on, feeling a wave of guilt rise up from his stomach.

I wished this.

I hoped for a crime. I wished for something to do, something to end the boredom.

It's my fault. I got my wish.

Crazy thoughts, he knew. But there they were.

"How's Duke doing? Is he okay?"

"He sounded real upset. Like he was going to cry or something."

Duke was squeamish, Garrett knew. The little guy never wanted to be a cop. He only took it up because his father's dry cleaning business went belly-up, and he couldn't figure out anything else to do.

Garrett grabbed his jacket. He clicked on the answering machine, then followed Walter out the door.

Into a cool, wet night. They didn't need their jackets. His gun pulling at his side. His heart pounding hard, hands cold as he slid them over the steering wheel.

"It's a girl," Walter said, slamming the passenger door. "A coed, maybe. Duke wasn't sure."

Garrett hit the siren and flashing roof light. The shrill wail made him wince. He hadn't heard it in a long while.

He backed the car out, spun quickly, tires skidding over asphalt, bounced over the curb, the car rocking hard, into the empty street.

"Was he sure she was murdered?"

Walter let out an odd sound, a sound Garrett had never

51

heard him make before, a choked cry from deep in his fleshy throat. "Yeah. He was sure."

The girl's face was covered with black, sticky tar.

That's what Garrett thought at first glance. And he could only glance before turning away. His whole body shuddering.

This was real. A real girl. Real death.

He wasn't sure he was ready.

The thick tar blackening her face? No. It was blood.

Red and black. Red and black.

The ground, the bushes, their faces all caught in the flickering glow of the squad car lights. Red then black. Red then black.

Duke stood awkwardly, his toothpick body strangely erect, the grenade of an Adam's apple bobbing in his long throat, his short black flattopped hair seeming to stand on end. He pointed to the bushes when Garrett and Walter arrived, then stepped back as if retreating.

"Where's Jimmy?"

"On his way. He had a flat. Out on Stowe Street. He'll be here."

"A flashlight," Garrett muttered, hesitating on the grass, eyes surveying the empty Circle, the campus buildings rising around it, dark, silent witnesses. "Did we bring a flashlight?"

Walter slapped his forehead. "Oh, shit. Forgot."

"Here. I got one," Duke murmured.

The white halogen light flooded over the grass like a bright river, making them squint. Garrett took the light from Duke. He needed something to hold on to.

He took cautious steps to the bushes. Walter hung back, a few feet behind Garrett.

Black tar over her face. So much blood.

Behind him, Duke's voice sounded distant and weak. "Her name's Charlotte. Charlotte Wilson. I found a college ID in her wallet."

Garrett stopped in front of the low evergreen shrub, unmoving in the windless night. He glanced back at Duke, a slender silhouette in front of the squad car headlights. "A student?"

"No. Employee."

"She was robbed?"

"No. Wallet has twenty dollars in it. And a MasterCard."

"She was raped?"

"Don't think so. Her panties are still on."

Very professional, Duke, Garrett thought.

Red then black. Red then black.

He took a deep breath and held it, then made his way around the evergreen shrub, gripping the metal-handled flashlight so hard his hand ached.

Walter's trembling voice behind him, surprisingly tiny: "Shouldn't somebody take notes or something?"

Garrett shut his eyes for a moment, still saw the red glare, the black, the red glare again through his eyelids. "We'll write it up later. First let's have a look, okay? Then—"

His breath caught in his throat.

He wasn't prepared. Not prepared for anything like this.

The black-tarred face. He knew it was blood. It had soaked into her eyes, puddled in the eye sockets. It filled her nose.

He couldn't see her mouth. Where was her mouth?

The beam of light trembled, making the ground appear to shake.

His knees buckled. Did that soft cry come from his own throat?

He squinted into the light. Forced himself not to blink.

One arm bent up behind her neck.

Do arms bend that way?

Short skirt up over her waist, revealing a V of black panties. Legs sprawled apart. Stomach torn open. Torn open. Torn open. Spilling . . . everything spilling.

And her back.

No!

Split in half? Bent in two?

No.

Shit no.

A trick of the light. His eyes gone bad.

Red then black. Red then black.

Swallowing once, twice. Forced to turn away. Duke and Walter right behind him now. Duke's pencil face a blank, eyes dazed. Nothing moving except for that sliding Adam's apple. Walter white and pasty even in this light, eyes half-shut, one pudgy hand resting on his gun handle, the other helplessly lowered, fingers clenching and unclenching.

Garrett forced himself to turn back.

A puddle of dark blood around the girl's broken body. Like a shadow. A dead shadow.

What a mess. A puzzle that can't be unscrambled, Garrett thought. The girl. Charlotte Wilson. She can't be rearranged, fixed up, put back in order.

"Oh fuck."

The quavering light rested on something on the ground. Garrett bent to pick it up, feeling dizzy. The light didn't make sense of it.

It was wrong. Something wrong.

"Oh fuck. What is it?"

Soft in Garrett's hot hand.

He gripped it tightly, held it high. Shook it.

"A wig?" he called out loud, his voice hollow, tight. "Was she wearing a wig?"

No. Not a wig, he saw, holding it close.

Too close.

Not a wig. It's her hair. Charlotte's hair. Still attached to her scalp.

Her hair and scalp. Gold in the bright light. Ripped from her head. Tossed aside like wrapping paper.

"Oh fuck."

The hair fell from his hand.

The flashlight fell too.

Garrett leaned over the bush and vomited up his dinner.

7

Sara tossed the *People* magazine onto the floor. "Do I really have to care about Keanu Reeves's problems? Mary Beth, why do you subscribe to this magazine?"

"My life isn't trashy enough."

Sara sprawled on her back on the green leather couch, her head on the soft arm, her knees in the air. She stretched both arms over her head. "I need some exercise. Want to come jogging with me?"

Mary Beth sat cross-legged on the faded Oriental carpet, her back against the coffee table. She shook her head. "No way. I'm not jogging across campus at night." She uncrossed her legs and reached for the magazine. "What does it say about Keanu Reeves?"

Sara stared up at the spiderweb of cracks on the low, white ceiling. "Did you see that girl on the news? It's so horrible. I can't stand to walk by that spot. You know. Where she was killed. They've got yellow tape stretched all over the bushes. To rope it off. Yesterday I saw two students with cameras, taking pictures there."

"Gross," Mary Beth murmured. She rolled the magazine between her hands but didn't open it. "I don't get it. Nothing like that ever happens in Freewood."

"That's what they keep saying on the local news."

"I never watch the local news." Mary Beth leaned back against the table edge. She yawned. "Why am I always so tired? I guess it's having to work for a living."

"That poor woman was murdered three days ago, and the police don't have a clue. It's just so creepy, don't you think? I have to walk past there every morning. It gives me the shivers every time."

"And you want to go jogging at night?" Mary Beth tapped the rolled-up magazine against the torn knees of her faded jeans. "It's safer to stay inside and get fat and flabby."

Sara frowned. "For sure." She shivered as the ugly images from the local TV news lingered in her mind. She saw the black plastic body bag being carried in a stretcher from The Circle. Saw the grim-faced policemen refusing to answer questions.

"How are your classes? You enjoying them?"

Mary Beth's question jarred her from her thoughts. "Guess who I got for my seminar?" Sara replied, brightening.

"I can't guess. I don't know anyone in the Psych Department."

"Boring."

"Excuse me?"

"Professor Boring. He's conducting the seminar."

Mary Beth laughed. "Is there really a Professor Boring?"

Sara pulled herself to a sitting position and swung her legs to the floor. "Do you believe it? If your name was Boring, and you decided to become a professor, wouldn't you change your name? I mean, do you know how hard it is to keep a straight face every time I have to call him Professor Boring?"

Mary Beth tugged a plastic barrette from the side of her hair. "I had a botany instructor named Plante. Greta Plante. We always thought it was a made-up name."

Sara chuckled. "Her first name should have been Ivy. Why did you take botany?"

"I thought it would be easy." Mary Beth clicked the barrette between her fingers. Her expression changed. She lowered her gaze to the carpet. "You know me. Always find the easy way.

Guess that's why I stayed here in Freewood. At least you took a chance. Moved to New York. Tried something hard."

Sara let out a short, bitter laugh. "Tried and failed. I always seem to make my decisions because of a guy." She stood up and crossed the small living room to the kitchen. "I'm getting a Diet Coke. Want one?"

"No thanks."

Sara returned, tilting the red and white can to her lips. "I came to Moore State as a freshman because of Michael. I left Freewood after college because of Rick. And now I'm back because of Chip." Said matter-of-factly, as if taking inventory.

"But I never left!" Mary Beth wailed. "Look at this apartment. It's like I'm still in college." She gestured to the posters on the wall above the couch. A Jim Morrison and the Doors at the Fillmore poster from 1967, in Day-Glo orange and red. Beside it, a Keith Haring, three of his bold, primitive figures dancing across a solid yellow background.

Sara's eyes surveyed the room. Besides the leather couch and the coffee table, donated by Mary Beth's parents when they redecorated their house in Shaker Heights, two beige futons on the floor comprised the only other furniture. A twelve-inch television rested on top of the white bookshelf against the far wall. The bookshelf held Mary Beth's stereo system and was crammed with CDs, paperback books, and stacks of magazines.

Sara had to laugh. "It does look a little like our old dorm room," she admitted. "Or that apartment we rented on High Street when we were seniors. Where's the waterbed?"

Mary Beth glumly rested her chin in her hands. "It sprung a leak. I had to swim for my life. Otherwise I'd probably still have it. I mean, I still listen to Pink Floyd, for chrissake! It's like I'm so determined not to grow up!"

Sara tossed her dark hair back with a flick of her head. "But at least you have a job, Mary Beth. I really *am* a student again."

She tried to think of a way to change the subject. In all the excitement of moving back to the campus and seeing Mary Beth again, Sara had forgotten about her friend's capacity to feel sorry for herself. Mary Beth was never as unhappy as she portrayed herself, Sara knew. It was just a way of keeping the conversation focused on her.

Mary Beth liked sympathy, liked to have her friends take care of her. In large part, their friendship in college had been based on practical, down-to-earth Sara watching out for intense, emotional Mary Beth.

But now, in a way, Sara realized, their situations were reversed. Sara was the one with the life crisis, the one who needed caring for. Mary Beth had come through for her as a true friend. But it must have been a stretch for her. They both had a sense that even though it was great to be back together, the relationship had changed. Neither of them had really sorted out what their new roles should be.

"Speaking of jobs . . ." Mary Beth reached up and pulled the soda can from Sara's hand. She took a sip, then handed it back. "Did you go to Dean Cohn's office?"

Sara nodded. "I went the other day. After my seminar. He wasn't there. His secretary said he was called away suddenly. I guess he'll be back in a few days."

"You going to try again?"

"Yeah. A part-time job three days a week sounds perfect. I can really use the money." She gestured with her free hand. "Talk about feeling like a college kid again. I can't even afford a futon!"

That made Mary Beth smile.

"You know," Sara continued, dropping back onto the low couch, "when I was leaving the Administration Building, I heard two kids in the hallway talking about him. They called him Milton the Monster." She snickered.

Mary Beth shook her head. "That's cold. That's really cold."

"Well, he kind of looks like a movie monster, doesn't he? He's so huge and menacing-looking. With that weird white hair that sort of stands straight up as if he's had an electrical shock." Sara took a long sip from the can. "Kids can be really cruel."

"I've heard he's a nice guy. The gossip is he's been married three times." She sighed. "Do you *believe* we have nothing better to do in our office than gossip about Milton Cohn?"

"Pretty sad," Sara agreed. She twirled the can between her hands. "Know who I ran into on the library steps? Liam. You know. Professor O'Connor."

Mary Beth's green eyes flashed. "You call him *Liam?*"

Sara laughed. She could feel her face growing hot and knew she was blushing. "Well, he told me to!"

Mary Beth leaned forward, interested. "Did you say hi to *Liam?* Did he remember you?"

Sara nodded. "Yes. I was so surprised. He remembered my name. He—he said my name was lucky. Because it means morning."

"Sara means morning?"

"No. Morgan. He said something about morning being a new beginning." Sara lowered her eyes. "I think he was *flirting* with me."

"Wow," Mary Beth murmured.

Sara suddenly felt sorry she had mentioned him. She felt somehow exposed. Could Mary Beth read her mind? Could Mary Beth tell how much she'd been thinking about Liam?

She didn't want to be teased about him. There really wasn't anything to be teased about. She had found herself thinking about him, feeling his hand brushing her hair, feeling the warmth of his brown eyes.

But so what?

"He was definitely flirting with you in the restaurant the other night," Mary Beth offered, shifting her weight on the floor and cupping her hands around her knees.

Sara played innocent. "Do you think so?" Her cheeks still felt warm.

"But of course he flirts with everybody."

"How do you know that?" A bit too defensively.

"Well, he flirted with *me* when I did that video of him. You know. He has that Irish charm. A bit of the old blarney, or whatever people always say."

She's right, Sara admitted silently.

I've been thinking about him all week, thinking about the way he looked at me, thinking about that old rhyme he recited, the way he held my hand.

The old blarney.

The old Irish charm.

Of course he's like that with everyone. What made me think he found *me* so special?

She tossed back her hair as if tossing away her thoughts. I'm the juvenile one. Not Mary Beth. I'm the giggling college girl. Twenty-four and still falling for the handsome professor.

Mary Beth pulled herself up straight. Her expression turned serious. "So what about Chip?"

"Huh?" Sara was still thinking about Liam, picturing him on the library steps, his brown eyes sparkling at her, the wind tossing his dark hair.

"You were going to tell me the whole story. About Chip," Mary Beth insisted, tossing aside the *People* magazine. "Come on, Sara. Stop keeping me in suspense. Why'd you dump Chip?"

Sara swallowed. "Well . . . he tried to kill me."

8

A shadow fell over Sara's desk. She finished typing the sentence, turned away from her computer. Stared up at Eliot Glazer, filling the narrow opening that formed the entrance to her low-walled cubicle.

Eliot Glazer, Executive Editor, Concord Publishing.

His thinning gray hair was slicked straight back. His bloodshot gray eyes peered down at her through silver-rimmed glasses perched low on his nose. His cheeks were always emblazoned with circles of pink, as if he were blushing. Or excited.

He wore unstarched white shirts, open at the collar. He never bothered to button the button-down collar buttons. His stomach sagged down over the belt of his blue suit trousers.

"Eliot. Hi. Catching up on some slush pile letters," Sara greeted him, gesturing to the stack of unwanted manuscripts. As editorial assistant, her job was to read them—at least a page or two—and send them back before they became a fire hazard.

Not her favorite part of the job.

Didn't these people know how *bad* their writing was?

Eliot leaned his bulky frame against the cubicle wall. "Sara, know why they call it the slush pile?"

"No. Why?"

"I thought you'd know."

He waited for her laugh. That was Eliot's kind of joke. So subtle it wasn't funny.

Sara laughed anyway. "Some great manuscripts today. I just finished one called *I Am a Martian*. It's an autobiography."

"You sending it back to Mars?"

"No. Wisconsin."

Eliot nodded. He peered over his glasses at her. "I've been to Wisconsin." She waited for him to continue, but he didn't.

Sara glanced at the little desk clock she kept on her shelf. Four-fifty on Friday afternoon. Was Eliot bringing her work for the weekend?

Please no. Please.

He turned and she saw the set of galleys in his hand. "Sara, these are late. Can you read them over the weekend?"

"Well . . ."

He pushed the stack of long sheets at her. He wasn't really asking. He was telling her to proofread them over the weekend. "They're pretty clean. It shouldn't take too long."

Sara glanced at the first page. "What is this? About soccer?"

Eliot nodded. "A soccer novel. Do you believe it? It's late, of course. Everyone's in a panic. You know. The drama of publishing. We work a year in advance, but everything has to be done in a mad rush." His cheeks brightened to scarlet.

Sara rolled her eyes. Flipped through the galleys. "This looks like fun. A four-thousand-page soccer novel."

A crooked smile revealed nicotine-stained teeth. "It only reads like four thousand pages." He turned, his stomach exiting the cubicle before he did. "Tense. Everyone's tense. I think it's the merger."

"Did you hear anything about it?" Sara demanded.

"See? You're tense too. What do you care if we merge or we don't merge? Think they'll take away your stock options?"

"That's cold, Eliot. That's really cold." As an editorial assistant, Sara's salary was somewhat under twenty-five thousand. No one had ever mentioned stock options to her. Or bonuses.

Or an expense account for fancy lunches. Or more than a two-week vacation.

He walked away. "Have a good weekend."

She stared at the space he left, rolling the galley sheets between her hands. Then she dropped the pages onto the desk and turned back to the rejection letter on the computer. *"I am sorry to say that your manuscript about your childhood on Mars does not fit in with our publishing plans."*

We should have a form letter for extraterrestrials, she thought.

A loudly cleared throat startled her, made her spin around. "Chip!"

Grinning, he stepped into the cubicle and dropped down on the edge of the counter, on top of some manuscripts. He swooped up her paperweight, a clear glass ball, and tossed it from hand to hand.

Just barge right in. Take whatever you want.

His straw-colored hair brushed her forehead as he leaned down to kiss her lips. His lips were scratchy, dry.

Take whatever you want.

She wanted the kiss to last a little longer. But she pulled away first. Most everyone had gone home, but Eliot was still prowling the halls.

What's wrong if he catches me kissing Chip? she asked herself.

Unprofessional.

She pushed Chip back with one hand, straightened the tan linen vest she wore over a cream-colored cotton sweater. "Chip—what are you doing here?"

He raised the glass ball between his hands and narrowed his eyes, peering hard into it. "Let's see what the crystal ball predicts. Hmm . . . I see water and sand. I see sun. I see a house in Southampton. A long weekend."

"Do you see your father in the house?"

He lowered the glass ball. "No. He flew to L.A. this morning. Some kind of crisis at the network. A production problem.

Some really big deal." His grin grew wider, revealing two rows of perfect teeth.

How does Chip always look tanned? Sara wondered. He spends so little time in the sun. Even his tennis club is indoors.

"No Dad. Just us." He reached into the pocket of his chinos, pulled out the keys to his Porsche, and dangled them in front of Sara's face. "That's why I came here. To take you away from all this."

Sara glanced at the clock. "It's five. We'll be in Friday rush hour. The traffic—"

Leaning down again, he ran his pointer finger tenderly down her cheek. "We'll be *together* in Friday rush hour. We won't care about the traffic—right?"

His touch gave her a chill. She grabbed his finger and squeezed it gently. She stared up into his clear blue eyes. Such innocent eyes. Baby eyes. So perfect, so touching in that open, American face. The young Robert Redford.

Chip Whitney, WASP Prince.

Sara still couldn't get over the fact that she was seeing someone prettier than she. Sometimes she ran her fingers over his soft, blond eyebrows, handling his face as if he were a doll.

A perfect face. A perfect life.

Well . . . almost perfect.

The scar on his chin made him human. A tiny, white line no longer than an inch. He had no memory of how he got it. It rose up from his tanned skin like a faint second smile. Sara liked to rub her fingers over it too.

And of course his nose was too small. Sara believed for months that some plastic surgeon had clipped it a little too close. But no. That slightly upturned stub was the nose Chip had been born with.

It made him look smug. He *was* smug, she had decided after knowing him only a few hours. But smug in a handsome, charming way.

He always managed to confuse her right from the start.

She always felt she was with him—and outside of herself

studying him—at the same time. But maybe that was her problem, not his.

"We have to stop at my apartment," she said. She turned back to her keyboard and tapped some keys, started to exit the word processing program. The Martian from Wisconsin could wait until next week to have his life rejected. "I mean, I have to get a swimsuit. Pack some clothes."

"We can buy you a swimsuit out there," he insisted. "We'll go shopping in town. Buy you everything you need."

"Chip, I can't just buy new clothes everywhere I go. I'm so broke, I've been packing my lunch."

Why did they spend so much time talking about poor Sara and rich Chip? Sara realized she was the one who constantly brought up their financial status. But what choice did she have? He was the Gold Card and she was Discover. Discover what it was like to try to live on one salary in New York City.

His broad shoulders slumped under the white polo shirt. He turned the glass ball in his hand. "You're always so good at thinking up excuses not to be spontaneous."

Ouch.

Could she let him get away with that? No.

"Maybe it's because *spontaneous* means doing what you want, when you want to do it."

Got him back. A good shot.

He nodded, grinned. An inappropriate grin, she thought. I was serious. It wasn't a joke. Not a funny comeback.

He set down the glass paperweight beside the stack of manuscripts. "Okay, okay. We'll stop at your place first. You can pack a bag. Then we'll grab dinner somewhere. Then we'll drive out to the beach. Do you like that plan better?"

She kissed his cheek in reply.

He jumped to his feet. The kiss didn't seem to please him. He glanced at his watch, an old Bulova from the 1950s she had bought him in a shop on Columbus Avenue for their six-month anniversary. It didn't keep good time. She suspected he only wore it when he was with her.

"Let's get going." He stepped out into the hallway and glanced impatiently down the long row of cubicles.

She wasn't surprised by his change of mood. He had been thwarted. Chip never reacted well to being thwarted. It wasn't just a matter of getting his way. It was an interruption in the smooth running of his life.

To Chip, even a small roadblock was a roadblock.

He wasn't totally spoiled, Sara realized. He had values. Growing up in Beverly Hills, the beach house in Malibu, the trips to New York and Europe with his father the network president, the glamorous TV and film stars and directors dropping by, sunning and shmoozing around the Olympic-sized pool in the backyard or using the clay tennis courts behind the two-story guest house—the Gold Card life hadn't kept Chip from becoming a caring, sensitive person.

It had only increased his expectations.

He expected a smooth, efficient life. He expected to ease through. He expected the sun to shine for every picnic.

Have a nice day. The phrase really meant something to him. He *expected* to have nice days.

And he expected people to say yes to him.

Yes, yes, yes.

No was a major disappointment. No was so unsettling for him. So unacceptable. He seemed to take every no so personally.

Sara saw him as golden and sunny. She loved to run her hand up and down the soft blond hair on the back of his arm. She loved to tug at the tuft of blond hair that poked through the open front of his polo shirts. The hair like tiny shafts of sunlight poking out of his skin.

She was so different. She was so dark, all gravity, all earth. She liked the shade so much. Sometimes when she was with him, she felt like one of those dark planets, invisible to the naked eye, until illuminated by the sun to become a star at night.

Yes, yes, yes.

No made the light fade from his eyes. He was so good-natured. So . . . mellow. Mellow yellow. They never argued over anything important. But the little nos set him off.

"No, I can't meet you until five-thirty."

"No, I don't want coffee. I have to get back to work."

"No, I love the dog—but you have to take it back. Pets aren't allowed in my building."

And then, who turned off the sun? She couldn't bear his muttered growls, the pained looks, as if the whole universe was conspiring against him, conspiring to destroy him with a single no.

She could still picture the pale, startled face on the waitress in that restaurant in SoHo. She could still see her frizzed-out purple hair. Still see her long plastic earrings start to jangle as she shook her head in disbelief.

"No, sir, I'm sorry but we're out of the risotto."

Chip's head had snapped back as if he'd been shot. Sara had really thought he was in pain. Then he jumped to his feet, nearly toppling the glass-topped table. Sara had no choice but to chase after him as he stormed to the door. She turned just before leaving, saw the waitress still at the table with her pad raised, her earrings swinging as if in an earthquake.

The earthquake had subsided when Sara reached the sidewalk. Chip was already studying the menu in the window of the restaurant next door. He smiled and pulled Sara close, as if nothing had happened, as if the sun hadn't gone out for a moment, as if he didn't really care about that little no. Just a joke, actually.

Sara still trembling in embarrassment. Sara, who hates scenes of any kind. Happy to bask in the shade. She wanted to say something to Chip, to scold him, to tell him that risotto just wasn't that important.

But he would only laugh at her. He wouldn't even understand.

Now she sees the long earrings shake. And every time she pictures them, it gives her a heavy feeling in her stomach, a heavy feeling about Chip.

Dread?

Chip took her hand and they glided into the next restaurant. People jammed three-deep at the bar. Every table filled. No reservation. But Chip got them a table, and they cruised into dinner.

It's so easy for him. He *demands* that it be easy.

It's all so easy, why does he need me? Sara wondered.

The only time he seems needy is when they are making love. Then he seems to need everything, all of her. He needs to cover her, to smother her, to swallow her, to please her, please her, please her.

Yes, yes, yes.

It doesn't last long.

And does she need him?

She likes him so much. Like a dark moth hovering close to the sun, daring to flutter closer, closer. She likes the parties in the mission-style townhouses or the chrome-and-white-leather penthouses, likes meeting the funny, vain people who stand with their wineglasses in such a practiced stance, who take such endless pains to dress so casually, such witty people who make each other laugh, for whom the purpose of life seems to be to look really good and make each other laugh.

They make Sara laugh too. She doesn't feel superior. She clings to Chip and watches from the shade.

She likes his Porsche. She likes the smell of his aftershave. Obsession. Obsession For Men. Isn't he embarrassed to buy it? Isn't he embarrassed to stand at the counter and pronounce the name?

No. It's easy for him.

She likes that about him too.

But does she need him?

Does she need to ask that question? No.

She clicked off the computer, stuffed the galleys into her canvas bag, and hurried to take Chip's arm. Past the double row of plum-colored cubicles. Past Eliot's office. She called in good night. Glimpsed him bent over the phone, one hand sifting through his gray hair. Looking up in time to see her with Chip, he gave a quick, dismissive wave.

Down the elevator. Chip humming. Starting to brighten after having to change his plans. Time for a kiss. She dropped the bag and pulled his face down to hers with both hands. Time for a long, sweet kiss. It's twenty-five floors to the ground.

Chip tapped the wheel impatiently with one hand, edging the dark green Porsche forward a few feet, braking inches from the bumper of the van in front of them. "Traffic," he muttered. He squeezed Sara's knee, then returned his hand to the wheel. "I hate going out to the beach on Friday night."

Sara raised her knees onto the dark leather of the glove compartment. "Some of us have to work for a living," she said pointedly. "Some of us can't leave earlier than Friday night."

"Work is overrated," he replied. The cars all moved forward a few more feet.

Sara saw red flashing lights around the curve. "Looks like an accident. We'll be okay once we get past it."

He didn't reply. He didn't seem to hear her. Where is he staring? Sara wondered, watching the harsh light from an overhead streetlamp roll over his face. They inched forward. Light then darkness. Light then darkness. His handsome face seemed to disappear, then glow back, but his narrowed eyes didn't blink.

"What are you thinking about?" she demanded softly.

"Huh? Oh." Why did the question surprise him? "Nothing, really. I get hypnotized by the traffic. You know." He sighed. "We could've gotten an earlier start if your mother hadn't called."

"Well, I had to talk to her. Poor Mom. All alone in that big house. She never used to keep me on the phone so long. But now . . ."

"You should get her a dog."

"She couldn't keep up with a dog. You know. Her arthritis." Sara blew her bangs out of her eyes. "I don't mind talking to her. She just always calls at the wrong time. And she's started to repeat herself a lot. She tells the same story three times. It's so sad."

Chip edged the car forward. "What about your brothers? Doesn't one of them live a few blocks away?"

"Yeah. But Mom and I were always close. I guess because I'm the youngest. You know, Mom was forty when I was born, and . . ." Sara's voice trailed off when she realized Chip wasn't listening.

The car on Sara's side had its interior light on. The driver, a round-faced woman with ringlets of orange hair, leaned forward, stretching toward the rearview mirror to apply dark lipstick to her lips. Behind her in the back seat, two little blond-haired boys shoved each other and wrestled.

"Did you talk to your father?" Sara asked, trying to regain his attention.

"Talk to Dad?" Chip shifted and lowered his foot on the gas. They bumped around the curve. Not an accident. Just a car about to be towed.

"Before he left," Sara continued, hands tucked in her lap. "You were going to talk to him. About a job, remember."

Chip nodded. Nibbled his lower lip. Kept his eyes straight ahead. "Oh, yeah. I was thinking about that. I had a different idea."

Sara waited for him to continue, watched him, studied him.

The light rolled over his face, revealed tension. The small scar on his chin caught the light, then dimmed. His eyes narrowed further as he concentrated on what he was about to say.

"I don't really want to work for my dad," he said slowly, thoughtfully, pronouncing each word distinctly as if he were having this thought for the first time.

Chip's lack of a job troubled Sara more than it troubled Chip. She found herself thinking about it all the time. She realized she had never met anyone without ambition before.

Most of his Harvard friends had moved to L.A. to write sitcoms. That's what the smart, serious Harvard grads seemed to be doing these days. In previous years, they might have become novelists or journalists or playwrights. But Chip's friends had a more contemporary ambition: they wanted to write twenty-two-minute scripts and become rich.

After graduation—not an honors student by any means, but somewhere near the middle of his class—Chip spent some time in Belize doing Lord-knows-what. When he returned, he stayed at his father's bungalow in Malibu, hanging out with sitcom friends when they weren't laboring over their keyboards, soaking up the sun, tanning his already-tanned skin. Partying—that California verb.

When Sara met him, at a publishing party in the Puck Building, of all places (Puck rhymes with luck, Sara thought, striking up a conversation with this grinning, tanned, confident guy who leaned so close to her while she tried to decide what to do with her left hand, the hand not holding the plastic cup of white Chardonnay), he told her he was writing a novel. But he quickly became frustrated. Novel writing was too slow, not gratifying, he told her, and besides, he had nothing to say.

Sara listened. He had a lot to say to her.

The places he talked about, the parties he swept her to, the friends he introduced her to—they made her tell herself, "Sara, you've come a long way from Indiana."

It was glamorous, exciting, romantic. All those things. Sometimes she felt as if she were living in one of those gauzy, dreamy perfume ads. Obsession. Obsession For Men. And for me too. But Chip still didn't have a job. He was twenty-four, and he had an allowance.

Was it just her Indiana upbringing? Doesn't everyone have to *be* something?

He turned the wheel, started to slide into the next lane, then changed his mind. He sighed, tapping the wheel. "We'll get there in time for a midnight swim."

She reached over, rubbed the shoulder of his polo shirt. "That'll be nice."

Horns honked around them. A motorcycle roared past, slipping between the lanes, a girl in faded denim, black hair flying behind her, hugging the back of a black-helmeted guy in leather.

"What's your different idea?" Sara lowered her knees, brushed a piece of lint off her jeans, stared out the passenger window. "I mean, about the job."

He hesitated. "Well . . . working for my dad would be a pain. He probably wouldn't want me underfoot, either. Instead, he'd farm me out. You know. Get me some kind of entry job at one of the production companies. They're always eager to kiss his ass. They'd make me an assistant producer. Which means I'd make sure the coffee machine was full. There's no way I'd get anything very interesting."

"So what's your idea?" Sara persisted.

He signaled, changed lanes. A dark oil truck rumbled past. Sara flinched. She always felt so low and tiny and vulnerable in the little Porsche.

"Check out that license plate." He pointed to the white Mercedes up ahead.

Sara squinted into the glare of headlights and read the license plate: EATME. She laughed.

Chip shook his head. "Some people have a lot of class, huh? Can you imagine putting a license plate like that on a sixty-thousand-dollar Mercedes? It ruins the whole car."

"So tell me your big idea," Sara insisted. "The suspense is killing me."

Chip shrugged, gestured with his right hand, steered with his left. "Well, I thought maybe I could start my own production company. You know. Start small. Maybe do features. Low budget. Under a hundred million. Or maybe even made-for-TV features. Quality stuff. Controversial. Things that would get noticed."

In the flickering light, he suddenly looked like a boy to her. An excited child. So *that's* why he doesn't have a job, she realized. Up till now, he hadn't figured out a way to start at the top. A little boy starting at the top.

The car lurched forward. He lowered his foot on the gas and they roared through an empty patch of highway. Sara felt loss. Felt as if she had left something behind. Lost something on that spot of road behind them where he had revealed his new plan.

Some part of her feelings for him had been left back there, she knew. Some part of her awe. Some piece of his sun-god hold on her. It had drained out of the car. And now she found herself riding beside a little boy. The innocent blue eyes. The little snub nose. A little boy planning what kind of lollipop he wanted.

She cleared her throat. "But starting a movie company— doesn't that take a lot of money?" The question came out more shrill than she intended.

"Well, yeah." He let out an unpleasant laugh. Scornful. "I'll need some start-up. For sure. That's what I'm going to talk to Dad about when he gets back from the Coast."

What flavor lollipop are you going to buy me, Dad?

Sara stared hard at him. Pictured him holding a long stick, licking a big, round peppermint lollipop.

9

She loved making love with the sound of the ocean outside the window. The sheet damp and salty against her back. Chip so light on top of her.

A soft roar. Then the crash of a wave on the sand. A lull. Then another crash. The perfect rhythm, she thinks, eyes wide open. Watching him slide over her.

Crash. Lull. Crash. Lull. The gentle wash of his body.

Eyes wide open. Trying to think about the waves . . .

Crash . . . crash . . . crash . . .

But thinking about something else. Listening . . . thinking . . .

Crash . . . crash . . . slide . . .

Why am I thinking?

"Ohhhhhh." Chip tosses back his head, lets out his warning groan.

The waves rise up hard and explode against the shore. She pictures white spray hitting a dark rock, splashing up to the night sky. He collapses on top of her, kissing her shoulder, her chest, her breasts.

Crash and then slide . . . slide . . . crash . . .

Outside, the waves don't stop.

She lies awake a long time, listening to his soft, steady breathing, watching the silvery moonlight beyond the billowing window curtains, thinking about the ocean, rolling to the shore, rolling so quietly, so softly, as if sneaking up on it—then rising up and crashing hard against the sand, crashing with such unexpected force, like a dark thought that rolls unwanted into your mind.

Breakfast on the deck, a hazy sun already high in the sky. Blueberry muffins and sweet slices of yellow watermelon from the farmstand on North Sea Road.

Chip, in a red bikini swimsuit, scratched the tufts of blond hair on his tanned chest, then stretched both arms above his head. "We slept late."

Sara smiled, brushed her dark hair out of her face with one hand. "I feel like I'm on vacation."

He poured himself another cup of coffee from the white pitcher. Raised the pitcher toward her. She shook her head, covered her cup.

"Did you sleep?"

"Like a log," she lied.

"It's the sound of the ocean." He turned to the water, leaned one hand against the wooden deck rail. "I always sleep like a baby out here."

Like a baby.

Baby want his lollipop?

What has happened? Sara asked herself, gulping coffee, nearly choking on it. Why do I keep thinking about that?

She adjusted the blue bikini top. Peered at herself over the dark sunglasses. I'm so pale. I'm the color of those seagulls down there.

She stared down the dune at the beach. The sand stretched blue-gold in the hazy sunlight. The sky appeared to end at a wall of dark clouds rolling from the horizon.

Chip grabbed her hand and tugged. "Come on. How about a morning swim?" His blue eyes flashing, teeth gleaming.

"It isn't morning. It's afternoon." She gulped the last of the coffee and set the cup down on the glass outdoor table.

"Even better." He tugged harder, pulled her to her feet. "The water is warmed up by now."

She laughed and rolled her hazel eyes. "Oh, sure. It's probably a hundred degrees."

He looked hurt. "I thought you liked cold water."

"Only when it's warm."

Those words made her think of Mary Beth Logan, her college roommate. That's the kind of thing Mary Beth would say, Sara thought. That's not the kind of thing I say. She made a mental note to phone Mary Beth. She hadn't talked to her in weeks, maybe months.

Mary Beth . . . still at Moore State. Some people never grow up.

Chip tugged her arm, pulling her off the deck toward the dune.

Some people never grow up.

"Ow!" Pine needles pricked her bare feet. "Chip—let me get my sandals!"

"No time. Run. You have to run right in. Otherwise you'll never get in."

She knows he's right.

Down the dune, the sand already dry and warm. A seagull standing at the shore tilted back its head and let out a shrill, throaty shriek. A warning? "Don't go in—it's freezing?"

The green-gold waves tossed gentle and low, breaking far out. The wall of dark clouds rolled in fast. In the distance, the ocean was dark beneath the clouds. She could see the line across the water where the sparkling sunlight stopped. The air grew cold.

She hesitated at the shore edge, cold water rolling over her bare feet. The water pulled back, leaving a strand of limp green seaweed around her ankle.

Sara shivered.

Chip grabbed her hand. "Come on! Don't wimp out!"

Water rushed over her ankles. She pulled back, struggled to free her hand from his. "Let go! It's too cold!"

He laughed. Swept her up in his arms, her feet shedding sand as she kicked in protest. "Let go! Let go, Chip! I mean it!"

Grinning, he started to jog, ducking away from her swinging arms, tightening his grip, surprisingly strong, surprising her, startling her, holding her with such ease.

Not taking no for an answer.

He splashed into the water. She felt the cold spray on her back, on her legs. "Let go! Let go! No! Don't drop me!"

Did prehistoric cave dwellers play this same dumb game at the ocean?

She started to scream, but the shock of the cold as he dropped her cut off her breath. She shut her eyes as she tumbled under a rolling wave, then scrambled to her feet, shivering, gasping. Her wet hair falling over her eyes, she playfully swung a fist at Chip. Missed as he ducked into the water.

"Ohh! I'm freezing! Chip—I'll get you for this!"

He ducked into a low wave, came up swimming hard. Several yards away, just beyond where the lapping waves broke, he motioned to her to follow him.

"I—I—I'm never going to warm up!" Water splashed into her open mouth. She tasted salt, tried to spit it out. Shaking her bangs from her eyes, she sucked in a deep breath, pushed herself forward, kicked her feet, and swam after him.

After a few seconds, she raised her head and saw him treading water, waiting for her to catch up. She felt herself pulled out toward him, didn't like the feeling. The undertow is stronger than I thought, she realized.

She was a good swimmer. She'd earned her lifeguard patch at the Y when she was fourteen. But she didn't like being pulled against her will, didn't like the feeling that she couldn't move where she wanted to move.

"Chip—I want to go back," she called, turning to glance at the shore, farther away than she thought. The purple clouds loomed over them, drawing a wide, gloomy shadow across the ocean. "I want to go back. The undertow . . ."

"It's shallow here, Sara. You can stand." He pointed down. "There's a sandbar here."

He reached out for her hand as she swam close, and pulled her beside him. She lowered her feet slowly, carefully. Found the narrow sandbar and stood, the water rippling at her shoulders.

He grinned at her, holding on to her hand. He had a string of green seaweed tangled in his hair. They both jumped to float above a high, rolling wave, then settled back onto the sand.

"Great, huh?"

"It feels nice," she admitted. "But the undertow—I feel myself being pulled that way." She pointed.

"It's not so bad," he replied, eyes out to sea. A large red and black cargo ship shimmered into view, hazy on the darkening horizon. "Wonder where that ship is going."

She floated up, treading water. She tried to tug her hand free, but he held on to it. A hard shiver ran down her back. "I'm cold, Chip. I'm going back."

He didn't seem to hear her. "Do you think the ocean is romantic?" His eyes remained on the ship, a tiny rectangle where the water met the sky.

"Huh?" Water splashed against her face. She tried to float up as another high wave swept past. "Let go. I can't swim."

He pulled her closer, turned his blue eyes on her. Sky blue eyes. She could see the darkening clouds reflected in them. "The ocean is romantic, right?"

What was he getting at? Why was he acting so strange?

"Yeah, sure. Of course." One foot slid off the narrow sandbar. She caught her balance, struggled against the current, replaced her foot.

"I mean, it would be a good place for a proposal, right?" Chip persisted.

"A *what?*"

"A proposal."

"A *marriage* proposal?"

He nodded, unsmiling, solemn-faced. They floated up, their heads bobbing over an incoming wave.

She pushed her hair off her face. The shudder she felt wasn't from the cold water. The goosebumps on her arms weren't from the cold, either.

"Marry me, Sara," he murmured, dark clouds in his eyes.

I don't want to, she realized, trembling in the cold current. The waves swept past her, rolling to the shore. Rolling. Rolling endlessly. Like time.

"Chip, we've had a lot of fun—"

But you're a big baby.

Did I just realize it in the car last night? Or did I know all along that I don't love Chip?

"I really care about you, but—"

"I've been thinking about so many things," he said, pulling the seaweed from his hair with his free hand, the hand not holding her prisoner. "You know. Asking my dad about the production company. My future. *Our* future."

We don't have one, Chip.

I knew it last night. I've known it for a while. We have nice dinners. We go to fun parties. We enjoy each other in bed. We enjoy each other in the present.

In the past . . .

"I want to share it with you, Sara." He grabbed her other hand. Squeezed them both.

Cornball, she thought. *What a cornball line.* Like a line in a bad movie.

Such cruel thoughts.

Why is he ruining the weekend?

Thunder crackled in the distance. Sara turned to the horizon. The cargo ship had disappeared behind a curtain of gray fog.

Let go of my hands, Chip. I want to disappear with that ship. Slip away. Slip away into the soft fog.

"Marry me, Sara."

"I can't, Chip." She floated over another wave. The tide was coming in, she saw. "I care a lot about you. I'm very flattered. Maybe later—"

"No. Really." His voice shrill now, raised over the rush and splash of the pitching water. "I'm serious."

"I know, Chip. I don't want to hurt you, but—"

"Marry me, Sara."

"No. Please. Let go. I can't."

"Marry me, Sara."

"Chip, stop. Listen to me. No! I can't. Not now. No!"

He shut his eyes. When he opened them, she could see that he had finally heard her. Finally heard her no.

"Marry me, Sara." He released her hands. His hands slid up to her hair.

"I have to go back now. I'm freezing."

She expected some kind of caress. But he grabbed her hair roughly, pulled down the sides. "Marry me, Sara." His voice shrill now.

"No! Let go!"

"Marry me, Sara." He grasped her head. Pushed hard. Pushed her under the surface.

So unexpected. She gasped, swallowed water, started to choke.

"Marry me, Sara." His voice harsh, insistent, shouting above her. His hands pushing so hard, holding her down, holding her under.

"Marry me, Sara."

She kicked and thrashed, twisted her head. Couldn't twist free.

The hands pulled her up by the hair. Coughing, sputtering, she struggled for breath.

"Marry me, Sara."

"No. No—please—!"

"Marry me, Sara." The hands shoving her under again. Down, down. Holding her there.

"Marry me, Sara."

Let go! Let go! Thrashing, kicking, struggling to squirm free.

"Fuck you, Sara."

The hands pull her up.
"Marry me, Sara."
Push her down.
"Fuck you, Sara."
Pull her up.
"Marry me, Sara."
Push her down.
"Fuck you, Sara."
Hold her down. Hold her under.
Her last breath bubbles from her mouth.
"Marry me, Sara. Fuck you, Sara."
The last words she heard before she went under for the last time.

10

"Then what happened?" Mary Beth lowered her hands. She had been tugging at the sides of her streaked hair, her mouth hanging open, for most of Sara's story.

Sara let out a bitter, dry laugh. "Well, I didn't drown."

Mary Beth's green eyes narrowed on her friend's face, studying her as if seeing her for the first time. Reborn. Her third cigarette had burned down, untouched on the side of the cup she was using as an ashtray. "Finish the story, Sara. How did you get away from him?"

"I didn't."

She wiped her clammy hands on her jeans legs. Talking about that day still made her sweat, still made her stomach tighten, her legs tremble.

"He—he pulled me up," she stammered, shifting her position on the couch. "I guess he snapped out of it, came to his senses or something."

Mary Beth shook her head. "Wow."

Sara lowered her eyes. "I thought I was going to pass out. I mean, everything was spinning. I couldn't tell what was sky, what was water. It felt as if my lungs had burst. My chest—it burned. On fire. I gasped in breath after breath. I couldn't get enough air."

"And what did Chip do?" Mary Beth demanded.

"He held me. Just held me. And then he let out a cry, in a strange, hoarse voice. And he started to hug me, tighter and tighter. And I still couldn't breathe. I just wanted to breathe. But now he was hugging me so tight, I couldn't breathe again. I thought I was going to drown *above* the water.

"I was so cold, so frightened. He kept apologizing. Hugging me and apologizing. 'Sorry sorry sorry sorry sorry.' Like some kind of chant."

"It's so sick," Mary Beth murmured, shaking her head. She reached up to squeeze Sara's hand. "Really. The whole thing is so sick."

Mary Beth shifted uncomfortably on the floor. "So then you swam to shore?"

"Chip helped me back. I felt so weak, so shaken. He apologized all the way back. And in the house. He just kept apologizing. He said he just lost it for a moment. He promised it would never happen again.

"But I knew it was over. I knew I never wanted to see him again. He was just too scary. Too out of control." Sara kept her eyes on the wall behind Mary Beth. "I always made excuses for Chip. I thought I understood him. I was so stupid. I always said, well, he's a spoiled rich kid. An only child. His parents divorced. His father obsessed with his work. He's used to getting whatever he wants.

"He didn't grow up like me with three older brothers. He never had to fight for anything. Never had to compete. Never had to lose. That's what I told myself. But that was crap. All crap."

"He's just crazy," Mary Beth offered. She stubbed out the untouched cigarette.

"Yeah. Crazy." Sara sighed. "So then he wanted to stay at the beach. Pretend it didn't happen. Start all over again. I made him drive me back to the city. He begged me to stay, to forgive him. When I refused, I think he went into shock or something. I don't think he could accept that everything hadn't worked out the way he planned it.

"We drove all the way back to the city in silence. We didn't even look at each other. The tensest, most awful three hours of my life." Sara shuddered.

"So then you never saw Chip again?"

Sara rolled her eyes. "Are you kidding? He wouldn't leave me alone. He couldn't accept our being over. He called me ten times a day. He sent flowers. He sent presents. He showed up at my office. He showed up at my apartment. A couple of times I spotted him following me on the street."

Mary Beth's mouth dropped open. "He *stalked* you?"

"I guess you could call it that. He was insane, Mary Beth. Totally insane. I thought about calling the police. I really did."

"Then what happened?"

Sara shrugged. "Then I lost my job. The merger went through. Concord Publishing was sold. Half of the Concord staff was let go. Including me. There I was, alone in my apartment on East Eighty-second Street. No job and a psycho ex-boyfriend following me everywhere. And . . . and . . ."

"And then I called!" Mary Beth sat back against the futon and smiled, obviously relieved that Sara's long, unhappy story had concluded.

"Mary Beth Logan to the rescue!" Sara declared, also glad to have finished her tale of woe. She knew she would have to relate it in detail to her friend. Now that she had told it, she would never have to tell it again. She felt a hundred pounds lighter.

Now I can close that chapter, she thought.

Close that chapter and start a new one: *Chapter One Hundred Twenty: The Graduate Student.*

"Here I am, back in college," Sara said cheerfully. "Goodbye, New York. Good-bye, glamorous world of publishing. Hello, sleepy little town of Freewood. Hello, Psych Department. I can't believe I'm back here, getting my master's."

Mary Beth grinned. "You're always analyzing everyone anyway, Sara. Why not become a psychologist and get paid for it?"

Sara sighed. "Getting paid would be good. I'm so broke."
She raised her eyes to Mary Beth. "You're such a good friend. It
was way past the enrollment date. I can't believe you got me in."

"Hey—I'm the big-deal Media Director of this college, remember? I can pull a few strings from time to time."

"I don't know how I'm going to thank you. I really don't.
You saved my life. No joke."

"Well . . ." Mary Beth's cheeks reddened. She seemed embarrassed by Sara's gratitude. Her smile faded quickly. "So Chip
doesn't know where you are?"

Sara shook her head. "I never told him. And I didn't leave
a forwarding address. He's probably searching the streets of
Manhattan for me. I mean, I hope he isn't. I hope he'll go pick
on someone else and forget about me. But—"

Mary Beth narrowed her eyes thoughtfully. "You don't
think he'll figure out that you came back to Freewood, back to
your old college town?"

Sara started to reply. But the doorbell rang, startling them
both. Mary Beth climbed up from the floor, straightened her
navy blue sweatshirt, pulling it down over her jeans as she made
her way to the door. "Who could that be? Did we order a
pizza?"

Sara laughed. "No. But if the delivery boy is good-looking,
invite him in!"

Mary Beth leaned against the white door. "Who is it?"

Sara heard a muffled reply. A male voice.

"Oh. It's you." Mary Beth pulled the door open. A boy
with carrot-colored hair shuffled in. He kissed Mary Beth on the
cheek, raised one hand to her shoulder.

She backed away from him. "Eric. Hi. I wasn't expecting
you." She motioned to Sara.

He turned, his mouth dropping open for just a second as he
spotted Sara on the couch. "Oh. Hey—"

"My friend Sara," Mary Beth said, closing the door behind
him. "This is Eric."

Sara said hi. He looks about eighteen, she thought.

Eric moved awkwardly into the room, shoving his hands into the pockets of his baggy jeans. His gray sweater was torn at the collar. He had a silver stud in one ear. Brown freckles dotted his nose and cheeks.

Talk about robbing the cradle. Mary Beth is dating Huck Finn! Sara thought cruelly.

She'll probably tell me that he's just a friend. But that hand on her shoulder gave him away.

He stopped in the center of the room, between the two futons, and turned back to Mary Beth, still at the doorway. "I was at the gym. You know. Down the block. Doing weights. So I thought I'd come by."

Mary Beth kept her eyes on Eric, avoiding Sara's stare. "So, how's it going?"

He shrugged. "Okay, I guess. Coach says I still have to beef up."

Mary Beth twisted up her face. "Wish someone would tell *me* I needed to beef up!" She patted her stomach. Turned to Sara. Finally. "Eric's on the wrestling team."

"Great!" What a dumb response. But she couldn't think of any other way to react. Her eyes swept over his broad shoulders, his thick neck. She had been so startled by how young he was, she hadn't noticed his athletic build, obvious even in the loose-fitting sweater.

"Sara just moved here. From New York," Mary Beth told Eric.

"I know. You told me." He turned to Sara. "I was in New York once. I was twelve, I think. It was kind of scary."

Sara nodded. "Yeah. It's scary even when you're not twelve."

Mary Beth laughed, a little too hard.

Eric shifted his weight awkwardly. "I didn't mean to interrupt. If you two are busy—"

"No." Sara jumped up. She set down the soda can. "I've got to go. I have to get up early tomorrow morning and be at the library when it opens."

"Are you sure?" Mary Beth stepped up beside Eric, arms crossed in front of her. "We could order a pizza."

"No. Really. I'm not hungry. Thanks for dinner, Mary Beth. It was great."

Mary Beth rolled her eyes. "Right. Tuna salad. A gourmet treat. For sure."

Sara smiled. "Well, you added just the right amount of mayonnaise."

Everyone laughed.

Sara picked up her black wool cardigan and hurried to the door. Mary Beth and her secrets, she thought. All the time I knew her, she always had a secret or two. A few surprises up her sleeve. As close as we were, Mary Beth always held something back. Kept something for herself.

She stopped at the doorway and glanced back at Eric. He's a nice secret, she thought. Her own little undergraduate to play with. Well . . . Mary Beth *said* she felt like a college kid!

"Nice to meet you," she called to him.

"Same here. Mary Beth talks about you all the time." His cheeks reddened as a smile crossed his face. "But I don't believe any of it."

Mary Beth gave him a playful shove. "Shut up, Eric! I'll call you tomorrow, Sara. Take care. And listen—don't cut across campus, okay? Go the long way. There are more streetlights."

"Yeah. Okay. I'll be all right." And she was out the door. Down the narrow, tiled hallway. Out the front entrance of the apartment building—Campus Towers. How can you call a two-story building a tower?

The wind carrying a chill. A half-moon still low over the trees. Bare branches rattling over the sidewalk. Fat, dead leaves scuttling over her Doc Martens.

Thinking about Eric, Sara crossed the street. Mary Beth's freckle-faced lad. Wonder if he shaves.

Sara stepped into a pool of darkness. Glanced up at the streetlamp. Bulb burned out. She shivered. Shifted her canvas bag to her left shoulder.

In the next block, the illuminated green dome of the Administration Building glimmered over the dark structure like a lowering flying saucer. Sara hesitated, then turned into the campus, following the curving dirt path through the trees.

I'll be okay. I'm too tired to go the long way around.

Her eyes alert now. A white high-top sneaker on its side under a rounded evergreen bush. Sheets of the campus newspaper blowing across the ground like a stringless kite.

Maybe I should get an apartment on the same side of campus as Mary Beth, she thought, picking up her pace. Her shoes slipped over wet leaves. Did Mary Beth deliberately put the campus between us?

A rush of wind flattened the grass. Tree limbs rattled.

Why am I being so hard on Mary Beth? Is it because she didn't tell me about Eric? Because she deliberately kept part of her life a secret from me?

Since when have I become so demanding? Sara wondered. Since when have I become so needy?

I need someone I can trust right now. She answered her own question. I need someone I can believe in, I guess.

The granite and brick classroom buildings that hovered darkly around The Circle vanished as the path led into the trees. Another rush of wind sent a chill down the back of Sara's neck.

She heard a metallic rattle.

Then a scraping sound.

Thudding footsteps.

Hot, sour breath on her face as the dark creature leapt out from behind the trees and grabbed roughly for her waist.

11

Sara stumbled back as the enormous creature attacked.

She inhaled its sour breath, hot steam against her face. Red eyes glared up at her as it pressed forward.

"Down! Get down!"

A man's voice. Frantic but sharp. Somewhere in the darkness.

"King—get down! Now!"

The big dog's paws slid down from Sara's waist.

Her chest heaved. Her heart thudded. She stepped back in the grass, slowly regaining her balance.

"King—get away from her! Down!"

The dog uttered a short growl. Then turned toward its master. A middle-aged man in a brown leather jacket. A white baseball cap pulled low on his forehead.

"I'm so sorry. Did King frighten you?"

"Uh . . . yes." Sara glared down at the enormous yellow dog. "What is it—a golden Lab?"

Why am I asking that? Who cares?

"King never did that before. I'm really sorry. You're okay?" The man followed her into the cone of pale light from a low green lamppost. He was older than Sara had first thought. Fifty maybe. Fifty-five. He had a white stubble on his face. The collar of the leather jacket was pulled up around his neck.

"He—scared me to death!" Sara declared, fear giving way to anger.

"Really. I'm sorry." He glared down at the dog, who was sniffing the base of a tree. The dog took a step, then lifted his leg, letting out a heavy stream.

Charming dog, Sara thought angrily. "You should keep a big dog like that on a leash. He could've broken my arm."

"He's never done that before. Really. King is a very gentle dog." The man lowered his eyes. "Did he get mud on you? I'll be happy to pay for the cleaning. Really."

"It isn't necessary. I'm okay. Really." Sara's heart had started to beat normally, but she felt shaky. Trembly all over. She could still feel the heavy paws, pouncing on her, pushing her back.

The dog ambled back to the path, wagging its tail. The man reached a gloved hand down and petted its big head. He apologized five more times before he finally said good-night and walked away, the dog loping heavily beside him.

Sara turned quickly and began jogging toward her apartment.

Mary Beth was right, she decided. From now on, maybe I won't cut through the campus.

At least until the murderer is caught.

No way we're going to catch this guy, Garrett thought glumly.

He shut his eyes. Rubbed them with his thumbs. Pictured the young woman. Just a girl, really. Pictured her broken body, her bare, blood-soaked head. Like a cracked egg.

Three days and not a clue. Not a tiny hint.

Three days and his stomach still lurched when he thought about her. Charlotte Wilson. Just a baby once. Like Martin.

Now cracked and broken.

The coroner down from Medford the next morning, puzzled and quiet. "Never seen anything like this one. She had to be run over by a truck."

But there weren't any tire tracks, Garrett explained. And a truck can't tear open your stomach or rip off your scalp, can it?

"But no man is that strong," the coroner insisted, scratching his neck till it was red. He was a tall, toothpick of a man, in a cheap, shiny gray suit, narrow navy blue tie, pulled down at the open collar. "Unless he used some kind of tool."

"You mean to crush her?"

"To crack her spine like that."

"He could've used a knife to cut off her hair," Walter offered, elbows on his desk, round, pale head propped in his hands.

"No. It was torn off." The man scratched his cheek. "Not cut off."

Garrett moved to the window. All that scratching was making him itch. He stared out at fog and drizzle. Raindrops plunking at the smeared pane. "You did the autopsy?"

"Working on it. You need me to tell you a cause of death? She didn't drown."

The guy's a real comedian, Garrett thought.

"She had sex less than an hour before."

Garrett turned away from the window.

Walter raised his head. "She did? With the murderer?"

The man snickered. "You boys ever work a homicide before? Maybe you should take a book out of the library. Read up on it."

Garrett felt a surge of anger. "Don't call us boys."

The coroner's needle face turned scarlet. "I didn't mean anything. Hey. Take it easy. You got a situation here. Cool heads will prevail. Know what I mean?"

"We're cops. We're not school crossing guards," Garrett insisted. Too defensive. He scolded himself. You feel helpless and stupid and you're taking it out on this stranger who also feels helpless and stupid.

"Well, she had sex less than an hour before." He reached under his thick glasses to scatch his eyelids. "Maybe it's a clue. Maybe it's just a dirty secret we get to share."

Walter shook his head. His gray eyes watered over. "I had

to call her parents. I never heard such screaming and crying. I'll never get the sound out of my ears, I don't think. Those poor people. They screamed like animals. It sounded like horses. You know. When they tilt up their heads and just neigh?"

The coroner stared at Walter but didn't react. "I'll get you the full report tomorrow." He swept his gray raincoat around his tiny frame and hurried out of the station.

"He's a cold fish," Walter commented.

Garrett sighed. "Who *else* becomes a coroner?"

MILTON R. COHN

DEAN OF STUDENTS

Sara stopped and read the hand-painted black letters on the frosted-glass door. She pulled the bookbag off her shoulder and lowered it to the floor. Then, trying to see her reflection in the glass, she pushed back her black hair with both hands, then adjusted the short black skirt she wore over black tights.

She glanced back at the long row of offices. Two students in jeans and sweaters stretched out on the marble floor outside one office, knees up, cigarettes in their mouths, backpacks between their legs. Two blond-haired young women, secretaries probably, carrying stacks of papers and colored folders, walked hurriedly side by side down the hall, their heels clicking on the hard floor.

Sara turned back to the office. She pressed her face to the glass, trying to see if anyone was inside. He must be back by now, she told herself. I hope he remembers me. I'll be so embarrassed if he doesn't.

She pictured herself barging into his office. "Uh . . . Dr. Cohn, I really appreciate the job offer. It's just the kind of work I'm looking for. I'm ready to start anytime."

And Milton Cohn turns to her, screws up his face, and says coldly, "Do I know you?"

Sara rubbed her finger over the black letters of his name. She had the feeling they would rub right off the glass.

Stop stalling, she scolded herself. He offered you a job. Why are you acting like a nervous teenager?

She knocked lightly on the glass windowpane of the door. Too lightly. She could barely hear it herself.

She raised her hand to knock again but held it in midair as two men turned the corner. One wore a dark brown suit. The other wore loose-fitting chinos, a white shirt and dark tie. Sara sucked in her breath when she thought the one in the suit was Liam. But as they walked by, she realized she had been mistaken.

"What if there was no such thing as tenure?" Shirtsleeves said in a high, reedy voice. "Then what would you do?"

"Beats the shit out of me. I'm on the committee too. Do you want to be on the committee?"

"No thanks. I'm already over the legal limit for committees."

"You should be on the committee. It never meets. So it wouldn't take up much of your time."

Sara caught them both checking her out, looking her up and down as they passed. She watched them disappear into an office a few doors down from the two students sprawled on the floor.

She raised her watch. Three-thirty, Monday afternoon.

Her seminar with Professor Boring had just ended. She had been distracted the whole hour, unable to concentrate, thinking about her visit to Dr. Cohn.

What's the worst that can happen? she asked herself. He'll say he's changed his mind or he's hired someone else.

Big deal.

Some people sailed through life, as if riding one of those gliders her brother Gary liked to fly, taking off from the highest hill, not knowing where the wind would take him, but enjoying the ride the whole way.

Sara wasn't the gliding type. She always had to make things a little harder for herself. "You're always getting in your own way," Gary had told her after she had lost her job in New York and confided to him she didn't know what to do next. It wasn't exactly the advice she wanted to hear. But the words had remained with her.

She spent more time thinking about things than doing them. Another pearl of wisdom from brother Gary. Gary the freelance journalist. Gary the traveler. The glider.

Yes, I like to think things through, Sara realized. That's why I'm a psych major. No one had ever accused her of being spontaneous or impulsive or free-spirited. But free-spirited people aren't necessarily happier, she decided.

She rapped on Milton Cohn's office door, a little harder.

Silence inside.

The lights were on in there. She cleared her throat. Turned the glass doorknob, pulled open the door. She peered into an outer office. An oak desk, cluttered with papers. A computer and printer on a low counter behind the desk. A wall of books, mostly hardcover. A brass coat rack in the corner, empty except for a black umbrella on the top hook. A row of gunmetal gray filing cabinets.

No one at the desk. The computer off.

"Hello?" Sara's voice soft and high.

Hazy afternoon sunlight washed through the open window. Sara took a few steps into the room, closing the door silently behind her. Glancing outside, she could see windows of the Language Arts Building next door, gleaming like gold in the reflected sunlight.

She heard footsteps out in the hall. Laughter. Turning away from the window, her eyes stopped on the pale green wall to the inner office. Two long knives were mounted on the wall, blade tipped against blade as if they were fencing swords. The silver blades caught the light. They aren't kitchen knives, Sara found herself thinking. Not carving knives. They're weapons.

"Hello? Dr. Cohn? Is anyone—?"

She took a step toward the inner office. The door stood open. She could see more bookshelves inside. A wine red carpet on the floor.

Two brown shoes on the carpet.

Two brown shoes, toes pointed up. Dark socks stretching from the shoes. Brown trouser legs.

"Ohh."

Sara blinked several times before she realized it was a man. On the floor. Lying motionless on the floor.

Dr. Cohn lying dead on the floor of his office.

"Ohh."

Panic made her heart race. She turned to leave. Realized she couldn't. Took a deep breath and held it. Stared hard at the twin knives on the wall, willing her heart to stop thudding. Then made her way to the doorway of the inner office.

"Oh. Hi."

Milton Cohn, his white shirt unbuttoned, on the floor of his office. Flat on his back. A gray dumbbell in each hand. Arms in the air. Up, then down, then up again.

He groaned, smiled at her, his face red. His arms were more muscular than she had imagined. Boxer's arms. That enormous stomach. She remembered him as being fat. But she could see now that it was muscle. His chest is massive, his stomach hard. The thick gray hair on his chest glistening with sweat.

He set down the weights and started to pull himself up. "Sorry. I didn't hear you come in." His voice deep but breathless. On his feet, he lumbered toward the wide mahogany desk, pulled a white towel off the green leather armchair beside the desk, and mopped his forehead.

Sara cleared her throat. "Sorry to interrupt. I knocked, but—"

I can't believe I thought he was dead, she scolded herself. Why am I so *morbid* these days?

Milton toweled off his white hair. He tossed the towel onto the window ledge. Made no attempt to brush down his hair, which stood straight up over his red face. He turned to her, buttoning his shirt.

He's staring at my tits again, Sara realized, feeling her face grow hot. She remembered his eyes on her that night in the restaurant.

95

"Claire is out today. She's expecting her baby next month. It's hard for her to waddle in." He grinned, finally raising his eyes to Sara's.

"If this is a bad time . . ." Sara started.

His huge fingers fumbled with the shirt buttons. One shirt flap was out of his trousers, one tucked in. "No. No. I was just taking advantage of the solitude. I try to work out twice a day. It's part of the job." He backed toward the desk, motioned for her to sit in the green armchair.

"Part of the job?"

"Hell yes. You've got to be *strong* to deal with college students."

Sara couldn't tell if he was joking or not. His eyes were on her legs as she lowered herself into the chair. She tugged down the short skirt, wishing she had worn something a little more modest. She set her bookbag down in her lap.

"They don't dare give me any lip," Milton continued in his raspy voice. It always sounded as if he needed to clear his throat. He flexed his biceps, grinning.

Sara laughed. He *is* joking.

"Keeping in shape is one of my obsessions." He backed up, then sat on the edge of the mahogany desk, on top of some files. He stared down at her knees. "I have many obsessions. How about you?" He leered at her, as if he had just said something suggestive.

"No. I—I'm not the obsessive type," Sara replied awkwardly. "I don't know if you remember me," she struggled to continue, eager to change the subject, to get to business. "I'm Sara Morgan. We met at Spinnaker's. I—"

He leaned forward and patted her hand. His hand felt like an animal paw, hairy and rough. "Of course I remember you, Sara."

"You do? Well, I—"

"Liam mentioned you the other day."

"He did?" She fiddled with her bangs. Why was she squeaking like a little girl? She determined to lower her voice.

"He asked if you had come to see me about the job."

"Well . . . here I am!" Sara declared. She gripped her book-bag with both hands. "I'm still interested, Dr. Cohn. If you—"

"Milton. Please, Sara. Call me Milton, okay?"

"Okay. Milton."

He lowered his eyes to her knees again. *Am I making a mistake?* Sara wondered. *Is he some kind of a pervert?*

"Yes. Milton. That's better." He squeezed her arm through her sweater. Sara forced herself not to wince. *He's really kind of repulsive,* she thought. Then she corrected herself. *Not really repulsive. Just too big.* "If you call me Dr. Cohn, you make me feel like an old geezer."

Sara let out an uncomfortable laugh.

"Let me ask you a few questions." He grinned at her. He had a gold tooth to the side that gleamed when he smiled. He pulled himself up from the desktop and made his way behind the desk. The leather desk chair let out a long *whoosh* as he dropped into it. "Do you have secretarial experience, Sara?"

"Well . . . yes." She lifted the bookbag so that she could cross her legs. "I was an editorial assistant. At Concord Publishing. In New York."

He picked up a paperweight, a metal pyramid, and rolled it in his big hand, keeping his eyes on Sara. "That sounds like an interesting job."

"I was just a glorified secretary," Sara replied. "But of course the secretaries got paid a lot better than the editorial assistants."

That made him smile. He moved the metal pyramid from hand to hand. "And why did you leave?"

"Well, Concord merged with another company, and my job was eliminated. So—"

"No. I meant, why did you leave New York? To get away from some man?"

How does he know that? Sara's first thought. Her second thought: *Why is he being so personal? I thought this was a job interview.*

"Well . . . yes." She felt her face grow hot again, knew she was blushing.

The answer seemed to please Milton. He leaned over the desk. She could see beads of sweat, big as raindrops, in a line beneath the shock of white hair.

"You're very pretty, Sara."

"Thank you." Feeling very uncomfortable, she stared at the bookshelves behind Milton's desk.

"You like to go to the movies?"

"Sure. I go sometimes."

This isn't exactly the job interview I expected, Sara thought. She shifted her weight in the chair.

A long, heavy silence.

Milton cleared his throat. "Claire isn't married, but she's having a baby," he offered, raising his eyes to the window. Clouds rolled over the sun, casting the room in sudden shadow. Sara felt a gust of cool air, refreshing on her hot face. "I always thought she was gay. Maybe she *is* gay. I don't know. It's hard to know anything these days, don't you think?"

Is that a question? Sara wondered. "I guess."

He tumbled the pyramid in his hand. The beads of sweat began the long trip down his forehead. "I mean, how do you tell if a woman is a lesbian or not?" he rasped. His eyes searched hers.

Sara shrugged. "Ask them, I guess."

He tossed back his head and laughed hard, as if she had just made a truly funny remark.

He's totally weird, Sara thought. I should get up and get out of here as fast as I can. She tightened her grip on the book-bag. But I need the money, she decided. I'm so broke. I can't keep borrowing from my brothers. This job is perfect. If only . . .

Another gust of wind through the open window. It blew over a small, plexiglass-framed snapshot on his desk. When he stood it upright, Sara saw a smiling, round-faced young woman with ringlets of blond hair.

"Is that your wife?"

Smiling, he tapped the young woman's face with a finger. "No. That's Jennifer. My daughter." His smile faded quickly. "I don't have a wife now." Said in a somber, low voice, his eyes dull and far away.

Sara lowered her head. "I see." This is all too personal, she thought. I just want to be his secretary. I don't want to be his friend. Or his . . . She couldn't bring herself to think of any other alternative.

"Tell me your schedule," he said, suddenly businesslike, as if reading her thoughts. "Let's figure out what hours you could work."

Sara went over her schedule. Milton removed a white linen handkerchief from his pants pocket and mopped the perspiration off his forehead. Replacing the handkerchief, he picked up the metal pyramid. "Could you work Tuesday mornings, Wednesday, and Friday afternoons?"

Sara nodded. "That sounds fine."

They discussed her pay, an hourly rate. Better than Sara had expected.

"I have to give two speeches," Milton told her. "One's a fund-raising thing. For an alumni group. The other is a pep talk to student advisers. Maybe you could help me write them?"

"Sounds like fun." She stood up, eager to leave. Lowered the bookbag to her side. Pulled down the hem of the short skirt with her free hand.

"Did you ever write speeches or anything?"

He stared at her legs. Was he deliberately being so obvious? Or did he think that Sara didn't notice?

"Well . . . no. In my job in New York, I wrote mostly letters. Rejection letters."

He nodded. "Well. Good. I'm glad to have found you, Sara. You can start tomorrow morning? At nine?"

"See you then. Thank you, Milton." She turned away, then quickly turned back.

And stared at the object in his fat hand. The metal pyramid. He had crushed it nearly flat.

Milton followed her gaze, glanced down at it.

"Oh. Sorry." A strange, guilty smile crossed his face. "Sometimes I don't know my own strength."

Sara ran into Liam as she stepped out of the Administration Building.

"Oh. Hi!" In unison.

They both laughed.

His overcoat was unbuttoned, revealing a black turtleneck and black slacks underneath. His brown eyes caught the fading afternoon sunlight.

"We have to stop meeting like this," he joked.

I love his smile, she thought. "I was just—" she started, motioning with her head to the door.

"It's fate. I think it's fate that we keep meeting," Liam interrupted. His smile faded. "Do you believe in fate, Sara?"

His seriousness caught her off guard. "I—I don't know." Stupid reply. She scolded herself, feeling her cheeks go hot. Can't you think of something interesting to say?

He didn't seem to notice. "I believe in fate." He snickered. "Of course, I believe in just about everything."

Sara raised her eyes to his. "Everything?"

He nodded. He didn't seem to be joking now. He tucked his leather attaché case under his overcoat sleeve and reached for her hand. His hand felt warm against her cold hand. He studied her palm. "Good lifeline."

Sara couldn't hold back a laugh. "You *do* believe in everything!"

His expression didn't change. He raised his eyes to hers but held on to her hand. "You have a wonderful laugh." His eyes lingered on her face.

She turned away, feeling her heart start to pound.

He returned to her hand. "I'm trying to see if there's a

reason why we keep meeting." Said playfully. "Sometimes two lines intersect and—"

"You're tickling me!" She tugged her hand away.

Liam apologized. He brushed back his thick hair, eyes on hers. "Would you like to get some coffee or something, Sara?"

He really likes me, she thought. He isn't just flirting.

Of *course* he's flirting.

She scolded herself again. Don't make a big deal of this. Don't get all muddled because he asked you out for coffee.

"Yes, I'd—" she started.

But a young man and woman came rushing up to Liam. They both started talking at once, excitedly, something about a Language Arts Department meeting. Sara gathered that Liam was supposed to attend, that they had been frantically tracking him down.

Liam turned and gave Sara a helpless shrug. "I'm so sorry. I seem to be keeping several of my colleagues waiting. Perhaps another time?"

"Yes. Great!" Sara replied, a little too enthusiastically. She felt her cheeks grow hot again.

She watched Liam being dragged away. He turned back once and shrugged again. Then he allowed himself to be pulled toward the Language Arts Building.

Fate, Sara thought. It wasn't a word she used or thought of often. But now it repeated in her mind, like a hopeful chant.

Mary Beth set her straight that night.

She phoned Sara after dinner. "Did Liam find you?"

"Huh? What do you mean?"

"He was trying to track you down," Mary Beth replied casually, unaware of the startling effect her words were having on Sara. "He called my office this afternoon."

"Liam did?" Sara's voice high and shrill.

"He said he was trying to find you. He asked me if I knew your schedule. I told him I thought you were going to see Dean Cohn. About the job. Did Liam find you?"

"Well . . . yeah." Sara's temples throbbing. "But he—he said it was fate."

"Excuse me?"

"He pretended it was an accident. You know. Us bumping into each other."

Silence at Mary Beth's end. Then: "Weird."

It's not weird. It's wonderful! Sara told herself.

"Weird," Mary Beth repeated.

12

Andrea DeHaven stepped back into the shadow of the tall hedge and stared at the curtained window across the street. A glimmer of light behind the curtain offered promise.

Liam, are you home tonight?

Liam, do you think about me?

She pulled up the collar of her fur coat, rabbit dyed gray, as headlights rolled over her. A van rumbled past, four young men outlined in the windows, all talking at once, gesturing with their hands, tapping the seats.

She straightened her red-orange hair, pulling a lock of it down over one eye. Sexy that way. At home, she had pulled it back and tied it, then changed her mind and let it fall free. Free and wild.

For you, Liam.

She had been thinking about him all week. Obsessing? Well, maybe. But what else did she have to think about? Real estate? Showing apartments and houses to these college students and their tacky professors, none of whom had a dime? Counting out the rent money on the three houses her father had left her?

Actually, he had left her five houses. But that weasel Scott sold two of them to pay off his debts before he ran off with his secretary.

Andrea sighed. Stared up at the starless sky, fighting back tears.

Don't smear your mascara, honey.

Coke isn't supposed to make you weepy. Coke is supposed to get you up.

Andrea rubbed her nose. Maybe I didn't do enough . . .

She shook her head, biting her lip, tasting the sweetness of the red lipstick.

Get a life.

That line was written for *me*, she thought bitterly. That's the title of my autobiography.

Talk about thin books.

Some life I carved out for myself. One husband runs away with a cheap slut. One husband drops dead into his dinner. Couldn't even wait till after dessert.

I'm forty-two going on sixty.

At least I've got my friends. Delia, who clips recipes like a 1950s housewife but never cooks. And still manages to weigh over two hundred pounds dripping wet.

Dripping wet? What a thought. I'd rather see *you* dripping wet, Liam.

And Esther. My pharmacist. What would I do without Esther?

Andrea sniffed. No. I didn't do enough.

What would Delia and Esther say, seeing me out here, about to throw myself at the handsome professor? Do I care? I don't think so.

Besides, he threw himself at me.

I knew what was going on. That first day last August, the day I showed him the house. I could feel his brown eyes on me. I knew what he was thinking. It wasn't like he was subtle or anything.

The way he brushed against me in the dining room doorway. And then he acted as if it had been an accident. Some accident. He practically felt me up. Those dark eyes on my face, then on my tits. Those soulful eyes, penetrating me.

104

Talking to me so softly, so sexily with that Irish lilt or whatever it is. Teasing me, flirting with me, brushing my hand as we stepped into the kitchen.

I remember each time he touched me. Each time.

And then I could feel his eyes on me as I led the way up the stairs. I knew what he was looking at. I knew he was enjoying what he saw.

So hot upstairs. The heat—the heat was between Liam and me. I could feel it. I could see by his smile that he felt it too.

I led him into the bedroom. If there had been a bed in there . . .

And last week. The night I just "happened" to drop by. He let me know we were on the same wavelength.

A mutual attraction. That's what a professor would call it. He's not like the other cold fish professors. Wimps and weasels, with their limp wrists and pasty white faces. Liam is hot-blooded. Like me.

I have some Irish blood in me too. On my mother's side. I think that's what she told me.

Tonight I want some Irish in me, Liam.

Wow. You're making me think evil thoughts. Very evil thoughts—and I love it!

Hot and Horny. Maybe that's a better title for my book.

You were having evil thoughts too last week. You were so obvious, Liam. So obvious and charming at the same time. The way you stared into my eyes and held on to my hand as you showed me out the door.

I remember each touch.

Do you remember too?

I've been thinking about you so much. Tonight I just couldn't bear to sit home alone. I'm so tired of sitcoms, Liam. They never make me laugh. Who *are* those people who sit there in the audience, laughing like morons?

I want *you* to make me laugh, Liam. That's why I decided to get dressed. In my sexiest sweater. I know you like this sweater. I know you like the way my tits look in this. I saw you staring at them, fondling them with your eyes. And they're for real, Liam. No Wonder Bra for Andrea. No way. No bra at all. You'll find out.

I got dressed up for you, Liam. I'd been thinking about doing this since last week. It wasn't just the coke. The coke just helped to clear my mind.

Did the curtains move? Are you looking for me, Liam? I'm here. I'm right here across the street. Waiting. Waiting for the right moment. Just catching my breath. Getting my shit together, as the college kids say.

Andrea tottered back against the hedge as the door to Liam's house suddenly opened, sending a rectangle of yellow light over the concrete stoop.

She grabbed the fur collar of the coat with both hands. Was he coming out?

No. It was the sister, Andrea saw. What was her name? She couldn't remember. Did it start with a B? Barbara? No.

Andrea felt her heart pound as the sister closed the door behind her, shoved her hands into the pockets of her trench coat, made her way down the three steps to the sidewalk, turned sharply, and hurried away, shoes scraping the pavement.

Yes! Thank you!

Andrea shot up both fists in triumph. Her black leather pocketbook fell to the sidewalk. As she bent to retrieve it, a wave of dizziness swept over her.

Steady, girl.

Don't blow your big chance now.

She grabbed up the pocketbook with both hands, righted herself, and stepped carefully across the street. The sister was considerate enough to leave us alone, Liam. While the cat's away, the mice will play.

She jabbed her finger at the bell.

She could hear it ring inside. Then she heard footsteps.

She pulled her hair down over her blue eyes. Cleared her throat. Wondered if her breath was okay. Wished she had sprayed on a little more cologne. *Poison.* She liked the heavy fragrance, didn't care much for the name.

"Who's there? Margaret? Are you back?"

The sister's name was Margaret?

The door opened before Andrea could answer. And there he stood, tall in the rectangle of light from the hallway. Dark hair slicked back, wet, as if he had just taken a shower. A white wool sweater over loose-fitting brown corduroys. He peered at her over rimless reading glasses. "Andrea?"

"Surprised to see me?" She tried to breathe the words sexily, but a strained giggle escaped her throat. The sleeve of her coat brushed against his chest.

"Andrea, I—would you like to come in?" He pulled off the reading glasses, his eyes still studying her. Those penetrating eyes.

Be friendly, Liam. Be nice to me. Be glad to see me.

But he still hadn't smiled.

Had she made a mistake?

He stepped back to let her enter. She stepped into the hallway, stumbled against him, her heavy coat pushing him against the wall. "I was thinking about you." She meant to say it in a teasing way, but it came out serious, kind of businesslike.

He finally smiled. The brown eyes flashed, catching the hall light. "Is it rent time already? I'm sure I'll be able to scrape up the money somewhere." He laughed.

I'll take it out in trade, she thought.

"No, you don't understand," she insisted. The hall light was too bright. She could only see him in silhouette now. This wasn't going the way she had imagined. She needed to sit down. Collect her thoughts. "Could I have a drink?"

He edged away from the wall, started toward the living room. "Water?"

Water? No! How romantic is that?

What is your problem, Liam?

"Do you have any wine?" She followed him into the living room. Anything to get out of that bright hall light.

Books stacked on one side of the couch. Desk lamp throwing a cone of light onto an open book on the desk against the wall. Low music from the CD player on a bookshelf.

"Is that Van Morrison, Liam? Do you *love* Van Morrison too?"

He nodded. "I like the old albums. Before he found religion." He started across the room. "I just opened a bottle of Chardonnay. May I offer you a glass?"

That's more like it, honey, she thought. She slid out of the coat. So hot inside it. Unbearable. "Yes. Thanks." She spread the coat out on the one uncluttered couch cushion and sat down on it.

"Is that real fur?" He crossed to the small table at the dining room entrance and picked up the bottle of wine.

"Bunny rabbit," she replied in a little-girl voice.

He snickered. "Looks like *several* rabbits." He motioned with a wineglass to the corner of the room. "Don't let Phoebe see that coat."

Phoebe? I thought his sister's name was Barbara. Or something.

It took her eyes a while to focus on the creature inside the cage. "You keep a rabbit?"

He stopped pouring. "I'm sorry. Do you have a rule against pets?"

It was meant as a joke, she knew. But she felt a stab of pain. Why does he keep thinking of me as a landlady?

"Maybe someday I'll turn Phoebe into a coat," he continued brightly. "A little coat for a leprechaun." He came up behind the couch and slipped the stem of the wineglass into her hand. Then he raised his own glass as he made his way toward the desk. "Cheers."

"Cheers." Andrea took a long sip. Good wine. Smooth. Lots of flavor. Not cheap, she decided. Another sip. "Do you believe in leprechauns, Liam?"

He chuckled. "Doesn't everyone?"

She shook out her hair. Stuck out her breasts. Why doesn't he look at me?

He stood in the center of the room, between the couch and the desk. Eyes on his wineglass.

She had an impulse to pat the cushion, invite him to sit beside her. But his cold stance discouraged it. " 'Tupelo Honey,' " she murmured. "Wow. I remember buying the single." She raised her eyes to him. "I like your sweater."

He smiled, rubbed the sleeve with his free hand. "Irish wool from good Irish sheep."

"Were you working? Did I disturb you?"

"I was reading the folktales I'm going to lecture on tomorrow." He picked up the book. "Quite enjoyable, actually. It's so wonderful. Just when I think I've read them all, I find one that's completely new to me."

"Wonderful," Andrea murmured, staring into her nearly empty glass. She tried to change the subject. "When did your family come to America, Liam?"

His scowl surprised her. "My family didn't come. Just me."

"And your sister?"

"Yes. My sister. Of course."

He answered so curtly, she let out a low whistle.

He didn't seem to notice. His expression slowly softened. He picked up the book in his free hand. "I think you'll enjoy this story, Andrea. It's about money."

Another stab of pain. There he goes again, thinking of me as his landlady. What am I doing here? Making a fool of myself?

But then he dropped down beside her. Leaned close. Clicked his glass against hers. Flashed her the smile she expected, the smile she had pictured, had remembered so often since that hot day in August.

He smelled soapy. She inhaled his shampoo. Sweet and coconuty. Why did he shower in the middle of the evening?

He set the wineglass down on the floor and let his eyes skim over the words of the book. "This story is about a fairy."

I'm not interested in fairies, honey, she thought, trying to look interested. Why not just forget the damned book and put your tongue in my mouth?

She thought of the two gay guys she had rented an apartment to that afternoon. Their smooth-skinned faces flashed into her mind. Fairies. Oh, well. At least they always kept their apartments neat.

Liam set down the book. He leaned close, grinning excitedly at her.

He's more turned on by the stupid folktale than by me, Andrea thought miserably. How can a grown man get so excited about fairies and leprechauns?

Liam seemed oblivious to her lack of enthusiasm. Eyes locked on hers, he launched into the story, speaking with the animation that made him such a popular teacher.

"There was a man named Sean O'Doole who lived many years ago in the tiny town of Carrick. Sean was a good Catholic lad and went to Mass every Sunday. But one Sunday morning, Sean felt faint. He made his way out of church and out onto the street.

"He still hadn't recovered when an old gentleman, dressed all in black, came wandering by. 'You do not look well,' said the old gentleman to Sean. Sean pointed to the church and replied, 'I was at Mass but I started to feel faint.'

"The old gentleman slipped a gold florin into Sean's palm. 'Go over to Muldoon's pub and take a stiff drink of whiskey. It will do your heart good, lad. You will soon be hale and hearty once more.' "

Andrea stifled a yawn. The wine was making her feel sleepy. The story wasn't helping matters. She shut her eyes. Liam continued enthusiastically.

"Sean thanked the man, went into the pub, and asked for the best whiskey in the house. He drank a good drop of whiskey and paid for it with the gold florin that the old gentleman had so generously given him. A short while later, he felt fine again.

"The next day, Sean found himself in need of tobacco. He went into the local shop and asked for a pouch. And when he reached into his pocket to pay for it, what did he find? The same gold florin the old gentleman had given him!

"He paid the store clerk with it and went on to his fishing boat. That evening, he returned tired and sore and wet. He stopped in at Muldoon's and ordered a whiskey to warm his spirits. When he went to pay for it, he found the gold florin in his pocket again.

"Sean began to wonder about the old gentleman who had given him the coin. Was he one of the fairy people not of this earth? Should Sean continue to use the coin? He used it for many days, always spending it and getting it back.

"But the more he used it, the more worried he became of it. Finally, one day, he decided he could no longer take the strain of owning it. He ordered a whiskey from Muldoon. He tossed the coin down on the counter and cried, 'May the devil go with you!'

"Muldoon put the florin in the till and asked Sean what he was so riled about. And Sean told him the whole story. 'You fool!' cried Muldoon. 'Keep the coin. You are a rich man!' He went to the till to return the coin to Sean—and it had vanished. No one ever saw it—or the old gentleman—again."

Andrea opened her eyes to find Liam staring at her. What was he waiting for? Was she supposed to laugh? Or cry? Or what?

Van Morrison's voice rose and fell as if gliding over ocean waves. Andrea pulled herself up. Her hand brushed Liam's sleeve, lingered there.

"I don't really get it," she said, squinting at him. It was so hard to concentrate. Why did the lights have to be so bright? Why couldn't the music be louder?

Liam laughed. "Typical Irishman. Can't stand it when something goes right."

"But why did he give away the coin?" Andrea demanded. "He was poor, right? He needed the money."

"But it could be a curse, don't you see?" Excitement in Liam's eyes, the excitement of a teacher with a trapped pupil in

111

his net. "Sean didn't know who the old gentleman was. Was he a devil? Some kind of fairy? Even the finest gift can become a curse if you don't know where it came from. It could have been bad luck. Sean had no way of knowing."

Andrea shook her head. The story didn't make a whole hell of a lot of sense, she decided. Why did Liam think it was so terrific? "Do you think the Irish are more superstitious than most people?" Asked casually.

Liam reacted with surprise. His cheeks reddened, circles of bright scarlet. "Why do you ask that?"

"Well . . . the guy in the story. He was superstitious, right? He believed in curses and bad luck."

Liam nodded thoughtfully.

Enough of this bullshit, Andrea decided. Are we going to get it on or not, honey?

It's now or never.

She reached up both hands and spread them over his still-blushing cheeks. His face felt surprisingly hot. Gently, she started to pull his head down to her. She shut her eyes. Opened her lips.

A cough behind the couch. Footsteps. A cleared throat.

Andrea gasped.

Liam pulled away from her headlock. Turned toward the sounds. "Margaret! You're back!"

Andrea turned to see the sister standing a few feet behind the couch, her expression disapproving, eyes on Liam, a brown paper bag tucked in her arm. Margaret raised the bag in one gloved hand. "I got the ice cream. I didn't know we were having a party." Said to Liam.

Andrea jumped unsteadily to her feet. She sucked saliva off her lips. The kiss. We didn't kiss. He wanted to. But the sister . . . The room tilted. "I just stopped by for a second. Really. I—"

Why was she explaining to the sister?

A smile on the woman's face. A mocking smile. Amused.

I'd like to rub it off with my fist, Andrea thought.

"Andrea, it's so nice to see you," Margaret said, finally taking her eyes off Liam and turning to her. "Please don't go."

"No. Really. I have to get home." Liam smiling at her too. She searched for any warmth in his smile, in his eyes. Was he laughing at her? Or was he smiling because they shared something now. A secret. Their own conspiracy.

I'm not a lovesick teenager. Why do I feel as if Mom has just barged in and caught me making out on the couch?

Her right temple throbbed. She tried to rub away the pain as she grabbed up her heavy coat and started for the front hallway. Liam caught her by the elbow as she tripped over the edge of the Oriental rug.

"Careful now," he murmured. His eyes peered questioningly into hers. She still couldn't read his smile.

He's holding on to my arm so tenderly. He cares about me. I was right.

"I'm putting the ice cream in the freezer and going up to my apartment." The sister still behind the couch. "Please don't hurry off because of me."

But Andrea had reached the front door. The hallway light so bright overhead. Bright as morning sunshine. It hurt her eyes, made her temples throb harder.

"I'm so glad you're both enjoying the house."

What a stupid, phony thing to say. What's *wrong* with me? It's the wine, I guess. The wine and the coke.

Not enough coke.

Liam pulled open the door for her. "Will you be okay?"

What does he mean?

"Can you get home okay, Andrea?"

She nodded. "It's a short walk. The other side of campus."

He took the coat from her arm and held it for her. She slipped into it, turning her head to smile at him.

He smiled back, his hands still on the shoulders of her coat. "Take care, okay?"

"Good night, Liam."

The door closed so quickly behind her. She felt a shock of

cold air on her face. And then the door shut so hard, she nearly toppled off the front stoop.

As her eyes adjusted to the darkness, she pictured his smile in the doorway, his dark eyes, his hands on her shoulders. "Take care, okay?" In that soft voice, smooth as honey.

He wanted me too.

He really did.

Leaning on the iron railing, she made her way to the sidewalk. Tucking her hands into the deep coat pockets, she leaned into the wind, started for home, eyes watering from the cold, tears burning her cheeks.

"Take care, okay?"

I could almost taste him.

Next time I will. Next time. Without that damned sister lurking about.

Why does a man like that live with his sister, anyway?

13

A young man took Liam's coat and cap. Then Milton ushered him through the living room, down a long mirrored hallway toward the den. Outside the French doors, a red afternoon sun lowered itself behind the bare trees. "Milton, you have your own forest out there," Liam declared.

He stopped to say hello to two graduate assistants in short skirts and tights. They smiled and raised their wineglasses as if toasting him.

"Nice of you to throw a party for no reason at all," Liam told Milton.

"It's sort of traditional. The Dean of Students has a party every fall. I thought it would be nicer to have it here than at some stuffy room in the Administration Building."

Three student waiters made their way through the room, offering plastic cups of red or white wine and crackers with some kind of white cheese spread on them.

Milton guided Liam by the elbow. "Sometimes I can stare out at the woods for hours. Just watch the light change."

Liam snickered. "Sounds like you have too much time on your hands, Milton."

Milton didn't smile. He adjusted the neck of his maroon turtleneck. "I'm so glad I found this house up here. You know, the whole back is glass. My bedroom looks out on the woods too. I can lie in bed and feel as if I'm outside."

Liam waved to a middle-aged man leaning on a cane in the corner. Then turned back to Milton. "You're a little far from the campus. How do you get up these hills in the winter?"

"Luckily, it didn't snow much last winter. That was my first year. But I've got four-wheel drive. It isn't too bad."

Liam stopped to admire a travel poster on the wall. "Is that British Rail?"

Milton nodded. "I collect British Rail posters. I have some beautiful ones from the 1930s." He sighed. "But no walls for them. That's one of the problems with having so many windows. And my other collections take up space."

Liam followed his gaze to the far wall. Glass display cases mounted on the wall reflected the red light of the setting sun. "Oh, yes. You told me about your knife collection."

"I have some very rare ones," Milton confided. "Historic. I'll show them to you later."

Piano music from the CD player followed them into the den. One of the waiters poked his blond head in. "Wine?"

"Not just yet," Liam replied. The young man disappeared. "Milton, I had no idea you were such a collector."

Milton reddened. "There's a lot you don't know about me, my friend."

He studied Liam's outfit. Liam wore a collarless black shirt, buttoned to the top, tucked into pleated, loose-fitting black slacks.

I guess that's supposed to be stylish. But he looks like a priest, Milton thought. When he walked in and greeted everyone, I expected him to give a benediction.

Milton always found himself amused by people who needed to be stylish. What was the point of it? Why not just be comfortable?

Liam's a good-looking guy, he decided. I guess most women would consider him really handsome. What does he need a costume for?

He saw Liam staring at the two crossed sabers on the wall above the stone fireplace. Saw Liam's eyes wander over the bookshelves, the rows of books on weaponry, ancient and modern. The shelf of true crime books. Milton's addiction. One of his addictions, anyway.

Liam's eyes stopped on the human skull on the corner of the mantelpiece. He turned to Milton, his eyes narrowing. "Is that real?"

Milton snickered. "Yeah. It's my grandmother. I saved it after her funeral."

Liam hesitated. Studied Milton. Decided Milton was joking. They both laughed.

"I picked it up in a flea market," Milton confided. "You believe it? I named him Maurice. After my old dean at Binghamton."

"Very nice. Gives the room some atmosphere." Liam raised the white box in his hands. "Here. I almost forgot." The box had a pink ribbon around it and a pink ribbon flower.

"I'm really sorry Margaret couldn't come," Milton said. "What a shame."

Liam pushed the box into Milton's huge hands. "I'm sorry too. She had the worst headache. One of her migraines. Nothing she can do about them but go to bed and try to sleep them off."

Milton gazed down at the gift box. "You weren't supposed to bring a present. It isn't my birthday, you know."

Liam smiled. "It isn't much. A little housewarming gift. Go ahead. Open it."

Laughter from out in the hall. Loud voices drowned out the piano music. More people had arrived, Milton realized. He wondered if Leila Schumacher from the French Department was coming. I'd like to give *her* some French lessons, he thought. The last time she walked past him swinging that fabulous ass, it was all he could do to keep from grabbing her.

Masturbating in the shower before the party, he had fantasized about Leila Schumacher. Not for the first time. He pictured her there in the shower with him, hot water running down her

117

skin. Spreading her legs. Spreading them. The hot water rushing down. Oh. Man. Sometimes the desire was just too unbearable. Maybe he could get her to stay after everyone left. Show her the view of the woods from his bedroom . . .

"Go ahead, Milton. Open it."

Milton fumbled with the pink ribbon. Realized he had an erection. Stepping behind the desk, he pulled the lid off the box, tore away two layers of white tissue paper—and stared at a football-shaped lump of black coal.

"Coal? I don't get it."

Liam's brown eyes flashed. He didn't smile. "It's very special, Milton. I want you to have it. It fell off a coal truck when I was nine."

"Excuse me?" Milton lifted the coal from the box, let the box drop to the desktop. "Don't you give coal to kids at Christmas when they've been bad?"

Liam took the coal from Milton and smoothed his hand over it. "This will bring you good luck. It's a Scottish superstition. If a piece of coal falls off a coal truck and you are the first to pick it up, you must toss it over your right shoulder."

Liam handed the coal back to Milton. "I did that back home when I was nine. I chased after the coal truck until it hit a bump. I watched the coal tumble out. I was so excited. I grabbed the coal and tossed it over my shoulder. I've kept it ever since. And now I give it to you."

Milton eyed Liam skeptically. "You sure you want to part with this treasure?"

"I never enter a new house without bringing some good luck." Said earnestly, without irony.

Milton grunted. "You really believe in this stuff?"

A thin smile spread over Liam's face. "I have to. It's my job."

Milton tumbled the black oval in his big hand. "Some of your students think the old stories you tell are pretty wild."

Liam's face registered surprise. "You've been talking to my students?"

Milton chuckled. "I have to. That's *my* job."

"Some of them have the effrontery to think that folklore is irrelevant today. I try to dispel them of that notion in the first few weeks. And the way I do it is to tell them—"

"Oh. Hello."

The door to the den swung all the way open, and a pretty young woman with frizzed auburn hair entered, wearing a long, loose-flowing faded denim dress. Her three top buttons were open, revealing creamy white skin.

Milton raised his eyes from her breasts to her face and recognized her at once. "Devra. Hi!"

Her eyes were on Liam, wide with surprise.

Milton turned to Liam. "Do you know Devra Brookes? She's an instructor in our Language Arts program." Surprise on Liam's frozen features too. The back of his neck suddenly red.

"Dr. O'Connor!" Devra exclaimed breathlessly, rushing forward and taking his hand. "You left Chicago in such a hurry, I didn't get a chance to say good-bye."

"Well . . . good-bye *and* hello!" Liam cradled her hand between his. That warm smile. "So nice to see you again, Devra. Such a surprise."

Fucking charm, Milton thought with some bitterness. How does he turn it on and off like that? Then, a more interesting question: How does Liam know our little graduate instructor here? Why did he look so hot and bothered when he first recognized her?

I'll bet he was fucking her. Back in Chicago.

"I came here at midterm. Last year," Devra explained, sliding her hand from Liam's, shoving both hands into the pockets on the front of the dress. "What a change from Chicago! Moore State is so much smaller. It was like moving to a little village high school or something."

"Ouch!" Milton declared. "Don't say high school."

"It's rather strange for me too," Liam confessed, beaming at her. "So nice to see a familiar face. Where are you living, Devra?"

"I have an apartment on Tremont." She twisted her face, her green eyes sparkling. "It's two bedrooms. But I have three roommates. Luckily, we all like each other."

"And your dog—?"

"Sparky didn't make the trip. He's living in the lap of luxury with my parents."

They chatted on. Boring conversation, Milton thought. But Liam kept his eyes locked on hers, as if entranced by every dull detail of her life. And she was eating up his attention.

Milton let his eyes wander down the front of her dress. She had a nice, firm body. Tits weren't bad. And that creamy, lickable skin!

I wouldn't hurt you, Milton thought. I know I'm too big. You could be on top, Devra. He pictured her on top of him, fucking him, fucking him, green eyes wide open, auburn hair falling over his face, brushing over him, tickling him—he loved redheads. He imagined the soft rhythmic slap of their wet bodies, her creamy white butt bouncing, bouncing in the air, slowly, slowly.

Oh God.

I should have been a monk. Why do I choose to work around all these luscious young women? How does *anyone* work around them?

Liam was holding her hand again. Milton struggled to focus on their words.

"So nice to see you."

"You'll drop in on my class? We'll have coffee?"

"That would be great. I can't believe you're here. For the whole year?"

"Yes. I'm teaching two classes and I'm doing research for a book. The library is really okay. And they have computers. I can go online. You know. Get onto the Internet and search more extensive libraries around the world."

She frowned. "I'm still a computer illiterate. I guess I should learn."

Liam nodded. "It isn't as hard as people tell you. If I can learn it, anyone can."

So *boring*, Milton thought impatiently. She's so pretty and so boring. I'd have to tape her mouth before I fucked her. I really would. He stared at her mouth. Tried to picture her lips dry and swollen.

"I guess I'd better go mingle," Liam said finally. "Take care, Devra. See you soon, dear." He nodded to them both, then made his way to the noisy living room.

Laughter in the hallway. Raised voices. People greeting Liam.

Devra turned to Milton, hands returned to the pockets below the waist of the denim dress. "Thank you for inviting me, Dr. Cohn."

"Please. Everyone calls me Milton."

"Guess I'll go get something to drink. This is a really nice den. Do you work in here?"

Milton nodded. "It's very comfortable. I like being surrounded by woods." He cleared his throat. Took a few steps toward her. "Liam left Chicago in a hurry?" Trying to sound casual.

Devra raised one hand to tuck back a curl of hair. "Yes. One day he just vanished. Like one of his leprechauns."

Milton pursed his lips. "He's an interesting man. How well did you know him?"

Devra blushed.

14

Mary Beth stepped into Milton's already crowded living room, waving to someone she recognized. Sara hesitated at the door. Is Mary Beth going to desert me before we even get inside? she wondered. I won't know anyone here—except for Milton, of course. Why did I let her talk me into coming?

Because Liam might be here. She answered her own question.

A chance to talk to Liam. To *flirt* with Liam?

A chance to gaze into those soft brown eyes, to listen to his beautiful voice, enjoy the radiant smile.

Sara, Sara. Don't get carried away.

He might not even be here.

She stepped into the crowded, noisy living room. Watched Mary Beth in the center of the room, already helping herself to a glass of wine from a tray, playfully grabbing an hors d'oeuvre from the hand of some guy she obviously knew and popping it into her mouth.

Sara's eyes flashed from face to face. Liam? Are you here?

Is it our fate to meet again?

Fate was Liam's word, she knew.

Where *is* he?

Sara studied the other outfits. Am I overdressed? She wore a black flannel blazer, single-breasted, soft and easy-flowing, over a cream-colored merino turtleneck, and matching flannel trousers.

Too New York? she wondered. Too stylish for these graduate instructors and young academics? Mary Beth appeared so much more casual in her bulky turquoise tunic sweater, pulled down nearly to her knees over navy leggings.

A burst of laughter drew her attention to the fireplace. A low fire glowed dully, orange and blue. One of those fake wax logs, Sara thought. The sun had set, the sky stretched out in royal purple behind the French doors. A very skinny young man in a black T-shirt and black denim jeans demonstrated a dance step, his arms high above his head, his hips grinding, the demonstration greeted by laughter and catcalls.

"I get embarrassed when white people try to dance," Sara heard a woman say.

"That's a rascist remark," a young man replied. "Have you ever seen *me* dance?"

Before Sara could hear the reply, she became aware of someone at her side. She turned to discover Milton, red-faced as usual, leering at her. No. That's unkind, she thought. That's just his smile.

But why does he always look so hungry?

"Milton, hi." She smiled back. Actually, she felt glad to see him. "What a beautiful house."

He took her hand, squeezed it hard. "So glad you could come, Sara. Did you have trouble finding it?"

"No. Mary Beth—my friend—drove us. I didn't realize it was so far from campus."

He chuckled, still holding her hand. "Sometimes it isn't far enough!"

She laughed, a little too loudly. She tugged her hand free. Noticed his face redden a little deeper.

"By the way, I found those files," he said, bringing his face close to be heard over the music and voices, so close she could smell the wine on his breath. "Claire filed them in the wrong drawer."

"Oh. Good." Glad it wasn't me, she thought. The work in his office had been boring, unchallenging to say the least. Then yesterday the new students files had been lost. Misplaced. And Milton had exploded. Only briefly. But it gave Sara a glimpse at another side of him. Frightening when he lost his temper. Not because of the words he shouted or his slamming the door so hard the windowpane shook. But because he was so big. A raging elephant.

The anger had subsided quickly. It was only a few files, after all. Now Sara was glad they had been found. Glad she hadn't been the one who had screwed up.

He took her arm and pulled her into the room. "Let me give you the tour. Do you know anyone here?"

"I don't think so." She gazed from face to face. A beautiful, dark-haired young woman on the arm of the couch tilted up her head and sent a perfect smoke ring floating up from her open mouth. A grinning boy wearing a baseball cap leaned over the couch and stuck his finger through the hole of the ring. "Just my friend Mary Beth." Where *was* Mary Beth?

"I'm reading the new Joyce Carol Oates," Sara overheard.

"Oh, really. What is *this* week's book about?" Said snootily. Followed by hooting laughter.

Milton's body brushed against hers as he led her to the French doors. His heavy lips formed a pout. "Aw, it got dark. I wanted to show off my woods."

Sara stared out at the tangled, reaching trees, black against the purple night sky. Faces reflected in the glass, making it appear as if the party was going on outside too.

Stepping carefully around three people sitting cross-legged on the floor, he led her through a long hallway, mirrored walls on both sides, to the den with its skull on the mantel. Then to the long, narrow kitchen. "My only dark room. No sunlight at all. If I decide to stay, I'm going to knock out that wall and replace it with glass."

She pictured him lowering his shoulder and battering the wall down with his own body.

"I like to cook. My daughter sent me a wok for Christmas last year, and I have become a great Chinese cook. I don't look it, do I! But I am Mr. Slice and Dice." He made rapid chopping motions with the hand not holding on to Sara.

She chuckled. "I love Chinese food. Back in New York, every Chinese restaurant delivered. We had it three times a week."

She spotted Mary Beth at the back of the long kitchen, leaning one elbow against the stainless steel refrigerator, tugging at her streaked hair, deep in conversation with a weedy young man in denim. He had a high tuft of brown hair on top of his needle-thin face. Reminded Sara of Lyle Lovett.

Where is Eric tonight? Sara found herself wondering. I guess Mary Beth doesn't take him to parties. Maybe there was some kind of rule about college employees dating students. She wondered if Mary Beth ever saw him outside her apartment. Outside her bedroom?

Mary Beth didn't see Sara. Milton tugged her into the back hall. A woman with long white hair stepped out of a bathroom. Sound of a toilet flushing behind her. "Dr. Cohn himself! There you are. I was looking for you. I have a bone to pick with you."

"Get in line!" he joked. He didn't stop. Turned back to the white-haired woman. "See you in a few moments, Liz. I'm just giving Sara the grand tour. Is Arnold here?"

"He's in Washington. He sends his regrets. He said he'll see you at the gym."

The room at the end of the hall turned out to be Milton's bedroom. More views of the woods. Sliding glass doors on the far wall. "This is where the tour ends. There's another bedroom, where I tossed the coats. And a little closet of a room I call my gym. I have some equipment squeezed in there."

He worked out every spare moment, she had learned. "Got to stay strong for the students." His constant line. But what exactly did it mean?

Sara nearly burst out laughing when she saw his bed. A canopy bed, all purple organdy. Without realizing it, she clapped a hand over her mouth. The idea of this big rhino sleeping under the frilly purple canopy struck her as hilarious.

He didn't seem to notice. She turned away from the bed, glimpsed matching purple velvet drapes over the window beyond the bed.

And then her eyes fell on the knives.

The silvery blades gleaming in the light from the ceiling fixture. A whole wall of knives, mounted nearly from floor to ceiling, all horizontal, blades to the right.

How many knives? Her eyes moved from top to bottom. At least two dozen. Long and short, thick-bladed and thin. All polished and silvery bright.

"You're admiring my collection?" Milton glowing like the knives. His hand on the shoulder of her blazer, he maneuvered her toward the wall.

For some reason, she suddenly felt stunned. Giddy.

So many blades? So many weapons? Or is it the contrast to the canopy bed?

"They're beautiful—aren't they?" He stared at her eagerly, urging her to react.

She nodded. "Beautiful? Yes. It's quite a collection." She swallowed. Trying to respond satisfactorily. "They're all old, right?"

He beamed like a proud papa. "Some of them are very old." He lifted a thick-handled knife from its mounting and raised it toward her. The blade appeared heavy, dull. "This is an original Bowie knife. I mean, one of the originals. Jim Bowie himself might have carried this knife."

"Really."

Come on, Sara. You can do better than that.

He slapped the blade against his fat palm. Smiled at her, almost a guilty smile.

Were the knives some kind of guilty pleasure for him?

"Some of them are much older than this." He carefully replaced it on the wall. "There is nothing more beautiful than a knife. The design is so clean, the symmetry so pure. Such a perfect tool, and a work of art at the same time."

When he turned back to her, his eyes were wide, dilated. She realized he was breathing hard, his big stomach heaving up and down beneath the bulky turtleneck sweater.

"They're really amazing," Sara offered awkwardly. She stepped back, bumped the side of the bed.

His hand swept past a long-bladed specimen with an ivory handle. "This saber is a museum piece. Look at the perfect sheen of the ivory. Have you ever seen anything so clean and beautiful? And this—this one—!" Such excitement. He was breathless now. Panting.

He reached up, pulled a long-handled knife with a heavy blade off its mounting. "It's Macedonian. Do you believe it? Isn't it beautiful, Sara? Look at the perfection of the blade. It's double-edged. Sharp as the day it was forged. Watch."

Gripping the handle with both hands, he pulled his arms back. Eyes wild. Stomach heaving. Mouth set in an open grin. With a loud grunt, he swung.

Sara raised both hands to her face as the blade cut through the purple velvet of the drape. Sliced cleanly, almost silently through the heavy fabric. The bottom section of the fabric hit the floor with a soft thud.

Milton lowered the knife. Still breathing hard, he squinted down at what he had done. He stared for a long moment, the knife at his side. When he gazed up at Sara, all the color had drained from his face.

"Sorry." The word came out in a whisper. He mopped his forehead with the back of his hand. Then he uttered a dry laugh, almost soundless. "I know, I know. I get carried away."

He hung his head as if she had scolded him. "I'm crazy, right? I get one of these ancient weapons in my hand and I just lose control."

"How long have you been collecting them, Milton?" Sara, eager to get things back to normal, still picturing the wild swing, the silent slice, the small rectangle of fabric dropping like a child's body to the carpet.

He didn't reply. He had turned and was on tiptoe, replacing the Macedonian knife. Carefully. Carefully.

"They're really interesting," Sara continued, eager now to get back to the living room, to some laughter, some cheerful voices. The knives gleamed down at her. She imagined herself in some ancient torture room. A purple-velvet-lined dungeon, with the enormous dungeonmaster selecting his torture weapon. "They must be worth a lot of money."

He grinned at her, the color back in his face. "I'm glad you enjoyed them. I'm glad you appreciate them. A lot of people don't really understand. They don't see their beauty, their perfection."

Again she saw the large beads of sweat at the base of his hedge of white hair. Saw his bottom lip quiver. Saw his gray eyes light with excitement.

I don't like this, she thought, feeling a chill of fear. *I'd like to get out of this bedroom now.*

And then a voice from the doorway. "So *there* you are."

Liam. Stepping casually into the room. One hand in the pocket of his black trousers. Amber bottle of Coors in the other.

Milton mopped his forehead again.

Sara turned to Liam, eager for his smile.

Liam, I've been thinking about you. Liam, I can't *stop* thinking about you.

He disappointed her by speaking first to Milton. "Everyone is asking about you." But then he redeemed himself by turning his smile on Sara. "But I see why you're hiding away."

A high-pitched cackle escaped Milton's lips. "I'm not hiding. I was showing Sara my collection." He pointed to the sliced drape. "Afraid I got a little carried away." He turned back to Liam. "Do you remember Sara Morgan? We met at Spinnaker's a few weeks ago. Sara is working in my office now."

Liam took her hand, bowed his head with mock solemnity. His hand warm and dry. Dark eyes burning deeply into hers.

"Of course I remember. Sara and I have been running into each other ever since. You know, I've been meaning to go back to that restaurant and try the crab legs. They looked so colorful, piled on your plate."

Sara felt her face grow hot. "They were very good. Very sweet. They were as good as the ones I had out west a few years ago." She suddenly felt foolish. *What am I saying? I sound like an idiot!*

Why am I yammering on and on about crab legs?

"It's nice to see you, Professor O'Connor." Might as well start all over again.

"Please. Liam. Professor O'Connor is my father."

"Your father was a professor too?"

"No. A farmer. But the other men all called him Professor. I think it was because he could *read!*"

All three of them laughed. Milton picked up the section of cut fabric and folded it between his hands.

"You were born in Ireland?" Sara asked. He stood so close to her she could smell his aftershave. Piney, not sweet.

Liam nodded. "Yes."

"And when did you move to America?" Sara asked.

Liam's brown eyes appeared to fade. "A long time ago." He cleared his throat. "It's so delightful to run into you again, Sara. I—" He stopped. "You don't have a drink." Took her hand. "Come. Let's remedy that."

"I'm not being a good host," Milton murmured, following them from the room. "I'd better check on the ice. I bought two bags, but that may not be enough. Not with *this* crowd!"

They walked between the mirrored walls of the long hallway. Sara glimpsed her reflection and her reflection of her reflection. She saw all three of them, Sara, Liam, and Milton, duplicated forever, growing tinier and tinier, and darker as they stretched into the distance.

The buzz of voices grew louder as they entered the living room. More crowded now, Sara saw. A mix of administration workers and professors and grad students. Liam guided her toward the drinks table. They had to step through a group of students sitting cross-legged on the carpet, a heated political discussion in progress.

"There's no trust, no trust at all," Sara heard.

"But that's a *good* thing," someone insisted.

Someone had changed the music. Sara recognized Ella Fitzgerald and Louis Armstrong, remembered that her brother Frank always played this album.

She spotted Mary Beth against the window, starless blue-black sky beyond the glass now, leaning over, hands on her knees, talking animatedly to a gray-haired woman in a wheelchair.

Liam stopped in front of the couch. Sara nearly bumped into him. He pulled the lighted match from a young man's hand. The young man reacted with surprise. Liam blew out the match, frowned at the group standing there. "Three on a match. Very bad luck."

"That was my last match, Professor O'Connor!" the young man protested.

"I think I have a lighter," a red-haired woman offered, reaching for her bag. She glanced up teasingly at Liam. "Do you have any rules about plastic lighters?"

Liam pretended to think. "No. I think you're safe."

He stepped up to the drinks table. Bottles of wine, several half-filled liquor bottles, a nearly empty Lucite ice bucket, lemons and limes. Someone had spilled their glass. A red puddle stained the white tablecloth. "Sara, would you like some wine? A beer?"

"Wine would be good. Red, please."

He poured the wine, finishing the bottle. Pressed the glass into her hand and led the way to an empty spot behind the couch. He clinked the neck of his beer bottle against her glass. "Cheers." Then he took a short sip of beer, tilting the bottle to his mouth while keeping his brown eyes on her.

"And how are you enjoying working for Milton?"

She shrugged. "It's not very challenging. But I'm glad to

earn a little money." A flashback of Milton in the bedroom, swinging the antique knife, cutting the drape. "How long have you known Milton?"

"I don't know him. I met him when I arrived. That night at the restaurant was our first real conversation." Another short sip of beer. "He's an interesting man. Once you get past his gruffness. And his appearance. I mean, I wouldn't want to see him coming toward me in a dark alley, would you?" Liam's eyes flashed merrily. "Not my idea of a college dean. But he's surprising in a lot of ways. He has so many unlikely interests. For example." He gestured to the display case of knives behind them on the wall.

"I'm surprised he hasn't sliced all of his curtains to shreds!" Sara joked.

Liam laughed. Then his eyes narrowed on her. "Sara, what month were you born in?"

"Excuse me?" A laugh escaped her throat. "Dr. O'Connor, you're really disappointing me. First, you try to read my palm. Now, are you really going to ask me my sign?"

A sheepish grin.

"Don't tell me you're into astrology."

"It's a superstition, like any other. What do *you* believe in, Sara?" Teasing her.

"I don't know. A lot of things."

"Like what?" Those dark eyes, those beautiful eyes, sweeping over her face, making her skin prickle.

She raised the wineglass. "*In vino veritas.*"

He laughed. Clinked his bottle again against her glass.

She felt herself start to relax. It wasn't just the wine. She had made him laugh. He wasn't hard to talk to. Not at all. And he seemed to enjoy talking to her.

"So answer the question."

"If you insist. I was born in May. May twelfth."

"A dangerous month," he replied in a low voice. Suddenly thoughtful.

She tried to decide if he was serious or teasing. She couldn't tell.

He leaned closer and recited a rhyme. "March will search, April will try. May will tell if you live or die."

She drank some wine, then raised her eyes to him. "I don't think I like that rhyme."

"It's very old."

"Do you have a rhyme for every occasion, Liam?"

"I've got a million of them." That wonderful smile. Intimate, somehow. "But I keep forgetting you're a psychology major, Sara. I'd better be quiet. I can see those beautiful eyes studying me, filing me away in some aberrant behavior category."

She grinned back at him, surprised he remembered what she studied. "Just how weird are you?"

"Weird enough." His eyes crinkled, but he didn't laugh.

She followed his gaze across the room. In front of the fireplace, two young women had their hands raised. It took Sara a moment to see that one of them had string entwined in the fingers of both hands. They were playing cat's cradle. Four or five others huddled nearby, cheering them on with exaggerated enthusiasm.

Liam placed his hand on the shoulder of Sara's blazer. "Mainly, I know a lot of weird and useless information. Did you know, for example, that Eskimo boys are forbidden to play cat's cradle?"

Sara smiled, feeling the warmth of the wine. "No. Why not?"

"Well, it is believed that if boys play cat's cradle, when they grow up, they will get their hands tangled in the harpoon line."

Sara turned back to Liam. "You *do* know a lot of weird and useless information!"

He tossed back his head and laughed, gleeful, appreciative laughter, as if she had just uttered the funniest thing he had ever heard.

* * *

Milton emptied the bag of ice into the ice bucket, spilling a few cubes onto the carpet. He bent to pick them up, struggling as they kept sliding from his hand.

He straightened up, trying to decide what to do with the melting cubes in his hands, and saw a frizz of auburn hair. Devra Brookes turned to him, a puff pastry in one hand. "Oh, hi again, Dr. Cohn. Nice party."

"Thanks. Are you enjoying it? Do you know people here, Devra?" She had a lovely smile. Very pretty girl. Such creamy skin. Delicious.

"Yes. Some." She leaned closer, turned her gaze, half-whispered. "Who is that with Dr. O'Connor? I don't think I've seen her before."

"Sara Morgan," Milton replied, inhaling Devra's perfume. Very flowery and sweet. "She's a graduate student. Works part-time in my office. Just started, actually."

Devra studied Sara intently. Milton watched Liam squeeze Sara's hand, lean closer. Fast worker. Look at him pouring on the charm. Twinkling eyes and all.

"They've certainly spent a lot of time together tonight," Devra murmured, more to herself than to Milton.

"I didn't plan to invite her," Milton revealed. "But Liam insisted. He called me three times to make sure Sara was coming."

Milton watched Devra's eyes narrow. Her creamy skin turned pink. "He did?"

"I'm suddenly starving. Would you like to get some dinner?"

Sara blinked. Two glasses of wine and she was imagining that he asked her to dinner. Raising her eyes, she realized he was waiting for an answer.

I should never drink at parties, she thought, feeling warm and a little off balance. One glass should be my limit. The second glass always makes everything blur. Makes it so hard to think quickly.

She thought she'd have to think quickly to keep up with him. But their conversation had flowed as if they were old friends. She felt comfortable and relaxed right away, and it wasn't just the wine, or the laughter all around, or the bright, flickering glow from the fireplace.

Had she talked too much about herself?

He really hadn't given her a choice.

She tried to get him to talk about his personal life, about his sister, about moving from Ireland, growing up a stranger here, about how he became so interested in folklore.

But he seemed reluctant to reveal much. He kept changing the subject back to her, drawing her out, asking question after question, those dark eyes locked on hers, appearing so amused by her answers, so fascinated and charmed.

With great enthusiasm, he told her a story he had just uncovered, an old Irish tale about a man who is given a gold coin that keeps reappearing in his pocket after it has been spent. Sara didn't understand the point of it at first, but he carefully explained it.

And then he had reached into his pocket and produced a gold coin which he slipped into her hand. "The original florin," he teased. "Try to spend it. It will remain with you always."

"Because it's magic?" she asked, suddenly wanting to believe in magic as he obviously did.

"Because it's worthless!" he replied. And they both laughed.

Laughed together.

Together.

She tucked the coin into her blazer pocket.

People kept interrupting them, wishing to talk to Liam. He charmed them all, Sara saw. It was so easy for him. Sara watched with a combination of envy and admiration.

And now he had asked her to dinner.

"Yes, I'd love to."

She wanted to *shout* it at the top of her lungs. *I'd LOVE to!"*

His dark eyes lit up. He seemed so pleased.

"Won't Milton be offended if we duck out?" Sara whispered. She glimpsed Milton at the fireplace, so wide he nearly blocked out all the light from the flickering fire, standing close to a young woman with frizzy, auburn hair, talking animatedly.

"The party is breaking up soon," Liam replied. "Of course everyone will miss us. But I'm sure they'll get over it in time." His expression changed, his forehead furrowing. "Actually, I haven't been too sociable, have I? I've spent all my time with you."

Sara lowered her eyes. She felt her heart pound. "I've enjoyed it, Liam."

"Then I'll go get our coats and let's see where we can scavenge up some food."

"I have to tell my friend." Mary Beth. Sara hadn't said a word to her the entire party. A couple of times, she caught Mary Beth flashing her quizzical looks from across the room. But Sara and Liam hadn't left their positions behind the couch, except to refill their drinks.

Now, feeling excited and a little drunk, Sara searched the crowded room for her friend. She found her in the mirrored hallway, talking to two middle-aged men.

Sara tugged her aside. "I'm leaving with Liam. I mean, is it okay? We're going to get some dinner."

Mary Beth placed both hands on Sara's shoulders. "Whoa. How much wine have you had to drink?"

Sara giggled. "Do I sound a little giddy? It's just that Liam and I—"

"I warned you not to fall for that Irish charm."

"Stop looking at me like that, Mary Beth. We're just getting dinner. That's all."

"Hey—I'm teasing you!" Mary Beth exclaimed, squeezing Sara's shoulders. She let out a short squeal. "That's wonderful! That's why you came here, after all."

The two middle-aged men snickered. Sara felt a flush of embarrassment. Why were they eavesdropping?

Mary Beth gave her a quick hug. "Have a great time."

"I'll call you later. Okay?"

Mary Beth smoothed the lapels of Sara's flannel blazer. "Yeah. Call me. I want to hear every detail."

The two men snickered again.

Sara turned back into the living room and searched for Liam. Her eyes swept the room twice. No sign of him.

He ducked out. He left. He was just teasing me.

The cruel idea tightened her throat. She dismissed it with a shake of her head. *Just the wine. I'm not thinking clearly.*

He went to get the coats. But how will he know which is mine?

She made her way past Mary Beth and the two men, down the long, mirrored hallway. Found the spare bedroom where the coats had been dropped. Stepped into the room. Saw Liam at the foot of the bed.

Looking so troubled. His face contorted. One hand rubbing his jaw. His eyes narrowed. In fear? Staring at the pile of coats.

He didn't seem to see her, even when she stepped up close beside him. "Liam, what's wrong? What is it?"

"My hat. They left it on the bed."

15

Andrea DeHaven turned the key in the lock, then double-checked to make sure the door was locked. "Be careful." She pointed. "That step is crumbling."

Mr. Olsham leaned heavily on the iron railing. He had a gimpy leg, and the steep stone stairs of the front stoop were a challenge to him. He let out little grunts as he achieved each step.

He was a trim, elderly man with thinning white hair, pale blue eyes set far apart on a face that Andrea saw had once been handsome. A spiderweb of tiny veins reddened each cheek. White bristle filled the deep cleft in his chin. He wore a gray wool overcoat, buttoned to the collar despite the surprising balminess of the October evening.

"I'm too stubborn to carry a cane," he muttered.

Andrea waited for him to reach the sidewalk before she started her descent. She wore a floppy, wide-brimmed purple hat, pulled low on her head because she hadn't had time to wash her hair. She had quickly pulled on a black suit to make her appear more businesslike. "So what do you think of the house, Mr. Olsham?"

"Pretty run-down, isn't it?" The old guy, she had discovered, could be really blunt.

"Run-down if you plan to live in it," Andrea agreed, adjusting the soft brim of the hat. "But if you plan to rent it out to students, it doesn't need that much work. Students aren't that particular."

He bit his lower lip, raising his pale eyes to the peeling white paint of the old house. "I'm a little worried about those wet spots on the pantry wall. There's a leak there somewhere."

"Yes, that will have to be looked into." She could see his interest fading. The house needed at least twenty thousand dollars of plumbing and plastering and repair, maybe more. He wanted something he could rent out to students right away, a house that would start making instant profits for him.

"It's quite a bargain," she offered, wishing he would stop staring at the broken gutter tilting down the side. "I'm sure I could talk the owner down whatever it will take for the plumbing repairs in the pantry."

He clicked his tongue several times. Made a sour face. "I don't know, Mrs. DeHaven. Hmmmm . . . Nice of you to show it to me in the evening. I appreciate your time."

One last try. "I'd buy it myself, it's so cheap. Really. I'd snap it up and do the repairs a little at a time. But I already own three rooming houses. Enough for me to handle."

A thin smile creased his face. He winked at her. "Bet you say that to all the boys."

Sharp cookie.

A few moments later, she was walking home, one hand pressed over the hat to keep it from blowing off in the swirling gusts that were suddenly blowing down High Street. Mr. Olsham had offered her a ride home in his black BMW, but she had declined. Andrea always liked a long walk after trying to pitch a house. The fresh air helped to clear away the bullshit.

Dry brown leaves danced across the sidewalk, blown into the spotlight of yellow light from a streetlamp. Pink clouds covered the moon. A red sky. What did that mean? *Red sky tonight.* Rain or no rain? She used to know. Why couldn't she remember these simple, basic things anymore?

She stopped at the corner of Yale when Liam's house came

into view. Lights on upstairs. That meant the sister was home. But maybe I should stop in anyway. Apologize to Liam for coming on to him like that. Tell him I wasn't feeling well. Tell him I'd taken some medication that always makes me a little out of it.

Or maybe there's no need to apologize. Maybe Liam was as sorry to have his sister interrupt us as I was.

She glanced down at her suit. Unbuttoned the top button of the jacket. Pulled the lapels apart to reveal a little more cleavage.

When she glanced up, the dark figure stepped in front of her, blocking her way.

Where had he come from? How did he move so silently?

"Hey—!" She cried out when he grabbed her hat. So hard. It felt like a punch.

Dazed, she reached for the hat with both hands. But it sailed into the street.

"Stop!"

He was breathing hard, wheezing, breath so fierce, like hot, rotting meat. So dark. She couldn't see a thing. Except for his gray eyes, glowing blankly, no emotion at all.

"I'll give you my purse! Here! Take my purse!"

A harsh ripping. She felt herself tugged. Struggled to keep on her feet.

He tore off the suit jacket. Ripped it in two.

"Take my purse! Please—don't hurt me! Take everything!"

Her voice cut off when she felt the searing pain in her shoulder.

She saw his big fingers dig into her skin. Felt the warm blood flow down her arm.

Another loud rip.

He tore the skin off her shoulder. Dug his fingers deep and peeled the skin away.

So easy. Like unmaking a bed.

Cracked her neck.

Fingers deep into her throat. Around to the back of her neck.

But I'm still alive! Still alive!

Ripping the skin down her back, grunting and wheezing. Such delight.

Peeling the skin off. Peeling it all off.

PART THREE

16

Sara cradled the phone between her shoulder and her cheek. She pulled her hair high on her head with both hands, studying herself in the dresser mirror.

"I was going to cut it short, but maybe I'll leave it. Liam likes it long."

Mary Beth groaned on the other end of the line. "I don't believe this."

"It looks nice in a French braid, but I really don't have time to braid it. Do you believe I lived in New York City all that time and never had it styled? I still just pull it back and tie it like I did when we were freshmen. My bangs are right out of the 1950s. I saw them on someone in an old movie on TV the other night."

"Sara, speaking as one who is Hair Challenged, you're boring me to tears."

Sara let her hair fall and took the phone in her hand. She laughed. "Hair Challenged? What does that mean?"

"It means I can't just tie my hair back. If I do, it looks like I have a skunk sitting on my head. A blond skunk, but a skunk."

"Mary Beth—"

"I have to torture my hair. I have to beat it down, force it into submission. And when I'm done, it usually still looks like road kill. That's why I cut it so short."

"Mary Beth—"

"So I don't really want to hear you complaining about your hair. You have beautiful, silky, shiny hair. It looks like a shampoo commercial. And if you shaved it all off and walked around bald, you'd still look beautiful and you know it."

Silence for a moment.

Then Sara, softly: "A skunk on your head? I always thought it was a fox terrier!"

They both laughed. It sounded a lot like college days, Sara thought. Mary Beth always complained about her looks. But somehow she was the one who always had a guy around who was crazy about her.

Mary Beth was the first to cut the laughter short. "What do you *mean* Liam likes it long? You've only gone out with him twice. Is he already telling you how to wear your hair?"

"No. Of course not," Sara protested.

"You're out with this famous professor, and the two of you sit around discussing your hair?"

"No. Well, yes. I mean, he was telling me some bit of Irish lore. You know how he's always tossing off these things. And—"

"How would *I* know?" Mary Beth interrupted, an edge to her voice.

"It was some old superstition about people believing that if you cut your hair, you cut your life short. And then he—"

"Sounds pretty grim to me."

"Mary Beth, if you keep interrupting—"

"Sorry."

She deliberately interrupted Sara the next three times Sara started to talk, and they both laughed again. Giddy.

Sara didn't remember feeling this giddy in a long time. She had called Mary Beth the moment she got home. From their second dinner date.

Their second date!

The effect of the wine at dinner had worn off. But not the effect of Liam.

"Anyway, then he sort of touched my hair and told me how

144

soft it was. Lustrous, he said. He's very romantic. Sort of old-fashioned. I mean, he says things that most men don't say. And he just kept staring at my hair with those amazing brown eyes of his. I really—"

"Sara, you sound totally stoned."

"I'm not stoned, Mary Beth. I'm not even drunk. He just seems like such an amazing person."

Another silence, heavier this time.

"Sara, I know you're going to think I'm saying this out of jealousy or something."

"What? What are you going to say?" Sara, a bit too eager. Mary Beth is right, she told herself, taking a deep breath and holding it. Shutting her eyes as she slowly let it out. Calm down, Miss Morgan.

"I just think you should be careful."

"Excuse me?"

"You heard me. I don't want you to get hurt. I think you're really vulnerable right now. Am I right?"

"Maybe."

"Listen, I watched Liam when we made that video. He flirts with everyone."

"This is different." Trying not to sound too defensive, but it didn't come out as casual as Sara had hoped.

"Sara, he even flirted with an Irish setter that wandered over to us!"

They both laughed.

"This wasn't just flirting, Mary Beth. We really like each other. I mean, we just hit it off. You know how you can tell when you're really on the same wavelength with someone else. Well . . ."

"That's what I'm trying to tell you." Mary Beth suddenly impatient. "You *never* can tell. Admit it, Sara. You are the *worst* judge of men."

"Well, give me a break. I made a few bad choices, but—"

"A *few?* I'll bet I could name more than a few. There was

Chip. And there was Steve. And who was that guy our sophomore year, when we moved to the apartment?"

"You mean Boris?"

"Right. Boris."

"Mary Beth, you promised me four years ago you'd never mention that creep again."

"God, Sara, I haven't thought of Boris in years. What a total shit. Not only was he the most boring jerk on campus. But then he sold your stereo! He stole your stereo when you went home for Christmas and sold it!"

Sara groaned. "Thanks for reminding me, pal."

"I'm trying to do you a favor. Sara, you're the one they write those books about."

"Books? What books?"

"You know. *Bad Men for Good Girls*. All those books about what total assholes women are when it comes to picking men."

"Excuse me? Did you just call me an asshole?"

Mary Beth snickered. "Nothing personal. I'm just trying to make a point. In all the years I've known you, you have never—*never*—chosen anyone who was any good for you."

"You made your point," Sara grumbled. Mary Beth was definitely becoming tiresome. "Liam is different." And then she added, "You know, just because you rescued me from New York and got me into school here doesn't mean you're responsible for me."

"Okay, okay." The sharpness of Sara's tone must have persuaded Mary Beth to back down. "You never listened to me before. Whatever you do, don't listen now. Besides, I don't know anything at all. I'm sitting here giving you advice, my wonderful wisdom. Meanwhile I'm screwing an eighteen-year-old kid." She quickly added: "And having a hell of a good time!"

More hearty laughter.

"I noticed you didn't bring Eric to the party at Milton's last week," Sara teased.

"No. I had to burp him and put him down for his nap."

"You know, a six-year difference isn't very much."

"Yes it is if it's Eric and me. I mean, he still thinks Beavis and Butthead are cool!"

Sara giggled. "Mary Beth, did you ever think of doing stand-up?"

Her friend reacted with mock outrage. "You really think my life is a *comedy act?*"

Sara glanced at the bed table clock. "Yes, I do. And my life is a sitcom about a working girl who goes back to school. I'd better hang up. I've got some work to do before class tomorrow. I'm supposed to have a theme for a term paper I have to write."

"What are you going to write about? 'The Psychology of Picking Up Visiting Folklore Professors'?"

"Mary Beth—are you obsessed or something? Can't we forget about Liam for a minute? I'm beginning to think you *are* jealous."

"Yes, I'm *green*. No. Seriously. What *are* you going to write about? Is it Freudian or Jungian?"

Sara hesitated. "I thought maybe . . . something about grief."

"Excuse me?"

"Well, it's something that's been on my mind. After my father died the year before last, I went through some pretty heavy times. I mean, I was really surprised by my reaction. We knew he was going to die and everything. And I thought I was prepared for it. Then—WHAM. It hit me like a ton of bricks. Really sent me out of control. Totally fucked up my feelings, anyway." She took a breath.

"I'm sorry," Mary Beth murmured, her voice a whisper now. "I sent you a note when I heard about your dad. Then I didn't hear from you. I thought—"

"My mother insisted on taking us both to a grief counselor," Sara continued. "I thought the idea was really stupid. But I went along to help her. And the woman turned out to be really smart. She talked about the five stages of grief that everyone goes through, just spelled out the whole pattern—disbelief, anger, guilt, et cetera—and it was so accurate, it made it all so clear.

"So when I found out I have to write a paper for Dr. Boring's seminar, I thought of that grief counselor. And I thought maybe I could do something on the stages of grief."

"Sara, are you sure it won't stir up a lot of unhappy feelings? You know. Memories of what you went through?"

"Well, I don't really think . . . Hey—there you go worrying about me again! What is your problem, Mary Beth? Since when did you get this mother complex? You were always—"

Sara heard a beep in her ear.

"Oh, wait. My call waiting. I have another call." *Maybe it's Liam*, she thought, heart suddenly pounding.

"You have call waiting?"

"It's a free thing. The phone company put it in when they installed the phone. An introductory offer or something. Gotta go. Call you tomorrow, okay?"

Another beep.

"Okay. Bye."

Sara eagerly pushed down the button to bring up the other call. "Hello?"

The voice on the line was hoarse. The caller spoke just above a whisper. "*Is this Sara?*"

"Yes. Yes, it is."

"*Do you want to live, Sara? Do you? Stay away from Liam!*"

17

Garrett's stomach lurched. He struggled to keep his dinner down.

Swallowing hard, he shut his eyes.

Another murder, ghastly beyond description.

I have to look. I have no choice. It's my job.

Open your eyes, Garrett. Do your job.

"Garrett, can I help you?" Walter's concerned voice, from somewhere behind him.

Garrett's legs trembled. He swallowed hard again, swallowed down a sour taste that choked his throat.

How are you going to help me, you fat moron? This woman has been *picked to pieces* right on the sidewalk, and all I want to do is shut my eyes. Or run away. How are you going to help me?

He took a deep breath. Held it. Waited for his insides to stop churning.

How come Columbo never puked his guts out?

Opening his eyes, Garrett squinted into the flickering glare of red lights. Sirens wailed in the distance. An ambulance tilted onto the curb, front wheels on the sidewalk a few yards from the body, lights and engine off.

No need for an ambulance, Garrett thought bitterly. We need a vacuum cleaner to pick this one up.

Onlookers stared from the shadows, huddled in silence against the brick apartment building wall beyond the sidewalk. Their faces tight with horror, lips pressed together, eyes wide.

Watching Garrett stand there frozen in helpless horror?

"Walter—get them out of here! Put up some barricades. Let's pretend we're cops! Move them away! Hey—you people! You're standing in a crime scene! Get *away* from here!" His throat tight and aching.

Walter bounced toward the crowd, waving his flabby arms. "Get back, everyone. Get moving! Nothing to see here. Go home—now. Nothing to see here."

Nothing to see?

Garrett blinked. The white-uniformed medics from Freewood General were crawling over the pavement, picking up pieces of skin with surgical tongs, dropping the pieces into sterile specimen jars. Garrett didn't trust his own men for this job. He insisted the hospital handle it.

Some skin fragments were small as feathers. Others were larger, resembled bloodstained strips of foam rubber, but dried and curling at the ends.

He had arrived on the scene less than two minutes after the call had come in. He had been talking to Angel, arguing with her about taking his brother's offer and moving away, when the call interrupted. A shrieking woman on the phone, hysterical and incoherent, shouting out the street names. So close to the campus. So close to the other ugly murder.

Garrett's eyes had landed first on the blood-soaked carcass, the ribs, white as moonlight, poking up through ripped skin. Legs bare. Sprawled in an unnatural V. Clothing ripped away. One knee bone raised up through torn flesh of the leg.

Trying to look away, Garrett had caught her face, the eyes wide, staring up accusingly at him.

How long did she live? Had she been alive when the murderer tore her body apart?

Had the murderer mercifully killed her first? Or did she see her skin pulled off, ripped away like wrapping paper?

That had been the thought that sent Garrett lurching to the curb, eyes tightly closed.

Now his stomach had calmed, but he still felt as if he were swimming in the flashing red current, struggling to keep his head up, the sour taste lingering in his throat, each breath a conscious effort.

The body had been gutted like a fish. Organs lay draining on the sidewalk. Entrails coiling into High Street. Garrett forced himself to concentrate on the white-uniformed medics, combing the ground, retrieving the skin specimens with their silvery tongs.

"Think the guy is some kind of cannibal?" Walter bobbing up beside him like a porpoise in a water show.

Garrett swimming, swimming in the current.

He wanted to lash out at Walter. *Do something useful!* But it wasn't Walter he was angry at.

It was his own helplessness.

Even he knew that.

"Some kind of cannibal," Walter repeated, shaking his head. As if that explained it.

Garrett heard a wrenching groan. Someone being sick, around the side of the building. One of the medics.

How could *anyone* keep his dinner down? he wondered, swallowing hard.

If only there were someone to question. Or maybe a clue to pick up. A gun with fingerprints on it.

But this person didn't use a gun.

What did he use? Some kind of knife? Did he slice and chop the skin off her bones?

Wouldn't that take a very long time? Wouldn't someone have come by? Driven by, maybe? Wouldn't someone have seen?

An eyewitness.

Garrett raised his eyes to the crowd of onlookers. Walter had managed to herd them back to the next building. They clus-

tered in the dim yellow light of a small, rectangular grassy courtyard.

The criminal always returns to the scene of the crime.

Was that just in movies?

Was the murderer standing there among those grim-faced
spectators? Enjoying the show? The blood of the victim still on
his hands?

"Walter, go check out the crowd." Garrett gestured with
his head.

"Huh?"

"The gawkers. Go check them out. Look for bloodstains.
Anything suspicious."

Walter's mouth dropped open. Instant excitement. "You
think—?"

"No, I don't think anything. Just check them out."

Walter obediently made his way toward the courtyard, lowering a hand to the handle of his revolver.

Do I *really* allow Walter to carry a gun? The question invaded Garrett's more solemn thoughts. Am I totally out of my
mind?

"We have an ID, Chief." Ethan, pale, his face locked in a
grim frown, jaw clenching and unclenching.

Garrett narrowed his eyes at the officer. Ethan's bald head
flashing in the red cruiser light. Where is his uniform cap? Did
he lose it? "An ID?"

"Yeah. From her purse."

"The wallet was still there?"

Ethan nodded. "Nothing taken, as far as Harvey and I can
tell. It wasn't a robbery."

No. It was a drive-by skin-slashing.

Garrett sighed. "Who is she, Ethan? I mean, who was she?"

"Name was DeHaven. Andrea DeHaven. Lived across campus. On Forrest.

"You put the purse in an evidence bag?"

"Yup. I was careful too, Chief. Not to mess up any fingerprints. But, jeez—" A sudden burst of emotion, the hard expres-

sion falling apart. "I'm going to be seeing this in my dreams for a long time to come." The narrow shoulders twitched as if suffering a powerful chill.

"Me too, Ethan."

Garrett saw the doctor approaching. Tried to remember his name. He'd seen him a million times. Never could remember. Grim nods in greeting. "What have you got for me, Doc?"

"The woman was skinned alive, then gutted, Detective."

He gets right to the point, Garrett thought, swallowing again. He tried to reply, but the words caught in his throat.

When he found his voice, a somewhat unprofessional question blurted out. "Doc, what kind of a person commits a crime like this?"

The doctor raised bloodshot eyes to Garrett. He replied through gritted teeth. "A very strong person."

18

A heavy knock on the door startled Sara from her thoughts. She had been staring at the same page of the book in her lap—a Camille Paglia treatise that had been assigned for Sara's Psychology and the New Woman class—for nearly half an hour, thinking about the whispered voice, the hissed threat over the phone.

Obviously a stupid prank. But by whom?

Most likely someone who had been at the party at Milton's last week, Sara figured. Someone who had seen her and Liam spend so much time together, who saw them leave together. Maybe someone who saw them tonight at Spinnaker's.

A jealous colleague?

Liam had been at Moore State for less than a month. Was that long enough for some woman in the Language Arts Department to have become possessive toward him? To have such strong feelings for Liam that she would call Sara and make such an ugly threat?

Was it a woman?

Sara couldn't really be certain. The connection had been bad. The line had crackled. The whispered words so soft and hoarse.

Feeling chilled, Sara had changed into long-sleeved pajamas, Chip's old pajamas, woolly white socks, and her warm, flannel robe. She put on the kettle for some tea.

The wind howled outside, rattling the windowpanes, one of the disadvantages of a corner apartment. Sara rubbed her sleeves, pacing back and forth from the tiny kitchen to the front room, waiting for the kettle whistle, thinking, trying to remember faces.

Faces from the party.

So many people had come up to greet Liam. He had been friendly to them all, warm, but not overly affectionate or effusive to anyone. Sara tried to remember if any of the young graduate students or instructors had lingered. She tried to picture any sign of shared intimacy, any closeness. Anyone staring at Liam from across the room, keeping watch on him.

No. No one.

The floorboards squeaked under her stockinged feet. As the kettle began to squeal, she felt tempted to call Liam. To ask him his theory about the caller. An excuse to talk to him.

Pouring the boiling water into the mug, feeling the hot steam warm her face, Sara began to feel calmer. She poured honey into the cup, watching the water darken. Soothing. She warmed her hands on the mug, carried it to the soft, low armchair beside her bed, and opened the Paglia book to the assigned chapter.

Something about changing sexual appetites. It should have interested her. But the words faded, seemed to recede into the distance, as her thoughts returned to Liam.

Was he just flirting? If so, why had he singled her out? She had felt an instant attraction to him at the restaurant that night. But she didn't expect him to even remember her.

At dinner tonight, he had been so charming, with his funny little superstitions. He seemed to know so many of them, superstitions Sara had never heard of.

What was the fuss he made about her napkin when they were about to leave? Oh yes. She had removed it from her lap and started to fold it back up. But he had reached across the table to stop her. "Folding a napkin after a meal means that you are folding up the friendship. I shall never see you again." A mock pout on his face. Such sad eyes.

155

She quickly balled the napkin up and tossed it down. They both laughed.

Earlier he had insisted they pour the tea together, his hand on top of hers. The warmth of his hand, the surprising strength of it on the back of hers, sent an electric tingle down her arm, down her whole body.

But why did he insist on holding the small china teapot and pouring together? What superstition was this? He refused to divulge it. A pleased grin on his handsome face, his eyes dancing, as if he had just played the most marvelous trick on her.

Sara stared down at the same two pages of the book in her lap, the tea cold now, a dark puddle on the bottom of the mug. *Don't I have a book about superstitions? Somewhere in those two cartons of books I haven't unpacked?*

The hard knock on the door made her slap the book shut. Her eyes moved to the bed table clock. Nearly midnight. *Who could it be this late? Mary Beth?*

And then an exciting thought: *Liam?*

She jumped up, tugging at the robe, pulling the belt tight, fixing it over the baggy pajamas.

Another knock, harder.

She checked her hair in the mirror. Hurried to the door. "Who's there?"

No reply. And then a breathless, "Sara?"

She pulled open the door and gasped. "Milton?"

He stood on the doormat, breathing hard, an elephant in a gray jogging suit. Sweat beading down his forehead despite the autumn chill, the swirling, cold winds. His face red in the dim overhead hall light. Normally upright white hair wet and matted on his head.

"Milton—what's wrong?"

"Nothing. I was jogging and—" Uttered between gasping breaths, his stomach heaving beneath the bulky gray sweatshirt.

"Oh. You frightened me. I thought . . . I thought . . ."

I thought you were having a heart attack. She doesn't finish the sentence. "Sure you're okay?"

He took a deep breath, swallowed. He pressed both arms against the door frame, supporting himself. "Yes. Fine. I had some work to do at my office. Then I felt restless. Sort of keyed up. So I decided to jog. I jogged across campus. Then I was passing your apartment, and . . . " His gray eyes on her, on the open neck of her robe.

"Milton, it's so late."

He shrugged massive shoulders. "Running relaxes me."

Why had he come to see her? Did he expect to come in?

He was so big. She had a sudden frightening image in her mind of him pushing his way in.

His silvery eyes locked on hers, as if searching for something. "Sorry to bother you so late. You weren't asleep, were you?" His eyes moved over her shoulder, past her into the apartment. Checking to see if anyone else is in there? Checking to see if Liam is here?

"Sara, I wanted to bring you some keys. Something came up. Family business. I have to go to Atlanta for a few days. But I'd like you to keep the office going. You know. Just answer the phone and check the mail."

"No problem, Milton. I—"

He held out a key chain with three or four keys on it.

"Milton—you're bleeding!"

He raised the back of his hand to his face. Reacted with surprise. "Oh. Yeah. Well. It's mostly dried."

She grabbed the hand, pulled it toward her to examine it. "It's a really deep cut. How did you do it?"

He reddened even more than usual. "I don't know. Must have cut it on something. I don't remember."

As she let go of his hand, Sara noticed the dark stain down the side of his sweatpants. More blood?

"I can't believe you didn't even feel it. There's so much blood."

A strange smile creased his face. His eyes trained on hers. "I'm a macho guy, Sara. It takes more than a little scratch to get my attention."

He pressed the keys into her hand. "The silver one is for the outer door. This one is the inner office." He picked through them with bloodstained fingers. "This small one, the one that's different from the others—that's to the locked file."

Sara pushed back her hair with her free hand. "I probably won't need that one."

"Just in case."

She raised the fourth key, brass, shinier than the rest. "And this one?"

He squinted at her. She suddenly felt as if his eyes were trying to penetrate her skin, stare into her brain. "It's my house key."

"Huh?"

"Maybe sometime you'd like to come by." Those silvery eyes beaming at her like searchlights. What was he trying to do—hypnotize her? "Maybe come visit . . . surprise me . . . I mean—"

"Milton, I really don't think—"

"Just hold on to it." Suddenly abrupt. Then softer: "Hold on to it just in case." He squeezed her hand shut around the key chain. His eyes finally let go, finally lowered, to her throat. "I could use a drink. How about you? I know it's late, but maybe . . ." Breathing hard again.

Sara felt a chill of fear. *I really don't want to let him into my apartment. Am I being silly? I work for him, after all. What would happen?*

Yes. What?

She didn't want to find out.

"I'm sorry. I don't have anything in the house. I haven't had time. I . . . well, it's really late, Milton. You can see I was getting ready for bed." *You've been staring at my pajamas hard enough!*

Milton sighed. Scratched his matted hair. Leaned forward. *He's going to push his way in,* Sara thought, feeling her stomach tighten. *I was right.*

She grabbed the door, preparing to slam it shut.

Milton frowned. Raised the bloodstained hand again. "I

should get home and wash this. Get cleaned up. I'll take a rain check on that drink." A dry laugh, as if he had said something funny. "You and Liam have a good dinner tonight?"

Sara felt another chill. *Why is he asking that? Is he spying on me? Spying on Liam and me? Is that why he's here?*

"Yes. Liam is really nice."

Nice? Great vocabulary, Sara.

Milton breathing hard again, let out a wheezing sound from deep in his throat. Another glance into the apartment. *Looking for Liam?* "He insisted that I invite you."

"What?"

"To the party last week. He insisted."

"He *did?*" Genuine surprise. Sara felt her face grow hot.

"Of course I already planned to ask you to come." His eyes up and down her. "Well. Liam's a charming guy. Very bright too. A real lady-killer, I understand."

Sara let out an awkward laugh. "Well, I'll be careful." *Please leave, Milton. Please—go home.*

"Yes. Well . . ." He studied the cut hand again. "Sorry to bother you so late, Sara. But I'm leaving early tomorrow morning. Be back on Wednesday. How *did* I get this cut? It's really nasty."

"Go wash it carefully," she said, relieved as he started down the hall. "You're lucky you don't need stitches."

She closed the door, locked it, and chained it. Pressed her back against the door and shut her eyes. She squeezed her hand shut, feeling the key chain and keys against her palm.

Why did he bring his house key? What did he mean in case I wanted to surprise him?

Such a strange man. All that blood and he didn't even notice.

She opened her eyes and thought about Liam. *"Liam insisted that I invite you."* That's what Milton had said. "What's going on, Liam?" Sara murmured out loud.

Was this some kind of crazy love-at-first-sight thing happening to her?

Careful, Sara. Careful.

Listen to Mary Beth. You've never picked a man who was good for you.

But what if he picks me?

Passing the kitchen, she glimpsed the tea kettle on the stove. Remembered the superstition book. Did I pack it? I'm wide awake now and not in the mood for Camille Paglia. I might as well check.

She had packed four cartons of books, including all of her old college books. The bookshelves in the living room held only two of the cartons. The other two boxes were shoved under the bed.

I think I remember seeing it, she told herself, getting down on her knees to drag the nearest carton out from its hiding place, pulling out a thick layer of dust with it. Some kind of dictionary of superstitions. Listed alphabetically. She had used the book for a comp lit course in her junior year.

I got an A in the course, she remembered, tugging open the carton, lifting books out, piling them beside her on the bedroom carpet. Such a good student. Maybe I'll stay a student for the rest of my life.

Or marry Liam and spend a quiet life living on college campuses.

Not an unpleasant prospect.

She found the book at the bottom of the first carton. Shuffling through it quickly, her eyes darted over the tiny, dense type.

Bet there are a thousand superstitions about tea.

There were three pages of them. Her eyes swept past "tea leaves, tea brewing, tea bubbles, tea stirring."

They landed on "tea pouring." There *is* a superstition about tea pouring! See, Liam, you thought you got away with something. You thought you could pull something on poor, ignorant, unaware Sara. But let's see. Let's see what your superstition is.

She brought the book closer and read:

"Romney Marsh, Kent. 1932. If a man and woman pour out a cup of tea from the same pot, a child will be born to them."

19

The white china teacup clinked against the saucer. Liam set it down on the low coffee table and turned as Margaret entered the living room. "Here you are."

"Yes. Here I am." She removed her black velvet hat, bowler-shaped but with a broad, floppy brim, and shook out her hair. She tossed the hat onto the chair against the wall and began to work at pulling off her green leather gloves. "Cold out there. It really feels as if it could snow."

Liam raised an arm to the back of the couch and watched her struggle with the gloves. Her hands were large. Gloves were always a tight fit. "Where did you go?"

She tugged one off and tossed it on top of the hat. Her hair fell over her eyes. She brushed it back. "I drove up to Northport. There's a whole row of antique stores up there. Very quaint, very charming."

Across the room, the TV droned. A Coca-Cola jingle. Flashing two-second images. Everyone drinking Coke. "Did you buy anything for the shop?"

"No. Just browsed. But I may go back." She sighed. "I know you think I'm foolish for opening a shop in this small town." She pulled off the second glove and tossed it beside the first. Then she undid her black wool coat. "But if I sell just a few large pieces a month . . ."

He didn't hear the rest of it. He sighed and shifted on the couch, turning back to the TV. "Want some tea? The kettle is still warm."

She didn't answer. He heard the front closet door swing open, pictured her hanging up her coat. A few seconds later, she dropped down beside him, the outdoor cold clinging to her sweater and long skirt. She patted his hand with a cold hand and offered him a smile, her eyes searching his. "And what did you do this afternoon?"

"Not much." He concentrated on the TV screen. The early evening local news was about to come on.

"Did you eat dinner?"

"Not yet."

She kept her hand on the back of his, warming it. "Liam, have you moved at all? Did you sit here all afternoon?"

He sighed. Pulled his hand away. He tried to shrink into his gray turtleneck. "Yes. I suppose."

Margaret bit her bottom lip. "So glum."

"Margaret—"

She jumped up to avoid his sharp stare and walked to the other side of the coffee table, blocking his view of the TV. "You did nothing the whole afternoon? You wasted a perfectly good Sunday?"

He didn't reply.

"Why didn't you call Sara? She might have cheered you up."

Liam waved a hand. "I can't see the news."

Margaret let out an impatient groan, but stepped aside.

"I did call Sara," he offered, eyes on the screen across the room. "We talked about what a wonderful time we had last night."

Margaret cut short a sarcastic laugh. "Two dinners with the great professor and the poor girl is head over heels in love?"

A bit of life flashed in Liam's eyes for the first time that evening. A thin smile. "I think she might be."

Margaret smiled back at him. "Who could resist you? Especially when you're pouring on the charm."

"It comes naturally, Margaret. I don't exactly have to work at it." His smile revealing his perfect teeth.

"And such modesty. That's your most charming quality."

"Sarcasm doesn't become you, my dear." He gazed past her to the TV. More commercials.

"Do you really like her?" Margaret's arms still crossed over her chest, her eyes not letting him escape.

He rubbed his smooth jaw. "Like her? Why, yes. She's wonderful."

"I'm very happy for you."

"I made another date for next Saturday night. She sounded quite delighted. We didn't have any other plans, did we?"

"No. No other plans. Sara is your most important project now, remember?" A scolding tone slipping into her usually gentle voice. "You have to succeed this time, Liam."

Liam patted her hand. "I have a good feeling about this one."

She shivered and pulled her hand away. "Maybe I will have a cup of tea. I don't know why you didn't take the offer at UCLA. It's probably eighty degrees in L.A. today. And we—"

Liam raised a hand. "Ssshhh." He leaned forward, on the edge of the couch cushion, and narrowed his eyes at the TV screen.

"Another brutal murder in the campus area . . ."

Pictures of a shiny plastic gray body bag. Grim-faced medics lifting the bag onto a stretcher cart.

Liam jumped to his feet, hands clenched. His shins bumped the coffee table as he stepped around it and made his way toward the TV, eyes on the screen.

"Liam—" Margaret called sharply.

"Andrea. The poor woman . . ." he muttered, shaking his head, fists clenching hard, then unclenching again. He stood inches from the screen.

"The victim has been identified as a local rooming house owner and real estate agent . . ."

Margaret pulled Liam's arm. "Turn that off. Come away. I mean it."

He twisted his arm from her grasp, staring at the news footage. Bright lights in the night. Grim-faced policemen. White-uniformed medics prowling around.

"Police are following several leads. Police Detective Montgomery announced that an arrest may be imminent."

"That poor woman." Liam's eyes watery now.

"Liam—turn it off! I mean it!" Margaret repeated impatiently, reaching for his arm again. "There's no point in torturing yourself."

He turned to her, his dark eyes flaring. "I *have* to watch. I *have* to see it!"

Margaret sighed. "What's done is done, Liam. Listen to me. What's done is done."

The blue glare of the TV screen washed over the sorrow on Liam's face. The news story ended, he crossed to the rabbit cage.

He leaned over the cage, staring down at the rabbit, murmuring to himself, murmuring in Gaelic, the same phrase, again and again, the rabbit twitching up at him in response, eager for its carrot.

20

Sara spread her legs. Raised her knees. She wrapped her hands around Liam's warm back and shut her eyes as he slid into her.

"Ohh." A soft moan, the first soft moan of pleasure.

He didn't move for a long moment.

He smelled so sweet and soapy.

Is this really happening?

Is this really happening so soon?

Yes. He was kissing her small breasts now. Rocking on top of her.

"Oh. Oh. Oh God."

Her eyes shut, holding on tight as if holding on to a dream.

"Oh oh oh."

He was kissing her frantically, kissing her breasts, kissing the soft skin between her breasts.

Sliding so lightly. Sliding. Sliding.

Heavier now.

She held on and moved with him.

"Oh God."

His warm cheek pressed against hers now. Breathing in her ear. His breath so hot against her skin. Making her tingle.

So sweet and soapy.

His hair soft against the side of her face.

"Oh. Oh. Oh. Oh."

A steady rhythm.

It is really happening.

It couldn't be more real.

Or more wonderful.

She had to open her eyes and see for herself.

He had lifted himself on both hands. His brown eyes stared down intently, unblinking, as if they too were trying to penetrate.

No smile on his face. His lips set in a hard straight line.

She felt a pang of disappointment.

No smile. Just those big, brown eyes burning into her. Burning. Burning.

He moved faster now. Sliding. Down to meet her. Up. Then down to meet her. Their bodies damp against each other.

A rapid rhythm in time to their breathing. Breathing together.

And then he exploded without warning, with the tiniest of cries.

Buried himself in her. His face between her breasts.

She came with a soft tremble. Gentle. Her arms going slack, hands sliding to his shoulders.

She sighed.

After a few seconds, he raised his head, smiling. Finally smiling. The brown eyes softer now, like teddy bear eyes. Pulled himself up, damp skin against damp skin. And kissed her lips. His tongue over her teeth, pushing against her tongue.

Kissed her, still deep inside. Kissed her as if he didn't want it to end.

I've just made love to Liam.

So soon! So soon!

I'm so happy!

The jonquils started it, she decided, returning his kiss, smoothing back his wet, brown hair with both hands. Yes. The jonquils.

* * *

He had arrived at her apartment with a bouquet of jonquils, golden as a July sun.

Sara raised both hands to her face. "Where did you find jonquils in October?" she squealed. She had taken a deep breath before opening the door, composed herself, put on her mask of sophistication.

But the jonquils made her lose her cool.

"How did you know that jonquils are my favorite flower?"

"Magic!" he replied, his smile revealing how much her response had pleased him. He pressed the flowers, wrapped in white tissue paper, into her arms. "Magic is the answer to both questions."

She giggled. "Well, I had no idea I was having dinner with a *magician* tonight."

He followed her into the apartment, his eyes surveying the small living room. "Yes. You had no idea."

"They're beautiful! Did you grow them yourself, Mr. Magician? Did you wave a magic wand and—poof—they appeared out of a top hat?"

He grinned. Rubbed his cheek. "I waved a magic Master-Card. And they appeared, probably from somewhere in South America. Nice apartment, Sara. Cozy."

"You mean tiny."

"Yes. I mean tiny."

They both laughed.

He followed her into the kitchen. "I think I brought one vase with me," she said, pulling open a cabinet door. "But where did I put it? Half of my stuff is still in cartons. I guess I'm reluctant to believe I'm actually back here."

He chuckled, stepping close to her. "Spoken like a true psych major."

She turned to study him. He wore a cream-colored crew-neck sweater under a brown wool sports jacket, patches at the elbows. The sweater was pulled down over crisp, straight-legged jeans. The jeans fell over black, Western-style boots.

Very collegiate.

Sara was glad she had decided not to dress up. She wore a silver-gray chenille turtleneck over silky black slacks. A necklace of black glass beads that Chip had given her clicked as she reached for the vase on the top shelf.

Humming to himself, Liam began to unwrap the flowers. "We need to find two buds that haven't quite bloomed." Said with the utmost seriousness.

Sara turned to him. "Why is that?"

"We must put them in a glass of water by themselves. It is an old superstition to determine if two people will become lovers."

Sara half-filled the vase with tap water. "Go on. You've definitely captured my interest." Her cheeks suddenly felt hot.

"We take two buds that haven't bloomed and put them in a glass of water by themselves. If they turn to each other, if they intertwine, that is a sign of true love."

Sara smiled, partly because his expression had become so solemn. "And if the flowers bend away from each other?"

His eyes flashed. "Then we get two different flowers!"

I think he really likes me.

Sara felt her heart start to race. She lifted the jonquils by the stems, prepared to lower them into the vase.

But to her surprise, Liam lowered his head and kissed her. He nearly missed. His warm, wet lips brushed her lower lip. Feeling off balance, she raised her head to return the kiss.

And the jonquils fell from her hand, fell to the counter, the yellow flowers tumbling over each other, tumbling, entwining, tangling together, yellows and greens.

A young woman came up to their table at the restaurant. Liam had been holding Sara's hand on the table, but quickly let go.

"Dr. O'Connor—we keep running into each other!" the young woman exclaimed. She bumped up to the table and locked her eyes on Liam, as if he were sitting alone.

She was very pretty, Sara saw, with round, green eyes, high

cheekbones, and frizzed-out, auburn hair. She wore a long, dark green sweater dress over green tights.

"Sara, this is Devra Brookes," Liam said casually, not particularly surprised to see her. "Sara Morgan. Did you two meet at Milton's party?"

They both shook their heads. Devra gave Sara a hello, then immediately turned back to Liam. "Isn't this a great restaurant? I come here all the time."

"We just ordered," Liam replied, glancing at Sara. "So far, the water is fine." He raised his water glass in a toast to Devra.

She laughed. "I'm over there with some friends." She pointed to a table against the wall with three other young women. "I just wanted to say hi. I saw you come in. How are you enjoying Moore State?"

"So far, so good. I've made some new friends." He flashed a deliberate smile Sara's way.

Devra glanced back at her table. A waiter was setting down food, big platters of barbecued chicken and ribs. "I'd better get back. Call me sometime, okay? I mean, we could discuss the old days in Chicago." She laughed. "I mean. You know." She started away. "I'm on Tremont." Halfway to her table, Devra called back to Sara, "Nice to meet you." And returned to her friends.

Liam studied them for a while. His eyes lingered on Devra's back. Then he returned his gaze to Sara.

Sara took a sip of water. "Who's she?"

"Devra? A graduate student of mine. From Chicago. She transferred here last year. I ran into her at Milton's party."

"I *knew* she looked familiar. Yes. Now I remember seeing her there. It's hard to forget that red hair. It's pretty spectacular."

"Nice girl," Liam muttered, his eyes suddenly distant.

A waiter set down their margaritas.

"Have you been close to a lot of women?"

The words tumbled out of Sara's mouth before she could stop them.

Something about the way Devra gazed at Liam made her think the question. But she never intended to ask it out loud!

Her breath caught. She wanted to take the question back, pull back the words. She wanted to fall through the floor.

How could I have *asked* that?

She forced herself to raise her eyes to Liam. He leaned across the table, an amused smile on his face, not surprised or flustered at all.

"Sara, do you know the old Irish saying, 'Never ask a cat a question'?"

"Huh? No. I—" Sara flustered enough for both of them.

Liam leaned closer, his eyes twinkling. "Well, do you know *why* you should never ask a cat a question? Because it might answer!"

He waited for her to laugh, and then he joined in.

He slid her hand between his. "You have a delightful laugh. It's like music."

Maybe it wasn't the jonquils.

Maybe it was that moment, that time-stopping moment with her hand in his.

Maybe it was that moment that she fell in love with him.

In love?

Sara gazed around the bright, crowded barbecue restaurant. Pink and blue, 1950s-style Formica tables. Paper placemats on the tables declaring the restaurant's name in script letters formed in a rope lariat—TEXAS. Ten-gallon Stetson cowboy hats on the walls. Cattle horns over the mirrored bar. Country music on the jukebox against the wall. The smoky aroma of chicken and ribs floating out from the open pit kitchen in the center of the room.

What could be more beautiful, more romantic?

Was Liam as taken with her as she was with him? He seemed to be. They clicked margarita glasses in a toast to "new friendships."

They talked and joked so easily. He made her feel so comfortable. So comfortable, she didn't hesitate to pick up the sticky, sauce-dripping ribs with both hands. So *what* if her face got sticky and the thick, red barbecue sauce dripped down her chin?

They seemed to have so much to talk about, so much to

share. Liam made her laugh with story after story. How did he remember them all?

A booth in the corner erupted with raucous laughter. Sara turned to see three middle-aged women raising their beer glasses in a toast. One of them said something, and all three tossed back their heads and laughed again.

An amused smile crossed Liam's face. "Reminds me of an old Irish tale about a fox," he said. He set down a chicken wing and wiped his fingers on his napkin. "The fox had three youngsters, and he wanted to see which of them could survive in the world. So he took them to a big house on the edge of the forest.

"Stopping at the back of the house, the foxes listened. They heard chattering voices, much talk and gales of laughter inside. The old fox asked the first two young foxes to tell him who was inside the house. 'We can't tell you,' the two fox children answered.

"And so the old fox tried his third child. 'Who is inside the house?' The young fox listened to the loud talk and laughter inside the house. And then he answered, 'Either two women or twelve men.'

" 'You will do well in the world,' the old fox told him."

Liam grinned at Sara.

She gave him a disapproving frown and playfully slapped the back of his hand. "Why, Liam, that is an extremely sexist story!"

"I know. Are you surprised that the old Irish folktales are politically incorrect?"

"Well . . ."

His expression turned serious. "I've begun making notes for a book on the subject. Something about sex roles in Irish legends and how they have been mirrored in society. Bound to be a bestseller, don't you think?"

Glancing over Liam's shoulder, Sara saw Devra and her three friends pulling on their coats, preparing to leave. Devra turned and waved to Liam, calling out something that was drowned out by the clatter and voices of the crowded restaurant.

Sara wasn't sure that Liam had seen Devra. He was staring so intently, almost devotedly, at Sara.

"Your friend is waving—" she started.

But Liam reached across the table and clapped a hand over her mouth. He raised the pointer finger of his other hand to his lips. "Sssshhh."

Sara listened. She heard the chime of a clock. A grandfather clock, somewhat out of place in the Western decor, beside the dark oak bar. Liam pressed his hand gently over her mouth until the clock had chimed nine times. Nine o'clock.

After the final chime, he removed his hand, brought his face to hers, and kissed her lips. A gentle kiss. Only a few seconds.

"Why did you do that?" Sara demanded, breathless.

He smiled. "Because I like you."

"No. Why did you hold your hand over my mouth?"

"The clock was chiming. You should never talk while a clock chimes. It's very bad luck."

Something about his solemn expression made Sara laugh. "Do you hold your breath when you go past a cemetery?"

He nodded. "Yes, I do."

"Liam, where did you learn all of these superstitions? How do you know them all?"

"My father . . . he passed them on to me."

Sara reacted with surprise. "Your father? You told me he was a farmer."

"Yes. He was a farmer. There is a lot of time to tell stories when you live on a farm. My father was a simple man in many ways, a very stern, quiet man, but a wonderful teller of tales." He lowered his eyes, fiddled with the knife and fork he had crossed over his plate. "Coffee?"

"Huh?"

"Would you like some coffee or dessert? They have an astounding cheesecake here, as heavy as cement."

"Why don't we go back to my apartment for coffee?"

The words tumbled casually from her mouth. She knew when she said them that she was going to sleep with him.

When they stepped into her apartment, she reached for the light switch. But he grabbed her hand. They undressed each other in the dark, giggling at the struggle of it, the awkwardness, the eagerness. He tripped over his own shoes as she pulled him to her bedroom.

But the clumsiness ended when he was caressing her, kissing her, on top of her, inside her.

Afterward, they held on to each other, touching, patting each other, their hands sliding over each other's skin, as if not believing the other was real. Sara kissed the skin behind his ear, inhaling the sweaty sweetness of his hair. "Does this remind you of a story about a fox?" she whispered.

He smiled, his eyes flaring in the dim light from the street. "Actually, it does."

She pressed a finger over his lips. "Don't tell it."

Her hands slid over his back, surprisingly muscular. Holding him, touching him, she saw that she had aroused him.

They made love a second time. This time he closed his eyes. Their bodies, already damp and warm, moved slowly together. Already familiar with each other. Familiar strangers.

She moved beneath him, watching his face, the dark eyebrows floating over the closed eyes, the mouth frozen in a half-smile of pleasure. Such a handsome face bobbing above hers. She grabbed it with both hands, pulled him down into a long kiss, wet and hard, their tongues probing, probing.

She didn't want it to end. But he ended the kiss, buried his face beside hers, and exploded inside her with a low cry, muffled in the bedsheet.

They held each other. Didn't speak.

Then Sara, softly: "We forgot about the coffee."

They both laughed so hard, so giddily. It wasn't that funny, really. But it struck them as hilarious, and they laughed. Laughed their way back to the real world.

A few minutes later, Liam was dressed and kissing her good night. She pouted. "Why don't you stay? Are you worried about my reputation?" she teased.

"Margaret will worry about me."

Sara pointed toward the living room. "Phone her. Tell her not to worry."

"No. I'd better go. I don't want to overstay my welcome." So formal.

Another kiss. Another. Her bare arm draped over his neck.

And then he was gone. The apartment door clicking softly behind him.

Sara lay back against the damp pillow, her legs still tingling.

What am I doing?

What have I done?

How did this happen so fast?

And then: You're twenty-four, Sara. It didn't happen that fast. It took you so many years to find the right one.

The right man.

Liam.

She licked her lips, tasting him. Ran her hand down her bare stomach, feeling him.

The phone rang about fifteen minutes later, startling her awake. She hadn't realized she'd dozed off.

A second ring.

She climbed unsteadily to her feet. Dizzy. Legs shaky from lovemaking.

Liam?

Yes. How sweet of him.

Into the dark living room. Blue-gray light from the uncurtained window.

She picked up the receiver in the middle of the third ring, raised it to her ear, eager to hear his voice. "Hello?"

"Stay away from Liam!"

Not the voice Sara expected. The ugly, hoarse whisper, same as the week before.

"Do you want to die? This isn't a joke. Stay away from Liam."

"Who—who *is* this?" Sara stammered angrily. "Who is it? Who?"

174

21

Whenever Liam thought of his house in Ireland, he smelled bacon. Bacon, sliced turnips, and onions, frying on the stove in the big kitchen, the largest room in the small farmhouse that Liam's grandfather had built with his own hands.

In 1970, Liam was ten, Margaret was nine, and the farm stretched brown and bare, nearly as desolate as his father's blank stare.

"The luck has run out," Rory O'Connor told his son. All the explanation Liam would get. Unlike the Irishmen of the folktales Liam's father dutifully read and told to his son, Rory O'Connor was a man of few words.

"The luck has run out."

All the other farmers had moved one by one, to live in the towns, to find work, to leave the farms to the big companies that could manage them.

But Liam's father had steadfastly refused to move, had continued to live where most of the paved roads ended in dirt, where the stone-cluttered fields rolled unfenced. Rory had forced his family to continue in a rural life that had long died out all over Ireland.

As if hiding, Liam thought. As if hiding us away from all that is modern in the world.

"Father, why can't you harvest the potatoes?" Liam asked,

tugging up the straps of his baggy, hand-me-down denim over-alls. Liam, so thin and pale that he seemed lost inside all of his clothes, not round-cheeked and robust, like Margaret, but dark and serious, with eyes that seemed old beyond his years.

"The luck. It's all turned." Rory continued to stare at the wall.

The luck had turned bad *indoors* as well as out in the fields. Liam saw it in his father's tear-glistened eyes, heard it in his father's weary sighs. Felt the cold in the house despite the fire in the stone fireplace.

Liam hadn't reacted to his mother's death yet. She had been dead for nearly six months, but he hadn't been able to react beyond feeling a dull sadness. An emptiness. A dull ache in the pit of his stomach.

The house seemed darker without her, without her curls of blond hair, her pale, freckled face, her sky blue eyes.

The tears came easily to Rory. But Liam hadn't been able to cry. He had tried. After the wake, after the black-suited men from town and their solemn-faced wives had eaten their fill and toasted the dead and offered their prayers and condolences, heavy shoes thudding on the floorboards of the house (Liam knew he'd never forget the thud of those heavy shoes), after they had made their way into the wind-swirled storm of that gloomy night, Liam locked himself in his room, threw himself onto his bed, and struggled to cry.

Tightened his face. Squeezed with every muscle.

Tried to force the tears out.

He knew he felt sad. He knew he would never see his mother again, never hear her sweet, musical voice, never feel her hand on the back of his head, smoothing his dark hair.

Why couldn't he cry?

He tried pinching his cheeks, then biting his tongue.

No tears.

On the other side of the bedroom door, he heard a wail. His father. Sobbing loudly.

Liam opened his mouth, tried to imitate the sound.

He lay on his back, staring up at the low ceiling, at the spiderweb of cracks above his head. Tried to picture his mother. Tried to conjure up her face.

He wanted to stare into her face. Burn it forever into his memory.

Will I forget it? Will I forget what you looked like, mother? Will I forget your voice?

Even that frightening thought could produce no tears.

He pulled himself up, feeling even emptier. He wondered if she was watching him from heaven. He wondered if she saw him unable to cry.

Six months later, the pain had dulled. Liam knew the tears had to come. But when?

His mother died and then the bad luck had struck the crops. The potato plants withered and browned despite the careful watering and care that Rory gave them. "No luck left in this old soil," he told his pale, worried son.

The goats grew thin, their bleating weak and sorrowful.

"No luck left on this farm." Rory's mumbled refrain.

He kept two lighted candles beside the framed photo of his wife on the mantel, the only portrait taken of her, taken by a professional photographer in a store. The silver cross on a slender chain she wore around her neck was draped over the photo. Beside it, a carved, four-leafed shamrock, the green paint peeling.

Liam's dad spent more and more time in front of the fireplace, gazing wet-eyed and silent at the smiling young woman in the portrait, so blond and bright.

If it hadn't been for Margaret, Liam knew he would have sunk into a deep well of despair, knew that his life would be more bare than the potato fields.

With her high laugh, her flashing green eyes, her sun-gold hair, Margaret brightened the darkest, coldest days for Liam.

They spent every day together, chasing each other through the rocky pastures. Hunting for buried leprechaun treasure beneath the trees. Collecting jars and jars of fireflies at night, Margaret's "sparkling diamonds."

Even then Liam promised her they would always stay together.

Even then.

Even when Rory made plans to leave the farm, leave their old lives, and all the bad luck behind.

"Are we really moving to America, Dad?" Liam, his voice just changing, reluctant and eager at the same time.

Rory glanced up from the side of bacon he was slicing. The onions were already browning in the pan, sizzling and smoking in the gray light from the window. "I'm waiting for a letter from your cousin in Illinois."

Illinoise. Rory's father pronounced the S. What kind of a word was that? Liam wondered. What language did they speak there?

"What will we do there? Will we buy a farm?"

His father shrugged. Sliced the bacon with slow, deft motions. Liam watched the gnarled, callussed hands. Farmer's hands.

"Couldn't we move to Dublin?"

Rory stopped slicing, squinted across the room at his son. "What would we do there? Beg in the streets?"

"But the Sheas moved to Dublin. And the Reillys live in the city now too."

"Not for us, Liam." Rory took a dim view of city life. Born on Galway Bay, on a tiny green island, he had seen the city only once, and it had frightened him. "No place for the fairy people on those hard streets," he once told Liam.

Did he really believe in the fairy people?

Sometimes, Liam believed that he did. At night, Rory would make the fairy people come alive in the stories he told. Stories about the fairy people and the elves who lived just beyond their farm, about the leprechaun, the wailing banshee, the phouka or spirit horse, the merrow (mermaid), and the dullahan who carried his head under his arm. (How many of those had lumbered in pursuit of poor Liam in his dreams?)

Rory made the strange creatures all seem so real.

Some nights they read books together, sitting close in front of the fire, a book of Irish stories held between them on their laps, Margaret on the footstool beside the couch, pages flickering in the orange firelight. Sometimes Liam didn't really understand the stories. But he loved the language, the dark humor. And he loved hearing his father read, uttering complete sentences, whole paragraphs! Such enthusiasm. The only time Rory seemed to come to life.

But now they were moving away, away from the farm, from Ireland. "You cannot stay where the luck has run out," Rory explained solemnly.

Would the fairy people follow?

"So what will we do in Illinois?" Liam pronouncing the strange name carefully.

"You will go to school and become an educated man." Rory finished slicing, dropped the bacon into the crackling onions. Picked up a wooden spoon to stir.

"But American kids are all rich. They won't like me. And people ride around in big cars shooting each other."

Rory snickered. "You watch too much telly." The turnips sizzled in the pan. "Liam, what would you like for lunch today?"

Liam pretended to think about it. "How about bacon?"

"Good idea."

It was one of their running jokes.

The night Liam lost his childhood came a few weeks before his twelfth birthday.

A warm spring night, the sweet fragrance of clover floating in through the open bedroom window. Liam lay on his stomach on the worn wool rug, reading a book about space travel (preparing for his voyage to America?) by the fading sunlight.

A shadow fell over the book. Liam glanced up, expecting to see Margaret. Instead, his father, stern-faced, eyes weary, new

179

creases in his already lined forehead, peered down thoughtfully at him.

"Liam—come with me."

"I just want to finish this chapter." How many times had Liam said those words? His father always beamed with approval when he found Liam reading.

But this time his expression remained cold. "Come with me now, please."

Have I done something wrong? Liam struggled to understand the sternness of his father's expression, the cold urgency in his voice.

He closed the book, climbed to his feet, straightened the pale blue jersey over his jeans, and followed Rory down the stairs and out the back door.

The sun glowed red behind the fresh-blossoming trees. The unplanted field stretching pink in the evening light. Like bare skin.

"Where are we going, Father?"

No reply.

Rory walking quickly, taking long strides across the dirt. Liam struggled to catch up.

"Are we going to town?"

Some town. A general store and post office. A filling station. And two dilapidated shipping warehouses back by the railroad tracks.

Normally, they went out the front and walked along the highway. If a neighbor came driving by in his pickup, he'd stop and give them a lift. But tonight, Rory led the way to the farm road, the old dirt path that curved between the fields. It had rained the night before, a harsh storm for spring with winds that shook the fresh tree buds and sent the goats scurrying for cover in the barn. The path was still puddled and soft.

"Father, wait up. Are we going to town? What has happened?"

Rory, leaning his long frame forward, his gnarled hands swinging in wide arcs at the sides of his overalls, his dark hair flying around his head, didn't slow his pace.

Something weird, Liam knew. *Something wrong.*

The two setters came scampering after them, panting excitedly, crisscrossing each other, their rust-colored coats wet and tangled. Rory spun around angrily. "Go home! Home!"

Normally, the two dogs ignored his commands. But something in his voice told them today was different. They stopped, their tails sagging, lowered their heads guiltily, and stared, panting, waiting.

"Go home!"

To Liam's surprise, both dogs turned and obediently took off for the farm. Somewhere nearby a crow cawed. It started a symphony of caws. Liam saw his father wince. Crows were bad luck, Liam knew. Birds the color of death.

They walked through the barren fields in silence. The sky purpled, then faded to evening charcoal.

Liam heard voices as they approached the general store, a one-story wood structure on the corner of the only intersection. Excited voices. Shouts. He saw two black-suited men hurry around the back of the building.

They crossed the street, Rory slowing now and placing a heavy hand on Liam's slender shoulder, and made their way behind the store, along the paved path to the warehouses.

Two small cars were parked at the side of the store. A pickup truck, its headlights on, stood in the middle of the street.

As the barn-sized warehouse came into view, Liam saw the police cars. Two of them, parked in a V at the warehouse entrance. A white and red ambulance, red light flashing on its roof, stood to the right of the cruisers.

Liam heard shouting. Angry cries. A buzz of conversation.

His hand on Liam's shoulder, Rory guided them around the boarded side of the warehouse to the back.

So many people scurrying around in the gray light. It looked like a play to Liam, the way he imagined plays when he read them with his father. Everyone seemed to be playing a role. Dark-uniformed police officers, white-suited medics, a woman crying stage right, comforted by two men Liam recognized, the townspeople as bystanders off stage left.

What were they all doing here?

And why had his father brought him to this strange performance?

The police huddled in a tight circle near the warehouse wall. Rory led Liam closer, their shoes sinking in the soft, rain-wet mud.

The circle of dark uniforms broke apart—and Liam saw the man on the ground.

He gasped.

Was the man hurt?

Closer. Rory's hand squeezing his shoulder now, holding him tightly, as if determined to keep him from escaping.

Closer. Close enough to see his first corpse.

The man on the ground—his body lay on its side, the head bent, bent backward, the eyes wide open. No. One eye wide open. The other a bare socket. A black hole into the skull.

One arm. One arm completely ripped off. Still wrapped in its shirtsleeve. Lying like a package a few feet away.

Liam reached up to his shoulder and grabbed for his father's hand. "Oh. Oh no."

But his father pushed him even closer. Close enough to see the lake of blood around the twisted body. Close enough to see the flies—even in the gray light—the flies crawling on the face, jamming into the open mouth, into the dark, round opening where the eye had rested, buzzing louder than the hushed voices of the bystanders, louder than the muffled sobs of the woman, the buzzing flies sweeping over the body like a blanket, covering the severed arm, torn and bloody like a package of meat, buzzing excitedly over their dinner.

Liam turned away, buried his face in his father's shirt. "Father—why are you showing me this?" His voice trembling, muffled against the flannel.

He could feel Rory's stomach muscles tighten, feel his whole body go rigid. Rory's voice cold and hard: "Because, Liam, you are responsible."

PART FOUR

22

"Do you believe in fairies?" Liam asked.

Sara giggled and pressed her face against his arm. They had just made love. Now she snuggled close, pressing against his warm skin, wanting to stay near, part of him, still touching, still one.

"Well, do you?" His warm breath tickled her ear.

She shivered, pulled the sheet and blanket up nearly to her chin, squirmed even closer so that their sides melted together, damp and so warm.

"I believe in this." She kissed his cheek, her lips already soft from kissing. He brushed tangles of hair off her face.

"Well, this is a story called 'The Fairy Wife.' " Liam pulled himself up, reached to the bed table for his wineglass, took a sip of the Chardonnay.

Across Sara's bedroom, two slender white candles flickered on the dresser, their flames repeated in the oval mirror behind them. Liam always insisted on lighting two white candles before they made love. One of his superstitions, she knew—but so romantic.

She found a lot of his superstitions romantic. The idea of *being* superstitious in this day and age seemed so innocent and romantic to her.

She settled against him, her forehead on his shoulder, one

hand trailing lightly, tenderly—possessively—over his chest as he told his story:

A young man named Lonnie lived alone on a potato farm in the Rosses long ago. One evening, as he was standing in his doorway, gazing up at the stars—which are brighter over Ireland than everywhere else (this is a fact well known to science, Sara)—a beautiful woman appeared, as if by magic. Lonnie's eyes grew wide with excitement, and his heart began to pound at the sight of her. "Come in," he invited.

"I shan't come in today," said she with the coyest of smiles. The next night she appeared at the door again.

"Come in," he said.

"I shan't come in today," she repeated with the same coy smile.

On the third night, the beautiful young woman appeared again, her eyes twinkling brighter than the stars. "Come in," Lonnie invited.

"Very well," said she.

She floated into Lonnie's house and lived with him as his wife from that night on. A little more than a year later, she gave birth to a son. Lonnie and his family lived happily, and the potato farm prospered, as they once did when the Irish soil was fresh and the fairy people inhabited the fields.

Some time later, the harvest fair was to be held in the village of Glenties. "I think I shall go to the fair today," said Lonnie. "I have uncles living there I have not seen for many a year." And so he set out across the green fields, heading to the fair.

His uncles were there. But instead of greeting him warmly, they snubbed him every one. Lonnie was hurt by their coldness and decided to confront them. "What crime have I committed?" he cried. "Why do you not greet me, uncles?"

To which an uncle replied, "We cannot greet you with happiness, boy. We hear that you have married a fairy woman."

"Why didn't you come to us?" demanded another uncle. "We would have found a suitable bride for you."

"Here is a knife," said the third uncle to Lonnie. "You must take it home and kill your fairy wife."

Lonnie took the knife. He knew his uncles had spoken the truth. He knew he had done wrong. But he also knew that he could not kill his wife. He tossed the knife into a cornfield and returned home.

"How was the fair?" she asked.

"Very enjoyable," Lonnie replied.

"And in what mood did you find your uncles?"

"Good," Lonnie replied.

She gazed at him sternly. "You should tell the truth. Did they not give you a knife with which to murder your fairy wife?"

"Yes, they did," Lonnie confessed.

"And did you not throw it in the cornfields?"

"I did."

" 'Tis well that you did," she told him, "for I have loved you like a true wife. But now I am going to leave you. You can go to your uncles and let them select a wife for you." She left and took the child with her.

And Lonnie did just as she instructed. A short while later, he moved back into the farmhouse with his new bride.

He was a good and faithful husband to his new wife.

But every night, before they went to bed, Lonnie crept down to the kitchen, where he left a lantern burning and two plates of food on the table. Every morning he found the lantern dark and the plates empty. This he did until the day he left the farm for heaven.

Sara lifted herself onto one elbow and turned to Liam. "What a strange story. So beautiful."

He smiled. "It is, isn't it."

In the glow of candlelight, she saw her face reflected in his dark eyes. "I don't really understand, Liam. Is there a point to the story?"

His smile grew wider. "Of course. Do you think an old Irish tale exists that doesn't have a point to make?"

She lowered her forehead to his chest. Her hair fell over

him. "Well? Come on, Professor. Do your job. Explain to your student."

Liam gently lifted her head in both of his hands. "He was loyal to her, Sara," he whispered, his expression suddenly solemn in the shadowy light. "It's a story about love and loyalty. About bonds that can't be broken. About happiness and sadness. And how love brings us both of them."

Sara felt her heart start to race. She shut her eyes. She liked the feel of his hands on her face. "But why did you decide to tell this story tonight?"

"Because I want you to be my wife, Sara."

She jerked her head up. Sat up against the headboard, gripping the sheet with one hand, pulling it up over her bare breasts. "Excuse me?"

"To me, you are like that beautiful young fairy who appeared in the doorway, Sara," he told her, his voice rumbling with emotion. He sat up gracefully and raised his hands to her shoulders. "I want you to be my wife."

"Oh!"

The simple, astonished cry escaped her lips before she could stop it.

The room blurred. She realized she suddenly had tears in her eyes.

What a beautiful proposal. What a beautiful story. And what a romantic and innocent way of asking her to marry him. So much like Liam.

So . . . perfect.

Perfect.

His dark eyes glowed, staring hard into hers. "Well, Sara?"

"Oh!" Again. Realizing she had forgotten to answer him.

"Yes, Liam. Of course, yes. I—I hope our life together is—"

He interrupted her with a kiss.

His arms slid around her bare back. And then he was on top of her. Inside her. Hard inside her. Wrapped so tightly together. They made love till the candles, the twin white candles, burned low, melting, melting, melting . . .

23

Afterward, neither of them could sleep. Sara rested in his arms, her cheek pressed against his. Pale moonlight washed over the bed, soft light, warm. Sara felt so happy, she had an urge to jump up, to dance, to twirl and stretch and leap around the room.

"When shall we have the wedding?" Liam asked, one hand trailing through her hair, straightening it, smoothing her bangs. "I would like it as soon as possible. Tomorrow. Tonight!"

Sara laughed. "We aren't really dressed for it."

"Hmmm . . . maybe."

"We can have it in the spring, Liam. In June. My mother will come. And my brothers."

"No. That's too long to wait," he insisted.

"Well . . . how about May?"

His fingers stopped moving through her hair. She felt his body stiffen. "It can't be in May, my dear. That would be very bad luck. May is the month the Romans honored their dead."

Sara let out a soft laugh. "Well, we don't have to invite any Romans—do we?"

Silence. She expected a laugh but didn't get one. "The term is over at the end of January, Sara. Let's have the wedding then."

"Liam, it's practically November. I'm not sure all of my brothers can get away on such short notice."

His arms wrapped around her. He sighed. "I changed my

189

mind. I can't wait till January. How about Thanksgiving, Sara? Please don't say no. We'll get married at Thanksgiving." He moved a hand under her chin and tilted her face to his. "I'm ten years older than you, Sara. I can't afford the patience of youth. I want to enjoy every moment with you."

They kissed.

He's really very sweet, she thought. Have I ever been this happy before?

Have I?

The next afternoon, Sara was curled up on the couch, a woolly white afghan pulled up over her legs, textbook resting on top of it in her lap. Thinking about Liam, she hadn't turned a page in several minutes, hadn't read one entire paragraph.

The doorbell jarred her from her daydreams.

She slammed the book shut, set it on the floor, and jumped up, stumbling over the afghan, kicking it out of her way as she hurried to the door.

Liam?

No. She was startled to find his sister, Margaret, standing on the welcome mat, a bouquet of pink and yellow roses in a cone of white tissue paper in her hand. "Hi, Sara. Are you busy?"

"No, I—come in. How are you, Margaret?"

Margaret breezed past Sara into the apartment, her eyes moving quickly over the barely furnished living room. "Here. I brought you these. I was passing that flower stand on Tremont, and I couldn't resist them. Aren't the colors wonderful?"

She seems so bubbly, so lively, Sara thought, smiling as she took the flowers from her. "Thank you, Margaret. They're beautiful." She raised them to her face and took a long sniff. "Mmmm. They smell so sweet."

Margaret looks so different, Sara thought. So youthful. She had seemed rather drab and washed out, almost mousy the few times Sara had seen her.

Margaret had a new haircut, very short at the sides, down

over one eye in front, a new color too, much blonder, not streaked. She pulled off her maroon down coat to reveal a white mohair sweater pulled down over black leggings. Quite a nice figure, Sara decided. She wondered why she had never noticed before. Perhaps because her eyes were always on Liam?

Has Margaret changed her makeup or something? Sara wondered. Why does she look so much prettier?

"I only have one vase," Sara told her, crossing to the small kitchen. "I hope it's tall enough. This was so nice of you. I love them!"

Margaret tossed her coat onto the couch and followed her. "You can cut the stems if they're too tall. I can only stay a minute. I was on my way to my shop and I wanted to stop by. Busy day today. Liam invited me to join him at some kind of faculty tea." She sighed. "He never seems to get tired of these things."

Sara chuckled. "He's very social." She pulled down the vase from the cabinet. Then she began to unwrap the paper around the roses.

"I enjoy talking to people too," Margaret said, fiddling with one sleeve of her sweater. "That's one of the nice things about owning an antique shop. But whenever I go to one of Liam's faculty things, everyone just wants to ask me about Liam."

I want to ask her about Liam too, Sara thought, filling the vase with warm water. I want to know *everything* about him. Everything.

Does she know that Liam asked me to marry him last night?

Of course she does. That's why she's here. That's why she brought the flowers, to show that she accepts me, that she's happy about it.

"Liam is fascinating," Margaret continued, picking up a yellow rose from the bunch and sniffing it. "But sometimes I'd like to talk about some other subject. *Any* other subject." She laughed. "Sorry, Sara. You're not interested in my social problems. I'm sure that—"

"Yes," Sara interrupted. She turned to Margaret, suddenly

feeling awkward. "I mean . . . I do want to get to know you." Why do I sound so stiff, so formal? "I hope you and I can become good friends."

Margaret smiled and patted Sara's hand. "Liam told me the good news at breakfast this morning. That's why I stopped by."

"Oh. Well—" Sara, suddenly tongue-tied, felt her cheeks start to burn.

Margaret twirled the yellow rose in her hand, her eyes on Sara. "I'm so happy for both of you. I'm just so glad Liam found you, Sara. I think you are just what he needs."

"Oh! Oh, thank you!" Sara felt her chest tighten with emotion. "What a lovely thing to say!" She had to struggle not to burst into tears. Margaret's words had really touched her. She dropped the roses and wrapped Margaret in a short hug.

It was Margaret's turn to appear embarrassed. She raised the yellow rose she had been holding and tsk-tsked. Sara had crushed the stem during the impulsive hug.

"Oops." Sara took the broken flower from her, tried to make it stand up in the vase.

Margaret straightened her short hair, tugging it back in place over one eye. "That's all I came to say, really. You and I should have lunch sometime soon. Have a really long talk."

"That would be great," Sara replied with enthusiasm. "I would like that, Margaret."

"I know you're going to make Liam very happy." Margaret's expression changed. Her smile faded. "And I'm going to try really hard not to be in the way."

"In the way?"

"Especially after the baby comes."

Sara let out a sharp laugh. A little too loud. "Baby? What baby?"

Margaret glanced at her watch, then crossed to the couch and picked up her coat. "Oh. It's late. Time to get to the shop." She slipped into the coat, tugging the sleeves hard to get them over the mohair sweater. "I'm sure Liam has told you how eager he is to have a child."

Without waiting for a reply, Margaret hugged Sara again, the heavy coat sleeves wrapping around Sara's shoulders, Margaret's cheek pressing softly against hers. Sara inhaled a flowery, powdery fragrance.

"I'm really excited, Sara. Welcome to our family. This is the *best* news! We'll get together soon—okay? Just the two of us. Bye."

Sara held open the apartment door, and Margaret breezed out. "Thanks again for the flowers."

Margaret hurried down the long hall. Sara watched her until she disappeared around a corner. She closed the door, then leaned back against it, taking a deep breath.

How weird. How totally weird.

Margaret seemed like a changed person. She was so warm, so animated, so happy.

Sara blinked, thinking hard, rerunning the short visit in her mind.

What was that about a baby?

Was Liam really eager to become a father?

If so, why hadn't he mentioned it to her?

24

A week later, Sara tugged the hood of her raincoat over her hair, ducking her head as a cold drizzle became a steady rain. A sharp wind pushed open the coat. She struggled with the large plastic buttons, her shoes thudding softly on the path as she picked up her pace.

She shivered. She could still feel Liam's warmth on her skin, his face pressed against her cheek, his body on top of hers.

To her right, the green dome of the Administration Building appeared to float in the dark mists. The trees in The Circle danced in the wind, shimmying and shaking, a silent, graceful tango.

Sara felt like dancing too. The cold rain invaded her hood, but she barely felt the water on her cheeks. She wanted to toss off the heavy coat, grab the lamppost up ahead and swing herself around on it, tap dance and sing like Gene Kelly in the rain.

Real love made you feel crazy, she decided. A new feeling for her.

Liam. Liam. Liam. Like a schoolgirl, she found herself saying his name, writing it over and over on the lined pages of her seminar notebook.

Mrs. Liam O'Connor.

Sara Morgan-O'Connor.

I *am* a schoolgirl! she told herself. The thought made her giggle like one.

The schoolgirl who marries the Great Professor.

She had spent every night of the past week with Liam, talking with him, laughing at his stories, his funny superstitions, making love with him, serious love. Making plans.

Mary Beth continued to warn her. *"You're acting crazy. Jumping into this too quickly. You know these things always end badly for you, Sara."*

These things?

"It isn't a *thing*. I'm getting married! I'm marrying Liam at Thanksgiving."

Poor Mary Beth. She didn't know what it felt like to want to toss off your coat and dance in the rain. I'd resent her advice, Sara decided, if I didn't feel sorry for her.

These days—this week—this moment—she felt sorry for anyone who didn't know the feeling, the feeling of wanting to explode, to burst apart, to leave the ground and fly up into the cool, sweet air.

I could fly. I really could!

The footsteps brought Sara back to earth.

At first, she thought she was hearing the patter of rain against the path. But the steady rhythm, the scrape of one shoe and then the other, told her someone was behind her.

A stab of fear made her turn her head, quicken her pace.

The rain hood blocked her view.

The darkness seemed to surround her, sweep over her. The black trees danced in the wind. She splashed through a puddle, felt icy water slide over her ankle.

She pushed the hood down with both hands. Running now.

The footsteps close behind her.

Who is it?

So dark and foggy.

A blurred figure, running fast. A dark overcoat. Head low.

He's running too fast. I can't outrun him.

She stepped into a pale, shimmering triangle of light from a lamppost, raindrops sparkling in the light, pearls, a shower of pearls. Unreal. All unreal.

Except for the dark-coated figure. Who caught up to her. Breathing hoarsely, his body heaving under the heavy black coat.

He reached out for her with both hands. Raised his eyes, angry eyes, frantic eyes almost glowing in the dim light.

"Chip!" Sara cried, rain pelting her face, her hair. "What are you doing here?"

He held on to her shoulders, his eyes locked on hers, accusing eyes, held on as if holding himself up, waiting to catch his breath. And then uttered, "Hi, Sara." Almost shyly.

So wrong, she thought. So out of place. As if he still didn't catch on.

I'm gone, Chip. I'm long gone. I'm not "Hi, Sara" anymore.

"I . . . followed you." Still holding on to her coat shoulders. Did he mean to squeeze so hard?

His white-blond eyebrows caught the light. Beneath them, his blue eyes lost their focus, appeared to swim.

She smelled alcohol on his breath. Just beer?

The face had seemed so familiar a few months ago. And now she felt as if she were staring at a stranger. The stub of a nose, the scar on his chin—familiar landmarks in New York seemed foreign now, the face unpleasant and unwanted.

"Chip, what are you *doing* here?"

"We have to talk."

"No, we don't." He tried to drown me. He nearly did drown me. And now he followed me here.

To do what?

"Let's get out of this rain, Sara. Let's go somewhere and sit down and maybe—"

"No. Please, Chip—" She reached up with both hands to pull his hands off her shoulders. His right hand slid into focus. She gasped. "When did you get *that?*"

Her finger grazed the small tattoo on the back of his hand.

Just an inch long. A tiny black dagger with a drip of blue blood at the tip of the blade.

He lowered his gaze, bobbed unsteadily, as if confused, as if seeing it for the first time. "This?"

"I don't believe it. Why did you get a tattoo?"

He pulled his hand close to examine it, frowned at it. "After you left, Sara. After you disappeared. Just disappeared without a word. I got drunk one night, I guess. I don't know. I was with some friends. Some guys. I was crazy. I didn't know what I was doing."

So the tattoo is my fault. Sara felt a chill, not from the rain. She struggled with the hood, managed to tug it over her hair.

"Chip, you shouldn't have come here. You—"

"But I have to talk to you. I miss you so much, Sara." He raised pleading eyes to her, to show his sincerity. How many times had she seen that expression? She had fallen for it before. Now it seemed too slick, too practiced. Shallow. Immature.

"You know why I left. I had to leave." The coldness in her voice surprised her. She had never heard it there before.

He pulled up his coat collar, feeling the cold too. "Can't we get out of the rain? There's a coffee shop . . ." He pointed toward the Dale Street Coffee Shop.

Rain glittered on his blond eyebrows. Like diamonds.

The Golden Boy, she thought, surprised at how much she disliked him now, at how fast her bitterness had surfaced, at how powerful an emotion it was.

He's a Golden Boy. He has everything. Such a great guy.

Just don't ever say no to him.

"No, Chip. I can't. I mean, I don't want to talk to you." She sucked in a deep breath. "I want you to go away. I really do." She could feel her neck muscles tighten. Feel the blood throb at her temples.

She turned quickly and walked away, slowly but with long strides.

He jogged up beside her. She knew he would. He reached to take her arm, but she jerked it away.

"Sara, please—"

"Go home, Chip. Be a man. Go home." Tough talk. Did she really say that? Was this really her? She had run away to avoid facing him, had run off without a word, so eager, so desperate to avoid any kind of confrontation.

Now here she was, toughing it out.

He grabbed her arm. He wouldn't let her get away. "That professor is too old for you!" He practically shrieked the words.

She turned to face him. His blue eyes wild and unfocused. Were those raindrops on his broad forehead or beads of sweat?

"How do you know about Liam?" she demanded through clenched teeth. "How long have you been in Freewood, Chip? Have you been spying on me?"

"He's too old for you. You belong with me."

The wind swept back her hood. Her chest heaved. She struggled to breathe. Rain pelted her face, made her squint, her eyes studying him, searching for answers. "How long have you been in Freewood?"

"Long enough." Suddenly coy. Angry and coy at the same time. "You're ruining your life, Sara. You know you belong in New York. With me."

"How do you know about Liam?" She would repeat the question until she forced him to answer it. But then another question, more urgent, forced its way to her mind: "Have you been calling me?"

The blond eyebrows arched as he squinted back at her. "Huh?"

"Have you been calling me? Late at night? Threatening me?"

"Hey—no way."

He's lying, she decided.

What a lying face. It always was a lie. So handsome, so pretty, so perfect. And so ugly underneath.

All a lie.

"You made those calls—didn't you!" Her mouth trembling, her tongue suddenly thick and heavy.

"No way, Sara. I didn't call you."

Liar.

Holding her arm, he pulled his face near. She inhaled the alcohol breath and a sweet fragrance, a flowery aftershave, a new aftershave, heavy even in the rain-drenched air.

Sickening, she thought.

And what was he trying to do? Kiss her?

Yes. The blue eyes wide now, trained on her. The grip on her arm tightening. The blond hair, matted by the rain, gleaming under the light. The half-smile. The lips parting. Pushing toward her.

"No! Let go!" Her scream appeared to startle him. His head shot back. The eyes shut.

But he didn't release her arm. "Come back with me, Sara. Come back to New York. I need you. I really do."

"No, Chip—"

"Would I follow you all this way if I didn't need you? Would I humble myself like this? Would I plead? Would I beg? Sara—"

"No. It's over. That's it. *Ouch!* Let go. You're *hurting* me!"

"It's not over. Listen to me. It's going to be great. Remember that production company I wanted to start? Well, my dad said he would help me with the start-up. And I'm getting a new apartment, Sara. With the most amazing river view. You've got to see it. You're going to love it. And—"

She tried to tug free. "Let go of me, Chip. I'll scream. I'll get the police. I'm warning you."

"It's not over. No way. I've changed, Sara. Really. You'll see. I'm a different person. *Listen to me!* I can't live without you. I can't—"

His fist came up. The tiny black dagger with its drop of blue blood floated in front of her.

How dangerous is Chip? she wondered. How insane?

"It's not over," he repeated. "No way. It's not over."

"Let *go* of me! Oww! What are you *doing?* Let go of me!"

25

Detective Garrett Montgomery was on the phone long distance with his brother when the report of the third murder came in.

The job at the furniture store had been filled, Duane Montgomery had reported in solemn, low tones usually reserved for funerals.

As if this had been Garrett's last chance.

"There'll be other jobs," Garrett told his brother. "Cheer up, Duane. What if I had come down there and taken the job? Then Angel, Martin, and I would be moving in with you!"

Keep it light, Garrett told himself. It isn't exactly a tragedy. Except that it had been his one avenue of escape.

Escape from this tiny hick town. Escape from staring across the desk at doughnut-devouring Walter, powdered sugar down the front of his bulging blue uniform shirt. Escape from the murders, the horrors that shouldn't be happening in a quiet town of young people and staid academic types.

Horrors that kept Garrett awake at night, staring at the shifting shadows on the low ceiling, listening to Angel's soft, steady breathing beside him, and picturing body parts, severed arms, broken backs, exposed bones among the shadows.

Murders he didn't think he could solve. Murders that made him feel helpless and weak—and made escape so much more inviting.

Of course, Angel wanted no part of Atlanta. And if he tried to persuade her, she would probably accuse him of trying to run away from the biggest, hardest challenge of his life.

And she'd be right.

But the investigation was going nowhere. All the hours he'd put in, he and his men. All the thinking. All the questioning and searching and hard work—had all turned up nothing.

And as the days dragged into weeks, the murders still haunted him. Day and night.

They didn't prepare me for anything like this at the training academy, he told himself. They didn't prepare me for the sight of gray bones poking out through ripped flesh. For the blood. Dark lakes of blood.

How *could* they prepare me?

How could you prepare someone for the sight of these torn and broken bodies? People didn't *do* that to people—did they?

And now Walter was staring across the desk at him, phone pressed to his round face, mouth open, chins trembling, gesturing urgently to Garrett with his free hand.

Garrett had seen the expression before. "Got to go," he told Duane. "Kiss Barbara for me." He slammed down the receiver. Jumped to his feet. "Walter—what?"

Walter even paler than normal under the fluorescent light. "Another one."

The next morning, Garrett had the photos spread across his desk. Want to wake up fast? he thought bitterly. No problem. Just line up the snapshots of three murder victims on your desk.

That kid Anders is a damned good photographer, Garrett thought, sipping black coffee from a cardboard container as his eyes swept over the newest batch. Anders was still in high school, but he was the main photographer for the local paper, and he did police photo work whenever it was needed.

Last night, Garrett had watched the skinny kid snap away as if he was photographing Miss America. Garrett had tried to concentrate on Anders to keep from seeing the subject of the photos.

Not a bad job, he thought now, setting the coffee container at the edge of the desk and leaning close to get a better look, to see if he had missed anything. The black-and-whites were kind of grainy, but they captured the highlights. And the color Polaroids—they were clear enough to keep a person awake forever.

This third murder was as ugly as the first two. More devastating to Garrett, maybe because the girl had once been so lovely.

She had creamy, white skin dotted with pale freckles, and frizzed-out auburn hair, cascading down her back nearly to her waist.

When Garrett and Walter had arrived at the scene—on the campus, less than a dozen yards from where the first murder occurred—she lay stretched out on her back and her hair had fallen over her face, like a soft, protective blanket.

Garrett had been the one to crouch down and pull the hair away. Garrett had been the one to discover that the girl's eyeballs had been gouged out and stuffed into her mouth.

The two green eyes stared up at him from between her lips.

Garrett had toppled backward, landing hard against a tree trunk, gasping for air, his heart pounding so hard his chest ached.

Is this what a heart attack felt like?

Now he leaned over the metal desk, staring at the grainy black-and-whites, thinking about . . . nothing. Unable to think clearly about anything.

Except escape?

Devra Brookes.

The girl's name was Devra Brookes. Once again, the victim hadn't been robbed or raped. Her wallet, her cash, her driver's license, her credit cards were all in her bag.

Devra had been a graduate assistant at the college. Language Arts Department. The Dean of Students sounded very shaken when Garrett called for information. Garrett didn't blame him. Three murders on or near the campus.

Three gruesome, inhuman murders.

Devra Brookes hadn't been at Moore State long, the Dean had revealed in a trembling, hoarse voice. She had moved to Freewood last year from Chicago.

A bad move, Garrett thought, shaking his head at the black and white corpse on his desk.

He had held on to Angel so tightly all night. Held on as if she could keep him afloat. She hadn't said a word. She knew.

But now there was nothing to hold on to but the desk. A container of coffee as murky and dark as his thoughts.

"Chief, we've got something here." Walter's voice, excited, loud for so early in the morning.

Garrett glanced up slowly, the transition from black and white to color painful for his tired eyes. Walter's white-blond hair was still wet from the shower. He had shaving cream behind one ear. It stained the blue collar of his uniform shirt.

"I got the prints from the guys in the lab in Somerville," he announced, holding up a large manila envelope.

Garrett sighed. "They get any clean ones?" He didn't expect much. The last two bodies didn't produce a single usable fingerprint.

Walter reached across the desks to push the envelope into Garrett's hand. "You look like shit, hoss. You been here all night?"

"Please don't call me hoss." Garrett through gritted teeth. "I didn't sleep. Kept seeing eyeballs." He groaned. "I'll never eat another hardboiled egg."

His hand fumbled with the envelope flap. Why did they seal them so tightly. "So? Any good ones? What did O'Brian tell you?"

"We got some this time," Walter reported, scratching his nose. "We got good clear ones. Off her face and off her clothes." Walter stood tensely, watching Garrett struggle with the envelope. "I didn't see 'em. That's just what O'Brian told me."

Garrett yanked hard and tore off the flap. "Did he think we could get an ID?"

Walter shrugged. "Didn't say."

Holding the edge of the black film carefully, Garrett slid the prints out of the envelope. A single contact sheet. Several different prints.

A first clue, he thought. Three murders and we finally get a break.

He held the sheet up to the light. Squinted up at it.

Squinted harder.

"Hey, Walter—what's the joke?" he demanded sharply. "Is O'Brian getting cute up there?"

Walter edged his bulk around the desk. "Huh? What's wrong, Chief?"

"These fingerprints—they're not from a human."

26

Liam lowered his thumb onto the black inkpad. The secretary, chewing gum with a fast, steady rhythm, guided his hand over the card, then gently pressed the thumb into the correct square.

Liam gazed down disapprovingly at the black smudge. "Do I have to do both hands?"

"Just your right." The young woman's breath smelled of Juicy Fruit. She guided his forefinger onto the inkpad. "You're maybe the last one."

Liam frowned. "The last one to be fingerprinted?"

The secretary nodded, chewing hard. "We never did it at Moore State before this year. But I think it's a requirement now." She pressed the finger into the square beside the thumbprint.

Liam gazed up to see Sara enter the small room. Her shoes clicked on the hard floor. Under a gray trench coat, she wore a short blue wool tunic dress over navy blue tights.

She looks about eighteen, he thought. Especially with those bangs and her hair pulled back like that.

She laughed, her hazel eyes flashing with amusement. "Liam—you're under arrest?"

He raised his hand, showing off his black fingertips, and flashed her a smile. "Remind me to wear gloves tonight when I rob the bank."

The secretary didn't laugh. She lowered her head, concentrating on getting the last fingerprint.

"This is soul stealing in some societies," Liam said. "Take my fingerprints, you take my soul." Then he added lightly, "Lucky I don't *have* a soul—right?"

Sara stepped up to the table and patted his other hand. "Oh, I think you're very soulful."

Liam squeezed her hand gently.

"You're finished, sir," the secretary announced. "Here." She pulled a roll of paper towels from the desk drawer, tore off two sheets, and handed them to him to wipe the ink off his fingertips.

He thanked her and led Sara into the hall, wiping his hand. "Quaint custom. Fingerprinting," he muttered. The ink smeared but didn't come off. "I really did feel like a criminal while she did it."

Sara tsk-tsked. "Guilty conscience, Liam?"

"Fingerprints are actually a thing of the past," he told her as they made their way down the long, brightly lit hall of the Administration Building. "Very crude. Someday soon the college will require that we leave some DNA. A hair maybe. Or a piece of skin. Maybe test tubes of blood, saliva, and urine."

"Liam—please!"

He laughed. "Why not? Why do you find that more offensive, more intrusive than having prints of your fingertips kept on file?"

Sara didn't reply. Her mind was elsewhere. "Are you packed?"

He shrugged. "Just about."

"I still have a few things to take care of. I want to bring Mom a Moore State sweatshirt."

Liam chuckled. "Is your mother the sweatshirt type? I pictured her in a gingham housedress, with a lacy white apron over her skirt."

Sara gave him a gentle shove. "God, Liam. What century do you live in?"

A hurt expression creased his face. She kissed his cheek. "I'm going to run to the campus store. Then I'll finish packing. The flight is at five. Can you pick me up in a taxi at four?"

Liam nodded. "No problem, as my students say." He grabbed her arm. "Do you think your mother will like me?"

"Liam, she's already nuts about you. I've given you such a big buildup. Half the population of Indiana will probably show up at the airport to welcome you and—"

As they rounded the corner to the building exit, Milton Cohn appeared in an office doorway.

"Hello!" His eyes lingered on Sara, then moved to Liam.

"You're back," Sara cried, surprised. "Liam and I are going away. I didn't think you were back from Atlanta, Milton. The office—"

"I never left. Because of that girl," Milton interrupted. Liam could see that his eyes were red-rimmed, weary. Thatch of white hair in disarray over his red forehead.

Milton heaved a sigh and shuddered. "I just got off the phone with her parents. It—it was hard." He lowered his eyes. "Tore me apart, actually. Parents shouldn't have to endure such . . . such grief."

He raised a hand to scratch his hair. Liam saw the flesh-colored bandage around the wrist.

"Milton—is that *another* cut?" Sara demanded.

He nodded. Held the bandage in front of him. "One of my knives. It slipped off the wall while I was taking it out to clean. Gave me a nasty cut." He shook his head.

Liam glanced at his watch. He took Sara's elbow. "Better get going. We haven't much time." He turned to Milton. "Be careful, okay? Those knives of yours . . ." His voice trailed off.

Milton swallowed. "I can't stop thinking about Devra Brookes. Such a wonderful girl."

Liam lowered his eyes. "It was a shock."

"She was at my party—remember? You were so surprised to see her, Liam. I can't believe she was just in my house. And now . . ."

207

"I saw her more recently," Liam said softly, eyes on Sara. "We were having dinner. Sara and I. At that barbecue restaurant—Texas. Devra came over to our table."

Sara gasped. "The red-haired girl? Oh my God! I didn't remember her name."

Liam squeezed her arm, rubbed it soothingly. "Yes. That was Devra. A nice girl. A good student. Pretty and very bright."

"I didn't realize," Sara repeated, hands pressed against her cheeks. "Oh, how awful." She raised her eyes to Milton. "I heard everyone talking about it this morning. I didn't realize . . . I mean, everyone on campus is so upset. So frightened."

"Students are afraid to walk on the campus at night," Milton said, tugging the cuff of his white shirtsleeve over the bandage on his wrist. "I've got parents calling me, asking me what's being done. I don't know what to tell them. What am I supposed to say? I'm sure the police are doing their best. But they're not used to this type of crime. This is a small town." He shook his head again. "What am I supposed to say?"

"We're all helpless," Liam murmured. He glanced down at his ink-stained fingertips and frowned.

"There's a crazed killer out there," Sara said softly, holding on to Liam's arm. "They said on TV that there doesn't seem to be any connection between the murders at all. They're just random. A crazed killer."

"We're holding a meeting later," Milton said. "We're deciding whether to move the Homecoming Game next week from night to afternoon." He sighed. "Will that make it any safer? Maybe we should cancel it completely. I don't know."

"We've got to go." Liam raised a hand to the back of Sara's shoulder. "Sara and I are catching a five o'clock flight. See you Monday, Milton. Get some rest. You look exhausted."

"Be careful, okay? I've got some more calls to return." Milton turned and walked slowly back into the office.

Liam eagerly guided Sara out the door. They stepped out into a gray afternoon, dark storm clouds on the far horizon beyond the campus, the air heavy and damp. Liam watched his breath steam up in front of him. Cold enough to snow, he thought. Hope the plane takes off.

They were halfway down the wide concrete steps when, to Liam's surprise, Sara moved in front of him and threw both arms around his waist. She pressed her cheek against his. "Three women murdered on campus. Oh God, Liam. It—it's so frightening."

"Yes, it is." He liked the warmth of her cheek on his, the feel of her arms tightening around his coat. He pressed his lips against her ear. "Don't worry. I'll protect you, Sara," he whispered. "I'll take good care of you."

Sara shut the clasp on the suitcase and tugged it off the bed. She set it down on the floor, then crossed the room to the dresser. Gazing into the oval mirror, she brushed her hair again.

Why do I feel so nervous?

She wiped a lipstick smear off her chin with her thumb. "Mom is going to adore Liam. No way she won't fall for that Irish charm. Frank and Laurie will love him too."

Frank, her oldest brother. How old is Frank now? She had to add it up. Fifteen years older than Sara. That made him thirty-nine. Frank was a teenager when Sara was born. We never had much of a relationship, Sara thought wistfully. He always seemed more like a second father than a brother. And his wife, Laurie, always seemed somewhat distant.

She glanced at the bed table clock. Liam would be there any second. She grabbed the suitcase handle, intending to carry it to the front door—when the phone rang.

"Hey—!" Calm down, Sara, she instructed herself. You nearly jumped out of your shoes.

She crossed the room and picked up the phone. "Oh, hi, Mary Beth. I was just on my way out. You know. To the airport. Muncie, here we come. I—"

"The airport can wait," Mary Beth interrupted. "I need to bitch to someone."

Sara glanced again at the clock. "Wow. You sound great."

"These murders are going to kill me!" Mary Beth wailed.

Sara held the phone a few inches away from her ear. "Was that some kind of pun or something?"

"I'm not joking," Mary Beth insisted. "The phone doesn't stop ringing. I've got photographers jamming my office—my little cubicle—can you imagine? And reporters from everywhere. There were two TV crews this afternoon. They both arrived at the same time and they started to fight over who got to film the murder scenes first!"

"I don't understand. Why do they all come to you?"

"Because I'm the college Media Director—remember? But this is just insane! It's supposed to be a quiet little unimportant job. I'm supposed to make videos that show how exciting the campus is and publish pretty little brochures. Instead I've got reporters sticking microphones in my face, asking me who *I* think is killing these poor women! And—and—"

"Calm down, Mary Beth. At least—"

"I've got to go out and get totaled. Really. I'm just so wired, Sara. I'm sputtering like an idiot. My head is spinning. I need to get loaded. Fly to Indiana tomorrow. Come meet me at The Pitcher—okay?"

"Huh? Are you serious? You know my mom. She's probably standing at the front door, watching for me already! Liam and I have to—"

"I want to talk to you about Liam too. I'm very happy for you. Really. But I just don't want you to rush into something—"

"Mary Beth—we can't talk about this now. I'm late. And—"

"You really don't know anything about Liam, Sara."

"I just know that he's a wonderful man, and this time it's right. I know it. This time it's right. But I don't have time—"

"That's why we have to get totaled. Get totaled and talk about everything. Sara, you have no idea what it's been like on campus."

"Hey, I know. I'm on campus too, you know. I hear people talking about how frightened they are, how they—"

"No. I mean in the Administration Building. Everyone is just scared to death. And these reporters and TV people are descending like . . . like locusts. Luckily, they decided to shift some of them off on Milton. Starting tomorrow. I mean, they knew I couldn't handle it all. These TV people are crazy. They're all so pumped. Like it's the Super Bowl or something. So since Milton is Dean of Students, they're going to—"

She stopped short, changed gears: "Hey, Sara, you work for Milton, right? Do you ever get the feeling he's kind of a lech?"

Sara snickered. "Yeah. Kind of. He never looks you in the face. He's always looking—"

"Yeah. Right. And he isn't too subtle, *is* he. This morning, I had to bend over to tie my shoe, and he—"

"Listen, Mary Beth, I'm sorry. I've really got to go. Really. Can I call you later? From Indiana?"

"No, I don't think so. I hope I won't be in any condition to talk by that time. Maybe I'll call Eric. He always knows how to relax me. Ha ha!"

"Mary Beth—"

"It's been a nightmare, Sara. A real nightmare. But go ahead. Tell your mom I said hi. Call me when you get back—okay?"

"Okay. Bye." Sara set down the phone, glanced again at the clock.

The doorbell rang.

Sara jumped even though she was expecting it. She hurried to the front door. Liam! He's early!

She pulled open the door. "Liam—is the taxi—?"

No Liam.

No one there? Was someone playing a joke?

Footsteps far down the hall.

She was about to close the door when she glimpsed the box on the welcome mat. A silvery gift box with white ribbon and bow.

"Huh?" A present from Liam?

But he knows we're in a hurry.

So it *can't* be from Liam. But who?

One last look down the long, empty hall. Then she carried it into the apartment in both hands, a big box but very light.

She bumped the apartment door shut with her behind. Dropped onto the couch with the box in her lap. Untied the bow. Lifted off the silvery lid. Pulled away the layers of tissue paper.

"Hey." What were they?

Four cottony white little powder puffs?

So sweet-looking.

She picked one of them up between her fingers—so warm.

She raised it closer to examine it.

And started to scream.

27

The cottony thing fell from her hand. Tumbled back into the box.

Bone and gristle poking up from the bottom.

Pink stains on the tissue paper. Bloodstains, warm and wet.

Her scream ended in a shudder. She shoved the box across the table.

The four rabbit feet bounced against each other. Again she saw the caked blood and yellow gristle beneath the cottony fur. She shook her hand as if trying to shake away the feel of the foot she had held.

Still warm.

It had still felt warm. Ripped off the animal, she realized, swallowing hard. All four bunny paws torn off—not cut. Gristle and veins hanging down from the stained fur.

"Ohhhhh." A moan escaped her throat. "How sick."

And then she saw the envelope. A small, square white envelope, like a greeting card envelope, tucked into the tissue paper at the side of the box.

I should leave it there, Sara told herself, staring at the envelope until it blurred. I should leave it there and call the police.

She blinked. The envelope came back into focus, along with the four furry paws. She grabbed up the envelope with a trembling hand and spun away from the disgusting sight.

A smear of pink blood on the back of the envelope. She tore it open. Pulled out a small note card, lined in black. Held it in both hands to stop it from shaking, and read the words printed neatly in red ink:

IF YOU MARRY LIAM, YOU WILL NEED ALL THE LUCK YOU CAN GET.

Sara crumpled the note in her hand, the hand suddenly cold and wet. She took a deep breath. Shut her eyes and tried to think.

Who sent this? Who?

Chip?

The whispered phone calls—and now this sick, disgusting gift. Is Chip so totally deranged that he'd tear apart a living animal to scare me?

No. He can't be.

He didn't.

But . . .

Without realizing it, Sara had lifted the phone receiver. She struggled to focus on the gray pad beside the phone where she had written Liam's number.

I've called it so many times, I should have memorized it by now, she scolded herself. Is he still there, or is he already on his way over here in the taxi?

She punched in the number, her heart pounding. Pounding as fast as a rabbit's, she thought. A wave of nausea rolled up from her chest, tightening her throat.

Three rings. Then: "Hello?" Liam sounding breathless.

"Liam, it's me. I—I—"

"Sara, what's wrong? I was just out the door. I'm not late, am I?"

"No. I—Liam—the most horrible thing." She wanted to describe the gift box and its sickening contents. But a different question came out in a shrill, taut voice: "That pet rabbit of yours—Phoebe. Is she okay?"

Silence. And then a loud breath in her ear. "Sara, you must be psychic."

"Huh? What do you mean?"

"Well . . . Phoebe *isn't* okay."

Sara felt a shock of surprise.

"She came down with some kind of fever," Liam continued. "The vet had to put her to sleep. Yesterday afternoon." He uttered a humorless chuckle. "It's funny how attached you get to pets. I've been thinking about Phoebe all day.

"Sara . . . I . . . well . . ."

Sara's eyes fell on the silvery gift box.

"How did you know about Phoebe?" Liam demanded. "I didn't mention it earlier. I didn't want to spoil—"

"The most horrible thing!" Sara interrupted in a cry. "Someone sent me a package. A gift box. With a ribbon and bow and everything. And inside were four rabbit's feet. All bloody and warm. They—they were *torn* off the rabbit, Liam. They were soaked with blood. And—and—" A sob escaped her throat.

"When? Today?" Liam demanded.

"There was a note. In red ink," Sara continued. "Warning me about you."

"Good lord. What did it say?"

She took a deep breath. If only her heart would stop pounding. "A warning. It said I'd need all the luck I could get if I marry you."

Silence. Then: "I'm horrified, Sara. I'm so sorry. Truly I am."

"What should I do, Liam? Should I call the police?"

"I don't know. This should be such a happy time for us. But someone . . ."

"Who?" Sara demanded. "Who?"

"I'll find out," he told her. "I promise you. I'll find out. And I'll put a stop to this."

28

The white clapboard house looked smaller to Sara each time she returned for a visit. Patches of gray snow appeared to float over the square front lawn like icebergs in a still, dark ocean.

She wrapped her hand in Liam's arm and rang the doorbell. Their breath steamed up in the heavy, wet air, puffs of yellow in the bright porch light.

Frank pulled open the door, a beaming smile, eyes crinkling behind rimless glasses. He's almost totally bald! Sara saw. She forced her eyes down from his gleaming, endless forehead.

"The prodigal sister returns!" Frank declared in his high voice. A hug for Sara. A manly handshake for Liam. She caught Liam's wince. Frank being unusually exuberant.

They stepped into the front room, the cold sweeping in with them. Good smells from the kitchen. The house hot as a blast furnace. As always.

Sara tried to shake off the cold. She glanced quickly around, pleased that everything looked the same. The dark-paneled walls. Green crushed velvet armchair and matching couch. Sunburst clock over the mantel. Picasso prints on the walls—from the Blue Period. A black and white photo of her dad, smiling up from the end table beside the couch.

Across the living room, her mother, grinning like Frank,

struggled to lift herself off the big armchair. Laurie, Frank's slim, pretty wife, bent to help her.

"Whoever invented knees really screwed up!" Mrs. Morgan declared loudly. Finally on her feet, she swept Sara into a hug. "You're freezing! Take off your coat."

A hug for Liam too. "Welcome to the family. You're a fast worker—aren't you!"

Sara had to laugh. Liam actually appeared speechless. "You look so much like Sara," he offered finally.

"I know, I know. I could be her sister." Mrs. Morgan rolled her eyes. She introduced Laurie to Liam.

Laurie stood awkwardly, hands on the waist of the short black skirt she wore over black leggings. "We've heard a lot about you. From Sara. My cousin took a course of yours. A few years ago."

Liam grinned. "I hope I didn't flunk her!"

Laughter.

Sara could see Liam's eyes studying her mother. Mom does look a lot like me, Sara realized. Mrs. Morgan wore a loose-fitting navy blue sweater over faded jeans. Her hair—Sara's hair, only streaked with gray—was pulled straight back into a girlish ponytail. She refused to get a short, "old lady" cut.

She was wearing more makeup than usual, Sara saw. She saw tension in her mother's cheeks as she took a few steps. The arthritis in her knees had gotten so much more painful since Sara's father died.

"I'm always surprised by how closely daughters resemble their mothers," Liam offered, handing his overcoat into Frank's outstretched arms. "But Sara doesn't have that beautiful dimple." He grinned at Sara's mother.

Her hand went up to her chin. "Beautiful? I was always embarrassed by it. You know how, when you're young, you want to look like everyone else? I always wanted to cover it up or fill it in!"

"There's an old rhyme from Yorkshire," Liam told her. He

closed his eyes, trying to remember it. "Dimple in your chin, your living's brought in. Dimple in your cheek, your living's to seek."

Mrs. Morgan laughed. "Well, mine must have slipped down or something. I'm still seeking!"

More laughter.

"Please—don't encourage him," Sara chimed in, grabbing Liam's arm. "Liam has a silly rhyme for everything!"

Liam flashed her a surprised glance. "Silly?"

Frank still held the coats in his arms. "Are you going to take lip from her?" he demanded of Liam. "Sara never used to talk like that before she lived in New York!"

More laughter. Everyone but Sara.

She growled at Frank. "Hey—are you ever going to stop with the digs about New York? I was evil *before* I lived in New York."

"Come sit down. Don't stand there," Mrs. Morgan ordered. She turned back to her chair against the wall. "I wanted to greet you with a roaring fire. But we don't have a fireplace!"

Liam grinned at Sara, appreciating her mother's humor, probably surprised since Sara seldom tried to be funny.

"You keep it so hot in here, a fire would probably cool the place down!" Laurie offered.

"I like it toasty," Mrs. Morgan replied. She took a few painful steps toward the chair.

"Mom, are you still taking the medication?" Sara demanded. "You look like you're in pain."

"It didn't stop her from going to the Dead concert in Indianapolis last week!" Frank exclaimed, returning from the front closet.

"No shit. I don't believe it!" Sara declared.

Frank to Liam: "She didn't talk like that before New York."

"Once a Dead Head, always a Dead Head," Mrs. Morgan grunted. "Listen, Jerry Garcia is almost as old as I am!"

"He sounds it too," Frank grumbled.

"I didn't need you and Laurie tagging along," Sara's

mother snapped playfully. "If you're too out of it to appreciate—"

"No, we had a great time, Mom," Laurie broke in, frowning at Frank. "It was . . . *awesome*."

Mrs. Morgan turned back to the new arrivals. "I read about the murders. The horrible murders on campus, Sara. I was so worried. They haven't caught the guy, have they?"

Sara sighed. Why did her mother have to bring up the murders first thing? "No. They haven't caught him," she murmured.

Mrs. Morgan tsk-tsked. "Are you being careful?"

"Of course."

Sara's mother stared thoughtfully at her daughter. Then she seemed to snap out of her dark thoughts. "Are you two hungry? You didn't eat that airplane food, did you? Let's eat."

She grabbed Sara's hand and pulled her toward the dining room. "I have a little surprise. I made a Thanksgiving dinner."

"Mom! Why—?" Sara started.

"We'll all be at your wedding on Thanksgiving—won't we?" Sara's mother grinned at Liam. "So I thought we'd do Thanksgiving tonight. You know. Turkey, stuffing, the works."

"It sounds wonderful," Liam said. "Flying always makes me ravenous."

"We're used to eating at six," Mrs. Morgan offered. "Here in the Midwest, people like to have their dinner early."

"I'm quite acquainted with the Midwest customs," Liam told her. "I lived in Chicago until this fall."

"I love Chicago," Mrs. Morgan gushed. "Dave and I went there every chance we had." She sighed. "We spent our honeymoon there at a hotel with a wonderful view of the lake. Perhaps you and Sara . . ."

"No, we won't have time," Sara cut in quickly. "After the wedding, we'll only have a couple of days until classes begin again."

"Maybe you two should hold off the wedding till spring," Mrs. Morgan suggested, making careful eye contact with Sara.

"Then you could take time to have a real honeymoon. You'd have all summer—"

Sara bit her lower lip. Mom was never the most subtle person in the world, she thought. This is her "clever" way of telling me I shouldn't be rushing into this marriage.

"Mom—look at this table! It's beautiful! Why did you go to all this trouble?" Sara exclaimed, changing the subject. She could be "subtle" too.

"Laurie and Frank helped," Mrs. Morgan replied. But her eyes still burned meaningfully into Sara's.

"That was wonderful!" Liam exclaimed, stepping into the living room and pulling up a stiff-backed chair beside Mrs. Morgan's armchair. Sara dropped down on the nearest end of the couch. "Best meal I've had in years!"

"Liam, flattery will get you everywhere!" Sara's mother declared, patting his hand familiarly. She chuckled.

"I'm not a flatterer," Liam protested. "Ask Sara."

Sara rolled her eyes. "You can't believe a word he says, Mom. He tells folktales, remember."

"I enjoyed that story you told at dinner," Mrs. Morgan said to him. "I'm going to go to the library on Monday and take out all your books, Liam."

He thanked her. He leaned toward her, talking in a low near-whisper. Charming her.

Sara struggled to hear what they were saying. "Sara was always the quiet one," Mrs. Morgan murmured. "She was my baby, but she always seemed so grown-up."

Behind the words, Sara heard the rush of water in the kitchen sink. Laurie and Frank were doing the dishes. Sara had volunteered to help, but they insisted she go talk to her mother.

She yawned, feeling satisfied, happy. "Mom, it's so hot in this house, it's putting me right to sleep."

"I wish Gary and Rich were here," Mrs. Morgan sighed. "I haven't talked to either of your brothers in weeks. I hope they'll be able to come to your wedding."

"I'm glad Frank and Laurie are coming," Sara replied. "I know they usually go to her mother's for Thanksgiving."

"It's going to be a beautiful wedding," Liam said softly, leaning close to Mrs. Morgan. "We're having the ceremony outdoors. At the edge of the woods, behind the dean's house."

Sara's mother reacted with surprise. "Outdoors? At the end of November? Won't we freeze?"

"It'll be a short ceremony," Sara promised. "I told Liam he's crazy, but he insisted . . ."

Liam started to say something. But he stopped when a dark form darted silently from behind the couch—and leapt onto his lap.

"Oh—!" A sharp cry escaped Liam's throat.

Sara watched Liam jerk back stiffly against the chair. And stare down in startled amazement at the large black cat on his knees.

"Flint—I wondered where you've been hiding!" Mrs. Morgan exclaimed. "You crazy cat. Why are you picking on Liam?"

Liam's dark eyes bulged. He appeared to be having a staring contest with the yellow-eyed cat.

"Just give him a good shove," Sara's mother instructed Liam. "Flint doesn't know how heavy he is. Just push him right off."

Liam didn't move. Didn't blink.

The big black cat tilted its head and continued to stare. It raked a claw lightly over the knee of Liam's trousers.

Liam stared down at it. Arms lowered stiffly, helplessly to the floor.

Sara saw the cat's eyes reflected in Liam's dark eyes. She caught the terror on Liam's face. Saw his chin quiver.

"Just shove that fat cat off, Liam," Mrs. Morgan insisted. "Liam? Liam? What's wrong?"

"Uh . . . Mom . . . It's nothing, really," Sara explained softly. "Liam . . . is a little superstitious."

29

Tugging down her flannel nightshirt, Sara met Liam in the dimly lit upstairs hallway. She stifled a laugh. His baggy, striped pajamas looked to be out of a 1940s movie.

He gestured toward the bathroom with his toothbrush. "You want to go in first?"

"No need to whisper, darling." Sara kissed his cheek. Then she slid her mouth along the side of his face, until she found his lips.

The floorboards squeaked beneath their bare feet. Sara peered down the stairs. The house was dark. Her mother had gone to her downstairs bedroom a few minutes after Frank and Laurie left for their home a few blocks away.

Sara pressed her lips against Liam's ear. "You can come to my room. You don't have to sleep in that little closet."

Liam shook his head. "No, I don't think so," he whispered. He hugged her tightly, pressed his face against hers. His cheek felt burning hot.

"Mom won't hear us," Sara whispered. "Really, Liam. We're not teenagers. We don't have to sneak around. She knows we sleep together."

"I . . . I'd feel uncomfortable," he confessed. He offered a helpless grin.

She laughed. Caressed his face tenderly with both hands. "You're so quaint and silly sometimes."

"That's what you love about me."

She kissed his upper lip. "Mmmmmm. One of the things." Another long kiss.

"Sorry about Mom's cat."

"It—it startled me."

"Startled you? You totally freaked." Another kiss. Her hands pulling his hot face down to her. "If I hadn't picked it up off your lap, what would you have done?"

He kissed her eyelids. "It just surprised me, that's all. It appeared out of nowhere. I didn't even know your mother had a cat."

"A black cat," she teased. "You don't like black cats, do you."

He pulled away from her, his features suddenly rigid. "Good night, Sara. Sweet dreams." He turned and started toward his room, floorboards squeaking beneath each step.

She trotted after him, grabbing his pajama shoulder. "You're really not coming to my room? I'm sorry, Liam. I didn't mean to make fun of you. Of your superstitions. It's just that . . . well . . . you have to admit the black cat thing is kind of silly."

"See you in the morning," he whispered. He gave her forehead a peck and disappeared into his room, closing the door softly behind him.

"What did I do?" Sara whispered in after him, bringing her face close to the door. "Really. What did I do? What is the big deal here?"

When he didn't reply after nearly a minute, she turned and stomped off to the bathroom.

Sara vowed she would not allow herself to get sentimental about sleeping in her old bedroom. She turned off the lights so she wouldn't have to see her old posters, her high school photos, all the things her mother had saved up here in the holy Sara Shrine.

I know I'm supposed to have all these warm, fuzzy thoughts about sleeping in this room—this room of my childhood—for the last time as a single woman, Sara thought.

But I'm just too tired. And upset about Liam. Liam and his dumb superstitions. And I don't want to get all weepy and start hugging my old panda bear and act like a five-year-old.

I do wish Daddy was here, she thought, adjusting the pillow under her head. Daddy, I miss you so much. I wish I could talk with you. I wish you could meet Liam. You'd like him, Daddy. He's not at all like you. But you'd like him just the same.

Thinking about her father, she drifted into a heavy, dreamless, childlike sleep.

She awoke to a scream—and cries of alarm.

Sat straight up in the narrow bed. Eyes wide. Heart pounding.

Heard the cries. Downstairs.

"Mom?"

Sara tossed the blankets away. Scrambled out of bed. Pulling down the nightshirt, she flew along the narrow hallway to the stairs. "Mom? Mom?"

She glimpsed Liam emerging from his room, pajamas twisted, hair sleep-tousled, rubbing his eyes. Then she plunged down the stairs, following her mother's cries to the kitchen.

Gray morning sunlight washed in through the kitchen window. Sara saw the dark puddle on the floor. Then the soft heap at her feet. A black yarn ball beside it.

Her eyes still sleep-clogged, Sara thought at first that her mother had dropped a black sweater.

But then she saw the four stiff legs poking out from the crumpled pile.

And realized that the black yarn ball was the cat's head.

"F-Flint," her mother stammered, pointing down at the black pile of fur. She kept blinking her eyes, as if in disbelief, as if trying to blink the gruesome scene away.

"F-Flint."

Sara's knees suddenly gave way. She grabbed the Formica countertop to hold herself up.

The cat's head had been cleanly ripped off. The furry black body soaked in a puddle of its own blood, a tangle of red veins sprawling from the open throat.

"F-Flint."

"What is happening?" Liam burst into the kitchen, bare feet slapping the linoleum as he hurried up beside Sara.

Sara grabbed his arm. "It's Mom's cat. He—"

"Someone killed Flint," Mrs. Morgan uttered, staring down at the round head.

Liam let out a startled moan. He moved quickly across the room and squatted down beside the corpse. He studied the body, then his eyes trailed over the blood puddle to the head.

"An animal," he muttered. He pulled himself up, shaking his head. "Raccoon, maybe. Or a big dog." He pointed. "Look. The back door is wide open."

Mrs. Morgan gasped, raising her hands to the sides of her face. "The door?"

All three of them stared at the open door.

Sara's mother turned to Liam. "But do you really think some animal came in the back door, killed Flint, then went back out the door?"

Liam nodded, his expression solemn. "What *else* could it have been?"

30

Liam stepped into the mirrored hallway to adjust his black bow tie. He heard laughter in the front room, the rustle of coats, the click of high heels on the wood floor.

Leaning toward the mirror, his fingers fumbling with the tie, he glimpsed Margaret's reflection. Dressed in a cream-colored skirt and white, high-collared lace blouse beneath an open cream-colored jacket, she stood tensely in the hall doorway, one hand in the jacket pocket, then down at her side, then adjusting the yellow and white corsage pinned to her jacket lapel.

Margaret, you're as nervous as the groom, Liam thought, a smile cracking his face for a second, more like a tic. I feel perfectly calm. More calm now that the wedding is about to begin.

He heard new voices in the living room. The front door slammed. Shouted greetings. Voices he didn't recognize.

He had wanted to keep the wedding small. Four or five people at most. Just enough to make it legal. Just enough to make it romantic for Sara.

But Sara had insisted on a real wedding. She had to invite her family, her mother, her brothers and cousins, her high school and college friends.

It had been Milton's idea to hold it at his house. And Sara leapt at the opportunity. "What a beautiful setting! What a beautiful place to begin our life together! So romantic!"

Romantic.

Liam patted the pocket of the tuxedo jacket, feeling for the hairpin he planned to give Sara. The minister from the campus chapel had agreed to give the standard service. That was fine with Sara. But Liam wanted to add something special.

He thought about their phone conversation the night before. Sara had sounded so nervous, so schoolgirlish. Surrounded by her family, she was the baby once again.

He had phoned on the pretext of making sure she was calm and in good spirits. But his true purpose was to make sure that she had arranged for items old, new, borrowed, and blue. And to make sure that she would arrive at Milton's house before he did, so that he would not see her or walk with her before the wedding.

No slip-ups, Liam told himself. No slip-ups. A solemn promise.

But then Mary Beth had had car trouble. She arrived late. Had pulled up to Milton's house—with Sara beside her—a few seconds after Liam and Margaret. Some friend she was!

Liam had cursed silently and averted his eyes—in time?— while Mary Beth shouted her apologies, her breath sending up smoke signals against the dazzling blue afternoon sky. Liam had turned away as Mary Beth hustled Sara and her bridal clothes into the house.

No slip-ups.

Liam glimpsed Margaret in the mirror once again, still by herself, fixing her smile.

Don't worry, Margaret, we're almost there, he thought. It's going to be okay. If I can just manage to knot this tie.

A hard slap on the shoulder destroyed Liam's efforts. "I've been looking for you, Liam," Milton boomed, grinning like a proud father. "How's the groom?"

"Not bad." Liam smiled back at him. Milton looked Dickensian in his shiny black tails. Liam wanted to call him "Squire."

"Let me help you with that."

Before Liam could protest, Milton's fat fingers were tangled in the bow tie. "Milton, please—"

"It's cold out there," Milton reported, oblivious to Liam's discomfort. "It isn't too late to bring the ceremony indoors, my friend."

"It's cold but beautiful," Liam insisted. "A clear blue sky. Sunlight sparkling off the snowy trees. Much more romantic."

"Okay, okay." Milton gave the tie a final tug, edged back to admire his work. "Perfect. You're a lucky man, Liam. I envy you. I really do."

I *know* you do, Liam thought without humor. "It was so nice of you to offer your house," he said. "The most beautiful setting I can imagine." And then he added, "Sara is eternally grateful too," which made Milton's smile spread.

He brushed a speck off Liam's tuxedo lapel. "You have no family here today?"

"No. No family," Liam replied softly. "My mother died when I was twelve. Before Margaret and I came to America."

"And your father—?"

"I haven't spoken to him in years. Margaret and I—we sort of ran away from him. We—we had to escape. We ran off to America and haven't heard from Dad since."

"I'm . . . sorry," Milton offered somberly. He glanced at his watch. "I'd better usher everyone outside. The string trio arrived from the Music Department. They're already back by the woods. Don't want them to freeze their cellos off!" He lumbered away.

Liam remained in the quiet safety of the mirrored hall. He could hear Milton rounding everyone up, herding them out. Voices chattered over the rustle of coats. Liam wondered how Sara was doing. She and Mary Beth were headquartered in Milton's bedroom, preparing for Sara's entrance.

She'll be a beautiful bride, Liam thought wistfully.

He gave the bow tie a final inspection. Nearly straight. Then he uttered a low gasp as he glimpsed his eyes in the mirror.

Blue.

His eyes were blue. Not brown.

"No—please!" he begged aloud. "Please!"

He blinked once. Twice. Several times rapidly.

Still blue.

"No—not today! Please!" he begged.

His words were cut off by the fat purple tongue that flung itself from his open mouth.

The tongue uncoiled, purple as a jellyfish, forked at the end. Liam staggered back as it flicked at the mirrored wall, at least three feet long now, fat as a salami, rutted and splotched, it spewed from his open mouth. Battered the mirror wetly.

No! Please—not today! Not now!

He struggled to breathe.

Not now! Not now!

The tongue waved and curled like an octopus tentacle.

Get back! Get back—please!

Footsteps. He turned to see Milton crossing the living room, returning for him.

The heavy purple tongue slid back rapidly, gagging Liam as it retracted. As he gaped in horror, his eyes darkened to brown.

"Liam!" Milton exclaimed. "What are you doing in the hallway? Are you okay?"

Liam shrugged. He forced a smile. "Just wedding day jitters, I guess."

PART FIVE

31

"I can't believe I finally found a good man!" Sara gushed. "No. Erase that. A *perfect* man!" She twirled around gaily, letting the lacy veil trail behind her, looking like a happy bride.

"Sara—stand still!" Mary Beth scolded. "I had the veil perfect. Now you've fucked it up."

Sara giggled, an uncharacteristic sound. "Don't say 'fuck' on my wedding day."

Mary Beth's mouth dropped open. "Huh? Why not?"

"It's bad luck." Sara's eyes flashed under the filmy white veil.

Mary Beth groaned. "Now you're starting to sound like Liam."

Sara moved to the window. "I want everything to be perfect. I've had so much bad luck with men. But now I've found Liam. He's so good and so kind and so . . . so *brilliant*. And he cares about me so much. This time, I know it's right. I'm going to make sure it's right. I'm going to make sure that everything is perfect!"

Mary Beth applauded. "Now that you've made your wedding toast, how about having the wedding?"

"Oh my goodness!" Sara's hands flew up to her face as she stared out the window. "Everyone is outside already. Waiting."

"Freezing their butts off," Mary Beth added. She chased after Sara. "Wait up! They won't start without you! Really!"

It had snowed the day before, less than an inch but enough to spread a shiny white carpet on the ground and leave the trees sparkling as if covered by diamonds.

Sara walked into the sunlight, dazzled by the brightness, white on white and all gleaming, gleaming.

It was all so beautiful, so thrillingly beautiful, it brought a tear to her eye. And when she saw Liam waiting for her, so dark and handsome in his tuxedo, the bow tie slightly crooked, when she saw his hair flutter in the wind, when she saw him smile and reach out a hand to her, she wanted to burst out crying, and cry and cry for happiness, for the sheer sparkling beauty of it all.

The minister was a short bald, round-cheeked man who reminded her of a snowman. All he needed was a corncob pipe and two eyes of coal. He carried a Bible in one hand but didn't open it. His smile never left his face as he talked. His words were blown away by the wind.

The powdery snow swirled around Sara's ankles. The cold was thrilling. She gazed into Liam's brown eyes. They caught the sunlight and sparkled back at her.

The minister, beaming the whole while, finished his part of the ceremony and took a step back, gesturing to Liam. Had he spoken for just a minute? For ten minutes? Twenty? Sara couldn't be sure.

But now Liam had turned to her, his breath rising like white smoke. He pulled something shiny from his jacket pocket and held it toward Sara.

Sunlight? A spark of sunlight in his palm?

No. A gold pin. A delicate gold hairpin.

Liam turned to the onlookers at the edge of the woods.

Were there actually people watching them? Sara had forgotten all about them. Now she focused on them, saw her mother, her brothers, everyone huddled together, coats over their fancy clothes, smiling, blue shadows at their feet.

"Sara, I offer this to you," Liam announced loudly. He slipped the gold pin into her hand, then gently closed her fingers around it. The pin felt warm against her palm.

"The words are by Yeats. But the sentiment is mine," Liam said, smiling at her warmly. And then, taking her hand, he recited:

> "Fasten your hair with a golden pin,
> And bind up every wandering tress;
> I bade my heart build these poor rhymes;
> It worked at them, day out, day in,
> Building a sorrowful loveliness
> Out of the battles of old times.
>
> "You need but lift a pearl-pale hand,
> And bind up your long hair and sigh;
> And all men's hearts must burn and beat;
> And candle-like foam on the dim sand,
> And stars climbing the dew-dropping sky,
> Live but to light your passing feet."

Silence now. Sara felt the hush in her heart. Even the wind seemed to stop.

Gripping the gold pin, she kissed Liam's hand.

"I now pronounce you man and wife." The words seemed to ring from out of nowhere.

And then she was kissing him, kissing him, and the cheers echoed off the ice-sparkling trees.

Perfect, she thought. This is perfect.

And then she turned to see Milton trudging across the snow, blue shadows moving quickly. She saw the shotgun in Milton's hands, the long silvery barrel and then the wooden handle gripped so tightly, saw the shotgun and Milton's grim expression, saw him raise the shotgun to his shoulder.

No time to scream. Or duck. Or hide.

No time.

32

A shrill cry of birds as the shotgun fired. The crack of the explosion echoed through the trees, faded behind the flapping of wings.

No one moved.

Milton fired again. Again.

Sara felt her knees buckle. Her breath choked in her throat. So perfect. It had all been so perfect. And now . . .

Liam squeezed her hand. "Don't be afraid," he whispered.

"Huh?"

Another crackling shot into the air. The flapping birds distant now.

"It's an old superstition," Liam said, leaning close, his breath hot on the side of her face. "The gunshots will chase away evil spirits."

Sara let out a shaky breath. "It mainly chased away the birds."

"Flapping crows," Liam murmured. "In the old days in Edinburgh, young men would hide behind the hedges. When the bride and groom approached, they all fired their muskets into the air. It was called a *feu de joie*."

"Liam—you scared me to death! I nearly jumped out of my skin. Why didn't you warn me?" Sara scolded, shoving him.

"Uh oh." Liam grinned. "Our first fight!"

* * *

As Sara kissed him, she felt Liam's tongue slide into her mouth. Her tongue met his briefly, just a tap. She ended the kiss abruptly, pulling her head back. "Liam—everyone is watching us!"

He laughed. His brown eyes sparkled. "I married such a shy girl!" His hands slid around her waist.

"I'm not shy," she protested playfully. "I'm from Indiana, remember? People from the Midwest don't believe in public displays."

He hugged her close, bringing his lips to her ear. "How do you feel about *private* displays?"

She turned and kissed him again. Missed his lips but grazed his cheek. This is the happiest day of my life, she told herself for the hundredth time. Beneath the satiny white wedding dress, her heart fluttered in her chest. She felt so light, as if she could lift herself off the floor and float across Milton's noisy, crowded living room. She wondered if she would ever come down.

Mary Beth interrupted, spinning her around, raising a small flash camera. "Just a couple more, Sara. You look so beautiful."

Sara opened her mouth as the flash went off. "Mary Beth— you've already taken five rolls!"

Another flash. Sara blinked, momentarily blinded. The people around her were moving through bright yellow globes.

She heard Liam behind her, telling someone about their honeymoon plans. "We're going up to The Pines. I'm told there's a wonderful old hotel up there. Just for a couple of days. No. We can't afford any more time. Classes start again on Monday."

Only a couple of days, Sara thought. But they'll be wonderful. Just the two of us. No one else we know. No one else to talk to. Paradise.

Her eyes focused slowly. Margaret appeared from out of nowhere and hugged her. She smelled of gardenias, the perfume fragrance sharp and pungent, as if she had dabbed too much on, as if she had bathed in it. Her cheek felt hot against Sara's. "I'm so happy for you both. I've never seen Liam so happy."

Another hug. And then Sara's family surrounded her, hugging her, squeezing her hands, touching her dress, raising their wineglasses, grinning and talking, all talking at once.

So wonderful to be the center of the universe. And so unusual.

She didn't see Milton. Didn't realize he had cornered her until it was too late. His eyes swimming, red-faced and smelling of liquor stronger than wine, he backed her into the entry to the mirrored hallway.

"Beautiful bride," he said, beaming at her.

"Thank you, Milton." She smiled up at him. "It was so nice of you—"

His big hand pawed her shoulder. "If he gives you any trouble, you come to me."

She laughed. Milton was joking—right?

"No. I mean it. If you get tired of him. I mean, if it doesn't work out. I mean . . . well, I don't know what I mean." He shut his eyes for a long moment. When he opened them, he seemed to focus more clearly. His hand massaged her shoulder. "You still have the key—right?"

"Milton—" She looked past his broad body, searching for Liam. Her mother was feeding Liam wedding cake from her plate.

A leering smile crossed Milton's face. "Did I forget to kiss the bride?" And then his lips were pushing against hers, wet, spongy lips, the kiss too hard, too eager.

"I guess it's time for Sara and me to get on our horse." Liam to the rescue.

Milton backed away unsteadily. His leering grin returned, aimed at Liam now. Sara could still feel the taste of his lips on hers. Poor, lonely man. Did he really care about her?

She couldn't dislike anyone today. She couldn't disapprove of anyone, not on this day, the happiest day, the dreamiest day, the dream day, the day she walked across the sparkling, bejeweled snow to become Liam's bride.

"We had better leave now if we're going to get up to The Pines by nightfall," Liam said, taking her hand. He turned to Milton. "I can't thank you enough."

"A lucky man," Milton muttered. He said something else, but Sara couldn't hear him over the laughing voices behind her.

Liam and Milton shook hands. Liam started to tug her down the mirrored hall to where the coats were kept. "Oh! My mom! My brothers!" Sara pulled away from him. "I have to say good-bye. They came so far."

More hugs and congratulations. Promises to do a better job of keeping in touch. Good-byes to others. Another hug from Margaret. Sara searched for Mary Beth but couldn't find her.

Liam appeared with her coat. "But I should change out of this dress!" she cried. "I'll freeze!"

"I'll put the heat in the car way up," he promised. "Change at the hotel. Let's sneak out—okay? I can't smile at another person. My face is frozen in place. I can't be charming for another moment. If one other person congratulates me and tells me how lucky I am, I swear I'll bite him!"

Sara laughed as he helped her slide into her coat. "Liam—*you*—not charming? Get serious."

His arm lightly on her shoulder, he guided her through the hallway toward the front. But Milton appeared at the other end, blocking their escape. Sara leaned back against Liam. Milton moved toward them unsteadily, trailing one hand against the mirrored wall.

"Ssshhh. Sneak out through this door," he instructed in a hoarse whisper. "This way." He pushed past them and, grinning, led them to a narrow side door. A hiccup erupted from his throat. He pulled open the door and squeezed against the wall to make room. "Have a nice honeymoon, kids." Another hiccup.

Liam patted Milton on the shoulder as he stepped past him, out into the yard at the side of the house. Sara took a deep breath, feeling the fresh air against her hot cheeks, luxuriating in the coldness, the sweetness of it. "Liam—look—it started to snow. How lovely!"

She heard the door close behind them. Grabbing Liam's arm with both hands, she took a step, then another, heading toward the front of the house and the street where Liam's green Volvo was parked.

Snowflakes fell lightly on her forehead and hair. She stuck out her tongue, hoping to catch one on it.

They were nearly to the front when she felt Liam's arm stiffen. His entire body tensed. He stopped so abruptly, she nearly tripped. "Liam—?"

His eyes stared straight ahead, not focusing. He stood frozen in place, his mouth open.

"Liam—?"

"Oh no." He uttered a low moan. "No. Oh no."

"Liam—what's wrong?" Sara demanded, squeezing his arm. "Liam— answer me. What *is* it?"

33

"The door," Liam finally choked out.

Sara held on to his arm, stared up at him, at his face, wrenched with fear.

"The door. We went out the side door." He swallowed hard.

Sara's mind raced. What was wrong with going out the side door? What could possibly be wrong?

"The side door," Liam repeated. He turned to her, squinted as if suddenly remembering she was still there. "Don't you understand? You have to leave by the same door you came in. You can't leave through a different door."

"But, Liam—we're already out. So what difference does it make?"

"All the difference, Sara. All the difference." Sadness in his voice. "We came in the front door. We have to leave by the front door."

"Oh, Liam—sometimes these superstitions of yours are totally weird!" she cried, holding on to him, trying to keep it light, wondering how he could be so upset, so . . . frightened. "Am I going to have to worry about what door I come in and out of every day when we're living together?"

He didn't seem to hear her. His eyes still wild, his features set in a hard frown, he grabbed her hand and, leaning into the falling snow, tugged her back toward the house. "We'll go out again," he murmured, talking to himself now. "It'll be okay. We'll go in the front door and come out again. It'll be perfectly okay."

"Ohhhh. Ohhhh."

Liam felt so light on top of her. She wrapped her arms around his neck and pressed his hot face against her breast.

"Ohhhh. Ohhhh."

Such a wonderful lover. She raised her legs, wrapped them around his back, tried to pull him closer, deeper. She wanted to wrap him up, wrap him inside her. She wanted him closer. Closer.

Harder now. Holding on to him, clinging to him, pulling him down, she rocked with him. His eyes were shut. His lips moved in a whisper. A language she couldn't understand.

"Ohhhhhh."

The candles darted and flicked their light from side to side as if rocking with them. Exactly sixteen white candles. Liam had unpacked them from his bag, had spread them carefully around their hotel room, a drafty room, dark and faded but comfortable-looking with its pine green wallpaper, heavy, darkwood furniture, calendarlike painting of the snowy Alps above the headboard.

"Why sixteen?" she had asked, still giddy, still excited on her wedding day, the ecstatic bride, not the least bit fatigued from the long drive through the falling snow to the old hotel. She watched his face, its concentrated expression, the dark eyebrows furrowed over the intense brown eyes. So serious. "Why not a hundred candles? Why not a thousand?"

He didn't smile. "Sixteen is a number of power, Sara. Sixteen is the fourth power."

She followed him to the dresser where he was arranging the silver candlesticks. "The fourth power? Am I your fourth wife?"

Come on, Liam. Joke with me. Don't look so serious.

But his features remained set in concentration. He ignored

her question. "Humans have sixteen teeth in each jaw. Did you think that was an accident?"

"Well . . ."

"Carpenters leave sixteen inches between the studs in the walls of a house."

She slid her hand down the front of his shirt. "You can be *my* stud tonight."

Not exactly a Sara joke. Having said it, she felt her cheeks grow hot. But it got a reaction from him. He pressed the final candle into its holder and raised his eyes to her. "We must make love until the candles burn down."

She kissed his cheek and chuckled. "I'm game if you are."

He still didn't smile. His arms slid around her waist. He pulled her to him and kissed her with startling urgency.

Then he whispered, his warm breath tingling her ear. "I want a child, Sara. Right away. I want us to have a child. A beautiful child. Do you want one too?" He pressed his cheek against hers, until her skin burned against his.

His words didn't surprise her. She had been expecting them, thinking about them, waiting for him to say them, thinking about a child for weeks, his child. Their child.

"Liam, I want what you want."

A cry of joy escaped his lips. He kissed her again, kissed her with such feeling.

It took him several minutes to light the candles. He refused to let Sara help. She watched him murmur to himself as he held the match to each wick. Was he chanting?

They made love the first time before they were completely undressed. Uttering low cries, they tore at each other, slamming, thrusting breathlessly with an intensity that surprised Sara. They had made love many times, Sara realized, but it had never been this *physical*.

It ended quickly. The sixteen candle witnesses had barely begun to shrink.

Still inside her, Liam lowered himself over her, pressed his lips against her ear. "I am so happy now, Sara."

The whispered words sent a shiver down her body.

When she started to reply, he covered her mouth with frantic kisses.

Moments later, they made love again. Slowly now, with a statelier passion. Shadows played over the high ceiling as the candle flames danced along with them. Sara clung to Liam, moving with him, listening to the low hum and hiss of his musical, murmured words.

"Liam—is that Gaelic?" she whispered.

He continued his soft chant, moving above her, inside her, his eyes shut, his lips curled in a smile.

"Is it Gaelic? It's so beautiful. What are you chanting, honey?"

He didn't seem to hear her.

34

Garrett glanced up from his Jumble puzzle as the squad room door opened.

LOCNORT. That should be an easy one. But it was hard to concentrate. His mind kept wandering back to the morning, to his argument with Angel.

Argument? No. Tirade? Yes.

And of course Angel was right. That always made Garrett even angrier. He hadn't been spending much time with Martin, true. He hadn't spent much time with Angel, either.

But give me a break, he thought. How about cutting me a little slack, seeing as how I've got three murders waiting to be solved? It's not like I've been out partying or enjoying myself or sleeping at night or been able to eat a single meal or think straight, or just sit and try to think clearly, or have one quiet moment, or—or . . .

Easy, man.

You'll get it all straightened out. You'll get everything in order.

LOCNORT.

Locnort. It sounded like some kind of lunchmeat.

That's it, Garrett. Stay cool. Keep control.

Control.

That's the word!

He picked up the pencil and filled the letters into the little circles as Ethan entered, his cap pulled down low over his bald head, a solemn expression on his face as he led in a young man in a bright yellow sweater.

The young man looks like a pencil, Garrett thought, tapping his fingers tensely on the desk as he studied him. The yellow sweater. Slender, reedlike body. Short brown flattop on top of a narrow head.

The troubled eyes, blinking, darting around the room, didn't fit the image. The kid was eighteen or nineteen, Garrett guessed. College student, most likely. He checked the hands. Clean, uncallussed. Yeah. College student. Bad complexion. Must have had acne in high school. A tiny silver stud gleamed in the kid's right ear.

The kid cleared his throat nervously. Cleared it again.

Garrett pushed the newspaper puzzle aside, and leaned over the desk.

Oh no, he thought, watching the young man hesitate before following Ethan up to the desk. No. Please. Not another confession. Not another phony confession.

There had been three "guilty" parties so far, one for each murder, each more pitiful, more laughable than the last.

What made these idiots confess? Was it some kind of a thrill? Some desperate need for attention? A grab for some sick idea of glory?

Leave that to the shrinks, Garrett had decided. Sickos. He just wanted them *out* of his police station. Out of his face.

"Got something here, Garrett," Ethan mumbled. He had taken to talking out of the side of his mouth, as if he had a wad of tobacco tucked in his jaw. Garrett decided he was trying to sound tough, hard, like the cops he watched incessantly on TV. But it just made him hard to understand.

Garrett kept his eyes on the young man, studied his pasty, pocked face. "How can I help you, son?"

The kid cleared his throat again.

Garrett gestured to the straight-backed wooden chair beside

his desk. The kid sank into the chair, twisted his hands in his lap.

"Says he saw something," Ethan offered. "Night of the last murder."

An eyewitness?

Garrett felt all of his muscles tense. He pulled himself up straight. "What's your name?"

"Craig Kline."

"Do you go to the college?"

He nodded. Shoved his hands into his jeans pockets. "I'm a junior."

"Did you see the murder, son?"

"No!" He gasped the word, a shrill cry of protest.

Garrett continued patiently, keeping his voice low and calm, studying the kid's eyes, searching for the answer to one question: True or False?

Everyone who came into his office was a True or False question. It was the question that had to be answered first.

"Well, what did you see?"

"I was on campus. Wednesday night. Crossing The Circle. I'd been doing some research in the library." This part had obviously been rehearsed. He seemed to be reciting it.

But that didn't mean it wasn't true.

"It was a dark night, kind of foggy. I remember because the lights on The Circle seemed dim, kind of shimmery."

"Very poetic," Garrett commented dryly. "You an English major or something?"

Kline blushed. "Sorry."

"Just tell Detective Montgomery what you saw," Ethan urged. He had grabbed the empty coat rack beside the other desk and was leaning against it.

Kline rubbed his nose. "Well, first I heard a scream."

"A girl's scream?" Garrett asked.

Kline nodded. "Yes. It was loud. Very shrill. But it didn't last long. It sort of stopped. Like it was cut off."

"Did you see the girl?" Garrett demanded.

"No. I looked for her. I mean, when I heard the scream, I tried to see who it was, where it was coming from. But it was too dark. I didn't see anyone."

Did he really come in here to tell me he didn't see anything? The question flashed through Garrett's mind.

Patience.

"Then what happened, Mr. Kline?"

"Then I saw a man in a costume. He was running really fast, in front of the row of evergreen bushes. By Weaver Hall."

Garrett felt his heart begin to race. He narrowed his eyes at the young man. "Costume? What kind of costume?"

"A monster costume," Kline replied. "He was wearing some kind of monster costume. He ran along the bushes, then cut through and disappeared."

"Whoa." Ethan let out a whistle. Of surprise? Of disbelief? "Weird, huh?"

Garrett ignored him. He kept his eyes locked on Craig Kline. "Can you describe the monster costume?"

Kline swallowed, making dry-mouth sounds. "Well, I couldn't see it too well. The mask had glowing eyes, I remember. Glowing red eyes. And it had long, pointed teeth."

"And what about the rest of the costume?"

"It seemed to be hairy. You know. Furry. Covered with dark fur, I think. It was so dark . . ." The kid's voice trailed off. He lowered his eyes.

"A guy in a monster suit," Ethan muttered, shaking his head.

Garrett shut his eyes, thinking hard. Was there a costume store in town? Any novelty store near the campus that sold costumes?

He couldn't think of any.

"Ethan, can you think of any costume store? A party store, maybe? A place where they sell masks?"

Ethan cupped his tiny chin in one hand. "Well, the K mart sells costumes at Halloween time. And some of the drugstores. That's about it, Chief."

Garrett grunted. "Check them out. And check out that guy on Tenth Street who rents costumes for the school plays."

He turned back to Kline. "That murder happened weeks ago. Why'd you wait so long to come in here?"

Kline cleared his throat. His pale blue eyes widened. "I was scared, I guess."

"Scared?"

"Scared you wouldn't believe me. I mean, after I saw about the murder on TV, I—well, I wasn't sure I believed it, either."

"So why'd you come in tonight?" Garrett demanded, leaning close, not letting the kid off the hook, testing, testing him.

"I couldn't stop thinking about it. I knew it was the right thing to do. I mean, I saw you on TV, on the news, asking anyone with any information to come forward. So . . ."

That was pitiful, Garrett realized. Anytime you see cops on TV pleading for help, it's pitiful.

But what else could he do?

Could he stand there with the camera nearly poking him in the eye and a dozen microphones jabbed in his face and say, "Look, folks, we don't have a clue. We've got a bunch of fingerprints that look like they were painted by Salvador Dali. And that's it. That's our one clue, after three ugly murders."

No way he could say that.

So he pleaded for help instead. And two days after Thanksgiving this kid comes in with a story about a man in a monster costume.

He leaned back in his chair with a sigh. "Thanks for coming in, Mr. Kline." He picked up the pencil, pointed it at Ethan. "Take him in the other room and write down a complete statement, okay?"

Ethan nodded, his big Adam's apple riding up and down.

Kline stood up quickly, straightening the cuffs of the yellow sweater. He started to follow Ethan out of the room, but turned back at the door. "Do you believe me?" he asked.

Garrett nodded grimly, twirling the pencil. "Yeah. Sure. I believe you."

After these murders, why wouldn't I believe in monsters?

35

Sara lifted an iceberg lettuce from the market shelf and squeezed it. I wish this were your head, Liam.

No. No, I don't. What am I saying?

I'm not still angry.

She tossed the lettuce into the shopping basket.

So we had a stupid fight this morning. Not even a fight. A few cross words.

Big deal.

She dropped two yellow peppers into the basket and moved down the aisle toward the cucumbers.

All newlyweds have fights. It's part of getting to know one another.

Sara nibbled her bottom lip. Married two weeks, and his superstitions are starting to drive me nuts.

No. Don't say that, she scolded herself.

But the incident this morning kept troubling at her mind. So *what* if she climbed out on the left side of the bed? So *what* if she forgot to say "Bless you" when Margaret sneezed?

Shouldn't Liam and I be fighting about something more interesting?

Doesn't he have better things to think about than which side of the bed I climb out?

Well, she had asked him those very questions this morning.

And they only made him sputter and start to fume. Okay, he was more than a little superstitious. He believed all that stuff for some reason. Fine. But there is a limit.

I mean, don't give *me* a hard time because I think it's all a load of crap, Liam.

And Margaret. Sister Margaret, standing there watching them argue with that doleful expression on her face. So silent, trying to blend in with the wallpaper.

Margaret was considerate. And kind. And helpful. She tried really hard not to be in the way. She spent most of her time at her little antique shop beside the bakery. And when she wasn't there, she stayed upstairs in her own apartment, surfacing only at meal times or when Liam invited her to join them.

Very considerate. But Sara felt Margaret's eyes on her, sensed her presence in the house, a third figure, another person when it should be just the two of them, having their newlywed arguments, their trivial fights, just the two of them. Eager to make up after the sharp, angry words.

The angry words repeated in her mind all through her seminar and as she tried to work on her research paper at the library. She rehearsed all the things she'd say to him later.

Then decided to let it drop. It was no big deal, after all.

Then she felt guilty for making it into a big thing in her mind. Felt guilty for thinking such harsh thoughts about him. Liam. Her husband. Her wonderful husband.

She decided to make dinner for him.

They'd been so busy with classes starting up the moment they returned from their two-day honeymoon. It had been pizza and Chinese food every night, or rushing out to grab a bite at one of the campus dives.

It seemed they hadn't had an evening—or a moment—to themselves. And it wasn't about to end. The student production of *Macbeth* tonight. Milton's dinner party to celebrate their marriage tomorrow night.

Hadn't Milton done enough by donating his beautiful house for the wedding? He didn't have to give them a dinner as well.

But he had insisted, had appeared hurt by her reluctance. "There was no time to give you a prewedding dinner," he announced in his gruff voice, his face beaming red. "So I'm giving the prewedding dinner *after* the wedding."

He really was a generous man, Sara decided.

She reached for a bottle of salad dressing, then lowered her hand. No. I'll make my own vinaigrette. I'm making everything from scratch tonight. My first homemade dinner.

Not because I feel guilty about this morning, Liam. But because I want to show you that I'm not just a college girl. I'm a real wife.

Shrimp scampi. Wild rice with spinach. A nice salad.

She had picked up the shrimp at the seafood store on Dale. Now she moved down the aisle of the little market down the block, picking up the remaining salad ingredients she needed.

Dropping the basket on the checkout counter, she glanced at her watch. Nearly five-thirty. There should be plenty of time to get dinner going and get changed for the play before Liam gets home.

Sara paid and, hoisting the bulging brown bag in her arms, stepped out of the market humming to herself. Humming a happy melody. Because she felt happy.

I'm making dinner for my husband.

Husband. Such a foreign-sounding word. Foreign and old-fashioned.

A short walk home along High Street. A cold December wind blowing down from the north, shaking the bare trees along the front of the campus. Sara shifted the grocery bag to her other arm.

I'll get the shrimp going first. Then I'll prepare the salad.

I can't wait to see Liam's face. "Sara—you can cook? You made dinner for *me?*"

No. Even Liam didn't sound that corny.

Sara had trouble imagining what he would say. Liam was one of the more unpredictable men she had ever met.

Unpredictable and brilliant, she decided.

He'll be happy with my little surprise. That I *can* predict!

As she turned the corner, their house came into view. A gust of wind nearly blew the grocery bag from her hands. Two girls Sara recognized from the campus passed by, wool mufflers wrapped under their chins, leaning into the cold wind, faces red, walking rapidly.

Sara climbed the steps of the low stoop to their house. Set down the grocery bag and searched her bag for the key. She rubbed her nose. Numb from the cold. Turned the key and stepped into the entryway, grateful for the warmth inside.

Balancing the bag against her chest, she carried it straight to the kitchen. And started to set it down on the counter—when she saw Margaret.

Margaret, at the stove. Stirring a steaming pot.

Margaret turned. Smiled. "Sara—hi!" Her smile faded when she saw the grocery bag. "What's that?"

"Groceries," Sara replied, feeling her chest tighten, the cold from outside lingering, hovering, swirling around her. "I thought—"

"I got home early," Margaret said. "So I made a nice veal stew for dinner. Liam's favorite."

"But—" Sara's voice caught in her throat.

Margaret gazed at the grocery bag again. Realized.

"Oh, Sara—I'm so sorry. You planned to make dinner? I didn't know."

She dropped the long metal spoon against the side of the pot. Hurried over to Sara, her face taut in apology. Wrapped Sara in a hug. "I'm so sorry. Really, dear. I'm so sorry. You should have told me."

Sara feeling ten years old. Sara starting to feel silly.

Margaret hugging her like an unhappy child.

No. That's unfair, Sara decided. Margaret is so sweet, so kind. It's not Margaret's fault. Margaret didn't do anything wrong.

And now I've made Margaret feel terrible.

"No problem," Sara said, forcing a smile, backing out of

Margaret's hug. "I'll put the shrimp in the fridge. We can have it Sunday."

Sara took a deep breath. "Mmmmmm, that stew smells wonderful, Margaret. Perfect for such a cold night."

Footsteps approaching rapidly. Sara turned to the door as Liam appeared, pulling off his overcoat. "Well. My two favorite women! Home early. What's for dinner?"

"I enjoyed it," Margaret said, following Sara onto the walk. "So wonderful to sit back and listen to Shakespeare's language." A gust of wind sent her coat flapping out like a sail. She grabbed the sides, pulled them together, and struggled to button it. "Hey—it really got cold."

Liam had stopped to talk to a student, and so they were the last to leave Ayers Hall. Through the open doors, Sara could see the auditorium lights dimming. The play had been well attended. Now audience members—student and faculty, mostly, joined by a few townspeople—were making their way in twos and threes and fours across The Circle, heading for the dorms, or restaurants, or bars, or home.

The wind cut sharply around the building. Sara pulled up the collar of her jacket. Her dark hair fluttered around her face. Liam was in the entranceway, still talking, gesturing with both hands. The student, a girl in a bulky raccoon coat that must have belonged to her grandparents, was laughing, a high, shrill laugh.

"The Lady Macbeth was wonderful—wasn't she?" Margaret moved closer to Sara, trying to step out of the wind. The bare trees across The Circle rattled and shook. "So expressive and so believable. I think that young woman has real talent."

"Yes, she does," Sara agreed, eyes on Liam. "I liked all that blood on her hands. That was a nice effect."

"A little gross," Margaret said, making a face. "Too bad that backdrop fell. It was so distracting. I felt so sorry for the poor kids who—"

"It's a jinxed play," Liam interrupted, jogging up to them, hands in the pockets of his black overcoat. "Did you know that?" He smiled at Sara, reached out a hand to straighten her jacket collar. "There's a curse on the play. Do you know the story? The actor who was supposed to play the lead in the very first production was found dead before the opening night performance. He never got to play the part. It is said that he has haunted the play ever since. Actors are very superstitious about appearing in it."

"Actors are very superstitious, period," Margaret chimed in. The lights inside the auditorium went out. The sidewalk grew darker.

"Actors who are performing in the play never mention it by name," he continued, taking Sara's arm. "They always call it 'The Scottish Play.' That's the only way they refer to it."

Liam hasn't said the name either, Sara realized.

"Is that what you were telling that student?" Margaret teased. "She certainly looked fascinated."

Liam grinned. "She thinks I'm fascinating."

Sara gave him a playful shove. "I guess *everyone* thinks you're fascinating, huh?"

He laughed. "Well? Can you deny it?"

They began to follow the path toward High Street, Liam between them, giving each of them an arm. They had gone only a few steps when a figure tottered onto the path.

Sara didn't see him at first. She was leaning past Liam to reply to something Margaret had said. Liam tugged her arm, trying to edge them past the stranger.

But the young man stepped with them, refusing to let them pass.

Sara turned—and recognized him. "Chip! What are *you* doing here?"

His blue eyes were silver in the dim light. Narrowing, they struggled to focus on her. His blond hair had been pushed straight up by the wind. His leather bomber jacket was open, revealing a stain down the front of his turtleneck. "Sara—"

He lurched toward her unsteadily, a strange, out-of-place

smile on his face, his eyes half-shut. The smile faded quickly. "Sara—"

"Chip—please!"

"Sara—look at him!" He pointed to Liam, his hand moving up and down, as if not quite in control. "He's too old for you, Sara!"

"Chip—"

She felt Liam tense at her side. He gripped her jacket sleeve. "Sara, do you *know* him?" Disapproval in Liam's voice.

"He's old enough to be your ffffather!" Chip still waving his finger in Liam's general direction.

"Go away, Chip." Sara said the words softly but firmly. "Just go away."

Chip squinted hard at Liam, trying to focus. "Your ff-father." He scowled. "Sara, I don't want trouble. I came to help you. I came to *warn* you. You don't know what you're doing. You don't—"

"Go away, Chip. You've been drinking," Sara said through gritted teeth, her voice low and hard. She could feel every muscle in her body tense. *This isn't happening. This can't be happening.*

She saw Margaret take a step back, off the path, her face pinched with fear. Or disapproval?

"Talk about robbing the c-c-cradle," Chip stammered, watery eyes still focusing on Liam. The wind fluttered his blond hair.

"Chip—I'm begging you—" Sara tried to keep her voice low and steady.

Liam let go of her sleeve and stepped forward. "She doesn't want to talk to you now." He raised a hand to the shoulder of Chip's bomber jacket.

Chip jerked away violently, so hard he threw himself off balance and nearly fell. "Keep your paws off me." Trying to regain his balance, he lurched forward.

Liam caught him, grabbing the leather jacket lapels. "Can we help you home? You need to sleep it off."

Chip uttered a hoarse cry of protest and pulled back, his eyes wild. Saliva glistened at the side of his mouth.

I've never been so embarrassed, Sara thought. How will I ever explain this to Liam?

"Liam—be careful," Margaret warned, on the grass several steps behind them, her arms crossed protectively in front of her.

"Liam, be careful," Chip mimicked. He let out a high-pitched giggle. His smile faded as he pulled himself up straight, smoothing the jacket collar with both hands, turning back to Sara.

"Chip—go away!" she insisted.

His blue eyes caught the light from the low lamppost beside the path. "I know why your professor had to leave Chicago."

Liam scowled, glanced at Sara. He took a step toward Chip, hands balled into fists at his side.

"Want to know why?" Chip taunted, sounding like a four-year-old. "Want to know why your *husband* had to leave Chhhhhhicago?"

Sara shut her eyes. She wanted to cover her ears with her hands. *This isn't happening. Please. Please—make him disappear.*

But when she opened her eyes, Chip stood there, leering at her. "Want to know the real reason?" he demanded.

Liam moved quickly. Margaret uttered a gasp of surprise. Liam grabbed Chip by the shoulders. Spun him around. Walked him away.

Chip protested loudly. Sara couldn't hear Liam's reply. To her relief, Chip didn't resist, didn't fight. He stumbled once, but Liam held him up. Liam walked him toward the street, moving him firmly, quickly.

Margaret crept up beside Sara and squeezed her hand. Margaret's hand was ice-cold. "An old boyfriend?" Margaret whispered.

Sara nodded. "He—he followed me from New York. I can't believe he's being such a creep. He knows Liam and I are married. Why is he still here?"

Liam returned with his hands shoved into his overcoat

pockets, his expression solemn. "A little real-life drama," he murmured, eyes on Sara. "Not quite up to Shakespeare."

Sara shook her head. "I'm so sorry. Really."

Liam's expression softened. "Not your fault. So that's Chip, huh? Every bit as charming as you described him."

Sara let out a long sigh. "Really . . . I'm sorry."

Liam chuckled. "I can't wait to meet the rest of your friends."

"Give Sara a break," Margaret chimed in. She shuddered, wrapped her coat around her. "That was really frightening." She flashed Liam a disapproving frown. "Mister Hero."

Liam shrugged. "Sometimes when my adrenaline gets flowing . . . "

"I'm just so sorry," Sara repeated, taking his arm. "I don't know how he found us. I don't know how he knew we were here tonight."

Liam patted her hand. "Don't worry about it. He was too drunk to do anyone any harm." He grinned at her. "Think I could use a drink myself."

They walked toward Yale Avenue. Sara's legs felt trembly. She kept picturing the pearl of saliva in the corner of Chip's mouth.

She stopped suddenly, raising her eyes to Liam's. "What was Chip talking about? Why *did* you leave Chicago?"

His smile was instantaneous. "To meet *you*, of course."

Margaret went up to her upstairs apartment. Sara settled on the couch in the living room. Liam poured out two glasses of port and, handing her one, eased down beside her, his free hand sliding around her shoulders. "Ooh, my dear. You are frozen. Drink this. It will warm you."

She took a sip. The dark red liquid felt good as it burned the back of her throat. She took another sip and leaned her head against the sleeve of Liam's sweater.

He told her about the first Shakespeare play he had ever seen, a production of *Henry V* in a small college playhouse when he was sixteen. He talked about the surprise of hearing such language for the first time, the frustration of understanding and not understanding, of wanting to know everything and digest it all—every line, every word—all at once.

Sara half-listened, nodding and smiling, letting the port warm her from the inside. Chip lingered in her mind. She couldn't shake away her embarrassment—or her curiosity.

Did Chip really know something bad about Liam? Or was he being the spiteful child once again?

Liam lowered his head to kiss her. But she pressed two fingers against his lips. "Why *did* you leave Chicago?" She had to ask it again. "Was Chip just being stupid, or . . . "

He pulled her fingers away tenderly. Smiled. "I *told* you—"

"No. Come on, Liam. Tell me. There's so much I don't know about you. What was the reason you left Chicago?" She poked him, flashed a teasing grin. "Was it some kind of juicy scandal?"

His dark eyes seemed to lose their glow. He twisted his mouth, glanced away. "I don't want to trouble you with my unhappy past."

She instantly regretted teasing him. "Unhappy past?"

Liam hesitated. He gazed at her thoughtfully, as if trying to figure out what her reaction would be if he told the story.

"Liam, if we can't confide in each other . . ." Her voice trailed off.

Liam sighed. "I had to leave Chicago. I don't know what your friend found out— if anything. I don't know why he was checking up on me."

"I'm really sorry about Chip, Liam. I—"

"There was a woman named Angela. I had to leave because of her." The words rushed out, all in one breath. His eyes locked on hers, studying her reaction.

Why is he so worried? Sara wondered. Doesn't he know that I love him? Why should I care about a woman back in Chicago?

"Liam—"

"No. Let me finish. Angela was my assistant. Actually, she was just a typist. She keyboarded the manuscripts to my last two books. One thing led to another—as they say. Angela was older than you, nearly my age. We had an affair. These words. They all sound so trite. It lasted nearly two years, I guess. It ended badly."

Sara brushed her head tenderly against his shoulder. He seemed so upset. Did he still care for this Angela? she wondered. Is that why he was acting so strange, so unlike himself?

"I broke it off," Liam continued, turning away. "I realized it wasn't going anywhere. I thought she had come to realize the same thing. But I guess I underestimated her. I mean, I underestimated the depth of her feeling. She . . . had some kind of breakdown."

"Oh, I'm sorry," Sara blurted out.

Liam shrugged. "She had to be hospitalized. I wasn't sure how to react. I mean, I felt terrible for her. And of course I was overwhelmed with guilt. But then I came to think that the breakdown was a kind of ploy, a way of holding on, of keeping me there beside her.

"To my surprise, I found myself angry at her. Angry that she would try to trick me that way. Angry that she would go that far to prove that she was a finer person than me, that she had more feelings than I had. Absurd thinking, of course. All driven by my guilt."

His eyes narrowed on her. A strange, humorless smile parted his lips, revealed his teeth, a smile she had never seen. "Guilt is the driving force in my life." Said without any emotion at all.

"Liam? What do you mean?" She felt a chill. The smile troubled her. She wanted to wipe it away. No. Kiss it away. "What on earth do you mean by that?"

He ignored her question. "I didn't want to hurt Angela anymore, but I had no choice. I had to leave. When the offer from Moore State arrived, I grabbed at it. Normally, I would have politely refused. But the timing was right. It seemed like a real escape."

The strange smile finally faded. The dark eyes regained their intensity. Sara leaned close to him, brushing her cheek against his.

"Angela was still in the hospital. I left without saying good-bye. It felt so good to get away. I admit it. As if I had broken out of prison chains." He shook his head. "I didn't really want to tell you."

Sara pressed her face against his. Hugged him.

"Hey." She pulled back. "Hey. Wait. Do you think that Angela is the one?"

He stared at her. "The one *who?*"

"Do you think Angela is the one who made those frightening calls and sent those bloody rabbit feet?"

Liam rubbed his chin tensely. Then he swept a hand back through his dark hair. "Perhaps. I can't imagine . . ." He thought a while longer, staring down at his port glass. "It could have been Angela. I should have guessed it. But I never think about her. I mean, I haven't thought about her since I arrived here."

Thank God, Sara thought, relieved that he wasn't still obsessed with the woman. And relieved that perhaps the mystery of the frightening threats had been solved.

"Maybe it *was* Angela," Liam continued thoughtfully. "The poor woman really is terribly disturbed. She's harmless, though. Believe me, Sara, she's completely harmless."

Feeling better, Sara curled her hands around Liam's neck and pulled his head down to her. "And how about *you?*" she teased. "Are you perfectly harmless too?"

He laughed. His eyes flashed. "Not when you're around." He kissed her. Tenderly. A long, sweet kiss. "When I'm with you, I'm truly *dangerous.*"

36

Liam stepped up to the sink and leaned close to the water-stained mirror. He pulled the pale blue shirt collar out from under the crew neck of his sweater. Changed his mind. Tucked the collar back in.

He heard the urinal flush on the tile wall behind him. Milton, zipping his black suit trousers, lumbered up to the sink beside him. "You shouldn't have dressed," Milton teased. He adjusted the crooked knot on his wine red tie. He sneered disapprovingly at Liam's sweater.

"Since it was Spinnaker's, I thought we'd all be casual," Liam explained.

"You know why I chose this place for your prewedding after-wedding dinner," Milton said, eyes on his reflection. He brushed back his thatch of white hair with both hands. The hair popped straight back up as if it were on a spring. "This is where you and your bride met."

Liam snickered. "You're so sentimental, Milton."

"And you're so lucky," Milton's reply. Said grudgingly, not the first time he'd said it. He grunted. "A lucky man. Sara is quite a girl. Wish I'd seen her first."

Liam let that subject drop. He tried to picture Sara with Milton. The thought made the muscles on the back of his neck tighten.

Milton leaned over the sink and turned on both water faucets. Too hard. The water splashed onto his suit jacket. He let out a sharp cry and fumbled to turn the faucet knobs. Then he began to wash his enormous hands.

Liam combed his hair. Replaced the comb in his trouser pocket. Then turned on the water carefully. "May I use that soap?"

Milton finished lathering his hands and handed the pale green soap bar to Liam. Liam absently began to rub it in his palms.

"Oh." The soap dropped into the sink. Liam scowled at himself in the mirror. "Damn. Oh, damn."

"Liam—what's wrong?"

Liam shook his head fretfully. "Soap must never be passed from hand to hand." He raised his eyes to Milton. "You should always set it down so that the other person can pick it up for himself."

Milton laughed, his chins bobbing under the tight white shirt collar. "You and your superstitions. You scared me. I thought you were really upset about something."

Liam chuckled too.

Milton dried his hands and made his way out of the men's room.

Liam heard the door close behind him. He stared down at the pale green bar of soap.

Stared down in growing horror at what he had just done.

Then he opened his mouth wide—as far as it would open—and let out a long, painful howl.

His hands shot up and he tore at his hair, tore wildly, frantically, pounding the sides of his head, pounding, ripping hair, beating himself, slapping himself, his eyes shut, head raised as the howl burst from deep inside him.

The fat, purple tongue uncoiled from his mouth. It made a wet *splat* as it slapped the mirror.

Liam's soapy hands shot out. He grabbed the writhing tongue with both hands.

And shoved it. Shoved it.

Shoved it, tugged it, slipping, sliding, fighting him, fighting.

Shoved it back down into his throat. And clamped his teeth shut over it.

A few moments later, his dark hair carefully combed, his hands in his pockets, he shambled casually to the table. Sara caught his eye, and he flashed her a happy smile.

37

Chip's breath fogged the window glass. He rubbed it clear with a gloved hand and peered into the restaurant. Sara's table was at the back, but he could see her face clearly. Could see her radiant smile. See her clutch the professor's sweater sleeve, toss back her head, and laugh.

Chip rubbed the pane clear again. Tried to hold his breath. The wind cut sharply around the building. The cold rushed into the front of his open overcoat. Intent on the silent pageant inside, he made no attempt to button the coat.

The back of his neck burned. The drinks—Red Label—from the bar across the street tasted sour, but it was what he needed—still warmed his throat.

Through the window, he watched the big, red-faced elephant stand and raise his champagne glass in a toast. Suddenly dizzy, Chip pressed both gloved hands to the glass, leaned hard against the pane. Glasses touched silently across the table. Chip imagined the fragile clink. Smiles all around.

A tall waiter with a blond ponytail blocked Chip's view. He motioned impatiently with one glove for the waiter to move. Cars rumbled along the street behind him. Narrowing his eyes, squinting through the fogged glass, Chip didn't turn away.

The waiter finally lowered his tray and moved. Chip saw that the professor had climbed to his feet. He was talking with a smile plastered on his weasely face, gesturing with his champagne glass. A woman with short, blond hair—Liam's sister?—smiled up at him.

Another sharp wind flapped Chip's overcoat. Staring at Sara, watching the gleam of her eyes, watching her laugh so appreciatively at whatever the professor—her Liam—was saying, Chip felt only the heat of his anger, of the liquor that had failed to soothe.

"Liam," he whispered the name with disgust. He smeared the fog off the glass. Why am I out here in the cold, Sara? You know you belong with me.

He tottered unsteadily, nearly fell forward onto the glass. But his gaze remained steady. He saw her raise her eyes to Liam, saw her cheeks flush, saw the admiring, fawning smile.

"No. No way."

You're not staying with him, Sara. No way you're staying with that phony.

Everyone at the table laughed. So merry.

But the laughter will end quickly, Chip predicted, eyes on Sara. The laughter will end, Sara, when you end the marriage. No more toasts. No more witty self-congratulatory speeches by the great professor.

And you *will* end the marriage. You *will* leave him.

You *will* leave him and return to me when I tell you what I know. What I found out about your brilliant professor.

"Liam. Liam." Chip murmured the word, watching it fog the windowpane. "Liam. It rhymes with . . ."

He couldn't think of anything.

Inside, they clinked glasses again. More cheers and laughter. Sara blushed prettily. She offered a short comment, and everyone laughed. Liam kissed her on the cheek.

No. Please—no.

Chip decided he needed another Red Label. Maybe two. Two for courage. His throat felt dry. He needed it to be smooth. He needed to be loose when he told Sara what he knew. When he walked into the restaurant, moved casually to their table—and ruined their life together. Clink clink.

A toast to me.

A toast to me and Sara.

I'm going to save you, Sara.

You cannot live with the professor, and I know why. I'm going to save you from him. I know all about him. All.

I should be angry at you, Sara. I should punish you for running away, for making me chase after you, for making me fight for what is mine. I have some pride, you know.

I asked you first, remember? I asked you to marry me.

You do remember—don't you?

Oh, never mind.

That's in the past. I'm going to be very forgiving. You'll see. I'm going to forget my pride, Sara. No punishment. No hard feelings. I'll take you back, back to New York. Or maybe we'll move to L.A. when my company gets rolling. And we'll never talk about this. Never. I promise.

Someday, maybe we'll even laugh about it. About the mistake you made.

Chip squinted into the restaurant. The waiter was setting down their dinners. Liam had a hand in Sara's hair, brushing it behind her shoulder.

Chip's throat tightened. You don't own her, Professor. At least, not for long.

The big, red-faced man with the swirl of white hair began eating as soon as his plate was set in front of him. There were four or five others at the table. Chip didn't recognize them. He hadn't paid them any attention.

He turned away from the window, surprised to find that he was breathing hard, noisily. He needed to warm himself, to calm himself before his big moment.

Plenty of time to step back across the street, he decided. The Pitcher had a red neon beer pitcher in the window. Fake wood slats across the front of the building. Cactus plants in big clay pots out front. Western-style swinging doors. A lame attempt to make the bar look like an old-time Western saloon.

Not Chip's kind of place. Not the kind of bar he frequented on Third Avenue back in New York. But the phony atmosphere couldn't harm the scotch.

He pushed through the swinging doors and moved across the dimly lit front room—mostly college students sitting around small round tables holding foamy glass pitchers of beer—and up to the bar. The young woman bartender with the long red hair and the rhinestone stud in her nose eyed him familiarly. "Red Label neat?"

He chuckled. "You're a mind reader?"

She twisted her mouth. "You just left fifteen minutes ago."

He nodded. "Oh." Seemed like much longer.

She poured the glass half-full. Slapped it in front of him. "Better fill it," he said, eyes not quite adjusted to the darkness.

The first drink burned. The second warmed him.

Leaning heavily on the bar, he stared at a couple caught in the blue light of the jukebox. College students. The girl, in jeans and oversized flannel shirt, sat on the boy's lap. Boy or man? He looked older. Or was it just the neon blue light? She kissed him. And kissed him. Kissed his cheeks. His forehead. Kissed his eyes. As if they were alone. As if no one could watch.

It made Chip angry.

His head felt about to explode. He lowered himself to his feet. Knees surprisingly rubbery. Throat knotted. All that good scotch wasted. He tossed a twenty, then another onto the bar.

Stepped into the blue light. Watched her kiss the guy. Kiss him again. Short kisses but sweet. Kisses that made Chip's face itch.

Into the night. A shock of cold. Wind in his face. A flattened orange juice carton skipping across the sidewalk.

Across the street to peer into the restaurant window. Tripped over the curb but kept his balance. The blue light following him across the sidewalk, sweeping around him, cold blue light, making him shiver.

Careful not to bump his forehead on the window glass. He raised his eyes almost shyly. Focused on their table at the back.

Empty.

No one sitting there. Two white-aproned busboys cleaning up.

No!

How long had he been across the street in the bar? He tried to think, tried to read his watch, but the blue light curtained it from view.

No!

How many scotches? How long? How long? Too long.

But he could catch up with them. He could still ruin their night. He could still wipe away those smug, leering smiles. He could catch up to Sara and tell her what he knew.

He pushed himself away from the window with both hands. Turned and lurched unsteadily to the corner. The cold of the window glass remaining on his hands.

My gloves. What did I do with my gloves?

He was still thinking about the gloves when he felt the first stab of pain in his shoulder.

The blue light flared.

The shoulder felt cold before the pain made him shout.

He saw the blade. Then the dark-gloved hand.

The blade slid from his shoulder, down, down nearly to his waist, slicing easily through his shirt, through his skin.

Cold. Then wet.

The warm blood—*his* warm blood—hissed as it bubbled against the cold air.

He swayed. Lowered his eyes to see the blood splash onto his shoes.

Another slashing tear. Down the other side of his chest. Shirt and skin ripping together.

He opened his mouth. Could only gurgle.

His eyes rose up from his shoes to follow the knife.

But the blue light went out.

And he no longer felt the cold or the pain.

38

"Yes, I know. Yes, I know." Detective Garrett Montgomery ran his finger over the framed photograph of his son, Martin, as he leaned over the desk, the phone cradled between his shoulder and ear.

Across from him, Walter, eyes narrowed on Garrett, moved his lips as if taking part in the conversation. Garrett spun around in his chair so that he wouldn't have to watch Walter's face.

"I know, sir. But you have to remember—" Garrett said quietly. He sighed as the shrill voice of the state marshal up in Medford invaded his ear.

"Yes, I know. I know, sir." Another frustrated sigh.

"We're a small force," Garrett finally managed to say. "Only six men. We're not equipped, sir. I'll be the first to admit it. And the national attention—all the TV cameras and reporters . . ."

His voice trailed off. The fourth victim *would* have to be the son of a bigshot network TV exec. The reporters and camera crews had swarmed to Freewood almost gleefully, Garrett thought. Swarmed like ants to a crust of bread, hopping over the campus, over the murder sites, hopping and chattering, talking to everyone, all talking at once, talking, talking, fixing their hair and then talking some more. A woman from one of the so-called news magazines had even offered Garrett ten thousand dollars if he would tell gruesome details about the murders on camera.

He had turned her down. Too quickly, maybe. Later, Angel had conjectured about all the things they could do with ten thousand dollars. She had argued that it wasn't unethical to divulge details that everyone already knew anyway.

But everyone *didn't* know the details.

The reporters had never been told just how grisly, just how violent and inhuman the murders had been.

Inhuman. Good word, Garrett thought.

Inhuman. No one had been told about the fingerprints. With their wild zigzagging whorls and sharp slashes that followed no human pattern anyone had ever seen. The computer upstate had nearly flipped its disc drive when they had tried to match the fingerprints with those on file.

Of course Garrett and his officers had been accused of total incompetence, of not being able to collect a simple fingerprint, a police skill that had been around since the middle of the nineteenth century.

Yes, Garrett knew the TV reporters would pay a lot to hear about the fingerprints. And the bodies ripped to pieces. Ripped and shredded, body parts strewn on the campus like groceries that tumbled from a torn paper bag.

And they'd go crazy for the eyewitness account. Of the story of the kid who saw the murderer escaping in a monster costume.

How much would they pay for that one?

"I couldn't sleep at night if I sold the story, if I made a penny from it," Garrett told Angel.

But he already didn't sleep at night.

So what was the big deal?

"Okay, sir. I understand. Okay," Garrett said into the receiver in a flat voice. No emotion at all. He replaced the phone.

"What was *that* about?" Walter demanded, leaning forward, making the chair squeak under him.

The sound reverberated in Garrett's ear. Every sound was exaggerated these days. He rubbed his temples. "We're being replaced. Big surprise."

But Walter reacted with surprise. "They're taking us off the murders?"

Garrett nodded grimly. "He didn't quite say it. But the Feds aren't going to want to play with us. They're going to take the ball away from us and play their own game."

Why was he suddenly talking as if it were a ball game? Was he more upset about failing than he admitted to himself? Was he trying to turn it into something not real?

Give me a break! he scolded himself. Am I a shrink or a cop?

Or either one?

"But—but—" Walter sputtered, gripping the gray-metal desktop with both chubby pink paws. "We've done all the work."

Garrett frowned. "We haven't done much. Mostly stared at corpses, then stared at photos of corpses."

Walter rubbed his chins. "You're just upset because of all the TV reporters."

"You're damned right!" Garrett snapped. He tossed a pencil across the room. It hit the wall and bounced to the linoleum floor.

Walter's mouth dropped open in shock. When did Detective Garrett Montgomery lose control? Never. "Four murders," he muttered, shaking his round head. "Four murders and we haven't been able—"

"I'm not sure it *is* four murders," Garrett murmured, still rubbing his temples. Not a headache. Just a dull throbbing that wouldn't go away.

"Huh?" Walter stared across the desks.

"Maybe it's three murders and one murder," Garrett replied softly, struggling to think, wondering why he was suddenly sharing this theory with Walter.

"I don't get it," Walter confessed. Not the first time Garrett had heard him make the remark. "We've got four bodies torn to pieces, Chief. Count 'em. One. Two. Three. Four." He counted them off on his fingers.

"We've got three bodies torn to pieces," Garrett corrected him. "And one body *slashed* to pieces and cut up."

Walter thought about this for a long moment. "You mean—"

"I mean, I don't think we can be certain that the fourth murder is related to the other three. That young man—Chip Whitney—was attacked with a knife. Yeah sure, he was slashed and mutilated. But he was *cut* up—not *torn* up."

"You mean there could be *two* murderers in town?" Walter grew even paler than usual.

Garrett stood up and crossed the room to retrieve the pencil. "I don't know. I only know that there was no indication of any weapon with the first three murders. Those corpses were a fucking mess. I get the heaves just thinking about them. And I think about them all the time."

He bent to pick up the pencil. "Whitney's corpse was a mess too. But the guys in the lab determined that the murder weapon was a knife with a four-inch blade. That makes it different from the first three."

Walter's mouth slowly fell open as he stared wide-eyed at Garrett. "Two murderers here in Freewood? *Two* murderers?"

39

"I—I just keep thinking it's my fault," Sara stammered. She lowered red-rimmed eyes to her lap, where her hands were tightly knotted.

Mary Beth reached out and cupped Sara's hands in hers. "How can you say that?" she replied in a hushed whisper. "You know that isn't true."

"But Chip wouldn't have been in this town if it wasn't because of me," Sara wailed. A single tear rolled down her swollen cheek. There weren't many tears left, she knew. She had cried all night.

Clung to Liam and cried. Not because she still loved Chip. But because she felt so guilty.

She and Mary Beth sat side by side on Mary Beth's couch, white mugs of coffee steaming untouched on the low table in front of them. Mary Beth, in a black skirt and crewneck black sweater, had hurried home early from work to meet her when Sara had called.

Sara's faded jeans were wrinkled, her long-sleeved blue T-shirt stained in front. "I came straight from the police station," she murmured, pulling her hands free from Mary Beth's grasp and raising them to brush back her dark hair. "Liam didn't want me to go. But I had to tell them I knew Chip. I had to tell them why Chip was in Freewood."

Mary Beth leaned forward and picked up her coffee mug. "Liam didn't want you to go?"

Sara shook her head. "He saw how upset I was. He—he was so wonderful last night. He held me all night and just let me cry. He kept telling me I had nothing to feel guilty about."

"Well, you don't," Mary Beth said firmly. The mug tilted in her hand. Coffee trickled down the side. Her eyes were on Sara. "You didn't invite Chip to Freewood. And you had nothing to do with . . . with his death."

"But it's just so weird," Sara replied, wiping the tear stain off her cheek. "It's just so weird *knowing* someone who was murdered."

Mary Beth nodded. She took a quick sip of coffee and replaced the mug on the table. "What happened at the police station?"

Sara sighed. "I talked with a detective. Detective Montgomery. I think that was his name. Black, with a very soft voice. He was very nice. Very understanding. He wanted to know when I saw Chip last. And if I knew anyone who might want to kill him. Some other questions." She shifted her weight on the couch, stretching her back. "He saw that I was upset. He didn't ask me very much. He seemed pretty upset too."

"He was upset?"

"Yeah. He said the local police were being taken off the case. The FBI or someone was coming in. He said he wasn't up to finding a serial killer. I don't know why he told me all that. I guess . . ." Sara's voice trailed off.

They sat in silence for a while. Sara heard the ceiling creak. Someone was walking around in the apartment above them. She heard the thud of drumbeats from the stereo next door.

Life was going on all around. For most people it was a normal day.

"Chip's father was arriving at the police station as I left," she confided to Mary Beth. "I saw a white limo pull up in the parking lot, and he climbed out slowly from the back."

"What did you say to him?"

"I—nothing. I couldn't face him," Sara confessed, avoiding Mary Beth's stare. "I went the other way. Before he could see me. I mean . . . what could I say?"

"Were Chip and his father close?" Mary Beth asked.

Sara nodded.

More footsteps overhead. Outside the window, a cloud passed over the sun, dimming the light. Gray shadows slid over Mary Beth's small living room.

Sara sighed again. "Why would someone kill Chip? I mean, why would someone—some stranger—come up to him on the street—and just murder him? It's all so horrible, Mary Beth. So weird."

"Sara, have some coffee. You've got to stop thinking about it. Somehow you've got to distract your mind. You've got to—"

"But how? I mean, I *know* someone who was murdered. Brutally murdered. And—*oh my God!*" Sara's hands flew up to her pale cheeks.

"Sara—what?" Mary Beth demanded.

"I knew *two* of them!" Sara exclaimed. "Four murders on campus. And I knew *two* of them. Chip—and that graduate instructor. Devra Brookes. I met her. I met her at a restaurant. Just before she was killed. Oh, my God, Mary Beth. My God. How can I know *two* people who were murdered? How?"

40

Sara tugged the belt of her blue cotton bathrobe tighter as she stood across the breakfast table from Liam. "Grrrrrrr. I'm growling at you, Liam." She tossed back her unbrushed hair with both hands.

Liam, already dressed at seven-thirty in loose-fitting chinos, a white sport shirt with a brown wool sweater vest pulled over it, his hair neatly brushed, still wet from the shower, shrugged and offered a placating smile. "I cannot eat the eggs. I'm truly sorry." He shoved the plate toward the middle of the table.

"Grrrr." She coiled her hands and clawed the air, an angry tigress.

"You can growl all you like. I warned you not to buy eggs after dark. It's a very old superstition, but—"

"Yes! A very old superstition!" Sara cried, as if proving her point. "Very old and very dumb."

"Sara, please—don't be upset. Sit down."

She didn't feel like letting it drop this morning. She hadn't slept well. Chip had been dead for two weeks, but she still saw his face at night, saw him when she closed her eyes, saw him whenever she relaxed her mind.

Two weeks. And she hadn't enjoyed a normal night's sleep in all that time.

Chip, why are you haunting me? Will you ever go away?

This morning, watching Liam carefully climb out on the right side of the bed and circle the room three times before counting his steps to the bathroom had just about sent her over the edge.

"Liam, I had no idea you had *so many* superstitions," she had groaned, her voice still clogged by sleep.

He didn't reply.

She pulled herself up, even though her first class wasn't until eleven, and made him scrambled eggs on toast, which he had casually rejected when told she had bought the eggs after studying in the library the night before.

"Just because a bunch of ignorant Irishmen were afraid to buy eggs in the dark three hundred years ago doesn't mean you can't eat my scrambled eggs!" she cried, and started to cough. She poured herself a mug of coffee and took a sip, burning her tongue.

He flashed her his little-boy smile. He knew it usually worked with her. "Please don't be annoyed with me."

She was determined not to be so easily charmed. She slammed the black mug onto the table. "When am I supposed to buy eggs? Why don't you tell me the right hours when the egg luck is good?"

He reacted to her sarcasm with a scowl. Then he reached for the coffeepot. "Don't worry about eggs, my dear. You have your research paper to think about. Let Margaret buy the eggs."

As if on cue, Sara heard Margaret's footsteps descending the back stairs. A few seconds later, Margaret, a woolly beige sweater pulled over black tights, stepped reluctantly into the kitchen. "Okay if I join you?"

"Why? Are we falling apart?"

Sara groaned. That was an old joke that Liam had read somewhere. For some reason, he loved it. He and Margaret repeated this routine just about every morning. And every morning—until now—Sara had laughed. This morning, it just added to her bad humor.

Why can't Margaret have breakfast upstairs? she asked herself angrily. Why can't Liam and I ever have one morning alone? Why can't we ever have a fight without Margaret standing there watching us?

Maybe I'm premenstrual, she thought, sipping coffee. Margaret is perfectly pleasant. And she tries so hard not to interfere.

And I shouldn't be so impatient with Liam. He's been so wonderful, so warm and caring, so loving. He seems so happy with me. And he's been so understanding about Chip.

Margaret poured herself a mug of coffee. She crossed the room to the refrigerator for some milk. Sara stepped up behind Liam, leaned over him, slid her arms around him. She took a deep breath, inhaling his aftershave. Then she kissed the back of his neck.

He turned to kiss her lips.

"The two lovebirds," Margaret muttered from the refrigerator. She shook her head, smiling.

"Coo coo," Sara offered. Her best bird impression.

They moved to the living room after breakfast. Margaret pulled open the curtains, allowing pale gray morning light to invade the room. Sara gazed out at an overcast winter day, dark storm clouds beyond the trees.

Liam settled on the couch and glanced through a stack of papers. "Lecture notes," he said, answering Sara's silent question. Margaret disappeared into the kitchen. Sara could hear water running into the sink.

Why is she doing the dishes? Sara wondered impatiently. I *told* Margaret I will do the dishes. Why does she always hurry to do them if I don't take care of them instantly?

Sara moved to Liam's desk. She glimpsed the rabbit cage. Empty now. Why didn't he get rid of it? Maybe I'll just do it for him, she thought. Sometime when he's out.

She started to pull open the top desk drawer, then thought better of it. "Liam, where do you keep the scissors?"

"Top drawer on the right." He didn't look up from his

notes. "I've lived here two months and I still feel like a visitor," Sara complained. "I don't know where anything is."

"You need your own desk," Liam muttered.

She pulled open the drawer. Scissors, pencils, a ruler, packs of index cards, all neatly arranged. She had a momentary urge to mess it all up, just shake her hand around inside there until it was in disarray. I have to bring a little messiness, a little disorder into Liam's life, she thought.

Then she scolded herself for such childish thoughts. What is *wrong* with me today?

She lifted out the scissors.

He lowered the lecture notes to his lap and smiled at her. "What are you doing?"

She closed the drawer with her hip. "Oh, I have those wedding snapshots that Mary Beth finally got developed. You know. I showed them to you yesterday. I thought I'd send a few to Mom. And I'm going to cut the wedding announcement out of the campus paper and—"

The scissors fell from her hand and bounced across the carpet. She bent down to retrieve them.

"No!" Liam shrieked. He leapt to his feet, the lecture notes tumbling to the floor. "Don't!"

"Huh?" Startled, Sara straightened up. "What's wrong?"

Liam moved quickly across the room. "Never pick up your own scissors."

"Excuse me?" Sara croaked.

"If you pick up your own scissors, your life will be cut short."

"Don't be ridiculous!" Sara cried.

"Someone else has to pick them up for you."

"No way!" Sara shouted. Liam dove for the scissors, but she was closer. As his hand swiped at them, she grabbed them up from the floor.

Liam uttered a cry, as if in pain.

Margaret appeared in the doorway. "What's going on?"

Liam straightened up, breathing hard, glaring at Sara. She

raised the scissors high, like a trophy. "Liam, sometimes you take this superstition thing too far."

Slowly his expression softened. He flashed his boyish smile again. "You're right. I'm sorry." He took a step back. "I'll try to be better. Really, I promise."

"What on earth happened?" Margaret demanded.

"Nothing, really," Sara replied, eyes on Liam. She already regretted acting so defiantly. The poor man seemed so distressed. Why shouldn't she let him pick up the scissors for her if it meant so much to him?

"I got a little carried away," Liam told Margaret. He started to say more, but the doorbell rang. He turned to Sara. "Are you expecting anyone this early?"

Sara shook her head. She set the scissors down on the desktop. Liam started to the front door.

Margaret moved to the window and peered out at the front stoop. "Oh!" She uttered a short cry of surprise. "Liam—it's a police officer."

41

Garrett pressed the doorbell again and stared up at the darkening sky. Storm coming, he saw. Was it cold enough to snow?

He pulled off his black leather gloves and stuffed them into the deep pockets of his overcoat. The overcoat was open to reveal his police uniform. He had his department photo ID clipped to the clipboard he carried. People always asked to see ID these days. A uniform wasn't enough.

He saw movement in the front window. A flash of color. A woman half-hidden by the reflection of the sky, peering out at him. Then footsteps inside the house.

Only nine o'clock and he had already done twenty houses. It was good to get an early start, Garrett knew. Catch people before they hurried off to work.

He thought he would hate this house-to-house detail. Canvas every house and apartment in the campus area? Question every resident? What could it possibly turn up?

Sandusky, the baby-faced FBI unit leader, said that Garrett might be surprised. Garrett hated the way Sandusky put his hand around your shoulder, talked to you like you were six. So patronizing. How old was *he* anyway? He looked about fourteen with those smooth, white cheeks and baby blue eyes. And since when was the FBI supposed to be so touchy-feely?

Maybe he's gay, Garrett thought, snickering. Maybe he's got a thing for big, black cops.

No. He's just a patronizing son of a bitch, really impressed with himself because he's a big-deal federal agent, not a pitiful campus play-cop who can't even get a fingerprint off a corpse that's been torn apart by hand.

At least, I'm out of the station house, Garrett thought. That's why he was happy the FBI guys had assigned him the house-to-house detail. At least I'm out here getting some fresh air and exercise. I'm not sitting in that stifling room, watching that fat clown Walter spill powdered sugar down the front of his shirt, eating doughnut after doughnut.

Shit, yes. It felt good to be outdoors, going from building to building, accomplishing nothing. Time to think. About his life. About the murders.

Angel hadn't laughed at him when he told her his theory. That the murders were committed by an inhuman monster. But he could see the doubt in her green eyes. Doubt and concern. Doubt about his *sanity?*

Well, why not?

He hadn't felt the same since he'd seen that first corpse. That poor girl with the top of her head ripped off, her hair in a clump on the grass, the torn blood vessels falling around her skull like withered snakes.

He hadn't felt the same. He hadn't been able to look at people the same way. He couldn't see anyone without thinking about their skull, their veins, how they'd look with their hair ripped off in a single clump.

Insane? Probably.

What was sane about these murders? How could the murderer *not* be a monster?

He heard a lock being turned. The front door started to open. Garrett waited for the surprised stare, the fearful expression. People were afraid to find a cop at their door. He had to be bringing bad news.

A dark-haired man, somewhere between thirty and forty, academic-looking in a brown sweater vest over a white shirt, peered out at him. Garrett caught the surprise in his eyes. Fear too? Garrett wasn't sure.

"Good morning, Officer. Can I help you?" The man had a smooth, pleasant voice. A slight foreign lilt.

"Professor O'Connor?"

"Yes." Eyes narrowing on Garrett.

"Your wife was in to see me recently. Regarding the murder of Chip Whitney?"

"Yes. I know. Sara was terribly upset. So was I, of course."

"You knew him?" Garrett demanded, shifting his clipboard.

"No, I didn't. I was upset that Sara was upset." He brushed back his dark hair. "And of course, we're all upset about . . . the other murders. It's all so frightening."

Garrett raised his eyes to the professor. "I'm on a house-to-house detail, Professor. I'll only keep you a minute. You knew one of the other victims, right?"

He didn't wait for a reply. He flipped through the pages on the clipboard. Stopped at the color snapshot of the second victim. The woman smiled out at him, dressed in a lemon yellow sundress, an ocean beach stretching behind her, hair down, blowing slightly in the breeze.

The professor squinted at the snapshot and nodded. "Mrs. DeHaven. She was our landlady. She owned this building. What a terrible shock."

"When was the last time you saw her?

"Did she ever tell you about any arguments or disputes with any of her tenants?

"Do you have any idea of anyone who might have had any trouble with her? The previous tenants? Any other tenants in this house?"

Dr. O'Connor answered the questions without hesitation, in a soft, thoughtful tone. He had no clue, no idea of any trouble. He didn't know any other tenants. Never heard the landlady mention or complain about any other tenants. He claimed to have had a "most cordial" relationship with her.

No help at all, Garrett thought. He could hear women's voices inside the house. The wife and the sister, he remembered from his interview with the wife. He'd have to talk to them too.

Two young men, students probably, came jogging around the corner. They slowed when they saw Garrett on the stoop, squinted to see who he was questioning, turned their heads as they trotted past the house.

"I don't think I'm going to be of much help to you, Officer," Dr. O'Connor said, showing the first sign of impatience.

Garrett turned to the photo of the first victim. Charlotte Wilson. It was a school photo. Senior year in high school. She looked about twelve. "Dr. O'Connor, did you know this young woman? Charlotte Wilson?"

Professor O'Connor squinted down at the photo. He swallowed. "Well, actually . . ."

"Yes?"

"I met her briefly. That's the young woman who was supposed to be my secretary. But she . . . It was when I had just arrived in town. My sister and I were so occupied with moving in and getting settled here, I barely had time to go into my office. I think I spoke only once or twice to the poor girl. And then . . . when she was murdered . . ."

Garrett felt the muscles on the back of his neck tighten. He stared hard at the professor. Caught the discomfort in the man's brown eyes. "So you knew Charlotte Wilson? You knew all three victims?"

Dr. O'Connor's cheeks reddened. "Well . . . yes. But I didn't know any of them well. They were barely acquaintances."

Garrett tried other questions, scribbling a note on the bottom of Charlotte Wilson's fact sheet as he talked. "Did you ever meet anyone Charlotte Wilson knew? Did you ever see her with any friends? Do you know of anyone else who knew her? Did she ever say anything to you about any of her friends or acquaintances? Did she ever act frightened or strange in any way?"

The professor could offer no help at all.

But Garrett felt his heart begin to race. Something going on here. Something fishy? Just coincidence? But we're three out of three. He knew all three.

Is it possible he doesn't know anything more? Is it possible?

Questions flew through Garrett's mind. He cautioned himself: Don't get excited. You haven't solved the case. You haven't found anything.

But three out of three?

Let's go for four.

A strong breeze fluttered the pages on the clipboard. The sky darkened. Both men raised their eyes to the clouds. Dr. O'Connor shivered. "I suppose I should invite you in, Officer. You'll have to forgive me." He glanced at his watch. "But I'm already late for my lecture. My class—"

"Here is the fourth victim," Garrett interrupted, raising the photo of Devra Brookes, the graduate instructor. Sexy in the photo, auburn hair down over one eye, a sly grin on her pretty face. Garrett had seen it a hundred times, but he shook his head. Couldn't they dig up a better photo?

The professor lowered his eyes to the photo. Appeared to study it. He shook his head. "No. Sorry. I didn't know that one. I've never seen her."

Garrett felt a stab of disappointment. "Are you sure, Professor? Her name—"

Before Garrett could finish, Sara poked her head out the door. She glimpsed Garrett, then lowered her eyes to the photograph. "Devra!" she exclaimed. "Liam, it's Devra."

"Oh. Yes." Circles of bright scarlet burned on Professor O'Connor's cheeks. "I *did* know her."

Four for four.

42

Sara followed Margaret into the house. She sighed, happy to be home. "What a horrible day."

She heard Liam close the front door behind them. He moved past Sara, his expression grim, weary, his eyes pouched, and tossed his overcoat over the back of the couch. "I will second that, Sara." He stretched his arms over his head.

Margaret picked up Liam's overcoat and carried it to the front closet. "Should we get a lawyer? Do you think we should have had a lawyer at the police station, Liam?"

Liam crossed to the window and peered out at the falling snow. "We don't need a lawyer. We haven't done anything. Those FBI men are grabbing at straws."

Sara dropped onto the edge of the couch. "A whole day at the police station. Answering the same questions again and again."

"It's all my fault," Liam said softly. "I shouldn't have lied about Devra. I don't even know why I did it. I guess it was that police officer, standing there, staring at me. He made me feel as if I really did have something to hide."

He stepped up behind Sara and began to massage her shoulders tenderly. "It's just such a horrible coincidence. And the police—they're desperate. They'll grab at anything. Even a ridiculous coincidence."

"Mmmmm. That feels good," Sara purred. "You have such soft hands for a murderer, Liam."

He stopped massaging. "Not funny, Sara."

"I'm going to make a pot of tea," Margaret announced, heading toward the kitchen. "Anyone want a cup?"

"I need something stronger," Liam replied.

"I need something cold," Sara said. "That police station was so unbearably hot. The radiator kept rattling away. It was driving me crazy."

Margaret disappeared into the kitchen. Sara could hear her running water, then the bang of the kettle on the stove.

Liam stopped kneading her shoulders and stepped back. "Well, we told them everything we know. Which isn't much. Perhaps now they'll sniff some other trail and leave us alone."

He pulled the sweater over his head and tossed it over his shoulder. Then he walked to the bar and poured himself a tall glass of scotch.

Sara watched him, thinking hard. What a dreadful coincidence.

Coincidence?

Of course it was a coincidence.

What else could it be?

Poor Liam. She hadn't realized that he had known all four murder victims. He had never mentioned it to her. In fact, he had never spoken about the murders at all, except to mumble about how horrible they were, how frightened his students were. But it must have troubled him a great deal, Sara realized. Four murders. Four people Liam knew in one way or another.

Yes, she decided. It *must* have troubled and upset him. Especially someone as superstitious as Liam.

Poor Liam. Poor, superstitious Liam. And yet he held his feelings in. Why? For her sake? Yes. That must be the reason.

She crossed the room and hugged him, caught him by surprise, made him spill some of his scotch onto the carpet. "Oh, Liam, you knew all of them."

"Not really," he murmured, his cheek warm against hers.

"I didn't know any of them well. Let's not talk about it, Sara. I really don't want . . ."

He backed away from her, drink raised in his right hand. "I'm going to change. Do you want to stay home for dinner or go out? Maybe a nice walk in the snow will cool us off, clear our minds. What do you think? All of those questions. Those men in their gray suits staring at us with their beady, ball-bearing eyes, asking us all those foolish questions. We'll have a nice dinner. We'll have some good wine. Maybe we'll get loaded. Calm our minds. What do you say?"

He was talking rapidly, nervously, in a voice Sara had never heard. He vanished from the living room before she could reply.

She stood in the center of the room and crossed her arms tightly in front of her. The poor man. He really didn't want to talk about it. She stared out the front window. The snow came down harder now, caught in the light of a streetlamp across the street. It got dark so early. She glanced at her watch. A little past five and already as black as midnight.

The phone rang, jangling loudly in the empty room. She crossed to the low table beside the couch and picked up the receiver. "Hello?" She cleared her throat.

"Is this Sara O'Connor? Is this Liam's new wife?" A woman's voice, tense, just above a whisper.

"Yes. Who's this?" Sara replied more sharply than she had intended.

"Uh . . . you don't know me. My name is Kristen Verret. But I used to . . . uh . . . be with Liam."

"Excuse me?"

"I used to live with Liam. Liam and Margaret. I have to talk to you, Sara. I have to warn you—"

Sara felt her stomach tighten. Felt a stab of dread in her chest. "Who *is* this? What do you want?"

"Listen to me, Sara. I called to warn you about Liam."

"Is this Angela? Is it?" Sara squeezed the receiver hard, remembering Liam's story about Angela back in Chicago, Angela so obsessed with Liam.

"Angela? No. I told you who I am. Kristen. Are you free? Can you come meet me?"

"Huh? Are you crazy? Why would I meet you?"

"I have to tell you about Liam. Please. You're in danger. You're in terrible danger. Listen to me."

"Angela, I know who you are and I know what this is about. I'm really sorry, but—"

"Can you come now? I'm at the College Inn. On Fairmont."

"No, I won't. Listen, Angela or Kristen whoever you are— don't call me again. I mean it. If you bother me again, I'll call the police. I really will."

"Sara, I'm trying to help you."

"I'm hanging up now. Don't call again." Her voice trembling with rage. And fear.

"Come tomorrow afternoon. Please. I'll be in my room. It won't take long. I have to talk to you. Tomorrow, Sara. Please."

Sara took a breath to reply. But the line went dead.

Then she heard another click on the line.

She ran up the stairs and burst into their bedroom. Liam stood leaning over the dresser, studying himself in the mirror, still in his chinos and white shirt. The scotch glass was empty in front of him. His eyes were watery.

"Liam—were you listening on the extension?" She stared at the phone on the bed table as if it would answer the question.

He turned slowly, his expression bewildered. "Listen? No. Were you on the phone?"

"Yes. I got another weird call."

He scratched his hair. He squinted as if trying to focus. "Angela?"

"I—I don't know," Sara stammered. "She said her name was Kristen. She said she used to live with you. Did you used to live with someone named Kristen?"

A grin spread over Liam's face. "The name doesn't ring a bell."

"Liam—"

"It's so hard to remember all the women," he continued, dark eyes flashing. Sara realized he was teasing her. "The truth is, I've had ten wives before you." He rubbed his chin. "Or was it eleven? I'm not sure how many. I've been meaning to tell you about them, Sara. But it just never seemed like the right moment."

He laughed. "Don't look so stricken. I'm joking—surely you can tell." He crossed the room and pulled her against him, wrapping his arms around her, pressing his face against hers. "Don't worry about other women. You're the only one, Sara," he whispered tenderly. "You're the only one. My only one."

He kissed her.

"Be serious, Liam. Please," Sara pleaded. "She frightened me. She told me to come meet her. She said I was in danger." Sara snuggled against Liam. She felt so cradled, so safe in his arms.

"Maybe it *is* crazy Angela. If Angela is in town, I'll deal with her," Liam replied softly, stroking her hair. "Perhaps we should have our phone unlisted."

"Do you really think it was Angela? Do you know anyone named Kristen?"

He continued to stroke her hair, petting her tenderly. Pressed against him, she could hear his heart beat. "No. No one named Kristen. It has to be Angela. Poor, mixed-up Angela."

He tilted her head up and smiled, his eyes tired and red-rimmed. "It's been a horrible day. Let's try to forget about it all. Let's go out and have a nice dinner. Just the two of us. And don't worry, Sara. There is nothing to worry about."

She forced a smile. "I know," she whispered. "I know."

43

"I'm worried about Liam," Sara said, nibbling her bottom lip. She shoved her hands into the pockets of her down jacket, wishing she'd remembered her gloves.

"What about him?" Mary Beth slipped on the icy ground, but quickly caught her balance. The snow was only a couple inches deep. But it had rained on top of it. The rain had frozen, leaving a hard, slippery surface. Now the late afternoon sun tried to burn through a thick covering of hazy, gray clouds overhead.

They were walking across The Circle, making their way down the center path toward the white-columned library at the other end. Sara heard screams. She turned and glimpsed a group of students near the line of evergreen shrubs trying to have a snowball fight. But the snow was too hard and icy. Backpack-carrying students, leaning into the sharp wind, moved in twos and threes along the crisscrossed paths between the snowy-roofed classroom buildings.

Mary Beth pulled her red and yellow wool ski cap lower on her head. They had been walking for only a few minutes, but her cheeks were bright red. "Oh, my God. The honeymoon is over? So what's Liam's problem? Are you about to divulge some horribly personal sexual problem?"

Sara snickered. "No. No way."

Mary Beth pretended to pout. "Too bad."

The ice crackled beneath their boots. "Doesn't the college ever salt these walks?" Sara asked, grabbing her friend's shoulder as she started to slip.

"Budget cutbacks," Mary Beth replied, watching some students pretend to ice-skate on the icy path. She stopped walking. Her breath steamed up in front of the bright ski cap. "Besides, we've got murders to worry about. No one can get too excited about salting the sidewalks." She turned to Sara. "Are you going to tell me why you dragged me out of my nice warm office, or not?"

"Well . . . it's . . . everything." Sara had been so eager to talk to Mary Beth. She had been thinking about it all morning, rehearsing in her mind what she would say. Then, after her seminar, she had hurried to Mary Beth's office and had forced her to come out for a walk so they could talk without being interrupted.

But now that they were alone, Sara's complaints about Liam seemed so trivial. He was so wonderful. He was so wonderful to her. She loved him so much. She suddenly felt that confiding in Mary Beth was too much of a betrayal.

"I'm supposed to be working in Milton's office," Sara said, glancing back at the Administration Building, its green dome capped by snow. "But I called him and told him I wasn't feeling well. Actually, I'm *not* feeling that well. After yesterday—"

"I know, I know. You told me all about yesterday," Mary Beth cut in impatiently. "Six hours at the police station. That must have been horrible. But what did you want to tell me about *today?* Come on, Sara—spill."

"His superstitions are driving me crazy!" Sara blurted out.

Mary Beth narrowed her green eyes at her. "Excuse me? His superstitions?"

"At first I thought they were so cute," Sara confessed, shaking her head, speaking rapidly, eager now—now that she had started—to get it all out and be done with it. "I mean, Liam spends so much time reading and talking about folklore and folktales and all that stuff. So it seemed cute that he'd be superstitious, that he'd believe in the old superstitions he reads about. I mean, I didn't take it seriously. I didn't think *he* took it all so seriously."

They stopped at the library steps. Mary Beth took Sara's arm, they turned, and started back in the direction they had come. "Well, what does he do?" she asked Sara, tightening her wool muffler at her throat.

"Everything," Sara moaned. "From the time he gets up in the morning—and gets out on the *right* side of the bed—there's some kind of superstition or ritual he has to observe. At first, I thought it was funny. Charming. Interesting. I don't know."

Mary Beth's eyes locked on Sara's. "Well, how bad is he? Do you think he's really obsessive-compulsive?"

Sara felt a pang of guilt. "Oh, I don't know. Maybe I'm exaggerating. Maybe I'm just noticing it more because I'm kind of on edge. I love him so much, Mary Beth. And I want everything to go right. But . . . well . . . we had another really bad morning."

"What happened this morning?"

Mary Beth gazed at her with concern. Sara felt relieved that she was taking her seriously, not making her usual jokes and ironic remarks. Mary Beth was acting like a real friend.

"Don't laugh. I forgot to say 'Bless you' after he sneezed."

Mary Beth didn't laugh. "Is that a crime?"

Sara nodded. "Liam got really upset. It wasn't the first time I'd forgotten. We'd had another fight about it before. Anyway, I apologized but that wasn't enough. He started explaining why we say 'Bless you' after someone sneezes. The sound of the sneeze attracts evil demons. We say 'Bless you' to keep the demons away."

Mary Beth let out a long whoosh of air. "And do you think Liam believes in evil demons?"

"No. Of course not!" Sara answered quickly. "I mean, I don't think so. How could he? Liam is so smart. He couldn't really believe in them." She nibbled her lip until she tasted blood on her tongue.

"But he got upset because you forgot to say it?"

Sara sighed. "That was only the beginning."

Two girls came running by, nearly knocking Sara and Mary Beth over. "Sorry!" one of them, long hair flying wildly in the wind, called back.

"After breakfast, I saw Liam coming into the house carrying a big bucket. The bucket was filled with dirt."

"How did he get dirt today? Did he dig under the ice?"

Sara shrugged. "I guess. I asked why he was bringing a bucket of dirt into the living room."

"And?"

"He said it was an old superstition from Sussex or somewhere. It's good luck to carry mud into the house in January. It's called January Butter."

"Uh huh." Mary Beth twisted her face. "I've got to remember to do that when I get home tonight."

"Please—it's not funny."

Mary Beth grabbed Sara's coat sleeve. "Sorry. Really."

"There's more. We hired this woman—Mrs. Layton—to come clean the house once a week. Actually, Milton found her for us. Well, this morning, I was upstairs getting dressed and I heard a loud racket down in the living room. Liam was screaming and carrying on about something. So I went tearing down the stairs—and do you know what he was so upset about? Mrs. Layton had opened the front door and was sweeping the dust outside."

Sara took a deep breath and let it out. "And Liam was shouting, 'You're sweeping out all the good luck. You're sweeping out all the good luck!' "

"I don't believe this," Mary Beth muttered.

"Liam grabbed the dustbroom from her and started sweeping the dust back inside. He was so frantic. He looked so . . . so *crazy!*"

Mary Beth shook her head. "Weird."

"Poor Mrs. Layton—she didn't know what to make of it," Sara continued breathlessly. "She burst into tears and quit. Got her coat and ran out of the house. Didn't even wait for me to pay her."

"Oh, wow. Then what did Liam do?"

"Well, after she left, he got real apologetic. I think he felt terrible. He kept telling me how sorry he was. He asked me to be understanding. He promised he'd try not to get carried away like that again."

"Sounds like a candidate for Prozac to me," Mary Beth said.

"Mary Beth—please!"

"It might help lighten him up, Sara."

"He *isn't* crazy. He's . . . he's just—"

Now she felt guilty for complaining about Liam to Mary Beth. She should have known that Mary Beth wouldn't take it seriously. Mary Beth made jokes about everything.

"You're the psych major," Mary Beth offered. "Maybe you could get someone in your department to talk to Liam. You know, just a friendly chat. Or maybe you could convince Liam to see a shrink."

I never should have told her all this, Sara thought unhappily. Never. First Mary Beth made jokes about it. Now she's taking it too seriously.

"A shrink? I don't think I could get Liam to see a shrink," she told her friend. "He's really okay. I guess he just enjoys all the superstition and folklore. And besides, it's all totally harmless—right?"

Garrett opened the door and poked his head into the outer office. No one at the desk. The computer behind it was on, a blue glare from the monitor.

"Dean Cohn? Are you here?"

Garrett heard a cough. Rumblings from the office behind the partition. "Dean Cohn? It's Detective Montgomery."

A few seconds later, Milton Cohn appeared from the back, adjusting a navy blue tie, then mopping beads of sweat off his scarlet forehead with a handkerchief. He stuck out a hot, moist hand to shake Garrett's.

"I was working out," Milton explained in his hoarse baritone. "Sorry I didn't hear you come in." He started to wipe his forehead again. But his beefy hand stopped in midair, and his eyes bulged. "Not another murder!"

"No." Garrett raised both hands, a signal to remain calm. "No. Thank God. As I explained in my phone message, I just need to ask you a few questions."

Milton let out a long whoosh of air. "Scared me for a moment." He motioned for Garrett to take the chair opposite the desk. Then Milton lowered himself heavily into the desk chair, leaning across the desk, still breathing hard from his exercise.

"It was nice of you to see me so late in the evening." Garrett gestured to the darkening sky outside the window. "You've been very cooperative." He pulled out a small pad and a pencil.

"I've tried to help your department in every way I can," Milton replied stiffly, silvery eyes studying Garrett. "No one is more upset about these murders than I am. Personally, and on behalf of the college." He cleared his throat loudly. "As I told you, I knew one of the victims. Devra Brookes."

Garrett nodded. He pretended to check over his pad. But he had nothing written on the page he had opened to. "I need to ask you a few questions about someone on the college staff," he said, raising his eyes to Milton.

The dean's eyes flickered with curiosity. "Someone who teaches here? You don't think—"

"Just routine," Garrett interrupted.

Just a total waste of time, he thought, suddenly feeling foolish. Why am I here? Why am I following up on this? The FBI agents thought I was a jerk for hauling in that professor and his wife and sister.

So *what* if he happened to be acquainted with all four victims? So *what?* There's no way that meek, quiet guy is a psycho who tears people apart with his bare hands.

What am I doing here? Why am I being so damned stubborn about this guy?

"What can you tell me about Liam O'Connor?" he asked the dean. "He's a visiting professor here, right?"

Milton pulled himself up straight with a grunt. "Liam? Why are you interested in Liam?"

"The agents and I had a little talk with him yesterday," Garrett revealed. He wasn't sure if he should have mentioned it or not.

What the hell. This is a waste of time, anyway.

"Liam is a very accomplished, very well known, well thought of member of the academic community," Milton said pompously. "I really don't think—"

"He was acquainted with all four victims," Garrett blurted out. He didn't have the patience to listen to any speeches.

Milton's mouth opened in a small O of surprise. "But that doesn't mean anything, Detective," he replied after a long, thoughtful silence. "Freewood is a very small town, after all."

Garrett nodded. "I'm just grabbing at straws, Dean Cohn. Think hard. Is there anything you can tell me about Professor O'Connor that might—"

"I can tell you only good things about him," Milton interrupted. "Only good things. I—I can't believe you're even asking me about him."

I can't either, Garrett thought bitterly.

"Liam is a world-reknowned scholar. His books have been published all over the world. He—he's a teacher!" Milton declared, his face reddening as he became more excited. "He's not a—a—"

Garrett raised a hand again. "I know. As I said, I'm desperate. I just thought you might—"

"There's nothing I can tell you about Liam," the dean growled. "His record, his references, his reputation—all are impeccable. The administration at Chicago was so sorry to see him go. They made him promise that—"

"Chicago?" Garrett scribbled the name on his pad. "He came here from Chicago? And why did he leave the university there?"

"I—I'm not really sure," Milton sputtered. "I think he needed a break. He told me he needed a quieter atmosphere where he could concentrate on writing his next book. Really, Detective Montgomery, I assure you—"

Garrett climbed to his feet, snapping the notepad shut. "You're right, sir. I apologize. I'm wasting your time. You've been very good to see me. I hope—"

"I hope you have some better leads than chasing after Professor O'Connor," Milton said, shaking his head.

"I wish I did," Garrett muttered under his breath. He thanked the dean again, then quickly exited the office.

Milton hunched over the desk, head propped in his hands, thinking hard. The police, the FBI—they obviously don't have a clue, he told himself.

Four murders. Four brutal murders. And they're running around in circles, asking questions about a man who spends all his time reading about leprechauns and elves.

That detective couldn't hide how foolish he felt.

What did he expect me to say? That I've suspected for a long time that Liam might be a crazed serial killer?

Four murders. Four . . .

Liam has been in town for such a short time. He moved here about four months ago. Four . . .

Four . . .

Such a short time to become acquainted with all four victims. All four . . .

Milton glanced at the desk clock. A little after five-thirty. That meant it was only four-thirty in Chicago.

I wonder if Jimmy Pinckney is still in his office.

Jimmy might get a laugh at the local cops suspecting Liam of murder. Liam spent four years in Jimmy's department. At least four years.

Four . . . Four . . .

I've been meaning to call Jimmy anyway. Find out how his son's operation went.

Milton fingered through the Rolodex. Found the office phone number at the university. Tapping one shoe against the floor, he punched in the number in Chicago.

A secretary answered. "I'm sorry, sir. Dean Pinckney stepped away. I don't think he went home, but—oh—wait. Here he comes now. Hold on."

A few seconds later, Pinckney's surprised voice on the line: "Milton—are *you* still alive?"

"I know, I know. I've been meaning to call you for months."

A few minutes of chitchat. Yes, Pinckney's son was perfectly fine. A cold, merciless winter in Chicago. So what else is new?

"Jimmy, I'm calling to tell you a story about Liam."

"Liam? How's he doing? How's he surviving the culture shock?"

Milton hesitated. "Well . . . I'm not sure. We've been having some grim times here, Jim. You've read about them?"

"TV exec's kid got killed near campus? Some others? Yeah. We get the news from Pennsylvania. Especially if it's bad news."

"It's been really rough, Jim. You know—"

"Sounds like what happened here the last couple of years."

"Huh?"

"You know, Milt. The murders on campus. It was so horrible. We had three of them. One more gruesome than the last. Unsolved. Do you believe it? Three murders, and the guy got clean away." A pause. Crackling on the phone line. Then, Pinckney continued: "Funny you should mention Liam. I had two FBI guys in my office last spring. Asking me about Liam. Liam, of all people. Seems he knew all three people . . . all three who got killed."

Milton gripped the phone receiver so hard, his hand ached. Numbers roared through his brain.

Three?

Three? Four?

Three plus four?

Pinckney's voice faded behind the roar. "So what was the story you wanted to tell me about Liam? Huh? Milton? Milton? Are you still there? Milton? Janet—I think we were cut off."

Milton frantically paced the small office, hands behind his back. Impossible. It was impossible.

The only word.

But seven out of seven?

Impossible.

An impossible coincidence.

The back of his neck prickled. Perspiration leaked down his face, into his eyes.

Impossible.

But he knew them all. Liam knew them all.

One thing I have to do, Milton decided, reaching for the phone.

I have to warn Sara.

44

Sara closed the front door behind her and ran to answer the phone. "Anybody home?" Why didn't someone pick up the phone? She had heard it ringing and ringing from outside as she fumbled with her keys.

Breathing hard, she picked up the receiver. "Hello?"

She heard a click, then the steady drone of the dial tone.

Whoever it was had given up.

Her boots had left dark puddles on the floor. She bent to pull them off. The cold clung to her coat, to her skin. She shivered as she dropped her bookbag to the floor.

She turned to the living room. "Where is everyone?"

Dark in there. She peered up the stairs. Dark up there too. Margaret must not be home.

She tugged off her coat and tossed it into the front closet. Rubbing the sleeves of her sweater, she made her way into the living room and clicked on a lamp. Her eyes quickly surveyed the room. Sections of the morning newspaper spread over the couch. The vacuum cleaner against the wall. A yellow spray can of Pledge on the coffee table beside a dark-stained rag.

Mrs. Layton. She quit and stormed out of the house without finishing. The morning's drama with the housekeeper flashed back into Sara's mind.

She felt another pang of guilt. Why had she confided so

completely in Mary Beth about Liam? After all these years, she should know better than to open up to Mary Beth that way.

Mary Beth is a good friend, Sara decided, but I shouldn't be turning to her for help. I'm a married woman now—not an inexperienced college freshman. I should be able to confide my feelings to Liam. What was I thinking of? One unpleasant episode, and I go tattling to Mary Beth like a six-year-old.

She slapped her forehead with an open palm. What *was* I thinking of? She wished she could put the day on rewind—go back to the morning and start all over again.

Shivering again, unable to get warm, she checked the thermostat on the wall in the front hall, then walked into the kitchen and put the kettle on the stove for some tea.

A note on the refrigerator caught her eye. It was in Margaret's curlicued handwriting, informing Sara and Liam that she would not be home this evening. Margaret was having dinner with a woman she had met at the antique shop, then going to a concert of the campus string quartet.

Just Liam and me tonight. For once, Sara thought. She glanced at the clock. A few minutes past six—and she hadn't made any plan for dinner.

The phone rang. Sara felt her stomach tighten. I hope this isn't Liam, saying he'll be late tonight. I really don't feel like being alone. I'm really eager to see him.

She lifted the receiver of the wall phone. Maybe it's Mary Beth. If it is, I'm going to tell her to forget everything I said this afternoon. "Hello?"

"Hello. Mrs. O'Connor?"

"Yes?" Yes, I *am* Mrs. O'Connor. The sound of it still excited her. But then she felt a stab of cold dread. Was this that woman calling back? Was this Angela again?

"I'm sorry to bother you, but this is Cathy in Professor O'Connor's office."

"Oh. Hi, Cathy." Sara let out a silent sigh of relief. "What's wrong? Is my husband there?"

"No. He left early. But he asked me to confirm his flight to

Dallas. I forgot all about it. I want to call the airline before I leave, but I need the flight numbers. Can you find the tickets for me? If it isn't too much trouble?"

Flight to Dallas. Sara had forgotten about Liam's speaking engagement next week. He had agreed to do it before he knew he was coming to Moore State. He said he wasn't looking forward to it, but he had given his word.

"No problem, Cathy," Sara said. "It's probably on his desk somewhere. Give me a minute or two to find it. Just hold on."

She let the phone receiver dangle to the floor and trotted into the living room to Liam's desk. She clicked on the tensor light, her eyes surveying the desktop. Stacks of papers. A pile of professional journals and magazines. A book of Celtic folklore and myths. More papers. A solid glass paperweight. Everything very neat and orderly.

She didn't see the airline tickets at first glance. She inspected the first stack of papers, shuffling through quickly. Then the next stack. Then through the journals and magazines.

Maybe Liam stuck them in a desk drawer.

She pulled open the top drawer. Some notebooks. Several ballpoint pens. A paperback thesaurus. No. He wouldn't keep them in here. He's so organized, so methodical, I'll bet he has a file somewhere called TRAVEL.

She pulled open the second drawer on the right. More papers? No. Bills to be paid. This was Liam's bill drawer.

She pulled the drawer out a little further and spotted a rectangular white box, a stationery box. Did he keep travel papers and things inside it?

She pulled the box out of the drawer and lifted the top. Moved the box into the square of white light from the desk lamp.

Photographs. Snapshots. Old school photos.

I didn't know Liam kept photos here. Who *are* these people?

Liam, a very young Liam, nineteen or twenty maybe, with two fingers raised behind the head of a blond young man, giving him horns, both of them grinning. Liam, a little older, in an ill-fitting sports jacket, a hideous, woolly jacket with huge shoulders, standing uncomfortably beside a smiling young woman.

I don't have time to look at these. I shouldn't be looking at them, Sara scolded herself.

But another snapshot caught her eye. A dark-haired young woman in a revealing black bikini, on a beach somewhere, smiling coyly.

Who is *she?* Sara couldn't stifle her curiosity. The young woman looked a lot like Sara. Who was she smiling at so teasingly? Liam?

Sara turned the snapshot over. Handwriting on the back, smudged by time. She squinted to read the faded words: *Love, Kristen.*

In the kitchen, the kettle started to scream.

45

"Liam!"

Smiling, he strode into the room, his overcoat open, carrying a bouquet of red roses wrapped in tissue paper in one hand, a yellow plastic shopping bag in the other.

Sara had just hung up the phone. Cathy would have to wait for Liam to find the ticket. Sara still clutched the snapshot of Kristen in one hand.

Liam thrust the roses into her arms. "I'm so sorry about this morning, darling."

"Liam, I—"

"I know. I was completely in the wrong. I just went overboard. As my students say, I totally lost it."

His smile widened. "I'm going to make it up to you tonight. I promise." He kissed her, pressing the flowers between them. His face felt cold, but his lips were warm.

She pulled back. "Liam—I have to ask you something."

He raised the plastic shopping bag. "I brought dinner. I left early and stopped at Szechuan Garden." He inhaled deeply. "Mmmmm. Doesn't that smell delicious? I got two orders of the vegetable dumplings. Your favorite."

He moved closer to kiss her again. "Let's have a romantic evening, Sara. Let me make you forget about this morning."

She could feel her heart start to race. His smile always had

306

that effect on her. And those brown eyes, those soft, soulful brown eyes that seemed to be filled with so much love, so much adoration for her.

But she held the photograph in her hand.

She set the flowers down. And raised the snapshot. "Liam, I—I found this," she stammered, her voice trembling despite her effort to keep it low and calm.

His eyes narrowed at it. He lowered the bag of Chinese food to the floor. "What's that?"

"I found it in a box. In your desk drawer. I was looking for your plane ticket. And I thought it might be in the box. But instead I found this photo."

His dark eyebrows furrowed. He took the snapshot from her hand and brought it close to his face, examining it carefully, his eyes moving from side to side as if he were reading it. "Who *is* this?"

"It's Kristen," Sara choked out. "Read the back. It's Kristen. The woman who called me yesterday. You told me you didn't know anyone named Kristen. But there she is. Kristen."

He continued to stare at the photo. Flipped it over. Read the back. Turned back to the front. Then raised his eyes to Sara. "I've never seen her before."

"Liam—"

"Where did you find it? In a box? What box?"

She turned and led him back to the desk. The floorboards creaked under her feet as she walked. She hadn't noticed the creaking before, but as she crossed the room, every sound seemed exaggerated, every thud of her stockinged feet on the floor, every breath she took, every swallow.

The desk light glowed as bright as a spotlight. The box stood in the center of the desktop where she had left it. The lid of the box beside it. The drawer still open.

"There." She pointed.

Liam, eyebrows still furrowed, features still set in their bewildered squint, picked up the box and shuffled rapidly through the photographs.

After a few seconds, he replaced the box on the desktop and raised his eyes to hers. "These aren't my photos."

"Huh?"

"It isn't my box. It's Margaret's. Those are Margaret's old photos."

"They are?" Sara's voice came out high and shrill. She placed a hand over her chest, as if trying to slow her pounding heart.

Was he telling the truth? Was he?

He glanced at the photo of Kristen once again, then dropped it into the open box. "The movers must have put this box in the wrong desk. I don't know this Kristen. She doesn't look familiar at all. Must have been a friend of Margaret's. We can ask her later."

Sara swallowed hard. "Oh, Liam, I'm so sorry. When I saw the photo, I just—"

He covered her mouth with his. He kissed her lightly, then with real feeling. When he pulled back, he was grinning. "I do love having a jealous wife."

"No. It was wrong," Sara stammered. "I shouldn't have jumped to conclusions."

"I especially adore having a wife who can become jealous of a faded old photograph," Liam continued, holding her snugly in his arms. "I'm a very lucky man, Sara. A very lucky man."

"I'm the lucky one," Sara murmured.

As he lowered his face to kiss her again, her eyes fell on the photo of the coyly smiling young woman in the box. Was Liam telling the truth?

Of course he was.

After dinner, he led her up the stairs to their bedroom. "A special night," he whispered softly. His warm breath tickled her ear, gave her chills.

She reached for the light switch, but he gently pulled her hand away. "No lights tonight." Another whisper. His lips brushed her cheek. His hands moved down the back of her sweater. They slid under her sweater as he kissed her softly, so softly. His hands were warm on her, warm and tender.

He pulled off her sweater. He kissed her again, his tongue pushing lightly against hers. His hands, his warm hands, caressed her. He let out a small cry of pleasure.

"Get undressed. I'll be right back."

He vanished in the darkness. Blue light washed into the room from the window, pale blue on the carpet, as if she were standing on air, standing in the sky.

She felt as if she were floating. Her body still tingled from his touch. She tasted him on her lips as she tugged off the rest of her clothes, leaving them in a pile on the carpet, and slid under the covers.

Liam, I want you. Liam, where did you go? I want you so badly.

He reappeared a few seconds later in a flicker of orange candlelight. She could see his smile, see the dark, excited flash of his eyes.

He carried a long, white candle in front of him. As he set it down on the dresser, Sara could see the small box he carried in the other. He set the box down on the dresser top beside the candle.

And turned to Sara. So handsome in the dim light, all dark eyes and shadows. So handsome. I want you now, Liam. Please—climb in beside me.

"I promised you a special night," he said in a low voice just above a whisper. He spoke rapidly, excitedly, his eyes flickering with the candle flame. "A very special night, my beautiful Sara."

He picked up the box and held it in both hands. "I know you do not live in the world of magic and superstition as I do, my darling. But this is an ancient Irish ceremony that newlyweds have performed for generation upon generation."

Sara pulled herself up against the headboard, tugging the blankets up under her chin. What is he about to do? she wondered, suddenly anxious. She wanted to say, "Liam, put down the box and just come to bed." She wondered how he would react to that.

But he looked so serious, so intense, she knew she could never hurt him like that. He's so much more romantic than I am.

I will go along with this because he's so wonderful and I love him so much. I love him and his silly superstitions and ceremonies.

"Liam—what is in the box?" she asked softly.

Perhaps it was a present for her. A special present. Jewelry that once belonged to his mother, a ring passed down through the generations of his family.

He raised a finger to his lips, signaling for her not to speak. He moved through the dancing shadows to the CD player on the bookshelf beside the closet. A few seconds later, soft music floated across the room. She recognized Bach. A flute concerto.

So sweet, she thought. So romantic.

She heard him chanting over the music. Words in Gaelic? She couldn't really hear.

He raised his finger to his lips again. Smiled at her.

Then he pulled open the box.

Is it a necklace? she wondered. An ancient pendant? An emerald?

He lifted an object from the box and held it in the glow of orange light.

A human hand.

Sara uttered a low gasp.

"It's from a mannequin," he said softly, his voice barely rising over the lilting flute. He raised it toward her so that she could see it more clearly. "Only a mannequin hand, but it's so lifelike, isn't it?"

"Yes. Very," she murmured, gripping the bedcovers with both hands.

"It has to be lifelike, my darling, for the magic to work."

The magic? What was he going to do?

No emerald? No beautiful jeweled pendant handed down by his mother?

Why did he need a lifelike hand? What were those words he was chanting?

Sara leaned forward, reassured by his warm smile, by the dark excitement in his eyes. Lulled by the soft, lyrical chant of the strange words.

Liam turned to the dresser. He lifted the white candle from its holder. He stuck the candle into the mannequin hand. The hand now held the candle in its wooden grasp. Liam raised it high in front of him. The flame wrapped Liam in a warm orange glow.

He lowered the hand until the candle flame flickered in front of his face. As he began to speak, his breath made the flame bend low.

"Let those who are asleep be asleep," Liam recited. *"And let those who are awake be awake."*

A few seconds later, the mannequin hand rested on the dresser top, the glowing candle tucked tightly inside it. Liam slid beside Sara and silently and tenderly pulled her close.

He entered her quickly, almost roughly. She gasped, shut her eyes, raised her body to meet him.

They made love more passionately than they ever had.

The candle had burned low, rivulets of white wax flowing over the wooden hand, when Liam finally exploded inside her with a cry of joy.

46

Sara awoke feeling achy and stiff, her temples throbbing. She squinted into the bright yellow sunlight flooding in through the window and reached for Liam.

To her surprise, he wasn't there.

She pulled herself up, shutting her eyes, massaging her temples. Her legs felt weak. Perhaps from the lovemaking.

A long, hot shower will make me feel better, she decided. She leaned over to pat the indentation in Liam's pillow. Sweet Liam. She wanted him to hold her now. She thought again of the night before, the long, passionate lovemaking, so fierce and tender at the same time.

"Liam, where are you?" she murmured aloud, her voice still hoarse from sleep.

Then she glimpsed the bed table clock. Nearly ten! She had overslept. Why had he let her oversleep? Her seminar was at eleven. She had planned to be at the library when it opened to do some preparatory research and organize her notes.

Her head still throbbing, Sara pulled herself up from the bed and lurched toward the bathroom, tripping over the bedsheet tangled around her leg, pulling it with her.

A hot shower. A hot shower and some aspirin. And then I'm out of here, she thought. This day is not starting out well.

* * *

Milton let the phone ring six times. Seven. Eight. "Come on, Sara. Pick it up." His fingers thumped the desk. He slammed the receiver down in frustration.

He had tried to phone her all last evening, but the phone must have been off the hook. If only she would stop by the office . . .

What will I say when I *do* talk to her?

The question repeated unanswered in his mind.

"Sara, you're not safe. Your husband may be a crazed serial killer."

Liam?

Sara will laugh in my face.

How can I even be thinking it? Liam seems such a gentle, civilized person. It isn't possible. And yet it is possible.

He knew seven out of seven.

That's what I'll tell Sara. "There were murders in Chicago too. Horrible, inhuman murders. And Liam knew them all, knew all the victims."

I have to warn her, Milton decided. I have no choice. I have to convince her that she is in real danger. She won't laugh at me when she sees how serious I am. She won't laugh when I tell her seven out of seven.

Then what?

She can grab her things. Come stay at my house till we decide what to do.

Milton had a call in to the police detective who had visited him. Detective Montgomery was out of the station on street duty, he had been told. But he would call as soon as he checked in.

Milton tugged his overcoat from the closet. Wrapping it around him, he hurried from the office. Got to get some cool air. I feel as if I'm burning up. Burning up.

He stepped out into a gray, blustery day, dark storm clouds lowering rapidly, a sky that seemed to reflect his mood perfectly.

He jammed his hands into the overcoat pockets. Didn't

bother to button the coat. Leaned into the cold wind, feeling a wet snowflake on his hot forehead. Then another.

Taking long strides, he started across The Circle, not seeing the students on the crisscrossing paths, not paying attention to where he was walking, letting the cold fresh air soothe him.

Halfway to the library, Sara ran right into him.

They both cried out.

Flecks of snow in her black hair. Her eyes startled, red-rimmed. His hands flew up to the shoulders of her coat. "Sara—!"

"Sorry, Milton. I—I was hurrying. I'm late, and I don't feel well. I—"

"I've been trying to reach you."

"I know. I know. I'm sorry I didn't come to work yesterday. I think I have the flu or something. I don't think I can come today, either. I—"

She swept past him, her face pale in the gray light.

"I have to talk to you. Right away."

"No. I'm so late."

"But, Sara—it's really urgent. I have to—"

"My seminar!" She started to jog, backpack bouncing over her shoulders. "Sorry, Milton. Can I call you later?"

"No!" He started after her, snow in his eyes. "Sara—listen to me!" His voice brushed back by the wind. "No—wait!"

But he couldn't keep up. An elephant racing a gazelle.

"Sara—I have to talk to you!"

Kids shouting, calling each other across The Circle.

Did she hear him? Did they drown out his plea?

Why didn't she give him one second?

Milton let out a frustrated growl, feeling his heart pound. Jamming his hands back into the overcoat pockets, he leaned into the falling snow, turned back toward the Administration Building.

Maybe that detective called.

Maybe I can get Liam arrested, arrested before . . .

He didn't want to finish his thought.

* * *

Garrett rang the doorbell again. Listened hard. Silence inside. No one home. Probably everyone was still at work. He checked his watch. Nearly five-thirty. Already dark. Almost time to quit for the day. Maybe finish the houses on this block, then call it quits.

He stepped down from the stoop and stretched. His back ached. I'm used to sitting down all day, he realized. Walking around from house to house in the fresh air is going to really help me.

Or kill me.

Maybe I'll knock off a little early and get home in time to feed Martin his dinner.

He stepped under a streetlight and raised the clipboard close to his face to read it. His eyes scanned the list of houses and apartments. He'd covered a lot of ground today.

And turned up nothing.

Another day, another half-dollar.

No one had seen or heard anything. No one had a clue.

He kicked at a clump of ice on the base of the lamppost. It cracked under the weight of his black boot. Pieces flew into the street.

I had my day last week, Garrett thought dejectedly. Finding that professor who knew all four victims. That was my big moment.

The fantasies had begun to play out in his mind as he drove the professor, his wife, and sister to the station to turn them over to the Feds. Garrett Montgomery, local hero.

He imagined himself on the eleven o'clock news—no—on the national news, explaining how he found the murderer. "It was easy, actually. No problem. How hard is it to put two and two together? I've been a cop long enough to know when to play my hunches. I'm not really a hero. I was just doing my job."

What bullshit.

The professor had walked. Naturally.

315

Why would a fucking college professor—and a famous one at that, a visiting celebrity in town for just one year—why would he start murdering people on campus?

The more he had thought about it, the more Garrett felt like a total fool. The guy wasn't strong-looking or athletic in any way. How could he have ripped those poor woman apart?

No way.

Garrett had wasted everyone's time. "Just doing my job." After all, it was the only kind of lead he'd been able to find in all these weeks of trying. And the guy had a connection to all four suspects. And he looked kind of nervous about it.

And then I wasn't satisfied. I had to go see the dean at the college. What did I think he would tell me? "Oh, yes. We know the professor likes to murder people from time to time. But he's such a good teacher, he has such a good reputation, we thought we'd overlook it."

He must have thought I was crazy.

I *must* be crazy. Crazy or just plain stupid. Or both.

I should go back to that professor's house and apologize.

But real cops don't apologize—do they?

He turned the corner, heading back to the car. Where had he parked it? On Jackson?

The snow was falling steadily now. Most of the houses were still dark. A van rumbled by, skis poking out the back window. In the distance, Garrett heard tires squeal. Some poor jerk sliding on the icy road. Garrett figured that Walter and some of the other guys probably went on traffic detail today to deal with all the fender-benders.

He found himself wondering how Walter was doing. Hey—don't tell me I miss that fat slob. No way!

Maybe I'll drop in and see Walter tomorrow. Unless he's still out on house-to-house detail like me.

Garrett uttered a bitter laugh under his breath. He knew the house-to-house deal was a joke. Just the Feds' way of getting him out from under their feet.

He crossed the street, his boots sliding on the slick surface.

The trees glittered darkly, ice clinging to the bare branches like clothing.

The creature dropped down on Garrett from high in a tree.

Garrett let out a grunt. Caught the creature in his arms. At first, he thought it was a big chimpanzee. It wrapped heavy arms and legs around Garrett's body.

Garrett gazed into round, yellow eyes. The creature was covered in thick, rank fur. The odor rose up, so foul, such a putrid stench.

Not a monkey?

It brought its face close—to kiss him, he thought.

But the pain shot out from the side of his head, pain so intense it made Garrett shriek.

He heard the tearing sound over his own shriek. Another burst of pain. And he saw his ear in the creature's mouth.

My ear. It bit off my ear!

Its yellow eyes flashed. It spat the flat, brown ear into the air like a potato chip. Then caught it in a furry paw—and stuffed the ear into its mouth, chewing noisily, teeth bared, its heavy black lips pulled back in a gleeful grin.

"Nooooo!" Garrett howled in pain. Felt the hot blood flow down the side of his face.

He swung his fist—a wild, frantic swing, more reflex than plan—swung it hard at the creature's grinning face.

The mouth gaped open just as Garrett swung.

Garrett's fist plunged inside. Deep inside. Down the creature's wide throat.

Hot and wet in there.

The monster's yellow eyes bulged. It let out a startled *gulp*. Thrashed its rank, fur-covered arms above its head. Tossed back its head, trying to free itself from the intruding hand.

Garrett's fist plunged deeper. Grabbed something soft. Soft and spongy. Deep beyond the monster's throat.

The creature made a hoarse retching sound. Jerked its head back. Retched again.

Garrett gripped the hot, spongy organ inside the creature's belly. Then jerked back with all his strength.

A shrill howl escaped the monster as Garrett ripped out a pink, sausage-shaped organ, covered in thick, shiny mucous. With an angry cry, Garrett heaved the creature organ across the street.

The creature whimpered. Slumped to the snow, a pile of dark fur. Legs slithering away, carrying it into a thick hedge, whimpering, whistling as it scrabbled low, defeated. Garrett heard it retching, retching and whimpering.

The winter-bare hedge trembled as the wounded monster pulled itself through.

Garrett lowered his eyes to the snow, puddled red, red with his own blood. Felt the warm blood flood down his cheek, jolt after jolt of pain shooting out from where his ear had been.

Pain hotter than the flowing blood.

He raised a hand to cover the hole. But it hurt too much to touch it.

He dropped to his knees, surprised by how much blood can pour from an open head, surprised by how weak he suddenly felt, so weak he couldn't raise his hands from the bloodstained snow, surprised, so surprised, surprised by how well he could still hear his own terrified cries.

"Liam? Margaret? Anyone home?"

Silence.

She made her way through the dark house, clicking on lights. Then she turned up the thermostat and, trying to rub the cold from her hands, walked into the kitchen to make a pot of tea.

Sleet tapped steadily against the kitchen window. Wind rattled the pane. She had stayed in the library longer than she had planned. When she had emerged, the sky was evening black, the sleet continued to pound down, and the walks were icy and treacherous.

Sara filled the kettle and lowered it to the stove. Then she hurried upstairs to change into something warmer and more comfortable. Clicking on the ceiling light, she found the room in disarray, just as she had left it that morning. The bed was unmade, the blankets rumpled, the sheet pulled halfway across the room. Her nightdress sprawled over the chair, hairbrush on the floor beside the dresser.

Why am I surprised? Did I expect elves to come clean the place up while I was out?

She moved to the dresser, leaned against the dresser top and bent to pick up the hairbrush. Her hand bumped against something soft. She turned and saw the mannequin hand, a coating of white candle wax over the thumb and curled fingers.

Sara couldn't help but smile, remembering the night before, remembering the wonderful lovemaking while across the room, the candle burned low and the wax slid over the hand.

She smoothed her fingers over the coating of wax. It crumbled and slid off under her touch.

She picked up the hand. Not wooden, as she imagined. Hard but sort of leathery.

She turned it, pulled open the stiff fingers to investigate the palm. Then turned it over again to the back.

And as the thin sheet of candle wax broke away, she saw the tattoo.

A small black dagger with a tiny drop of blue blood at the blade tip.

"Ohhh." The hand fell to the dresser, the fingers spreading slowly.

Chip's hand.

Chip's hand.

Chip's hand.

PART SIX

47

How long did she stare down at it? At the leathery fingers spread over her dresser top. At the tiny black dagger on the back of the hand, fading into the browning skin. At the wrist so cleanly sliced, so carefully sewn together with heavy, black thread.

How long? How long?

Till the dagger darkened behind a curtain of teardrops. Till the hand blurred. Till she shut her eyes and kept them shut, feeling the room spin, feeling the floor tilt and sway like the deck of a rocking, storm-tossed ship beneath her.

Panic.

The panic, making it so hard to breathe, bringing up the waves of nausea, tightening her muscles, tightening every muscle until they ache, until they feel about to burst, my whole body about to burst, my legs so heavy, so heavy I can't move away, can't move away from this . . . thing . . . this thing that I used to hold, that used to hold me, that used to touch me. This hand.

Chip's hand.

Chip's hand.

Chip's hand.

On my dresser now. Holding the candle, holding it so tightly while Liam and I made love.

Why? Oh, why?

Why, Liam?

"I have to get out." Said aloud in a tight, low voice through gritted teeth.

So tight. Everything tight. Even her teeth. Her jaw clenched so hard.

She spun away from the dresser. Forced herself to breathe. Forced herself to take a step. Then another.

Mary Beth. I need Mary Beth.

I need help, Mary Beth.

I have to think. I have to think clearly. I have to make sense of it. It *has* to make sense.

Liam. Sweet Liam.

So good. So brilliant. So wonderful.

Liam loved her.

But . . .

Chip's hand. Chip's hand. Chip's hand.

It didn't make sense at all. Maybe Mary Beth could help.

You've *got* to help, Mary Beth.

Sara found herself in the living room. Wiped tears from her eyes with both hands. Pulled open the desk drawer. Her hands trembling so hard.

It didn't make sense at all.

She scribbled a note. She didn't mean to scribble. Normally, she had such nice handwriting. Her teachers always complimented her on her handwriting.

Her handwriting. Her hand. Writing. Her hand.

Chip's hand. Chip's hand.

How many times had she held that hand? Kissed that hand?

HAVE DINNER WITHOUT ME. I'LL BE HOME VERY LATE.

Her note to Liam. She started to the refrigerator with it. But returned to the desk. And added: LOVE, SARA.

I *do* love you, Liam. And I know you love me.

I know it's going to work out this time. I know this time it's right.

But . . . Chip's hand?

Mary Beth will know.

She stuck the note to the refrigerator. Grabbed her down coat. The gloves toppled out of the pocket onto the carpet. She didn't stop to retrieve them.

What if Liam came home? What if he walked in the door right now and asked her where she was going?

Would she be able to ask him about the hand? Would she be able to ask, "Why is Chip's hand on our dresser, Liam?"

No. Not until the panic faded. Not until she could breathe again. Not until she could blink, shut her eyes for a second without seeing that sewn-up hand with its dark smudge of a tattoo. The leathery fingers grasping, grasping . . .

Oh, Liam—why?

Out into the cold. The sleet had softened to a cold rain. The sidewalks glowed like dull silver under a layer of soft slush and ice.

Ignoring the slippery footing, Sara started to run. She knew she was running away. She told herself she was running for help.

I'll be back, Liam. I'll be back late, but I'll be back.

She ran all the way across the campus, hands tucked into the coat pockets, collar pulled up around her face, the cold rain soaking her hair. She ran over the ice, the slush, tripping, slipping, sliding on the icy walks. She was breathing hard when she reached Mary Beth's apartment, gasping, breath smoking above her, her side aching, stomach cramping, blood thumping at both temples.

Mary Beth pulled open the door, green eyes narrowed in surprise, streaked hair in disheveled tangles, wearing faded jeans torn at both knees, an oversized red and gray Moore State sweatshirt, sleeves rolled up. "Sara?"

"I—I've got to talk."

"Whoa. Catch your breath. You're soaked. Did you run all the way? What's wrong? Sara—what happened?"

Sara put a hand over her heart, struggled to take a deep breath, then another, slower, slower. She followed Mary Beth into the apartment. An open pizza box on the table, half a pizza left inside it. Bruce Springsteen on the stereo. Mary Beth moved to turn it off.

Then swung back to Sara. "What *is* it? What's wrong?"

Sara starting to breathe a little easier. She glimpsed the bedroom through the open door, spotted a suitcase open on the bed. "Are you—are you going somewhere?" Voice still breathless.

Mary Beth twisted her mouth, scratched the shoulder of the sweatshirt. "I have to go home. My dad fell down or something. He broke his leg. Mom is hysterical. For a change." She rolled her eyes. "Do you believe having to fly on a night like this? I hope the airport doesn't shut down."

She took Sara's wet coat, set it down on the bench by the door. "Can I get you something to drink? Something hot?"

Sara shut her eyes. Saw the hand again. "Do you have any wine?"

Mary Beth thought about it. "Just red. Is that okay?"

"Great."

Mary Beth produced two juice glasses of red wine. Sara took a long sip. It burned the back of her throat, felt so soothing and warm. She took another long sip.

"So what's wrong?" Mary Beth dropped beside her on the couch, sitting on the cushion edge. She pushed back her tangled hair. "What's happening, Sara?"

Sara took a deep breath. She swallowed hard. Took another sip of wine. The glass nearly empty already. "It's kind of hard to explain. It's about Liam."

Mary Beth rolled her eyes. "More superstitions?"

"Yes. No. I mean, yes." She struggled to tell her friend about the ceremony the night before. How romantic Liam had been. How tender and caring. She told her about the box, the candle, the flute music, Liam's soft, Gaelic chant.

And then the hand.

"Huh? He put the candle in the hand?" Mary Beth squeezed Sara's arm. Her fingers felt warm through Sara's sweater.

Sara nodded. And then the horrible part, the horrible truth burst out of her: "It was Chip's hand!"

Of course Mary Beth didn't believe her at first. "There has to be a logical explanation for this, Sara. Liam isn't a *ghoul!*"

Ghoul?

Sara repeated the word in her mind, as if she had never heard it before.

Ghoul?

"Listen, Sara—just because it had the same tattoo . . . doesn't mean anything. Daggers are a very common tattoo, you know. Someone could have painted it on the mannequin hand . . . as a joke."

Sara uttered a choked sob. "It wasn't a mannequin hand. I touched it. I picked it up. It wasn't wood. It was skin."

Mary Beth placed both hands firmly on Sara's shoulders. "You're shaking all over. You poor thing. You've gotten yourself all messed up over nothing. I'm sure. If we call Liam, I know he'll be able to—"

Sara sat up sharply. "That woman—she tried to warn me."

"Huh? What woman?"

"Angela. Or Kristen. Whatever her name is. She called me. She said she was with Liam before me."

"Whoa—!" Mary Beth's green eyes bulged. She opened her lips and let out a whoosh of air.

"She said I was in danger. Of course I didn't believe her. Liam said he didn't know her. So I didn't go see her. But what if . . . what if she was telling the truth? What if she really was trying to warn me?"

Mary Beth slumped back on the couch. She twisted a curl of blond hair in her fingers. "Someone called you? To warn you about Liam?"

Sara nodded. She stared down at the nearly empty glass cupped between her hands. "I got calls before. Before we were married. Liam said it was probably an old girlfriend who had a breakdown. He told me not to pay any attention."

Mary Beth shook her head. "Weird."

"Then she called again. Two days ago. She said her name was Kristen. She said she had lived with Liam. She really frightened me. I mean, I didn't know whether to believe her or not. I mean, I didn't believe her. I had no reason to believe her. But why was she calling me? Why?"

Mary Beth refilled Sara's glass. "Have some more. Let's finish the bottle. Take a deep breath, Sara. We'll figure this out. It can't be anything too terrible. Try to get control, okay? Look at you, shaking like a leaf. You're starting to scare me."

"Well, I *am* scared!" Sara shot back, tipping the glass without realizing it, spilling a little wine onto her lap. "I'm really scared, Mary Beth. I don't understand—"

"Maybe that woman is still around," Mary Beth interrupted, standing in front of the couch, glass in one hand, bottle still in the other. "Did she leave a number or anything? If you talked to her, maybe she could clear everything up."

Sara took a deep breath. She rubbed her throbbing temple with her free hand. "Talk to her? You mean call her? Well . . ."

"We could go see her together," Mary Beth offered.

Sara couldn't think clearly. She couldn't decide what to do. "She said she was staying at the College Inn. You know, the big old place on Fairmont."

Mary Beth set down the wine bottle. "The College Inn? Are you sure?"

"Yeah. That's what she said. Why?"

"Well . . . you know. With all the excitement over there." Mary Beth crossed the room to the phone. "Well, let's call over there. See if we can reach her." She picked up the receiver. "What did you say her name was? Angela?"

Sara shook her head. "No. Kristen." She thought hard, struggling to remember the woman's last name. "Verret. Kristen Verret."

She expected Mary Beth to start dialing, to get the number of the College Inn and dial it. But Mary Beth stared back at her, shock on her face.

"Mary Beth—?"

"Sara, say the name again. I don't believe this."

"Kristen Verret," Sara repeated obediently. She rose

quickly to her feet, feeling a little dizzy. She gripped the arm of the couch, thinking that she shouldn't have stood up so fast. "What's wrong, Mary Beth? Why are you staring at me like that?"

"It can't be Kristen Verret," Mary Beth moaned, her voice barely reaching Sara. "It can't be."

"Why? What are you saying?"

"Kristen Verret? You're sure? Kristen Verret?"

"Yes, I'm sure," Sara cried impatiently. "Will you please tell me what's wrong?"

"Sara, didn't you hear the radio this morning? That's the woman who was murdered this morning. At the College Inn. Kristen Verret? She was cut to pieces. Didn't you hear the radio?"

48

Sara grabbed her stomach. She shut her eyes against a sharp stab of pain. She swallowed hard, fighting back a wave of nausea.

"Mary Beth—are you sure?"

Mary Beth dropped to the edge of the couch. "You really didn't hear about it? It was the only thing on the radio this morning. You didn't listen to the news?"

She asked another question, but Sara didn't hear her. Instead, Sara heard Liam's voice, Liam assuring her he knew no one named Kristen. Liam explaining that the snapshot of the young woman had to be a friend of Margaret's.

You didn't lie to me—did you, Liam?

You didn't lie. It isn't *all* lies, is it?

No.

But what if Kristen Verret told the truth? Why did Kristen Verret call Sara? Why did Kristen Verret call Sara and then get murdered in her room?

Why did Liam know *everyone* who had been murdered?

No. Oh please, no. Too many *whys*, Sara thought, pressing her hands against the sides of her face. She shut her eyes again, tried to force the questions away. The questions that rolled one after the other, like dark, cold waves.

You lied, Liam. And I believed every lie.

Because I wanted to believe. I wanted desperately to believe.

I'm sick. I really feel sick.

Liam, I need you now.

When she opened her eyes, Mary Beth stood over her, talking rapidly, excitedly. Sara could see her friend's lips move, but couldn't make out the words.

Kristen Verret. The name repeating in Sara's ears drowned out Mary Beth's gruesome description.

Kristen Verret.

She called me and then someone cut her to pieces.

"Oh, God." Sara uttered a low moan.

Mary Beth leaned down and placed a hand gently on Sara's trembling shoulder. "We have to call the police. We have to tell them about the phone call."

"I—I don't feel well." Sara lurched to her feet. Pushed past her friend.

"Sara—?"

Into the bathroom, swinging the door shut behind her. She bent over the toilet bowl, doubled over in pain, and tried to vomit.

"Sara—are you okay?" Mary Beth's worried voice muffled by the bathroom door.

Sara coughed. Her throat tightened. I feel so sick. I can't believe this is happening.

I don't understand. I just don't understand.

Liam's face hovered in her mind, his smile, his beautiful smile, the warm brown eyes, so loving, so adoring.

Oh, God. I don't understand. Liam, will you explain it to me? Will you make me feel good again?

The pain dulled to an ache. The nausea faded. She stood up. She turned away from the toilet on trembling legs. Rubbed cold sweat from her upper lip with one finger.

When she emerged from the bathroom, she knew what she had to do. Mary Beth stood tensely in the hall, her green eyes studying Sara's face. "You look terrible. Should I cancel my flight?" She glanced at her watch. "I don't think there's a later flight to Cleveland. But I could go tomorrow."

Sara squeezed her friend's hand. Sara's hand was ice cold, Mary Beth's warm and dry. "No. Really. Don't miss your flight. I feel better now. I—I'm going home."

"Home? Sara—no. Let me call the police for you. You've got to tell them about the phone call, about that woman calling you. Before you go home to Liam. You have to."

Sara shook her head vehemently. The sudden movement made her temples throb. "No. I have to get home. I have to talk to Liam."

"But what if Liam—?" Mary Beth didn't want to finish her thought.

"I have to give Liam a chance," Sara told her, not intending to sound so shrill, so frantic. Then softer, "I have to give Liam a chance to explain."

She slipped past Mary Beth into the living room. Mary Beth hurried after her. "You sure you don't want me to stay? I could walk you home. You really don't look well. I could get my car and drive you home. I could wait for you—in case . . ." Her voice trailed off. She lowered her eyes.

"I'll be fine." Sara's voice trembled. She struggled to keep it low and steady. "Really. I'll be fine. I need some fresh air. That was such a shock. But I don't think that Liam . . . I mean, well . . . I don't know. I just know I have to give Liam a chance to explain. About the hand. About Kristen Verret. About . . . everything."

She moved to pick up her coat, but Mary Beth stepped in front of her. To her surprise, Mary Beth wrapped her in a tight hug, pressing her hot cheek against Sara's.

She's never this emotional, Sara thought. Is it the wine? Is she so wired because her father is in the hospital? Because she has to fly home tonight? She isn't *really* worried about me—is she?

"I—I'll call you from Ohio." Mary Beth backed away, her

eyes locked on Sara's. "It'll be late. The plane stops in Pittsburgh first. Why do planes have to stop in Pittsburgh?"

Sara laughed. "I don't know. But they always do." She pulled on her coat.

Mary Beth headed to the front closet. "Let me at least give you an umbrella. Look at your coat. It's still soaked."

Sara raised her eyes to the window. "No. That's okay. It turned back to snow. I like the snow. It'll cool me down." She made her way to the door.

Mary Beth bit her lip fretfully. "The flight will be canceled. I know it will. Look at it out there. It's a blizzard!" She pulled open the door for Sara. "I'd better leave now. I don't believe this. I'll call you. As soon as I land."

"I'll be fine. Really. Have a good flight. Give my regards to your father." Sara pulled the down coat around her as she stepped out the apartment door. Her boots thudded dully against the hard floor of the long hallway. Muddy shoeprints led to a door across the hall. Puddles of dirty rainwater dotted the floor.

Rotten night, she thought, tugging up her collar. In every way.

She stepped out of the building, out from the safety of the long awning in front, the heavy canvas flapping noisily in the stiff wind, stepped into the snowy night.

She usually loved walking in fresh snow, but tonight it did nothing to raise her spirits. The sharp, swirling wind blew the wet snow into her face. The rain had frozen beneath the snow, leaving a treacherous layer of slippery ice underneath.

Raising her eyes, she saw a car slide across the intersection. It spun all the way around, skidding over the icy pavement, then slid to a stop inches from a lamppost.

I hope Mary Beth makes it to the airport, Sara thought, lowering her head against the windblown snow, trying to pick up her pace. Driving is even harder than walking tonight.

Her face felt raw, her nose and ears tingly and nearly numb by the time her house came into view. The light over the stoop made the falling snow sparkle as it fell. She couldn't see any other lights on in the house.

Weird, she thought. It's nearly nine. Liam should be home by now. Shielding her eyes against the snow with one hand, she gazed up to the windows of Margaret's rooms at the top of the house. Her windows were dark too.

Did they go out? On a night like this?

Not very likely.

Sara slipped on the bottom step of the front stoop. Grabbed the iron railing to keep herself from falling. She fumbled in her bag for the front door key, her frozen fingers moving stiffly among all her junk.

She finally managed to unlock the door, pushed it open with her shoulder, and, stamping her feet hard on the rubber outdoor mat, stepped into the warmth of the house.

Darkness. "Hey—anybody home?"

The upstairs hall light appeared to be the only light in the house. Trying to massage the stiffness from her frozen fingers, Sara stared up to the top of the stairs.

Was Liam up there? Did he go to bed so early? Did he go to bed and turn off all the lights downstairs?

Or had Sara left the hall light on earlier?

"Hey—anyone here?" Her throat tight from the cold, her voice soft, almost feathery.

Silence.

Please be here, Liam. I need to see you, to talk to you. I need to hear you tell me everything is okay.

Her coat still on, snowflakes clinging to the wet collar, tickling her neck, she grabbed the wooden banister and started to pull herself up the stairs.

Her heart pounded as she reached the top. She took a deep breath, held it, then turned toward their bedroom.

Liam, please be here. Liam, please . . .

The bedroom door was closed.

She grabbed the glass knob, twisted it, and pushed the door open.

Light from the hall spilled into the dark room.

The room smelled steamy. Sweaty.

She stepped inside. Saw Liam in bed. On his back.

Arm around someone else.

Another figure. Another person in the bed. Face hidden in shadow.

Liam sat up quickly, blinking in surprise. His arm slid away from the other person.

Who stirred and sat up.

A woman.

Liam in bed with a woman.

The woman moved. Her face slid into the light.

Margaret!

Liam in bed with Margaret! His sister!

Margaret leaned over Liam. Her bare breasts fell out from under the sheet. She squinted into the light, cleared her throat, then spoke softly. "Oh. Sara. Sorry."

49

"Noooooooo!"

Sara let out a howl of protest.

Liam in bed with Margaret. Liam in bed with his own sister.

Sara stared at Margaret's breasts, pressing against Liam's bare chest. Stared hard at them, unable to look away. Why was Margaret naked? Why was Margaret in bed with Liam?

He spun around quickly, lowered his feet to the floor.

Naked too.

They were both totally naked, Sara saw. In bed. Brother and sister. My husband and his sister.

She felt a wave of revulsion wash up from her stomach.

I'm sick. I really feel sick. I just wanted to come home. I just wanted to hear an explanation. From Liam. An explanation. That's all.

But now . . .

She knew she had to move. She had to get away from them.

So why was she standing there? Why did her feet feel nailed to the floor?

"Sara, listen—" Liam starting to his feet, reaching out both arms to her. Behind him, Margaret pulled the sheet over her breasts. But made no attempt to get up. Or leave.

Leave. Leave. Leave.

"Liam—how *could* you?" Sara uttered in a hysterical shriek. It was sick. So *sick!*

Liam stood up. She could see his body glistening with sweat in the wash of yellow light from the hall.

They had made love. Margaret and Liam. Liam and his sister. They *fucked* each other!

Sara blinked several times, as if trying to blink away the whole scene, to blink them both away. Then she threw herself forward. Just to move. Just to get her legs working again.

Threw herself into the room. Stumbled forward. Off balance. Out of control.

Liam and his sister. Liam and his sister. Liam, my husband.

"Sara—wait!" Liam cried, bare feet thudding over the floorboards toward her. "Wait—!"

"Nooooo!" Another hoarse wail from Sara. And then she picked the hand up from the dresser top. Chip's hand. So leathery. So hard and bony.

She picked it up and, with another cry—a cry of horror, of disbelief, of *shame*—heaved it at the dresser mirror. Heaved it with the strength of her anger, her *fury*.

The curled hand, almost a fist, crashed against the mirror glass.

Shattered it.

She gaped at the spiderweb of cracks.

Then heard the cry behind her. Liam's shrill cry of protest. "Not the mirror! No!"

Sitting up in the bed, hands tearing at her hair, Margaret shrieked out her horror too.

Liam dove for Sara. She struck out both hands, hit him hard in the chest.

He uttered a pained gasp. Groped for her again.

She ducked away. Grabbed the bedpost and propelled herself to the door.

"Sara—wait! Sara—you don't understand!"

What a pitiful cliché, she thought, surprised she could summon such bitterness. Down the stairs two at a time. Breathing hard. Wheezing each breath. Ignoring the pain in her side. The pain behind her eyes.

"You don't understand!" Liam shouted from the top of the stairs.

She didn't understand! How could he fuck his sister?

Why was he fucking Margaret?

She didn't turn around, didn't want to see him standing naked up there, his dark hair tousled, his body glistening with sweat. *Her* sweat. His sister's sweat.

Oh, Liam. Oh God, Liam.

Why did you fuck your sister? It's not one of your damned superstitions—is it?

Oh God, Liam. Oh God.

"I'm coming after you, Sara!" The last words she heard before she pulled open the door and burst outside. Left the front door wide open and flew down the icy concrete steps to the sidewalk. And kept running.

Past cars sliding over the slick, silvery streets. Past snow-dusted windows with icicles hanging down like daggers from their tops.

Cold. The whole world so cold tonight.

Sara ran through the campus, empty and dark, the bare trees shivering in their snowy white coats. The dark buildings around The Circle hunched low under the pink-gray snow clouds, as if trying to keep warm.

Cold. Too cold.

Sara didn't feel the wind or the snow. She saw the white cold everywhere, but didn't feel it.

Numb. I'm completely numb now. My mind. My body. Dead and numb.

"I'm coming after you." Liam's cold words sent a fresh shiver down her back. She turned, as if expecting to see him behind her, running naked across the campus, running over the snow, calling to her, calling, "You don't understand!"

So lame for someone so brilliant.

"You don't understand!" Like a character in a bad sitcom. Not like a world-renowned man of letters.

A world-renowned man of letters who sleeps with his sister and then cries, "You don't understand."

"No, I don't," Sara breathed. "No, I don't, Liam."

The snow fell harder, pushed in all directions by cutting swirls of wind. Sara brushed snowflakes from her eyes, off her eyebrows.

Mary Beth's apartment building loomed across the street. The long awning at the entrance covered in snow. A man in a gray uniform and cap had his back to the street as he tossed salt from a bucket onto the walk.

Sara darted past him unseen. Her boots scraped over the rough salt particles. Into the building, sliding on the wet floor, gasping for breath. The cold followed her inside. She carried it in with her.

But she couldn't feel it.

Couldn't feel anything at all.

She rang Mary Beth's bell six times. Then she pounded the door. Pounded hard with her numb hands. Pounded and called. Pounded and called—until she remembered that Mary Beth was gone. Mary Beth was at the airport.

She's not here. Not here. Not here.

Of course she's not here. What's wrong with me?

Sara turned her back to the door. She slumped against it with a weary sigh.

Now what do I do?

Where do I go?

50

Back into the snowy night. The orphan. Homeless now.

I've got to think. Got to think clearly. Make a plan.

I can handle this. I really can. I just have to stop shaking. Can't stop shaking.

I'm so cold, so cold inside and out.

The snow fell more slowly now, large flakes settling on her hair and the shoulders of her coat. The wind faded to a hushed whisper. The campus spread before her like a dark photograph. Frozen and empty. Nothing moved.

She jammed her hands into her coat pockets and pressed her arms into her sides, trying to warm herself. Ignoring the cold touch of snowflakes on her face, in her eyes, she stepped out onto Dale Street. And saw the small coffee shop down the block, its pink and green neon sign providing the only light among the dark, closed shops.

Was it open?

Yes. Squinting through the falling snow, Sara saw lights beyond the steamed front window.

I've got to get warm. Got to stop shaking.

Got to get control.

I can handle this. I really can. I can handle anything.

Oh God. Oh God, Liam. Why?

She stepped into the small restaurant and shook herself like a wet dog. Snow puddled onto the black rubber mat at her feet. She felt the warmth on her face, took a deep breath, inhaled the aroma of strong coffee and stale grease.

Rubbing snowflakes off her eyebrows, she gazed down the row of tables and red vinyl booths. The restaurant was surprisingly crowded. Probably because it's one of the few places still open, she decided.

College students filled the nearest booth. Two old men at the next, grim-faced, nursing white mugs of coffee. A clean-cut-looking couple, also college students, wet coats draped behind their chairs, holding hands over the white Formica table, staring at each other dreamily, Cokes and plates of French fries being ignored in front of them.

Young love.

Sara turned away, feeling bitter. And cold. So cold.

Shivering, she made her way to the small booth under the Budweiser sign against the back wall. As she walked, clutching the collar of her coat, she had the feeling that all eyes were on her, that conversation had stopped, that all motion had stopped. And they were all staring, staring at her, studying her like some kind of lab specimen.

Because they knew.

They knew that her husband had fucked his sister. Had used her old boyfriend's mutilated hand in a bizarre, candlelit ceremony.

How do they know? she asked herself. And why are they watching me now? What do they want from me?

She reached the empty booth and glanced back. No one watching. No one staring at her. No one interested in her.

Unable to stop the cold shudders that shook her body, she slid into the seat. Remembered she still had her coat on. Slid back out and pulled it off. Stuffed it into the seat across from her.

The waitress, a weary-looking young woman with short, slicked-down white-blond hair, appeared before Sara could slide back into the seat. "Need a menu?"

Sara grabbed the seatback to support herself. Why couldn't she stop from trembling? Why couldn't she get warm?

"Just coffee, please. Black."

"Are you okay, miss?" Green eyes narrowed at Sara with concern.

Sara uttered a low gasp. Can she see me shaking? Do I look weird or something?

"I . . . don't feel very well. It's so cold."

"I'll bring the coffee. Anything else?"

"No. Uh . . . well . . ." Something to settle the turmoil in her stomach. Something to help make her feel normal again.

I'm normal. I know I am.

"Toast, please. Yes. Just some buttered toast."

The waitress nodded and hurried away. Sara heard the sizzle of grease on the griddle. The college kids squeezed into the front booth exploded with laughter.

She slumped into the seat and pressed herself against the warm wall. She rubbed the sleeves of her sweater, took a deep breath and held it, trying to stop the cold shakes.

I'm sick. I must have the flu or something. I'm sick and I have nowhere to go.

Still holding on to herself, she closed her eyes and tried to concentrate on the restaurant sounds. Normal sounds. I'm normal. Completely normal. The murmur of voices punctuated by laughter, the clink of silverware against plates, the scrape of a chair on the linoleum floor—it helped to calm her.

"Your coffee. Did you say milk?" The waitress's voice made her open her eyes.

"Yes, I—"

My purse!

I don't have my purse. Or my wallet. I ran out of the house without them.

She felt her throat tighten. Felt the shivers start up again. She jammed a hand into her jeans pocket. Felt a quarter and two pennies.

I can't pay for the coffee.

Sara scrambled up. Grabbed her coat and ran. Ran past the startled waitress, down the narrow aisle, past the long counter, past the grim-faced old men, the couple, the college students—all of whom *did* look up this time, to see who was running so fast, running so frantically, coat flapping and flying behind her.

"Hey, miss—! Your coffee!"

The waitress's hoarse voice cut off by the door slamming behind Sara. Sara, the orphan. Homeless Sara, in the cold again.

Penniless.

And now what?

Her boots slid in a deep pile of gray slush. She grabbed the side of an open phone kiosk to keep from falling.

I'm not going to cry. No way. I'm not going to cry till I'm warm and safe. A solemn vow of strength. And not an easy one to keep.

She held on to the metal phone kiosk, staring at the bell engraved in the side. And knew that she had to call him.

I have to get my stuff, she decided, suddenly seeing clearly despite the heavy white flakes, the low fog of pink-gray clouds. Suddenly seeing so clearly.

I have to get my purse. My money. I have to pack a bag with some clothes. Liam has to let me come home and get some things. He cannot leave me wandering all night in the snow.

Oh God, Liam.

Can I talk to him?

Yes.

I can be very businesslike. She started to rehearse what she would say when he picked up the phone. It all seemed so clear now. No discussions with him. Allow him no explanations. Just pick up the necessities and get out. Go to a hotel. The College Inn. It was big and always half-empty.

No. Not the College Inn.

That's where Kristen was murdered.

Kristen. Kristen. Who is Kristen, Liam?

Liam?

She pictured his face, pictured him with the phone pressed

against his ear, his brown eyes wide with surprise, with eagerness to see her and explain to her, dark hair disheveled, features intent. She pictured his face and realized it filled her with revulsion now.

The words ran through her mind as she rehearsed her speech. "Liam, I'm coming home to get a few belongings. But I don't want to see you or talk to you." Yes. That was good. She could say that.

"Leave the front door open and do not wait up for me. Or speak to me. It will take me only a minute or two."

Yes. She could say it. She could do it.

And not cry. Not cry. Not cry.

She squeezed the quarter tightly in her hand. Her only quarter. She didn't want to drop it in the snow. Her hand shook as she pushed the coin into the slot and pressed the cold receiver against her ear. The words—her rehearsed words repeated in her mind as she listened for the click, and then the buzz of the dial tone.

Oh God, Liam. Oh God. Why is this happening?

That's not what I'm going to say. I know what I'm going to say. But what is my phone number?

Oh God. How could I forget my own phone number? I really am losing it.

It came back to her as she fought down the wave of panic. She punched in the number carefully, slowly. No wrong numbers. Not now. I only have one quarter. One quarter to my name.

She heard one ring. Two.

She tried to swallow, but her throat felt as if someone had tied a knot in it. Her mouth now dry as cotton. The receiver so cold against her ear. A chill of snow down the back of her neck.

Three rings. Four.

Pick it up, Liam. I don't want to talk to you. But pick it up.

Five rings. Six. Seven.

The words of her speech repeating in Sara's mind. Am I shaking too hard to say them? Am I too cold to talk?

344

I'm going to freeze to death here. They're going to find me frozen stiff, standing in front of this kiosk with the phone stuck to my ear.

Eight rings. Nine.

He isn't home.

She stood listening to the steady ring, unable to react. As if her mind had frozen. As if her emotions had frozen too.

He isn't home. And Margaret isn't home.

Listening to the low, rhythmic buzz. Again. Again. And his words came back, the threat he shouted as she fled out the front door: "I'm coming after you."

Yes. He and Margaret are out looking for me. They're chasing after me. And I can slip home and pick up my belongings undisturbed.

If I have my key.

Her hand plunged into the other jeans pocket. She never kept the house keys in her pocketbook. Afraid of losing them, she always tried to keep them with her.

And they were with her now.

"Yes!" She dropped the receiver onto its hook. She could still hear the steady ringing in her ears. She pushed herself away from the kiosk. How long did she have? How long before Liam gave up and went back to the house?

She took a deep breath and started to run. In her panic, she hadn't fastened her coat. Now it flapped out like a cape as she swooped down the sidewalk, sliding, gliding, breathing loudly, snow battering her face, her arms in front of her as if reaching, reaching for safety.

A car rolled by slowly, side windows snow-covered, tires crunching over the icy street. The headlights washed over her, casting her in a harsh spotlight. She ran out of the light without slowing.

How long do I have? How long?

She turned sharply at the corner. The house stood in the next block. Snow swirled around her. She heard the soft crunch of her boots as they sank into wet snow. No other sound.

Silence all around.

Silent Night.

She reached into her pocket for the keys as she climbed the snow-blanketed stairs of the stoop. Do I really live here? Is this really my house? My house with Liam?

Not anymore.

The tears started to flow, hot on her frozen cheeks.

Why now? Why cry now?

She begged herself to stop. Scolded herself angrily. Forced the tears back, forced her chest to stop heaving.

She wiped her eyes with the palms of her hands. Such salty tears, stinging her eyes. Such bitter tears.

She raised the key to the lock. Thought better of it. Rang the bell instead.

What if they were back? What if Liam and Margaret returned after I called? I'd better make sure.

She kept her finger on the button. Could hear the bell jangling inside. She felt pleased with herself that she had been able to think so clearly.

The feeling didn't last long. She lowered her finger from the doorbell. Listened hard. Footsteps approaching inside?

No. Please—no.

"Hey—!" A shouted voice.

Sara gasped and spun around, slipping, nearly toppling off the stoop.

Two boys. Moore State students, probably. One in a long black coat, the other covered in a red hood, chasing each other across the street. A snowball flew. Loud laughter. They grabbed each other. Wrestled. Then started to run again.

Sara turned back to the house with a sigh. Some people are having fun tonight. She pressed the bell, letting it ring for nearly a minute.

All clear.

Get in there, Sara, and get out as fast as you can.

She shivered. The shiver convulsed her whole body. Her

hand was shaking so hard, she needed to use both hands to steady the key, both hands to slide it into the lock.

She turned the key. Took a deep breath. Pushed open the door.

And stepped into the hot, heavy darkness of the house.

51

Floorboards groaned under her light step. "Anybody home?" Whispered up the stairway.

She listened. Heard the refrigerator click on in the kitchen. Heard her own shallow breaths.

Her hand reached for the light switch, then dropped away. No. No lights. If they should return, why announce that I am here?

She grabbed the banister and started to pull herself up the stairs, her eyes raised to the dark landing.

"Let those who are asleep be asleep." Liam's chanted words suddenly returned to her. She heard them in his voice, drifting softly down the stairwell.

She stopped, one boot above the other, and gripped the smooth wood of the railing. It had sounded as if Liam were standing there, at the top of the stairs, standing outside their bedroom, reciting the words once more.

"Let those who are asleep be asleep, and let those who are awake be awake."

So romantic that night.

So romantic and beautiful. The pale, dancing candlelight, the floating shadows, Liam floating too, so lightly over her, inside her, the two of them so close, so together, as close as the sound of his chanted whispers in her ear.

"Aaaaghh." A groan of disgust escaped Sara's throat.

Her boots thudded on the stairs as she hurried to the top.

It wasn't romantic. It was *sick*.

And what did those words *mean* anyway? She had been so carried away, so happy, so disgustingly *giddy*—so eager to believe in Liam, so eager to make sure that this time it was right, everything was right, everything would work—so giddy and eager that she had never thought for a moment about the meaning of those recited words.

"Let those who are asleep be asleep."

Who was he talking about? *Who* should be asleep? And who should be awake?

Did it make any sense at all?

I really don't want to think about it now, she told herself, stopping at the landing, reluctant to let go of the banister, of its solid feeling of safety. I don't want to think about it. Or Liam. Until I am out of here.

As her hand finally released the wooden railing, she felt a wave of nausea roll up from her stomach. I don't want to think. Liam and Margaret . . . I have to go back in that bedroom. Liam and Margaret.

Were they laughing at me the whole time?

Were they fucking each other every time I left the house?

Margaret seemed so kind, so understanding. So . . . welcoming.

She seemed so perfectly pleasant and normal in every way. So tolerant of her brother's quirks and superstitions. So willing to fade into the background when I arrived. So eager to help me, to allow me to confide in her, to turn to her.

And all the while . . .

All the while . . .

How long a while? Sara suddenly wondered, swallowing hard and taking one step toward the bedroom. Two steps. Three. How long have they had this sick relationship? Their whole lives?

"Let those who are asleep be asleep."

The words made no sense at all to Sara. She shook her head as if trying to toss them from her mind. She had no use for words now. No use for explanations.

How could Liam explain such a betrayal?

How could he explain Chip's hand? How could he explain Kristen, murdered at the College Inn?

The other murders? All people Liam knew in one way or another? The other murders? Could he have had some hand in killing those people?

No.

He was too tender—too *weak*—to be a murderer. To be a mutilator. The bodies had been pulled apart, according to the lurid newspaper and TV reports, shredded like someone pulling apart a roasted chicken. Shredded and torn. Or cut and slashed until they barely resembled a human.

No. Liam couldn't do that.

He was too gentle. Too sensitive. Too *professorial*.

Or was he?

Did she really know Liam at all? Did she know *anything* about him?

All those stories he told her with such seemingly innocent pleasure. All those stories and old tales. They were all fairy stories. Sweet, old fairy tales.

They revealed nothing about Liam.

"I don't know you," Sara murmured aloud.

She was so mesmerized, so hypnotized by the romance of him, she hadn't learned a thing about him. Why was he so entranced, so delighted by the old stories of fairies and little people?

And why was he so superstitious?

Yes. Why was he so obsessed with every kind of superstition? Simple everyday superstitions. Strange, complicated superstitions she had never heard of.

Why, Liam?

Too late for questions now. She would probably never know the answers.

She no longer *wanted* to know the answers.

She stopped outside the bedroom door, open just a crack, pale light seeping out, and listened. Anybody in there?

A creaking sound. She spun around, turned back to the stairwell. Had they returned?

She listened hard, over the drumbeat of her heart.

No. Silence now.

She pushed open the bedroom door. She took a deep breath and held it. A bed table lamp provided the only light. The light washed over the bed, the wine-colored wool blanket tossed to the foot, the top sheet crumpled in a ball, pulled to one side—Liam's side. The bottom sheet wrinkled, still wrinkled, still wrinkled by their bodies. Liam and Margaret. The pillows piled together. Dented. Dented by her head. Liam on top of her. The two of them, wrinkling the sheets.

Staining them.

Sara moved to the bed and gasped. She could smell them. Smell his sweat. Smell her flowery perfume.

She could smell their lovemaking on the sheets, in the heavy, hot air of the room. Smell the two of them all around her. Smell them. Smell them.

"Oh." Had she ever felt such disgust before?

My husband and his sister. My husband.

Without even realizing it, she had grabbed up the bottom sheet, had pulled it from the mattress. She began to ball it up, the top sheet too, balling them up, as if preparing to toss them in the laundry hamper, balling them frantically, rolling the sheets in her hands, smelling them, smelling Liam and Margaret, balling them up, feeling her stomach roll with the sheets, feeling her stomach ball up, feeling the nausea roll up, roll up.

"Oh! What am I *doing?*"

Out of control, she suddenly realized. Her hands working on their own. Her stomach lurching. Out of control.

And then her hands tossed down the sheets. And her legs carried her across the room to the bathroom. Their bathroom.

She clapped her hands over her mouth, trying to hold back

the vomit till she reached the toilet bowl. One hand stabbed at the light switch. The overhead light flashed on.

She lurched to the bowl and heaved up the lid. Leaned low.

And heard the steady *drip drip drip* behind her.

What was that noise?

She turned to the tub. Saw the dark stain running down the open shower curtain.

Drip drip drip.

And then she forgot about her nausea and started to scream, a short, hoarse scream at first that became a long, shrill howl of horror.

52

Drip drip drip.

The bright red blood dripped in a steady rhythm from Margaret's nose and mouth.

Margaret. Naked.

Margaret stared down at Sara, wide-eyed, an expression of surprise on her face, her head tilted against her bare shoulder. Stared down at Sara. Stared down because she was hanging on the tiled wall.

Red smears of blood down the white tiles.

And what was that poking out through Margaret's chest?

Sara squinted hard, no longer able to scream, or make any kind of sound, or move at all, her hands pressed tightly against the sides of her face, her eyes trying to decipher the impossible sight, to make sense of it and deny it at the same time.

What poked through Margaret's blood-soaked chest?

Yes. No. Yes.

The shower nozzle.

Smeared with thick blood, the shower nozzle jutted out through her chest. The skin ripped and flapped. Blood rolling down her sagging breasts and belly.

She had been hung up there. The chrome nozzle shoved right through her body. No. Her body shoved right through the nozzle.

Margaret had been hung on the shower nozzle. Hung on a hook like a side of beef. Hung like a painting. A blood painting.

One arm had been ripped out of its socket. It dangled precariously on a single, thin tendon.

And the blood dripped and flowed down the tiled wall, into the tub, puddled in the bottom of the tub, clotted the drain.

Margaret. Margaret. Liam killed Margaret.

He killed his own sister.

Hands tugging the sides of her hair, Sara forced herself to turn away from the bathtub. Eyes shut, she hurtled from the room, legs trembling, rubbery. Head pounding. Pounding with each drip of blood into the tub.

He killed his own sister.

Why, Liam? Why?

There could be no answer. No suitable answer, no logical answer. No *sane* answer.

Liam is crazy. Liam is psychotic. Psychotic and deranged.

He killed Margaret. He butchered her.

He killed his own sister.

And now he's out looking for me.

The police. I've got to call the police.

But not from here. No time. No time at all. Pack my things. Pack just a few things.

Then *go*, Sara. Go.

Sara grabbed the glass knob and pulled open the closet door with such force that she nearly fell over. With a groan, she reached blindly to the top shelf, fumbling for the handle of the suitcase kept up there.

"Oh. No." She lowered her hands, spun away.

No time to pack. Just run, Sara. Grab your purse and run.

Get out of the house.

He's looking for you. He killed his sister. Now he's coming for you.

He'll be back. He'll be back here any minute. You've got to get out. Now.

She slammed the closet door shut. She took a step back. Turned.

Yes. Get out. Get out, Sara. Take your purse and get out of the house.

She was halfway across the room when she heard the heavy *thud* behind her—and knew Liam had returned.

53

With a low cry, Sara whirled around. She didn't want him to take her from behind. She wanted to face him, to face the murderer.

No one there.

Her knees buckled. She grabbed the bedpost to hold herself up.

Where is he?

Liam? Are you here?

Who made that sound behind me?

Her eyes darted to the bathroom. She glimpsed the arm, the bare arm, Margaret's bare arm, hanging over the side of the tub.

The arm had dropped off the body.

That explained the *thud*.

Hanging over the side of the tub, Margaret's bloodstained hand lay open, as if trying to reach the floor.

Sara's throat tightened. She struggled to breathe.

Move, Sara. Don't stand there.

She obeyed the stern, silent voice in her mind, turned away from the bathroom, and lurched out of the bedroom. Then down the stairs, boots clonking loudly, gripping the banister, trying to blink away what she had seen up there, trying to blink away the picture of the severed arm, draped over the blood-red tub, reaching, reaching for the floor.

Not a picture. But real. Really Margaret.

Liam and Margaret.

He killed her. Now he wants to kill me.

She grabbed her black leather purse from the hall table. Nearly dropped it. Caught it by the straps. Gripped them tightly. Pulled open the front door.

Would she find him standing on the stoop, waiting for her? Waiting to tear off her arm? To hang her up on the front door?

No.

She peered out into the pale yellow light from above the door. No one there. The snow drifting down, soft and silent.

No *drip drip drip*.

Soft and silent and white as a cloud out here.

Get moving, Sara. You can't stay here. The stern voice again. Thank God for the stern, commanding voice. Strength from somewhere within her, she wasn't sure from where. Thank God for the voice. Without it, she would have collapsed long ago, collapsed in tears and the cold shudders.

Collapsed and waited to die.

Why, Liam?

Why do I have to die? Why did Margaret have to die? Why?

Move!

But where? Where can I go?

Her boots sank into the deepening snow as she stumbled off the stoop and began to race along the silent, empty street.

Who will save me? Who will rescue me from you, Liam?

The police?

She stumbled to the phone kiosk on the corner, a thick blanket of snow over the top. Yes. The police. The police will come, Liam. The police will protect me. And stop you.

She brushed wet snow off the receiver, raised it to her ear.

Silent.

Dead and silent.

She slapped at the dial. Shoved the 0 again and again.

Silent.

No. Got to keep moving. Got to get away from you. Far away.

Her eyes narrowed at every doorway. Every shadow on the snow, even her own shadow sliding ahead under a streetlight then retreating as if in terror, gave her a start, a chill of fright.

She imagined she saw him a dozen times. Lurking beside a snow-covered hedge. Stepping out from behind a lamppost. Overcoat swirling around him, dark hair down over his forehead, dark eyes glaring at her—with hate?

Do you hate me, Liam?

Why do you want to kill me? I only loved you.

Loved you. Past tense now. *Loved* you. Her love as cold now as the snow beneath her boots.

As cold as Margaret's mutilated body, mounted on the cold chrome shower nozzle.

Cold. The whole world cold now. Cold and dark.

"Oh!" Her boots slipped on the frozen surface. She tossed out her hands to catch herself. Nothing to grab.

She fell hard, landing on her knees, then toppling into the snow. Her face plunged into wet snow. She jerked up her head, sputtering. Pain shot up her body from her right knee. She brushed snow off her eyes, her cheeks.

A sob escaped her throat. She struggled to cut it off before the tears began to flow. And flow. And flow.

"Damn it!" Pulling herself up, she saw her purse tilted into the snow. The top had opened. She saw her wallet in the snow. A lipstick tube poking up from the snow. A set of keys.

Stifling another sob, she bent to retrieve them. Stuffed them with a trembling hand back into the bag. The keys.

The keys.

They were the keys to Milton's office.

And Milton's house key.

Milton's house.

I saw Milton this morning, she remembered. He stopped me. He seemed so desperate. He wanted to talk.

Oh my God!

Did Milton want to warn me? Did he find out about Liam?

Was Milton trying to help me? Why didn't I stop? Why didn't I listen?

She grasped the house key tightly in her hand.

I'll go to Milton. I'll go to Milton's house.

The perfect place to hide from Liam. So far from campus. Back in the woods.

She stared at the key through the tears that had welled in her eyes. Stared at it as if it were a piece of silvery treasure. A piece of starlight. A star to guide her.

Milton will help me think clearly. Milton will help me stop shaking. Milton will protect me from Liam. We can call the police from Milton's house.

She pictured Milton, so big, so strong. He always wanted to help Sara. He always wanted Sara to come to him.

Well, this is the time. I need you now, Milton.

Yes.

Milton's house.

I'll be safe there.

54

Brushing snow from her eyes, Sara lurched toward the pay phone on the next corner. Milton, please be there, she prayed, grabbing the cold, wet receiver in her bare hand.

Please be there. I need you now.

She pressed the receiver to her ear.

Silent.

No. Not this one too.

An angry cry escaped her throat. She slapped at the dial, slammed the receiver down, listened again.

No dial tone. Not a sound.

Don't *any* of these phones work?

She tossed down the receiver, letting it dangle on its cord, and spun away from the open kiosk, heart pounding, not feeling the cold anymore, not feeling the snowflakes on her forehead, on her eyebrows, melting snow soaking her hair, numb now, not feeling anything but fear.

A car turned the corner, tires spinning. A single white light swept over Sara. When the light rolled past her, she could see the taxi, one headlight out.

Taxi?

Yes. *Campus Taxi.* She could make out the words on the top light.

She waved frantically, both arms raised over her head. "Hey—taxi! Taxi! Oh, please!"

It slid to a stop. A maroon and white Plymouth. A layer of snow over the top.

Sara slid into the back seat. The floor was puddled from the last occupant's boots. Despite the NO SMOKING sign on the back of the front seat, the car smelled of stale tobacco smoke.

Shivering, she wrapped her arms around herself. "Could I have a little more heat back here?"

The driver, a somber-faced old man in a plaid lumberjack cap, glanced at her in the rearview mirror. "That's all the heat I've got. You're very lucky. I was heading home."

"Yeah. Very lucky," Sara murmured bitterly.

"Directions, please," he demanded impatiently.

The wipers scraped the windshield, smearing a trail of white over the glass. The driver leaned over the wheel, his dark eyes squinting out, both hands at the top of the wheel.

As he slid onto the street, tires whirring, Sara turned and tried to see out the back window. Liam—are you back there? Are you following me?

She saw solid darkness. The rear window was blanketed with snow. Comforting, somehow.

You can't see in. You can't see me.

The car slid from side to side, like an ice skater, one step to the left, then glide to the right. Sara rubbed the fogged passenger window, watched the dark houses roll past, the snowy lawns, shimmery blue in the dim light of night.

The window fogged again. The world faded behind the glass.

Sara wished it would stay that way. Stay on the other side of the glass. Stay dark and silent and distant.

Liam . . . Liam . . .

She pictured Milton's surprise when he found her at his door. "Sara—what's wrong? Sara—please tell me." She could hear his hoarse voice, see his face redden with excitement. With concern.

She wondered if he would believe her story. She wondered if she could tell it. She wondered how much she could tell before she broke down and the tears started to flow.

I'm keeping it all back. I'm doing such a good job. But how long can I hold on?

A loud rumble made her heart jump. The driver spun the wheel, cursing to himself. The taxi swerved, avoiding a large snowplow, backing into the road.

Please don't plow this road, Sara thought as the driver spun back onto the road. Please don't make it easier for Liam to get to me.

I'll be okay, she reassured herself, watching the wiper blades scrape the windshield. I'm getting away. I'll be okay until the police arrive. Then they'll protect me. They'll keep Liam from me. They'll find him. They'll capture him. They'll—

The car jerked to a stop. Sara's shoulder bounced against the door. "What's wrong?"

The driver stared at the meter and didn't reply.

"Driver—what's wrong? Why have we stopped?"

He turned slowly, dark eyes studying her from under the wool cap, seeing her for the first time. He clicked on the light. "Six eighty, please."

"Oh." She lowered her head and squinted out the windshield. Was that Milton's house? Had they arrived so quickly?

Lowering her gaze, she realized she had been gripping the house key the whole time. Now she dropped it into her lap to search her purse for the taxi fare.

"You live here, lady?"

Sara pawed through the purse. My wallet. My wallet.

"You live here, lady? The house is really dark."

She found a bill crumpled on the bottom and pulled it out. A ten. "Here." She thrust it up to the front. "Keep the rest."

Her heart started to pound as she pushed open the door.

Milton's keys started to slide from her lap. She saw them and retrieved them in time.

The wind blew a blast of powdery snow into her face. She climbed out of the car and stared at the house. All the windows dark. No light over the porch.

The taxi backed away as soon as Sara pushed the passenger door closed. The tires crunched over the snowy driveway. The single headlight washed over the front of the house. Sara glimpsed a mound of snow topping the gutter, thick frost creeping up the front window.

She gripped the purse under the arm of her coat and tightened her fingers around the keys. She walked carefully, one step at a time, along the front walk, feeling a slick layer of ice beneath the wet snow.

Eyes on the dark windows. Then to the door.

Please be home, Milton. I need you to be home. I need you to help me, to keep me safe. From *him*.

The trees shuddered, sending down a shower of snow.

Sara stopped. Her eyes moved to the side of the house, to the tall evergreens standing now like white tree statues.

A sob escaped Sara's throat.

I was married here. Liam and I were married back between those trees. Such a happy time. Such a happy day.

Not so long ago.

I came here to marry the man I loved.

Tonight I've come here to hide from him.

Another gust of wind made the trees shudder, as if in sympathy with her. Gripping the key tightly, hunching against the blowing snow, Sara made her way to the front door.

Please be home, Milton.

Please help me.

Her hand shook as she brushed snow off the top of the doorbell. Then she pressed the button, pressed it in and kept it in, listening to the loud buzz inside the house, waiting for Milton to rouse himself and come open the door.

55

The wind tossed snow against the door. She felt the cold in her hair, on the back of her neck. She lowered her finger from the doorbell. Listened hard.

The shudder of the trees. The wind's harsh whisper.

No footsteps inside. No sign of life.

"Milton!" The name exploded from her. She could feel herself start to fall apart, feel the glue soften, melt, feel the delicate pieces start to crack, like china, like glass. "Milton!" Her voice so frail, so frightened.

She raised her finger and leaned into the bell. She could hear the steady buzz on the other side of the door. She pushed it. Pushed it. Three long buzzes. Then a longer one.

"Milton! Milton—please!"

She pounded on the door with both fists. Then pressed the doorbell again.

Silence inside. Not a creak. No light flashing on.

Maybe he's not home.

She shut her eyes and tried to remember. Did he tell me he'd be away?

"Milton—are you home? Are you a heavy sleeper? Are you going to wake up and let me in?"

The snowdrift against the side of the house shifted in the

wind. Sara raised the key to the lock. It took three tries before she realized she was holding it upside down.

She turned the lock and pushed the wooden door open. Stared into darkness. Felt the warmth of the house on her cheeks.

"Milton?"

Sara leaned her head into the silence.

She stamped her boots on the floor, then stepped into the house. The wind blew the door against her back. Startled, she shoved it shut. She blinked against the darkness, waiting for her eyes to adjust.

"Milton? It's me—Sara! Milton, are you home?"

She fumbled on the wall for the light switch. Couldn't find it. So she stepped into the front room. Dim shapes formed around the room. She saw the dull glint of knife blades against the wall. Milton's prized collection.

"Milton—wake up! It's me! Sara!"

Silence.

Check his bedroom, she ordered herself, moving carefully in the blue-black darkness. She remembered the long, mirrored hall. Milton's room was at the end of it on the left.

"Milton?"

So quiet. So warm.

She took a deep breath and held it. Then she started across the living room, eyes narrowing on the black rectangle that must be the hallway entrance.

She was halfway across the living room when her leg bumped something on the floor. Something heavy and soft.

"Unh." With a startled grunt, she fell over it. The big object gave way beneath her.

Not an ottoman. Too soft to be an ottoman.

The object moved under her weight. She felt warm liquid, sticky on her hands.

"Oh God."

She struggled to her knees.

"Oh God."

She didn't have to see it to know what it was.

She didn't have to see to know that she had found Milton.

The overhead light flashed on.

Sara blinked. Stared at her hands. At the thick, dark blood on her hands.

Then down at Milton's ragged body. Torn. Torn open.

Milton?

Torn open like some kind of package. Skin ripped open above the blood-soaked pajama bottoms. The red stomach pulled out. Pulled out of the body. Pink intestines rolling out onto the floor in a dark puddle of blood.

Milton's head tilted against the couch bottom, mouth and eyes wide open in a startled gasp.

"Oh God. Oh God." Sara's hands so sticky. The blood still warm.

She raised her eyes to the knives in the glass shelves. Then spun around quickly, remembering. Remembering that some-one—someone else—had turned on the ceiling lights.

And saw Liam.

In the entrance to the hallway. Gray overcoat unbuttoned over his sweater. Dark hair disheveled. Arms crossed in front of him.

Liam. Glaring down at her. Glaring at her so cruelly. Features set in a hard stare she had never seen on that face she thought she knew.

On that face she thought she loved.

I don't know him.

I don't know anything.

He's going to kill me now.

Sara, still on her knees. Tried to return Liam's stare.

But didn't want to see him.

Couldn't *bear* to look at him.

The face making her sick now. That stare filling her with dread. With terror.

So many murders, Liam. So many inhuman murders.

"Liam—you killed Milton." Somehow she found her voice.

She gestured with both bloodstained hands. "You—you killed him, Liam. And you killed your own sister."

Liam blinked. But his features remained set. Cold. Colder than the snow that brushed up against the front window.

"You killed your own sister!" she shrieked.

He spoke finally, through gritted teeth. "I didn't kill them, Sara. *You* did."

56

Sara stared up at him, struggling to think clearly.

His words were insane. Crazy. Liam is crazy, she realized.

I should have guessed. There were so many clues. All those crazy superstitions.

But how could I have guessed that he was a murderer?

How?

How could I guess that he tears people apart?

He remained frozen in the hallway entrance, arms still crossed, features set in a hard frown. Watching her. Studying her.

Waiting for her to react to his crazy accusation?

She pulled herself to her feet, wiping her blood-sticky hands on the front of her coat. Think hard, Sara. And think fast.

Her strong voice again. Willing her to get away from him. Willing her to stay alive.

But how?

Her eyes moved to the front door. Could she get there before Liam?

Probably not.

He was blocking the hallway, the only other avenue of escape.

Nowhere to run, Sara realized, feeling the panic tighten her chest, listening to her own rapid, shallow breaths.

I need a weapon.

Could she run to the glass shelves, open them, and pull out one of Milton's knives before Liam crossed the room to stop her?

No. Not a chance.

Her eyes stopped at the fireplace. The iron poker stood beside the basket of firewood.

Yes. The poker. Maybe I can get to it.

She choked back her terror. The room suddenly felt as if it were closing in. This room. This room where Liam and I first really talked.

Milton's party. We spent the whole time talking together—Liam and I—right over there across from the fireplace.

And now he's going to try to kill me.

And I'm going to grab the poker and—

"*You* killed them, Sara." Liam's low, steady voice broke into her thoughts. "*You* did. You don't believe me—do you?"

He suddenly sounded so lifeless. So drained of energy, so drained of everything resembling the Liam she knew.

"I believe you, Liam," she choked out. Anything to keep him calm, to keep him still, to keep him in that doorway. "Really. I believe you."

"Sara—!" Her name burst out of him in an angry cry.

The sound made her jump, made her move, made her plunge across the room. She reached the fireplace before he did. Grabbed up the iron poker, heavier than she thought.

She raised it with both hands—as he grabbed the other end.

"Nooo! Let goooo!" A frantic wail.

They wrestled with it, both pulling, both groaning as they struggled.

"Sara—listen to me! Let me explain! You must let me explain!"

"No! Let go! Let go! Owwww!"

He suddenly reversed himself. Both hands on the poker, he pushed forward. Shoved her off balance.

She stumbled back. He tugged it from her hands. Raised it

369

over her, pressed the bar down against her chest, forcing her back, back—onto the couch.

"Liam—no! Let me go! Please, Liam!"

He stood over her, eyes aflame, face twisted in fury, chest heaving as he struggled to catch his breath.

"Liam—don't!"

She couldn't move. She couldn't squirm away. He held the poker between his hands. He had her pinned to the couch.

No escape.

He was going to kill her now. He was going to tear her apart as he had the others. Tear her apart and hang her on the wall.

"Please. Please!" Begging was all that she had left. Had he no feeling at all? Was he so completely insane? Had he no feeling for her, no love left? Did he *ever* love her?

He leaned over her menacingly, chest still heaving, normally pale face a bright scarlet. "I have to explain. You must let me explain."

Yes, she thought. Explain. Keep him talking. Explain, Liam. Explain all night if you wish.

But then she lost control.

She had held herself in for so long. And now, pressed against the couch, staring up at him in fright, the words tumbled out of her, tumbled out in a breathless rush before she could grab them back, before she could bite her tongue, or hold her breath, or do *something* to stop herself.

"Liam—you slept with your sister! How can you explain? You slept with your sister—and then . . . and then . . . you *killed her!*"

"No, no, no," Liam lowered his voice to a whisper. "Margaret wasn't my sister. Margaret was my *wife.*"

57

What is he saying?

Sara gazed up at him, studying his brown eyes, the eyes she had loved. She couldn't read them now. She couldn't find any truth behind their dark stare.

Is he completely insane?

Or am I?

Why did he say that Margaret is his wife? I am his wife! Why is he telling me such a crazy lie?

The ceiling began to spin. Dizzy, Sara shut her eyes. But she couldn't stop the spinning. As if all her confusion, all her questions, all her fears were whirling inside her head, spinning faster and faster.

No way to make any sense of it. No way to understand.

When she opened her eyes, he had lifted the fireplace poker and had taken a step back, his eyes still wild, his expression taut. She pulled herself up to a sitting position on the couch. The room tilted again, rocking, spinning. She narrowed her gaze on him, concentrated on Liam.

"Are you going to let me explain?" he demanded softly. "Or are you going to attack me again?"

"I—I didn't want to attack you. I just want to leave," she stammered.

"Are you going to let me explain?"

"Yes." What choice did she have?

He dropped the poker to the floor. It bounced over the carpet and rolled to a stop beside the end table. He stood stiffly, arms tensed at his sides, staring down at her intently. She saw his eyes become distant, saw the concentration on his face, as if he were trying to decide how to begin.

Or trying to make up a good story, she thought with bitterness.

He is a storyteller, after all. His whole life is stories and fairy tales.

Are you going to tell me a fairy tale now, Liam?

He crossed his arms over the front of his sweater. "Margaret was my wife," he began tentatively.

Sara couldn't help herself. She interrupted, without meaning to. The hurt was just too much. "I—I thought I was your wife."

His gaze, she realized, was above her, distant, far away. He didn't seem to have heard her words of protest.

"Margaret was my love, my life." His voice trembled as he spoke the words. "It was always Margaret and me. Margaret and me—since I was four years old."

"Liam—"

He raised a hand to silence her.

What *was* that in his eyes? Sorrow?

"Margaret and I, we were neighbors. We weren't brother and sister. Her family lived on the next farm, a farm as barren and despair-ridden as my father's. We—we were always together. Always. I often thought we kept each other alive."

He uttered a low sob, his chest heaving. Sara watched him take a deep breath and hold it. "We left Ireland together. We ran away from my father. We ran away from the bad luck. The bad luck. The bad luck. At least, we *thought* we did. We were married here, as soon as we were old enough."

He stopped again to catch his breath. Sweat made his dark hair glisten, rolled down his forehead.

The silence lay heavily between them.

Sara wanted to protest again, to scream, to question him:

What are you saying—that you're a bigamist? If you were married to her, why did you marry me? You married me and continued to live with her?

It can't be true, she decided. He's deluded. Completely deluded.

Liam's eyes sought hers. "Do you remember the tale I told you on the night I proposed? The tale of the fairy wife? Well, Margaret was my fairy wife. I have been loyal to her all the years, as loyal as a man can be. But as in the old folktale, I had to take a second wife, Sara. That wife was you."

"Liam, please—" Sara protested.

"Listen to me!" he shrieked.

The violence of his cry made Sara gasp.

"Listen to me, Sara." Softer now. "We needed a child. I wanted to spare Margaret. I needed a child by someone else. And the child had to be born in wedlock. That's why Margaret and I needed you, Sara. We needed you to have the child."

"No!" Sara screamed. "I don't believe you, Liam. Why are you making up this horrible story? How can you expect me to believe such . . . such craziness?"

"It's the truth," he insisted, more sorrow than anger in his voice now. "What is the expression? The *bitter* truth?"

"Liam, please—"

"I loved Margaret so much, Sara. So much I would do anything for her. She was my life, my fairy wife. Margaret and I needed a child. *I* needed a child. To free myself of the demons." A cry of pain burst from deep in his chest. "You don't know what my life has been like, Sara. The demons . . . the demons . . . My father passed them on to me. My whole life, I . . . I . . ."

He swallowed. His eyes took on a glassy, faraway gaze. "My father . . . before Margaret and I fled, he taught me. He taught me how to keep them down. He taught me to be vigilant. And he told me how to free myself. By having a child in wedlock. The only way to free myself. But I couldn't do that to Margaret, could I? My mother died when I was twelve. I'm sure she *wanted* to die. I'm sure she willed herself to die, knowing the truth. Knowing what was about to happen to me as I reached manhood. So I couldn't do that to Margaret. I . . ."

"Liam, please—" She motioned for him to sit down beside her. The story, she could see, was torture for him. Was it the telling that was so painful? The act of making it up as he went along? Did he realize that it made no sense, that it was the ramblings of an insane person? Did he realize that—and was that why he seemed in such pain as he related it?

He ignored her gestures. He cleared his throat loudly. "I'm trying to make you understand, Sara. I had to get rid of the demons. I had to free myself so that Margaret and I could begin our life. But the demons—"

"Liam—what demons?" Sara interrupted. "What demons are you talking about?"

He swallowed again. And took a deep breath. "The demons of superstition. Didn't you wonder about my superstitions, Sara? Didn't you wonder why I was so strict, so vigilant, so watchful every waking moment? It was because of the demons. I had no choice."

"Liam, please. Sit down. I can help you. I—"

"All superstitions are designed to keep away evil demons. I told you that, Sara. Remember? Why do we say 'Bless you' when someone sneezes? It keeps away evil demons. Remember? When we knock on wood or throw salt over our shoulder—it's all to keep the demons away.

"But I can't! I can't keep the demons away!" He was screaming now, bellowing, pounding his chest with both fists. "I can't keep the demons away. Because all of them—*all the demons of superstition*—they all live inside me!"

58

He needs help.

I had no idea.

I should have guessed.

He was so compulsive, so obsessed. He was so careful, so careful to obey every rule of superstition. I should have realized.

Staring up at her troubled husband, Sara's guilt competed with her fear. I could have helped him. I should have seen how frightened he was. I pretended his superstitions were a joke. I pretended they were cute and quaint. I didn't want to face the truth about him. I could have helped him before . . . before it was too late. But . . . now what?

Now what?

Other thoughts flared through her mind: What about Margaret? Did Margaret realize that Liam imagined her to be his wife? Did she know about it and play along? Is that why she was in bed with him?

Yes. What about Margaret? Her role didn't make sense.

She must have known that Liam was deeply sick. Why didn't she try to get help for him? She was his sister, after all.

Wasn't she?

Staring up at Liam, who had started to pace, moving only a short distance, four or five steps one way, then back, Sara tried to remember her psych reading. There were so many cases of people who believed they were inhabited by demons. It usually stemmed from guilty feelings, from a dark secret they were keeping, from an act that they were ashamed of.

This doesn't help me now, Sara thought, watching his abrupt, frantic movements across the floor. It doesn't help me at all.

Liam stopped in front of her and lowered his gaze once again. He continued his story in a trembling voice. "You have to understand, Sara. You have to understand why I've tried to be so careful. Whenever I slip up, whenever I forget to observe a superstition—every time someone *near* me violates the rules of superstition, it gives a demon the chance."

He took another deep breath. Beneath the sweater, his chest was heaving.

"A chance to do what?" she asked softly.

"A chance to slip out of me," Liam replied, avoiding her stare. "A chance to slide out of my body. A chance to escape. Every time . . . every time . . ." He uttered a sob and shut his eyes as if in pain.

"The demons slide out of my body. They slip away—and kill. They only kill people I know. They—they live in my consciousness. They know who I know. When they slip out, they murder someone. A friend. An acquaintance. Someone I met only briefly. They murder. They murder. Then they vanish forever."

Sara was beginning to understand. So this was Liam's dark secret. He had murdered. He had murdered . . .

She shuddered.

Had he murdered *all* of those people?

He had murdered and he couldn't face the truth. And so he had created the demons to explain the murders. He had dreamed up the demons. Someone to blame, someone to help make him feel guiltless for the hideous crimes he had done.

Demons.

Of course someone who studied folklore, someone who

lived in a world of magic and fairies and leprechauns would dream up demons when he found himself in severe trouble.

And I'm sure the demons are very real to Liam, Sara thought, studying him intently.

"They're always waiting to get out," Liam continued. "They're always there, just at the edge of my consciousness. Waiting. Waiting for their chance to escape. I—I've lived with them for so long, Sara. You can understand why I was eager to pass them on, why I *had* to free myself of them."

He moved closer. She could see that his chin was trembling. Tears had welled in his eyes.

"I—I tried to warn you. Really. I did. Sometimes the demons let down their guard. Sometimes they go dormant. They go to sleep or something. Not very often, but sometimes. I can feel when they're not alert, when they're not awake.

"That's when I called you. That's when I warned you to stay away from me."

Sara gasped. *"You* made those frightening calls?"

Liam nodded. "Yes, I called. I tried to warn you away. And I sent the rabbit feet. Poor Phoebe. I sent the rabbit feet, Sara. I tried to scare you away. I tried to warn you before it was too late. Too late for you."

Sara pressed both hands against her burning cheeks. "Oh my God."

He's so much crazier than I ever could have imagined.

Keeping her eyes on him, she pulled herself slowly to her feet. "Liam, I'm going to use the phone now." Spoken softly, carefully, each word distinct. "I'm going to get help for you, dear. It's going to be okay."

"No." He moved quickly to block her path.

She felt a sharp tremor of fear, tried not to show it. "It's going to be okay, Liam. Really. I'm going to get help."

"Sit down, Sara."

She stared into his brown eyes, found no warmth there. With a sigh, she retreated to the couch, perching tensely on the edge. And glimpsed the iron fireplace poker at her feet.

377

"Don't patronize me, Sara. I'm trying to explain. I need for you to believe me."

"I believe you, Liam. I just—"

"*No you don't!*"

She jerked back, startled again by another sudden, angry explosion.

"I want you to know what I've had to live with, what my life has been like." His face reddened. His chin trembled. "A nightmare. There's no other word for it. Margaret and I—we had no choice. We had to find a way out. I had to free myself. So that Margaret and I could have a life. I want you to understand, Sara."

"Liam, please—"

"Margaret and I did everything to keep you happy. We tried so hard. Didn't we, Sara? Didn't we?"

Sara started to her feet again, eyes on the poker. "Liam, let me go. Let me make a call and get help. It'll be okay, dear."

Again, he moved quickly to block her escape. "We worked so hard to keep you innocent. To keep you from knowing. We didn't want to upset you. We loved you—because you were going to free us. You were going to have my child, Sara. The child would inherit the demons and free me from their grasp. Your child would take the demons away. We loved you for that, Margaret and I. We truly did. We were a family. A real family.

"And we didn't want anything to ruin our family. It was too important to us. *You* were too important. So when your old boyfriend showed up . . ."

"—Chip?"

"When your old boyfriend showed up . . . when Kristen came barging into town—"

"Kristen?"

"Kristen was my second wife. I married her two years ago in Chicago. Margaret and I hoped she would have the child. But she failed us. She failed us, so we had to try again."

"Oh my God," Sara murmured, hands pressed against her cheeks.

"When Chip and Kristen showed up to spoil our plan, Margaret insisted on taking care of them."

"She—she *killed* them?" Sara choked out.

Liam nodded grimly. "Margaret didn't like to kill. She was a quiet person. Like me. But she knew we had no choice. We couldn't let those intruders spoil our plan. We had to keep you innocent."

"They d-died because of me?"

Liam nodded again.

Sara's gaze went past him, to Milton's torn body, sprawled in its own dark puddle of blood, his insides heaped on the floor.

So much blood.

So much death.

How could you, Liam? How *could* you?

She couldn't sit still any longer. She leapt up, dove for the poker. Grabbed it in one trembling, slippery hand. Dropped it. Grabbed it up again and raised it toward Liam.

"You—you used Chip's hand. You—"

"I had to calm the demons. I had to try to put them to sleep." Liam raised both hands as if in surrender. "It was the only way I knew."

"Ohhhh . . ." A long, low moan escaped Sara's throat. "No, Liam. No. No. No. No more. You're very sick. You need help." She raised the poker, made sure he saw it.

Liam lowered his hands to his sides and took a step toward her. Beads of sweat trickled down both temples, down his cheeks. "We tried to keep you innocent. It was so important to us. But then you came home early tonight. And you saw us. You saw Margaret and me. And then . . . you killed Margaret."

"No!" Sara screamed, swinging the poker, trying to keep him back. "No! Stop saying that!"

"You broke the mirror, Sara. You broke the dresser mirror. When you did that, they slipped out—the demons. They slipped out of my body. They murdered Margaret. I—I c-couldn't do anything to save Margaret." Stammering now, his voice choked and tight. "I—I listened to her screams of agony. I couldn't bear to watch. I could only imagine what the demon was doing to her.

"I hurried out. I drove here as fast as I could, hoping—praying—the demons weren't going after Milton. I got here too late. Too late." His voice cracked with emotion. "Milton . . ." His voice trailed off. He covered his eyes with one hand and let out a loud sob.

"Liam, listen to me—there are no demons!"

"You released them, Sara!" he screamed. "You broke the mirror and let them out. You did. You did."

He made a clumsy dive for her. Missed. He caught himself on the couch and whirled around, breathing hard.

Sara backed away from him, holding the poker in front of her. "This is insane!" she cried, her voice shrill and trembling. "This is insane, Liam! There are no demons. No demons! Look—I'll show you!"

"No! Wait!" A desperate cry. She saw him stumbling after her.

But she was already at the hallway. She pulled the poker back over her shoulder like a baseball bat. "Watch, Liam—watch! No demons! No demons anywhere!"

"Sara—*please!*"

She ignored his frantic howls, pulled back the poker.

Swung with all her might.

And watched the mirrored wall shatter with a *crack* and then an echoing *crash*.

59

"No demons!" Sara cried. "Do you see, Liam? No demons!"

She swung the poker again. Shattered the next mirrored panel.

Again.

She plunged down the long hall, swinging the heavy poker, smashing mirror after mirror. "No demons! No demons! Do you see?"

The smack of the poker, the *crack* of the glass, the *crash* of the heavy, jagged shards hitting the wood floor—the sounds, so satisfying somehow, so real, so *final*, accompanied her screams. "Do you see, Liam? No demons!"

Behind her she heard his terrified wail, like a shrill siren. It rose over the crack and thud of shattering glass, rose over Sara's desperate shouts.

Liam's cry, revealing so much pain, so much horror, forced her to stop and turn around. He crouched at the entrance to the hall, head tilted back, eyes bulging wide, mouth open in his endless wail.

"Don't you see, Liam? There are no demons!" Sara let the poker fall. It clattered loudly on the hard floor and rolled to the wall. "No demons. It's okay, Liam. No demons."

He dropped to his knees. Raised his hands and clasped them in a prayer position.

Sara started toward him, back through the broken hallway, her boots crunching over shards of mirrored glass.

"Noooooo—!" Hands still clasped, he tilted back his head in another pained howl.

"Liam—"

Sara stopped as his wail was cut short.

Liam appeared to choke. Raised his hands to clutch his throat—as his tongue shot out of his open mouth.

No. Not his tongue.

Something wider than a tongue, and purple. Something purple unfurling from Liam's gaping mouth.

Two of them. Two tongues.

Stretching from Liam's mouth, longer, longer, stretching into the hallway, twisting, waving, as if reaching out to Sara.

"Oh my God. Oh no. Liam?"

Liam fell onto his side, clutching his throat with both hands, making ugly choking sounds.

Sara tore at the sides of her hair, staring in disbelief at the twisting, twining tongues pushing out farther, farther from Liam's mouth. "Oh my God. Oh my God. What have I done?"

Liam uttered a choked groan as yellow foam pushed out of his mouth behind the tongues. No. Not foam. A head. A spongy, yellow head.

"Ohhhhh." Sara sank against the wall, against a broken mirror pane.

The two tongues leaped out from the bubbling head. Two red eyes opened. The head poked through Liam's open mouth as he gagged and choked, his hands flailing the air wildly now.

A sour odor rose through the narrow hallway, heavy and rank. The air grew colder. Sara felt a sour dew on her cheeks that made her skin tingle.

Yellow shoulders slid up past Liam's lips, the flesh appeared spongy, glistening wet.

The twin tongues flapped against each other. The red eyes opened and shut rapidly, focusing on Sara. The yellow skin of the head appeared soft and craggy, like scrambled eggs. Soft scrambled eggs running wetly down onto the undulating yellow shoulders.

Liam lay sprawled on his back now, arms flying wildly, helplessly above him, feet kicking, head tilted back as the red-eyed demon, its tongues leaping out before it, slid the rest of the way out from Liam's mouth, making a soft *plop* as its yellow, taloned feet splashed onto the floor.

With a hard jerk, it pulled a yellow, lizardlike tail from Liam's throat. Then it straightened up, tongues twirling around each other, entwining like twin serpents, and took a heavy, wet step toward Sara.

"Nooo!" Her cry came out in a choked whisper.

The smell. I can't bear the smell.

She tried to hold her breath. But the heavy, fetid odor seemed to wash over her, creep into her pores.

The taloned feet made wet sucking sounds as they moved over the hard floor. The creature stood upright, as tall as Sara. It raised its spongy, wet arms as it made its way heavily down the hall, leaving a thick trail of wet yellow slime on the floor behind it.

One step. Another. Another. Tongues tangling around each other. Red eyes glowing brighter now.

It's real, she thought.

Oh, my God. It's real.

Staring in horror and amazement, it took Sara a few seconds to realize that it planned to attack her.

60

The sour stench rolled over her.

She staggered back. Turned. Tried to run the other way, toward the bedroom. Away.

Away.

Too late.

She felt the purple tongues, hot and sticky, wrap around her neck. Pull her back. Tightening around her throat. Tightening like twin boa constrictors.

The smell . . . the smell.

With a groan of disgust, Sara reached up, tugged, her hands sliding over the bumpy, wet flesh of the tongues, struggled to pull them off.

Felt the hot, spongy front of the demon press up against her from behind.

I . . . I can't . . . breathe.

Can't . . . breathe.

She heard a groan behind her. Heard scuffling sounds, the crunch of broken glass on the floor.

She spun around as the tongues loosened their wet grip on her neck.

And saw Liam's arms around the demon's spongy yellow middle. The tongues slapped the air angrily, like whips. The clawed hands swung hard, scratching at Liam's body, slashing his clothes, his skin.

But Liam held on.

He pulled it off me, Sara realized.

He tackled it. And pulled it away.

"Sara—run!" Liam pleaded.

She hesitated, staring at him as he desperately held on to the eggy flesh of the creature.

"Run! Go! Run!"

Obediently, she squeezed past them. Hurtled to the living room. Turned back.

In time to see the creature lift Liam in its arms, then raise one yellow knee.

It happened so fast. The demon held Liam high, then brought him down hard, raising his knee into Liam's back.

Liam made a splintering sound. The sound of a crab shell being cracked. The sickening *crack* seemed to linger in the heavy air of the hallway, linger in Sara's ears.

Liam groaned and slumped back in the creature's arms. His dark hair touched the floor as his head swung back, and his eyes, dull, faded now, nearly lifeless, fell on Sara.

"I—I'm sorry, Liam!" she called. "You told the truth. I can't believe . . . I can't believe what you lived with your whole life."

"I did one good thing." Liam's choked reply, a whisper, like the wind against dry leaves. "I saved you."

His head fell back. His hands slumped to the floor.

The creature dropped him to the floor, then vanished down the hallway, trailing yellow slime.

Liam sprawled on his back, his broken back. Sara could see his eyes, the brown eyes she had loved, staring blankly, lifelessly, at the ceiling.

Liam is dead.

Liam gave his life for me.

Oh God. He's dead and now . . . Now . . .

Liam moved.

His head jerked.

Sara gasped. She took a step back into the hallway. "Liam—are you alive? Liam—?"

No.

Dark fur poked up from Liam's open mouth. An ugly head lifted itself from his throat, simian-featured, green-eyed with a long snout, rows of jagged teeth, drooling thick, white slime from its gaping maw. Fur-covered shoulders raised themselves from Liam's mouth.

"No! Oh God—no!"

Sara grabbed the wall, her temples throbbing, her entire body convulsing in a shudder that stopped her breath.

The fur-draped demon climbed out of Liam's head, green eyes flashing, snapping its long jaws hungrily, stretching and grunting, craning its thick neck.

And then a shiny-skinned arm reached out of Liam's mouth. A sleek, glistening shoulder. Another arm. A hideous lizardy head, silvery with ugly brown spots, raised itself, eyes shut, wide mouth spread in a lascivious grin.

It plopped onto the floor, stood on sticklike legs, insect legs. Licked silvery lips with a serpentlike, forked tongue.

Another dark head poked up from inside Liam. With a soft, scraping sound it rose up quickly from the open mouth. Slender at first, it unrolled wide, opaque wings, flapping them, the wings crackling like dry paper. It tossed back a swanlike head in a shrill hyena laugh, revealing jagged rows of teeth.

All the demons of superstition.

That's what Liam had told her. They were all inside him. All escaping now. All sliding out, stretching and grunting.

Crowding against each other. Bumping. Flapping ugly wings. Snapping powerful jaws. Smacking purple lips with bulging tongues. Filling the narrow hallway with their growls and sighs. And their foul stench.

All staring at Sara.

All preparing to attack me next, she realized.

Why was it so hard to turn away from them? Was it turning away from Liam that she dreaded? Turning away forever?

She knew she had to run.

How far would she get?

How far would she get before they caught up with her, picked her up, broke her in half or tore her to pieces?

"Good-bye, Liam." She spun away from the hall, from the stretching, grunting creatures with their hungry faces.

Each step was a struggle, her boots suddenly heavy, heavy as lead, her head still spinning, her eyes still filled with the deformed bodies, the twisted ugly demon faces, her legs so weak, so rubbery and weak.

She made it to the front door.

Pulled open the door and burst out into the snow. The cold, white snow. Sweet smelling and fresh.

She was halfway down the driveway, snow-laden trees shivering on both sides, when she glimpsed the first demon at the door.

It raised its fur-covered head to the purple sky and opened thick lips in a long animal howl. Then it came galloping on four legs over the snow. After her.

After her.

Hah hah hah hah. Its heavy breathing like cruel laughter.

A winged creature at the door, black wings crackling, claws raised to attack.

Hah hah hah hah.

Sara forced herself to turn away, to run, boots sinking into the snow. Sinking.

Nearly to the road now.

She glimpsed them all hurtling, leaping, flying after her. Chattering and howling as they moved over the snow.

Hah hah hah hah hah.

Such an ugly parade.

So eager. So hungry. So *gleeful*. So sure they were going to catch her.

Catch her and kill her.

All the demons of superstition live inside me.

They killed Liam, and now they will kill her.

Hah hah hah.

She was running along the snow-carpeted road, pumping her arms, leaning into the wind, her dark hair flying behind her, her breath streaming up in puffs of white, when she fell.

One boot caught on something, and she toppled forward into the snow. She stuck out both hands to stop her fall. But landed hard on her left elbow, a shock of sharp pain shooting up her side.

And then they swarmed around her. Buzzing like flies. Chattering and grunting. *Hah hah hah.* Hot drool sizzling the white snow.

All the demons of superstition.

They circled and spun, moving faster and faster, trapping her in the middle, trapping her in their sour wind, darkening the snow as they whirled, darkening the world, her world, tightening the circle, dancing, dancing for her, moving in, bringing the darkness, bringing utter blackness, ugly, dark monsters over the white, white snow.

61

When Sara opened her eyes, she saw white.

She blinked.

Blinked again.

The white glowed above her, a white light soft as snow.

I'm dead, she thought. I've entered the white glow of death.

She coughed.

Whoa. Wait a minute.

The dead don't cough.

She tried to raise her head, but it seemed to weigh a ton.

She glimpsed white walls. A white door.

"You're awake?" A man's voice. Soft and low.

A face appeared above Sara. A black man. His head wrapped in bandages.

Sara squinted up at him. Recognized him. The police detective.

"She's waking up," he called to someone. "Better come. Let me know when I can question her."

The detective slipped from Sara's view. He was replaced by a pleasant-looking woman, round-faced, pudgy, with short, white hair tucked under a white nurse's cap. A starched white uniform. An ID badge pinned to one shoulder. Sara's vision was too blurred to read it.

"Am I . . . in a hospital?" Startled by the sound of her own voice. So real.

So alive.

The woman nodded.

"But—"

Strong hands on both shoulders pushed Sara gently down. "Don't try to sit up. Take it easy."

"But—how did I get here?"

The big woman shrugged. "That policeman—he found you and brought you in. You were here when my shift started this morning."

Sara coughed again. Her throat ached.

As if reading her mind, the nurse handed her a glass of water. "You had a terrible shock, poor thing. I checked out your chart when I came on duty. The doctors don't even know what happened to you. 'Undetermined shock trauma.' That's all it says on that thing." She raised her eyes from the chart. "Were you in an accident or something?"

"I—I don't really know . . ." Sara started. "I have to get up. I have to go—"

The nurse gently pushed Sara down again. "Sip that water slowly, hon. You're gonna be okay. But you'd better not be gettin' up just yet. At least not till the doctors do their rounds."

"But I—"

"You're lookin' a lot more perky than we thought you would. Really. You're gonna be just fine. I can see you're real worried. But everything's okay. And here's the good news." She smiled down warmly at Sara.

"Good news?"

"Yeah. Good news. You're going to be okay—and your baby is fine too."

"My . . . *baby?*"

The nurse nodded. A grin spread across her face.

And Sara started to scream.